"Scrumptious!"

—Eve Chase, *Sunday Times* bestselling author
of *The Midnight Hour* and *The Birdcage*

"It's easy to forget what a snooty, stuffy publishing world Jacqueline Susann and Jackie Collins initially faced when trying to sell their 'racy' books about modern women and their real desires. Gill Paul captures perfectly an imagined relationship between the two groundbreaking authors in this scandalously delicious novel—especially fun for anyone who loves books and publishing."

—Liz Trenow, *New York Times* and *USA Today* bestselling
author of *The Secret Sister*

"*Scandalous Women* is sensational! Honestly, I flew through the pages, adored it. It's a pacy, brilliantly written tale of two bestselling authors in the wildly sexist publishing industry of the 1960s."

—Tracy Rees, internationally bestselling author of *The Elopement*

"This book unlocked so many emotions in me. It made me woozy with nostalgia, remembering how much I adored and devoured Jackie Collins books growing up. . . . Gill has captured the essence of these two dynamic and groundbreaking female writers and encourages us to look again more deeply at their phenomenal achievements. . . . This is Gill at her absolute best, offering up a strong revisionist history with sparkling and propulsive writing. A fitting and empathetic love letter to the 'two Jackies.' Emotional, compelling, memorable."

—Kate Thompson, bestselling author of *The Wartime Book Club*

SCANDALOUS
WOMEN

ALSO BY GILL PAUL

SCANDALOUS WOMEN

A Novel of Jackie Collins and Jacqueline Susann

GILL PAUL

wm

WILLIAM MORROW
An Imprint of HarperCollinsPublishers

This book is a work of fiction. References to real people, events, establishments, organizations, or locales are intended only to provide a sense of authenticity, and are used fictitiously. All other characters, and all incidents and dialogue, are drawn from the author's imagination and are not to be construed as real.

HarperCollins books may be purchased for educational, business, or sales promotional use. For information, please email the Special Markets Department at SPsales@harpercollins.com.

FIRST EDITION

Interior text designed by Diahann Sturge-Campbell

Book illustration © BigJoy/Stock.Adobe.com

Library of Congress Cataloging-in-Publication Data has been applied for.

ISBN 978-0-06-324515-0

24 25 26 27 28 LBC 5 4 3 2 1

For all my scandalous women friends,
with thanks for the inspiration

Compared to Jacqueline Susann, Harold Robbins writes like Proust. . . . For the reader who has put away comic books but isn't yet ready for editorials in the *Daily News*, *Valley of the Dolls* may bridge an awkward gap.

—GLORIA STEINEM, *NEW YORK HERALD TRIBUNE*, APRIL 1966

Oh, Miss Collins, your books are filthy and disgusting and you are responsible for all the perverts in England.

—BARBARA CARTLAND, *WOGAN*, 1987

The Bookshelf, 1975

F ive, four, three," the floor manager counted down. The host, Barbara Walters, smiled directly at camera two and waited till a red light flashed on before speaking.

"Good evening. Tonight we're going to discuss women who write sexy books—a subject that divides opinion across the literary world like no other," she read from a teleprompter. "Authors such as Jacqueline Susann and Jackie Collins sell millions of copies, but attract unprecedented vitriol from the critics. Here to discuss this are the feminist publisher Nancy White and the journalist and author Truman Capote, a longtime adversary of Miss Susann's." She turned to Nancy. "Do you agree with the criticism that these books demean literature and should be placed on the pornography shelves rather than alongside the greats?"

Nancy took a deep breath before she answered: "Jacqueline Susann's and Jackie Collins's novels tell great stories and that's why readers love them. Yes, they include some sex scenes, because sex is part of life, but they are never gratuitous. I think we should be celebrating both of these authors as visionaries. Their books may get scathing reviews but they have introduced the reading habit to millions of men and women who hadn't previously enjoyed reading. Their stories empower women, and in my opinion these authors should be hailed as feminist heroes."

Truman Capote had been shaking his head as she spoke and now he harrumphed. "What utter baloney! These women are cynical creations of a greedy publishing industry, and I'm offended that they dare to call their work 'novels.' They're single-handedly knocking down the temple of literature and turning it into a house of ill repute."

Nancy started to reply but he spoke over her, in his strange, high-pitched Southern drawl.

"It's well known that Jacqueline Susann didn't write her own books. Everything about her is fake, from the wigs to the eye-lashes, the teeth and probably the . . ." He clapped his hands over his chest. "While Jackie Collins—let's just say that doesn't look like the nose she was born with."

Nancy was bemused. "Why do discussions of women's writing so quickly descend into critiques of their appearance? Should women who write novels not try to look good? I can't speak with authority on Jacqueline Susann's teeth or Jackie Collins's nose, but I can tell you for a fact that they both wrote their own books because I worked on both of their first novels. While they were tightened up during the editorial process, as most books are, the stories and characters were theirs alone."

"Yet Jacqueline Susann's publisher admitted to a *McCall's* magazine journalist that they virtually wrote *Valley of the Dolls* for her." Truman cocked his head to one side and gave Nancy a malicious smile.

"That's not what he said at all," Nancy replied. "But I'm curi-ous, Mr. Capote, because elsewhere I have seen you quoted as saying about *Valley of the Dolls*, 'That's not writing, it's typing'—yet now you claim the publishers wrote the book for her. Your position seems contradictory."

Barbara Walters intervened. "Is it the sales they've achieved that makes the critics so mad? I understand *Valley of the Dolls* has sold over sixteen million copies, and Jacqueline Susann is the only author to reach number one on the *New York Times* bestseller list three times in a row. She once accused you of being jealous of her sales, Mr. Capote. Is that the case?"

He was riled now. "I'm certainly not jealous of a *fake* author. The public may be conned by flashy marketing campaigns and expensive road shows but they don't know that none of it is real. It's the emperor's new clothes."

"It's strange you should raise this accusation," Nancy said. "Wasn't there a rumor that you received a lot of help with your book *In Cold Blood* from your friend, the novelist Harper Lee?"

"That's slander and I'll sue anyone who repeats it." He reached for a glass of water on the table in front of him and drank from it.

"I think men are unsettled by women writing about sex," Nancy said, turning to their host. "Sex is traditionally something that men do to women, while women submit, but the new generation of women authors has turned that upside down. Their heroines are gutsy, they get on top and take control in bed, and perhaps that makes men nervous."

"Oh, pur-lease," Truman said in a tone heavy with sarcasm. "You're not trying to tell me their sex scenes are supposed to be realistic, with all those thrusting members and swelling breasts and women who can perform unnatural tricks with their foo-foos."

"I would bow to Mr. Capote's expertise on many subjects," Nancy said, choosing her words with great care, "but perhaps not this one." Truman was openly gay, but homosexuality was still illegal in some states, so it would be libelous to blurt it out on national TV.

Truman stood abruptly and threw his water in her face. "Bitch!" he hissed before he turned and strode off the set.

"Are you alright?" Barbara Walters leaned toward her, looking concerned.

Water from Nancy's hair was dripping down her neck and she blinked, feeling her sooty mascara dissolve. She started to laugh and, once she'd started, she couldn't stop. It was the word "foo-foos" that cracked her up. Barbara Walters laughed too, and then Nancy heard the camera operators chortling. The floor manager appeared with a towel, and still Nancy couldn't stop laughing.

"That was television gold!" Barbara told her. "If the lawyers clear it, we'll use it for the trail!"

It was Nancy's first time on television, but she had channeled the two Jackies and she hadn't felt nervous, not one little bit.

CHAPTER 1

Nancy

Manhattan, 1965

Straight after graduating from college, Nancy caught a train to New York City with three letters that invited her to interviews for publishing jobs carefully folded in her handbag. She had arranged to stay with her cousin Louise, but when she got to Louise's Chelsea apartment block and rang the buzzer, no one answered. She double-checked the address, then loitered on the sidewalk for almost two hours before another tenant took pity and invited her into the lobby to shelter from a heavy shower.

There was no concierge, just a wall lined with metal mailboxes, and up ahead were the lattice-metal gates of the elevator. Nancy was alarmed to notice that Louise's mailbox was full, with envelopes poking out, as if she hadn't been there for some time.

She thought back to the invitation, rerunning the words in her head. It had been four months earlier at Nancy's mother's funeral. Louise had stood with a supportive arm around her waist as Nancy accepted condolences from a stream of family friends. She'd felt numb as she acted the part expected of her. The enormity of the loss hadn't struck home then; in many ways, it still hadn't.

"You graduate this year, don't you?" Louise had asked. "What are your plans?"

"I've always wanted to work in publishing," Nancy told her, "so I'm coming to Manhattan to apply for jobs."

Then Louise said: "You must stay with me. Finding your feet in the city is tough, but I'll look out for you. We'll have a swell time."

Louise didn't have a telephone at her apartment but wrote down the address and said she looked forward to welcoming Nancy at the end of May. That was a firm arrangement, was it not? Nancy had written to confirm her exact arrival date and time—but now Louise wasn't here.

She rode up in the clanking, groaning elevator to find Louise's apartment, 4B, on the top floor. It was a sprawling old building with windowless corridors that snaked off in seemingly random directions and lights that buzzed and flickered overhead. She knocked hard on Louise's door, called her name, and rattled the handle, then held her ear against the wood, but inside was dead quiet.

What could she do? She only had forty-eight dollars in her purse and she'd need that to buy food and subway tokens, so she couldn't afford even the cheapest hotel room. If she caught a train to Ossipee, New Hampshire, where her stepfather lived in the family home with her six-year-old twin stepbrothers, she'd miss her interviews. She ran through the alternatives in her mind but kept coming back to the fact that she and Louise had made a definite arrangement. Louise must be out for the evening. She was a singer, so perhaps she had a show and would return later.

Louise's door was set on an offshoot of corridor that came to a dead end. Nancy sat on the floor by her suitcase and ate a box of Sun-Maid raisins, then flicked through the pages of a Dickens novel, finding it hard to concentrate. Her heart leapt every time she heard the rattle of the elevator ascending, only to have her hopes dashed when it stopped on another floor.

After a while she fell asleep. When she wakened it was dark and she had a stiff neck. She could sense from the silence in the block that it was the early hours, maybe three or four a.m. She got up to stretch her legs, then felt an urgent need to urinate. Leaving her suitcase behind, she groped her way along corridors and up and down flights of stairs and finally found a caretaker's broom closet, where she urinated in the sink, then rinsed her face and hands and cleaned her teeth with a finger. She returned to doze fitfully in the corridor till she could hear other residents getting up to start their days. Still no Louise. Was she staying overnight with a boyfriend perhaps? Had she not received the letter?

Nancy's first interview was at ten thirty. She changed clothes and freshened up as best she could in the toilet at Penn Station, put her suitcase in a luggage locker, then made her way a few blocks north to the publisher's office on Fifth Avenue, near Bryant Park. Thank goodness for the numbered street system, and a dog-eared map she had purloined from her college library!

On arrival, she and four other candidates were given a typing test. Nancy did her best, but she could tell from the rhythmic clattering of keys that the others were far more competent. When the supervisor looked at her half-page effort with multiple crossings-out, she said sorry, they were looking for someone with more office experience.

One down, two to go, Nancy thought, disheartened.

She wandered the streets for the rest of the day, then went back to Louise's at five o'clock, heart in mouth. Please let her cousin be home now! But once again, there was no answer when she rang the buzzer. Another resident let her into the lobby when she said, "I'm staying with Louise in 4B." She'd bought herself a sandwich and a Coke, just in case, and consumed them sitting on the floor outside the apartment, then she read her novel till she nodded off. Once again, no one disturbed her.

Before the second interview, two days later, she managed to wash her hair and change her clothes at a local swimming pool in return for the fifty-cent entry fee. She turned up at the publishing company and gave her most sparkling interview to a lady in the sales department, who was friendly and encouraging, but said at the end that she was sorry, they were going to hire another candidate on this occasion. Nancy would be put on a waiting list for the next post that came up.

That was a Friday, and her third interview, at Bernard Geis Associates, wasn't until Monday. She prayed that Louise would come home over the weekend. Maybe she'd gone out of town for a singing engagement. Maybe she had been visiting a friend. Whatever the reason, she'd be mortified when she realized she'd left Nancy in the lurch.

Nancy spent the days walking the streets, buying cups of coffee in diners and making them last till the waitresses got snappy. At least the weather was warm and dry, so she could sit on park benches reading until a passing drifter tried to convince her the world was about to end, then begged her for spare change. Every evening there was an anxious wait for someone to let her into Louise's building, and she lived in fear of another resident discovering her in the corridor and throwing her out. It was a stressful existence. Finding toilets, eating and drinking, washing and brushing her teeth, changing her clothes—everything had to be carefully planned, and the cost counted out in nickels and dimes.

On Monday morning she returned to the swimming pool to shower and dress for her third and final interview.

"I have *oodles* of office experience," she told Bernie Geis. "I worked in a bookstore in college and I reviewed books for the college paper." She crossed her fingers, praying under her breath. She needed this job badly.

"There's one final test we ask candidates to take," he said, and Nancy braced herself for a typing test, which she would inevitably fail.

Instead, Bernie led her out of his office to a central lobby area where a brass fireman's pole led up through a hole in the ceiling to the floor above. She'd noticed it on her way in and wondered if this was a converted fire station.

"To work here, you need to be willing to slide down the pole," he said. "It's our initiation test to check if you're the right sort. Want to give it a try?"

Nancy was wearing a tight knee-length skirt and wasn't sure how she would manage, but what choice did she have? It was this or return to Ossipee. She let herself be shown up to the floor above and glanced down through the gap. A group of men had gathered alongside Bernie.

"Come on, sweetheart," one called. "Don't be scared."

"All the girls who work here have to do it," another said. "Prove you're a good sport."

Nancy clutched her handbag under her arm, grasped the pole with both hands, then gripped it between her knees, took a deep breath and slid. Her skirt rode up over her garters and her descent was clumsy, but she thumped to the ground below and wriggled her skirt down to general applause, hooting, and cheering from the spectators.

"I think she's earned the job, don't you?" Bernie asked the assembled men, and they all agreed.

"Will you sort the formalities, Mrs. M?" Bernie turned to an older woman with a gunmetal perm, who was watching them with pursed lips.

Mrs. M told Nancy that the salary for secretaries was a measly seventy dollars a week, with only two weeks' vacation a year, but Nancy was in no position to negotiate.

"When can you start?" Mrs. M asked.

Nancy took a deep breath and explained that she was new in

town and needed to find somewhere to live first. Also, she asked if she could possibly have an advance on her salary so she could pay the deposit.

"I think Barbara in accounts has a spare room," Mrs. M said. "Let me ask."

Nancy agreed to share the apartment on the Lower East Side, without even viewing it first. She took the subway home with Barbara that evening and winced when Barbara unlocked the door. Salubrious, it wasn't. Cockroaches scuttled in the kitchen and several strains of fungus grew on the ceiling, but at least she had a mattress to sleep on, a washroom, and her own key to the front door. Compared to the corridor, this was a palace.

CHAPTER 2

Jacqueline

Hotel Navarro, Manhattan, 1965

J osephine hadn't eaten for a couple of days, and Jacqueline Susann was worried. The vet had put her on a regime of low-calorie dog food, just half a can a day, because her weight had crept up to twenty-five pounds, which he claimed was a full ten pounds more than a poodle ought to weigh. But Josephine refused point-blank to touch the low-calorie food. She whined and begged when Jacqueline and her husband, Irving, ate their own breakfast, then slumped on her bed, listless and depressed. She had to be dragged out for her morning walk and, after doing her business, she sat on the sidewalk, refusing to budge.

Jacqueline couldn't bear the reproach in those beautiful dark eyes any longer. After making sure Irving was busy in his office, she dialed room service and ordered a plate of chicken livers—Josephine's favorite—and some creamed rice. Thank God for room service! They lived off it. Irving complained when she used it for her darling poodle, but this was an emergency.

Since getting married, they had always lived in apartment hotels. She'd made it very clear to him that she wasn't the kind of girl who would cook or clean, and he'd accepted that. The Hotel Navarro, on Central Park South, was huge: twenty-five stories comprising 118 apartments of varying sizes, with a laundry, gymnasium, kitchen, and a round-the-clock concierge. She and Irving had a three-bedroom penthouse apartment, very modern in style, with windows that overlooked the park along one wall of the open-plan living/dining area.

Jacqueline had designed the décor herself: ivory linoleum on the floors (practical if Josephine had an accident), black lamp bases shaped like human torsos and topped by red lampshades, and walls covered with framed photographs of Irving and her with their many celebrity friends from the world of movies, television, and theater.

A waiter brought the food, and Jacqueline lifted Josephine onto her lap and offered a morsel of chicken liver. Josephine sniffed it, licked tentatively, then gulped it down.

"I think Josephine's got her appetite back," Jacqueline called to Irving.

"I don't know why you were worried. That belly would keep her going through weeks of famine," Irving called back.

"Ignore him," Jacqueline whispered, stroking Josephine's inky black ears, then offering another chicken liver. "He's rude."

The telephone rang and she snatched up the receiver. She was waiting for her publisher, Bernie Geis, to call about a novel she'd written, which he'd had on submission for three weeks now. *Three whole weeks!* It wasn't Bernie on the phone, though, but Helen Gurley Brown, a friend who had recently taken over as editor-in-chief of *Cosmopolitan* magazine. She had called to moan about the recalcitrant attitudes and lack of imagination of the staff she'd inherited from her predecessor. Jacqueline put the whole plate of chicken livers in front of Josephine, lit a Lucky Strike, and curled her legs beneath her. It was a long call, as she listened and asked questions and sympathized, and in the back of her mind she worried that Bernie might be trying to get through.

She'd put her heart and soul into this novel. It had taken two years of writing solidly, from ten to five, Monday through Friday, sitting in a room at the back of their apartment with just a desk, a chair, and a typewriter. A large blackboard on the wall was covered in a diagram drawn in different-colored chalks that showed the characters' storylines.

She'd gone through five separate drafts: first draft on white paper was for the bare bones; second draft on yellow paper focused on characterization; third draft on pink paper was all about story; in the fourth draft on blue paper she cut, cut, cut anything extraneous; and the fifth draft, on expensive white paper, was the one she'd sent to Bernie.

It wasn't just the work it had taken: she'd spilled her life onto those pages. She'd included memories of her almost thirty years' career in showbiz and the colorful folk she'd met along the way. She'd included the wisdom she'd acquired about relations between the sexes, based on her own affairs and her long experience of advising friends on their romantic escapades. And she'd included lust—plenty of steamy, explicit sex. She still cringed every time she pictured her mother reading it, but she'd cross that bridge later. She'd even been nervous about Irving reading it because some of the sex scenes involved feats they'd never attempted in the marital bed, but he'd said he loved it. He always had her back, no matter what.

Now the novel had to get published, it simply had to. Irving made enough as a showbiz producer and publicist to support the two of them, and she got paid decently for her writing and TV work, but she needed more than that—a heck of a lot more. Big money. Serious money. Not for her, but for her beloved son.

Jacqueline glanced at the phone, willing it to ring. She knew Bernie had been expecting another funny book, a sequel to *Every Night, Josephine!*, which she'd written about her darling poodle, but she was convinced this novel had more bestseller potential. Once it came out, she would go on the road and sell, sell, sell it with all her energy and verve. Irving knew everyone who was anyone in the media, and they would put their all behind it. She was raring to go.

But why hadn't Bernie rung?

"Do you think we should nudge Bernie?" she called to Irving.

"Not yet," he replied. "Give him time. He'll bite!"

She sighed and gave Josephine the rice pudding, kissing the top of her silky head and breathing in her delicious doggie scent.

CHAPTER 3

Jackie

London, 1962

Jackie Collins was sitting at her kitchen table, pen in hand, trying to write a novel. The baby was asleep and her husband was at work, so the time was ideal—but the words wouldn't come.

She'd always wanted to write. Back in her teens she used to charge schoolfriends sixpence a time to read breathless sex scenes she'd conjured from her imagination. She'd kept diaries from the age of ten and held on to them all, thinking they might provide inspiration for her writing one day. What she lacked was a plot. She'd started dozens of novels, always with an initial burst of enthusiasm. She'd scribble a few chapters, then invariably run out of steam before she sank into despair and abandoned them.

Might this one be different? It was about a sixteen-year-old girl having an affair with her movie idol. The idea had been rattling around in her head for ages. She could describe vividly the emotions of the sixteen-year-old because she had been like that girl. She'd gone to Hollywood to stay with her sister, Joan, in the Chateau Marmont while she tried to get work in the movies. At a party a few days after her arrival she'd caught eyes with a chiseled and brooding young actor called Marlon Brando, whom she recognized from the movie *A Streetcar Named Desire*. There had been hardly any conversation—a few taciturn mumbles on his part—before she let him whisk her to bed.

For a week they spent most of their time in her attic room at the Chateau, ordering room-service cheeseburgers and liquor, occasionally slipping downstairs for a moonlit swim in the pool, then rushing back up, dripping all over the plush carpets. Marlon wasn't one for small talk: he didn't tell her she was cute, he didn't pretend he loved her, but he couldn't keep his hands off her, and she took that as a huge compliment.

At the end of the week, he said, "Gotta split, babe. I'm in a movie that starts shooting tomorrow." She'd been cool about it, saying, "You know where I am. Come over if you get time off." But he never had. No matter. She had the memories, and there were plenty more hunks in Hollywood. It had been a heady time, although the studio contract she'd hoped for didn't materialize before her visa ran out.

She had managed to write the beginning of her latest novel— the bit about falling in love—but she wanted the couple to meet up again years later, after life had put them through the wringer, and she couldn't figure out how her story was going to end. Statistically, actors must have a higher percentage of failed marriages than any other profession, but she wanted her fictional couple to fall genuinely in love a second time around. Maybe they had learned some hard lessons during their years apart and that had changed them, but she couldn't think how to make a happy ending plausible.

She reread the twenty-three pages she'd written so far in her loopy handwriting. It sounded trite, like a breathless schoolgirl romance. The sex was too saccharine. The hero was a cardboard cutout. She realized she didn't know him at all, just as she had never known Marlon in any sense except physical.

Her baby, Tracy, started cooing from her cot in the next room, a musical sound like a little bird. Jackie folded the pages in half and stuck them in the bottom drawer of the bureau before going through to lift her adorable five-month-old, kiss her plump cheeks, and inhale her shampoo-and-milk scent. "Hello, little boogaloo," she said, smiling at her, and was rewarded with a gummy grin.

There would be no more writing for the day. She would take Tracy for a walk, pop in to visit her mum, pick up chops for tea, then come home and play till bath time. Tracy was an angelic baby so long as they stuck to her routines.

Her husband, Wallace, got back at half past six clutching a carrier bag with the logo of his fashion company, Mornessa. He flung an arm around her neck and kissed her hard on the lips. "Got a present for my foxy missus," he said with a grin, handing her the bag.

She passed him the baby and pulled out a silky dress in ocelot print, sleeveless, falling straight to just below the knee, with a black faux-leather belt cinching the waist.

"Oh my god, this is divine!" she exclaimed. "Are you sure I can have it? Shouldn't you be selling it?" She held it under her chin, smoothing it against her body, and could tell it would fit.

"My lady wife likes big cats, and has an amazing curvy figure, so the minute I saw this, I knew it was for her." He put Tracy down on the couch so he could wrap his arms around her.

"I'm going to try it on," she said, pushing him away and heading for the bedroom. "Don't let her roll off."

The dress fit like a second skin. She stood in front of a mirror that was propped against their bedroom wall, turning around and peering over her shoulder at the back view. She loved it. "We need to go out so I can show this off," she called. "Shall I get a babysitter for Saturday?"

She strutted back into the living room, hips thrust out catwalk style. Wallace was by the fridge, pouring them gin and tonics and not watching Tracy at all. Fortunately, she hadn't fallen off the couch but was sitting, quite content, sucking the corner of a cushion.

"I knew it would suit you," Wallace said. "Everything suits you. You'd look amazing in a potato sack." He handed her a drink and she clinked her glass against his before taking a sip, thinking how lucky she was that the baby weight had fallen off; she was already back to the dress size she'd been before getting pregnant.

"How did the writing go today?" he asked, and she pulled a face.

"Like eating soup with a fork." Who was she kidding? She didn't have the talent to be an author. The fact she never managed to finish anything was a sure sign she wasn't any good.

"You'll do it," Wallace said. "I know you'll get published and be a massive success. I can feel it in my boner." He patted his crotch and winked.

She placed a hand over his erection, giving it a squeeze. "Let me get the little boogaloo off to sleep, then I'll see what I can do about that," she told him, feeling an erotic stirring in her loins. "I have a few ideas I think you'll like."

She turned to pick up the baby with a seductive wiggle of her hips in her fancy new dress.

CHAPTER 4

Nancy

Manhattan, 1965

O n her third morning working as a secretary at Bernie Geis's publishing house, Nancy was asked to take minutes at the editorial meeting being held in Bernie's office. She perched on a stool by the corner of his oversize oak desk clutching a notebook and pencil, feeling apprehensive as a succession of middle-aged men arrived carrying coffee cups and ashtrays. They settled on the available chairs, greeting each other, ankles crossed over knees. Latecomers were forced to stand behind, leaning against the wall. Several men lit cigarettes with a mass clicking of lighters.

"These are last week's minutes." Bernie handed Nancy a densely typed document, three pages long. "We'll go through them first and all you need to do is mark changes, then type up new business."

The men glanced briefly at her but no one asked her name or thought to introduce himself. She examined the minutes. They listed the titles and authors of books the company had been offered, the date the agent needed a response by, and whether or not the editor planned to make an offer, but staff names were given as initials. Once the meeting started, it was like a crossword puzzle as she tried to figure out whether Darren was DP or DZ, and if Tom was TS or someone else entirely.

"Did David Wilkerson accept the deal?" Bernie asked a latecomer, who shook his head.

"He wants five thou," came the reply.

"Jeez. Is it worth that?" Bernie asked the room in general.

"The film rights brought in ten last time," someone replied, "but does he have more to say that wasn't covered in the first book? That's the question."

Nancy was still scouring the minutes, trying to find David Wilkerson, and didn't like to ask for Bernie's help. She decided to write everything down on the back of the pages and try to figure out where it all went later. The men spoke so fast it was hard to catch every nuance and she wished she hadn't lied about her secretarial experience at the interview. "Shorthand? Yes, of course," she remembered saying blithely.

"We have to decide what to do about the new Jacqueline Susann," Bernie said. "Have you all read Don's report? He's pretty scathing."

Nancy found the name Jacqueline Susann in last week's minutes and decided Don must be the DP mentioned alongside.

"Sounds like a disaster," one man said. "A tawdry soap opera with lots of what she calls 'humping.'"

Bernie agreed. "I skimmed part of it yesterday and I was embarrassed for her. Poor Irving! Doesn't sound as if she's had much personal experience of 'humping.'"

Someone else chipped in: "Seriously, you wouldn't go there, would you? Those big horsey teeth are terrifying, and the eyelashes flutter like agitated tarantulas."

"All that false hair is a fire hazard," another man contributed. "I'm scared to light up near her."

"She dresses as if she's still in her twenties, but what is she—late forties? She's had work done—you can see the scars by her ears."

Nancy was astonished by the venom. Surely the author's appearance wasn't relevant to the decision whether or not to publish a book? If that were the case, the majority of male authors would never have gotten into print.

"She has a two-book contract, but we can wriggle out of it because the second book was supposed to be a sequel to *Every Night, Josephine!*" Bernie put on a sarcastic voice to say the name Josephine. "As far as I can see, this is unpublishable."

"*Josephine* sold well, though," another man chipped in. "Thirty-five thousand copies, and it made number nine on the *Time* magazine list."

Nancy wrote that down. She guessed the speaker might be in sales, since he knew the figures off the top of his head.

"Who would have thought it?" yet another commented. "A book about her goddamn poodle! And I came into publishing to work on great literature."

"The poodles subsidize the great literature," Bernie said, "but I don't think we need to let the fake humping onto our list. Who's going to tell her?"

The men lowered their heads, shuffling papers.

"Why don't you try the Scarsdale Test?" The speaker was the same man who'd told them the sales figures for *Josephine*. He had sandy-blond hair in a crew cut so short it looked as if he'd just left the army. Nancy would have to ask one of the other secretaries who he was. She scribbled down the term "Scarsdale Test" although she didn't have the faintest clue what it meant.

"Darlene will kill me," Bernie said. "But OK, I'll ask." He turned to Nancy. "Leave it in the minutes till next week."

"What's the book's title?" Nancy asked, the first time she'd spoken. Last week's document just said "New Jacqueline Susann."

Bernie consulted the first page of a manuscript on the floor by his desk before he replied, his tone withering: "*Valley of the Dolls.*"

* * *

"WHAT'S THE SCARSDALE Test?" Nancy asked Barbara as she scrubbed a pot in the sink so she could scramble some eggs for supper.

Barbara was sitting at the kitchen table, painting her nails a plum color. "Bernie sometimes takes manuscripts home to his wife, Darlene, to get a woman's point of view," she explained, "and they live in Scarsdale."

"Why doesn't he ask us?" Nancy wondered. She had come into publishing hoping to read manuscripts and help discover new authors, but all she had done so far was brainless typing and filing. That afternoon had been spent tracking down Bernie's wallet after he left it in a taxi following a long lunch. Minuting the editorial meeting had been the highlight of her week, although stressful at the same time.

"Darlene's an author of children's books," Barbara said, "so I guess he trusts her opinion."

Nancy vowed she would work hard and learn as much as she could so that one day Bernie would trust her opinion too.

After eating her eggs, she took out the editorial minutes and asked Barbara's help in identifying the men behind the initials. She found out that the one who'd suggested the Scarsdale Test was a sales executive, Steven Bailey—SB. Don was an editor called Don Preston—DP.

The next morning, when she got to the office, Nancy noticed that the *Valley of the Dolls* manuscript was still on the floor by Bernie's desk. He must have forgotten to take it home. She decided to make a Xerox copy, all six hundred pages of it, as a precaution in case he left it in a taxi or on a train. It would give her a chance to read it at the same time as Darlene, she thought, and hoped no one would mind. That lunchtime she took the first chunk of pages to the park and raced through them. She took the rest home that evening, and sat up reading till three a.m., her head filled with the adventures of Anne, Jennifer, and Neely.

Like her, Anne had just arrived in Manhattan hoping to forge an exciting career. She came from a sleepy hometown and was an innocent in the big city. It felt like Nancy's own story, with Anne taking a job in which she felt out of her depth. She could sense she shouldn't be trusting her friendship with the duplicitous Helen, an aging Broadway star. She could tell that Neely, the aspiring singer Helen had sacked from a production, was going to cause trouble. She knew that Jennifer was making a mistake by jumping into marriage with the crooner Tony Polar, who seemed strangely dependent on his sister. She felt she understood these characters.

The novel was flawed. The story jumped bizarrely. Sometimes Miss Susann appeared to have forgotten she'd left her characters in one situation and she picked them up somewhere entirely different. There were loads of spelling mistakes and grammatical errors. But the core of it was an incredible, fast-paced read about modern women. She wondered what Darlene would think. Dare she offer Bernie her own opinion, or would he be cross that she'd read it?

At the beginning of the following week's editorial meeting, Bernie thumped the manuscript down on his desk. "Bad news," he said. "Darlene insists we absolutely have to publish the Jacqueline Susann. She says women will love it and it's going to be huge."

Nancy suppressed a grin as she jotted this down in the minutes. Her instinct had been right.

"It needs masses of work," Bernie said. "Lots of structural editing, rewriting, a complete overhaul. I'm going to give Don six weeks off his other books to knock it into shape."

Nancy had made copious notes and felt she knew what the

story required. She was dying to speak up, and only held her tongue with difficulty.

"It's a tall order," Bernie said, "so I'll ask one of the secretaries to help with the retyping and ferrying queries back and forth to the dreaded Jacqueline."

Nancy jumped in: "I'll do it," she said, forgetting about her dismal typing speed. "Please. I know I can manage."

Steven Bailey caught her eye and gave a quick smile of encouragement.

Bernie shrugged. "I'm sure there won't be any other volunteers lining up, so why not? Let's give it a shot. But we'll have to change that title or booksellers will end up stocking it in the kids' department. *Valley of the Dolls* indeed!"

CHAPTER 5

Jacqueline

Hotel Navarro, 1965

When Jacqueline heard Irving answer the telephone and say "Hi, Bernie," she dashed to his side, leaning close to hear what was being said. "You will?" Irving grinned and gave her a thumbs-up. Bernie was going to publish *Valley of the Dolls*.

She punched the air in triumph, then twirled around the sitting room, Josephine yapping at her heels, while Irving discussed terms. *Dolls* was going to be published! She was ecstatic. It was the best news *ever*!

There was a proviso in the offer, Irving told her when he came off the call: she had to cooperate with them to revise and "tighten it up."

"Sure! I can do that," she agreed. She could listen to their suggestions; it didn't mean she had to accept them.

The following week Bernie and a young girl by the name of Nancy came to their apartment for the first meeting. Jacqueline clutched Josephine on her lap and stroked her as she listened to Bernie tell her what they thought was wrong with the novel. "Meandering plot," "lack of insight into characters' motivations," "clichéd descriptions": he didn't spare her feelings. She kept her face expressionless and pretended her orange-and-pink swirly-patterned Pucci dress was a suit of armor, her black wig a helmet, and her makeup a visor. He was a boring little man. What did he know anyway?

She noticed Nancy flinching at a particularly brutal criticism and warmed to her; at least one person in the room had some empathy. Irving was busy reading the fine print of the contract and wasn't paying attention to the conversation.

When Bernie finished his list, Jacqueline paused to steel herself before she replied. "As you know, Bernie, I'm always happy to accommodate editorial suggestions that improve the book. What I won't do is compromise my characters, because I know them better than you ever will." She pitied Bernie's wife; he certainly didn't demonstrate any understanding of female psychology.

"This kind of book needs a happy ending," Bernie told her. "Readers will want that. Not for all the characters, of course, but you can't destroy Anne. They won't stand for it."

Jacqueline noticed Nancy give a slight shake of the head. "What do you think?" she asked, turning toward her.

"Anne is an archetypal innocent," Nancy replied. "To give her an upbeat ending would be like Hardy having Tess of the D'Urbervilles live happily ever after with Angel Clare, or Tolstoy turning Anna Karenina and Vronsky into the perfect couple. It doesn't fit the narrative expectations."

Jacqueline had to restrain herself from grinning as she watched Bernie shoot daggers at Nancy for disagreeing with him.

"Have you ever taken amphetamines, Bernie?" Jacqueline asked. "Or tried LSD?"

"Of course not!"

"So you have no idea what effect pills have. I do, and that's why I will never promote drug use by having my characters emerge unscathed from addiction. It would be totally irresponsible." She turned to Nancy again. "What did you think of the book, dear? Did you enjoy it, despite what Bernie calls the 'meandering plot'?"

"I couldn't put it down," the girl replied. "Far from meandering, I think the jumps in point of view help to maintain pace, and the story arcs mesh together very satisfyingly."

She had an unusual mix of qualities, Jacqueline thought: achingly pretty, with strawberry-blond shoulder-length hair and sea-blue eyes, yet she clearly didn't care about her appearance, because she wasn't wearing makeup and her pale blue cotton frock and brown T-bar sandals were desperately old-fashioned. She was an intellectual, probably a literature graduate, but she could still appreciate a novel like *Dolls*, which had no literary pretensions. Most impressive of all, she had the courage to express her opinions when they contradicted those of her boss; Jacqueline was always drawn to women who weren't afraid to speak the truth to men in positions of power.

Irving looked up and winked at Jacqueline. "The girl has excellent taste!" he said, turning to Bernie. "We like her."

"What age are you?" Jacqueline asked.

"Twenty-two," the girl replied.

Four years older than her son. He was good-looking too, but there the similarities ended. While Nancy had the whole world in front of her, with choices of career, husband, home, and children, her son had no choices at all. His life would be forever limited.

"How long have you been working at Bernie Geis?" she asked.

Nancy gave a shy smile. "Just under three weeks and I'm loving it," she gushed. "I dreamed of working in publishing from the moment I learned to read. I'm addicted to books, every bit as much as your characters are addicted to pills."

She was adorable, Jacqueline thought, and still so innocent. "You've got a New England accent. Am I right?"

Nancy agreed.

"Weren't your parents worried about you coming to live in the Big Bad Apple?" Jacqueline asked.

"Both my parents are dead," Nancy said, a slight tremor in her voice. "And my stepfather is busy bringing up my stepbrothers, so he didn't really mind me being off his hands."

"Do you have any family in the city?" Jacqueline asked. "You're very young to be here on your own."

"My cousin Louise lives in Chelsea," the girl replied. "I was hoping to stay with her, but she seems to be away somewhere."

"That's too bad. I hope she gets back soon."

Bernie cleared his throat, signaling that he wanted to return to the business at hand. "We need to change the title," he said. "*Valley of the Dolls* won't work for bookshops. We'll send you a list of our ideas."

"Don't waste your time," Jacqueline told him, "because for me that's a deal-breaker. You want my book, you use my title."

Irving flicked to a page in the contract and began to argue with Bernie about the interpretation of a clause concerning titles.

As he spoke, Jacqueline continued to watch Nancy. Despite her surface assurance, she was clearly vulnerable. Bad things could happen to pretty, naïve girls alone in the city, especially motherless ones. She decided she'd keep an eye on her. It seemed Nancy was to be the go-between while Bernie's editor worked on *Valley*. That was good. They could get to know each other better.

* * *

THAT NIGHT, JACQUELINE couldn't sleep, although she'd taken two red pills and washed them down with a large whiskey. Irving was snoring and wheezing, with a sound like a death rattle. Her thoughts were with her son. She generally tried to avoid seeing friends' kids who were around his age because they highlighted all that he was missing. But if she was to work with Nancy, she would have to confront it because Nancy was his contemporary. In another lifetime, maybe she and her son could have dated—

or even married. Nancy could have been her daughter-in-law, could have produced grandchildren for her. Oh, how she would have spoiled those grandchildren!

She thought back to her pregnancy, which had been the happiest time in her life. Everything had slotted into place. Irving had come back from war uninjured, and she had gotten pregnant just under a year later. She'd had a healthy pregnancy and a straightforward delivery of the sweetest, most perfect baby she'd ever seen. Then a few weeks in, a suspicion began to creep up on her that all was not well. Her son didn't seem as responsive as other babies. He didn't babble and play the way her friends' babies did. Irving told her she was being paranoid, but the anxiety grew and she sought opinions from doctors. Then came the darkest period of her life, when her little boy was diagnosed with Kanner's syndrome, also known as infantile autism. The specialist recommended he would be best cared for in an institution, but at first Jacqueline rejected that out of hand. She would cope. She'd find a way.

She started reading all she could and learned that Kanner's children did not respond to external stimuli in the ordinary way; for them, everything felt brighter, louder, stronger, and more overwhelming than for the rest of the population. Kanner's children preferred to be alone and didn't interact socially, so it was difficult for them to form relationships. They didn't like physical contact, loud noises, or strong smells, and they were prone to repetitive actions like rocking and flapping their hands. Dr. Kanner's research claimed that parents of children with this syndrome were often cold and uncaring—he used the term "refrigerator mothers"—and for Jacqueline that was a brutal twist of the knife. Nothing could have been further from the truth. She'd showered that baby with love and affection from the second he was born. She adored every tiny bit of him.

"It's because you hired a nurse," her mother said, thoughtlessly. "You didn't get a chance to bond with him properly."

Deep down, Jacqueline would never forgive her for that. Rose had always been spiky and tactless, and they'd had a complicated relationship, but this was a new low. She wasn't about to cut ties with her own mother—she and Irving continued to visit her in Philadelphia a couple of times a year—but she held her at arm's length.

Truth be told, Jacqueline did blame herself for the Kanner's. Was it because she took sleeping pills and the occasional dexy during her pregnancy? Her obstetrician had said they were safe but doctors didn't know everything. Had she made mistakes in her son's early months that caused his disability? The specialist insisted it wasn't her fault, that Kanner had gotten it wrong about parents being responsible, but perhaps he was trying to comfort her.

When her darling boy was three, she finally had to accept that she and Irving couldn't cope. He got very distressed and screamed for hours on end, needing round-the-clock attention they couldn't give. It wasn't fair to keep him at home for selfish reasons when an institution with trained staff could help him better, but the pain of handing him over to strangers was excruciating. He didn't speak so he wouldn't be able to tell them if anyone treated him badly. He was totally at the mercy of staff hired by the institution, and it felt all wrong.

Jacqueline broke down after leaving him there. She drank too much and took too many pills, seeking oblivion in a chemical haze. Finally she checked herself into a sanitorium for a rest cure, and that at least helped her to wean herself off the self-administered anesthetics.

When she got home again, Irving suggested trying for another baby, as if they could simply replace their son, as if he were saying, *That one didn't work out but maybe the next one will*. She stared at him, open-mouthed. How could he imagine another baby would fix anything? She refused, because the specialist said there was a chance their next child might also have Kanner's, and she couldn't go through that again. It would kill her.

She didn't tell anyone but her closest friends about her son's illness because she held out hope of a cure one day and didn't want him to be stigmatized. Instead, she and Irving concocted a story that he was receiving treatment for severe asthma and that's why he didn't live with them. After a while, most people stopped asking.

As their son grew up, they chose the very best institutions for him, guided by the experts, but the fees weren't cheap. That's why Jacqueline was so determined to write bestselling novels. Her son could outlive both of them by decades and she needed to leave enough money to pay for his care for the rest of his life, however long that might be.

She had always enjoyed writing. She'd dissected Harold Robbins's bestseller *The Carpetbaggers* scene by scene and figured she could do something similar. With *Valley of the Dolls*, she'd given it her best shot.

* * *

A WEEK AFTER their initial meeting, Nancy came back to the Hotel Navarro with the first batch of edits. Jacqueline took the pages from her and invited the girl to sit down and have a coffee. Straight away Josephine climbed onto her lap, and that was a ringing endorsement because she was very choosy with her favors.

"What kind of work do they have you doing at the office?" Jacqueline asked.

"Typing letters," Nancy said with a flinch, and Jacqueline got the impression she didn't much like typing. "Filing what feels like years' worth of ancient correspondence. And organizing Mr. Geis's diary. He's prone to double-booking himself, then asking me to make excuses for him. Frankly, I don't know why he bothers with a diary because he never consults it anyway. He just relies on me to remind him where he's supposed to be."

Jacqueline smiled to herself. The girl was sweet and likable—and her indiscretion could make her a useful spy. Bernie was a hustler and she didn't trust him as far as she could throw him. She would get Nancy to tell her the decisions being made about her book, in time to countermand them if necessary.

"That doesn't seem a good use of your talents," she advised. "You're a smart girl and you should be in a more challenging role."

"My ambition is to be an editor of women's fiction," Nancy said. "Publishing houses don't focus on it enough, but when I worked in a bookstore at college I noticed that women buy the most books. They're often buying them for men but they'll slip in a novel or two for themselves, as a 'little treat.' My mom used to be a voracious reader and I guess she passed it on to me."

Jacqueline detected a wobble in her voice when she mentioned her mom. "You're very young to have lost both parents," she said. "What happened?"

"My dad died of cancer when I was thirteen," she said, "and Mom died suddenly of a heart attack in February this year." She blinked hard and Jacqueline reached out to take her hand. She'd been thirty-nine when her beloved father died, and she'd had Irving to comfort her, but still her world had been shattered. She'd been a doting daddy's girl, and it looked as though Nancy had been equally close to her mom.

"You seem very alone," she said. "Did your cousin Louise turn up yet?"

Nancy shook her head. "I've put a note under her door asking her to call my office number when she gets back."

"What's Louise's job?" Jacqueline asked. "Do you think work has taken her away?"

"She's a singer. She performs in clubs. I guess she must have gotten a new contract somewhere and forgot to tell me. Her parents are divorced and live out West—Nevada, or Utah, I'm not sure which. I don't have their numbers, so I'll have to wait till I hear."

"Have you made any friends in the city?" Jacqueline persisted, and Nancy scrunched her mouth to one side.

"Sort of," she replied. "I have a roommate, Barbara, but . . ." She didn't finish the sentence.

"I hope you'll consider me a friend," Jacqueline told her. "You've got my number. Don't be shy to call."

Maybe she'd invite Nancy for lunch somewhere swanky, the kind of place she'd never been before. Her clothes looked like they came from a thrift store, so she clearly wasn't flush. Someone should be looking out for her, and she would enjoy playing fairy godmother. With her bright-eyed ambition, the girl reminded her of herself back when she first arrived in the city all those decades ago.

CHAPTER 6

Jackie

London, 1962

J ackie was shocked when the landlord knocked on the door one afternoon and told her that they were six months behind on the rent. *Six! How could that be?*

"I'm sorry, I know you have a baby," he said, "but I can't let it slide any further."

"Of course not," she replied. "I'm sure there's a misunderstanding. I'll talk to my husband."

She'd thought Wallace made a good living from Mornessa. Had he simply forgotten to pay the rent? His memory could be erratic.

"I had to inject more capital into the company," he explained when he got home that evening. "I'm investing in new designs from India—but don't worry, they'll pay off soon." He opened his briefcase and pulled out some lengths of gold-bordered sari fabrics in lime green, shocking pink, lilac, and midnight blue, draping them across her playfully.

She stepped backward. "These are lovely but what will I tell the landlord? Can you pay him this week? Or next?" She'd promised to call him the following morning.

"Tell him he's lucky to have two such divinely sexy tenants and we'll pay when we're good and ready."

Jackie frowned. Soon after their wedding, Wallace had been diagnosed as manic depressive. She was initially relieved because it made sense of his extreme mood swings. When a "high" episode came on, he was spontaneous and great fun to be around, booking impromptu skiing holidays in Gstaad, or flying them to the South of France to have a flutter in a new casino; during the worst of his "lows" he was so depressed he couldn't drag himself out of bed. He didn't like taking the barbiturates the doctor prescribed, which made him slow and fuzzy-brained, and claimed he could deal with the unpredictable moods by himself.

Jackie was learning to recognize the warning signs when an episode was looming and the ways she could help him to manage it. She worried that getting so far behind on the rent might mean one of his "highs" was imminent and was about to say as much when she heard voices in the hall outside, followed by a loud knocking on the door.

"I invited a few friends from the pub," he said. "You don't mind, do you, darling?"

"What, now?" Jackie rushed to retrieve some pages of her novel, which she'd left on the kitchen table, and shoved them in a drawer so no one could laugh at her literary efforts. Next she threw Tracy's changing mat into her pram and wedged it against the wall by the coat stand. Wallace flung open the door and ushered in half a dozen folk who were laughing raucously, as if someone had just told a particularly good joke.

She knew most of the group and went around greeting them, cheek-kissing and fetching glasses for the bottles of hooch they'd brought. Wallace put a Ray Charles LP on the record player and one couple shifted the coffee table and began to dance.

Jackie had grown up in a household where impromptu parties were common. Her father, Joe Collins, was a theatrical agent, and often brought home a crowd after a show. Her mother, Elsa, was a good sport who always contrived to make guests feel welcome no matter what the hour, and Jackie did the same now, swallowing her irritation when a wail from the bedroom indicated that the baby had been wakened by their revelry.

She slipped next door to settle Tracy with a quick feed. She was breastfeeding, against the advice of the nurses at the hospital and almost all the childcare experts. To her, it felt natural and nurturing. Why else would a woman's body produce milk if it weren't the best food for newborns?

A banker friend of Wallace's burst into the room and took in the scene.

"I was looking for the bathroom," he said, "but may I say—cor! What incredible knockers you have!"

"Out!" Jackie ordered him with a forced smile. "Next door down the hall."

When Tracy fell asleep at her breast, Jackie laid her down in her cot and rejoined the party. Someone was making toast under the grill, using the last of her bread. She'd have to go to the shops before breakfast. She wandered from group to group, making conversation, and striving not to yawn in their faces. Tracy would be awake at dawn, and it was creeping ever closer.

Around two thirty, there was another knock on the door and Johnny Gold, a close friend of theirs, appeared with a floppy-drunk blonde on his arm. Jackie adored Johnny. He was the biggest lothario in London, squiring a different girl every night, but he had a heart as big as a castle.

"You look knackered, sweetheart," he said as he kissed her in greeting. "Want me to get rid of this lot?"

"Oh God, I'd love it. Have a drink first, then round them up, if you can."

Good as his word, ten minutes later Johnny called out: "Time for bed, ladies and gents! We've imposed on this lovely couple's hospitality for long enough."

He had an air of authority and the guests downed their drinks and trooped out.

Wallace turned to Jackie, his face accusing: "Did you tell him to throw them out?"

"Of course not!" She harnessed all the acting skills she'd gleaned from the dozens of British B movies she'd appeared in.

Wallace eyed her with suspicion but she disappeared into the bedroom before he could start a drunken row. She kicked off her shoes and collapsed into bed without bothering to undress or remove her makeup, and within seconds she was asleep.

* * *

THE NEXT MORNING Wallace sipped an Alka-Seltzer and water, clutching his temples and groaning, before heading for the office. Once he was gone, Jackie pushed the pram to the corner shop for bread, milk, and tea leaves—the guests had finished her tea as well. She mused that while she'd thought she was marrying someone who was the polar opposite of her domineering, unpredictable father, he and Wallace had certain qualities in common— such as a total lack of consideration for their wives and children. But at least Wallace was a loving and generous husband, while her father had been foul to her mother—and to her.

"Useless good-for-nothing," Joe used to call her when she still lived at home. "Shame you didn't get your sister's looks. How does it feel being the ugly duckling of the brood?"

"Silver-tongued as always, Pop," she retorted, pretending a nonchalance she didn't feel. Her elder sister, Joan, was beautiful, glamorous, and a successful actress, and she knew she could never hope to live up to her, but the repeated reminders from their father were bruising.

He didn't just deliver psychological blows but treated her poor mother as a punching bag on which to take out his drunken frustrations. He had sometimes raised his hand to Jackie when he was in his cups—just a slap on the backside or a clip round the ear, but they hurt.

Wallace had only hit Jackie twice, both times when he was

suffering one of his manic episodes, so she didn't consider them his fault. The first was after they had been married only a few months, when she broke the news that she was pregnant. She'd thought he'd be pleased but instead he exploded.

"Why weren't you more careful? I made it very clear I don't want children yet." His face twisted with fury.

"Babies tend to have their own timetables," she said. "Anyway, it's happened now."

"I don't want to come home to a flat stinking of dirty nappies and a grumpy, sleep-deprived wife. Maybe I'll feel differently in a few years, but we're young. We should be having fun."

"A *baby* will be fun. It will be an adventure," she insisted. "Besides, I'm twenty-three. I don't want to leave it too late."

"I fell in love with you because you weren't like other girls, Jackie. You liked living on the wild side. Don't let me down by turning into your mother."

Jackie flared up. She wouldn't hear a word against her mother, who in her eyes was a saint. Elsa had been ill recently—"just a virus," she insisted, but Jackie sensed it was something more. She seemed to be getting weaker, and she'd heard her retching in the bathroom.

"My mother is going to be thrilled to hear she's about to have her first grandchild," she told Wallace, "and I can't wait to tell her, so you'd better get used to it."

His fist crunched into her face so fast she didn't have time to duck. She was thrown back against the sofa, too shocked to scream. Her first thought was for her nose. She'd had plastic surgery two years earlier, swapping her big hooter for a neat, slim nose that she loved. It suited her face and gave her a boost. She touched it carefully, running her fingers along the bridge: she'd kill him if he'd broken it. Her whole face hurt, so it was hard to feel where the damage was. She licked her lip and tasted blood.

Wallace was watching her with a defiant look, fists still clenched as he waited for her reaction.

Jackie hauled herself to her feet, her head spinning, and staggered toward the bathroom to check the damage. She turned in the doorway and said, in a low, warning tone: "If you ever do that again, I swear I'll leave you."

"If you leave me, I'll kill myself and it will be all your fault," he replied straight away.

She slammed the door.

The second time he hit her, when she was eight months' pregnant, it was just a punch on the shoulder but she lost her balance and fell to the ground. Afterward she lay very still, trying to feel the baby moving, terrified it might have been harmed.

Both times Wallace was contrite. He cried, swearing it would never happen again. Old Joe had never apologized after he used his fists on her mother, and he didn't have the excuse of a manic depression diagnosis. There was no comparison between them in that sense. Wallace wasn't a violent man. It wasn't in his nature to hit women. He was a good person, and Jackie knew he loved her to pieces, just as she loved him.

* * *

A FEW DAYS after the impromptu party, Jackie wheeled the pram around to her family home. She took Tracy to visit several afternoons a week because her mum got so much pleasure from watching the baby play on the floor, even if she was too frail to hold her in her arms.

Jackie had to have a difficult conversation with her. Wallace couldn't predict when he might have enough money to pay the rent arrears and the landlord had said he had no choice but to evict them. She daren't ask her father for a loan—she could just imagine the sarcastic outburst that would provoke—but she knew her mother had a little money from an inheritance.

"I'll be able to pay you back if I get a book deal," Jackie explained, not adding that the chances of her ever finishing a novel seemed remote. "Or Wallace will pay you when the company is doing better." She felt humiliated asking. They should have been able to support themselves by now.

Without a word of recrimination, Elsa reached for her handbag and took out a checkbook and pen. In a whisper, Jackie told her the amount they owed, and she made a check payable to their landlord and handed it over. Then she wrote another check. This one was made out to Jackie and the amount was a staggering five thousand pounds. Jackie gasped.

"This is not for Wallace," her mum said firmly. "It's for you and Tracy. This is your nest egg. Put it in a private savings account and don't tell him about it. *Promise* me." Her voice was firm.

"I promise," Jackie said.

She was embarrassed to be taking money from her mum, embarrassed that Elsa knew Wallace wasn't managing to support his family. She would never let on about the rest of her marital troubles, though.

Wallace was still the love of her life. Their problems were all caused by the manic depression. She'd felt protective of him when he first got the diagnosis and determined to help him manage the illness, but now that she had a baby it felt as if she had two children to look after: a six-month-old and a twenty-four-year-old. She would have to be the strong, stable one. Somehow she would cope, because she loved them both so passionately.

If only she could find time to finish a novel and start earning herself, so that she didn't ever have to ask her mum for money again. She'd try to write during the baby's afternoon nap, she told herself, then yawned so widely her jaw clicked.

CHAPTER 7

Nancy

Bernard Geis Associates, 1965

Nancy was allocated a desk right outside Bernie's book- and paper-strewn office, on the edge of the uniform rows of the typing pool. She was nervous at first. How would this work? Dare she volunteer her own opinions on *Valley of the Dolls?* Would Bernie sack her when he realized her typing wasn't up to scratch? This was why she had wanted to get into publishing—to learn how books were made—but everyone was scathing about Jacqueline Susann's novel. "VD," Bernie rudely called it.

"You have to admit it's trash," he said. "As if she's vomited onto the page."

Don, the editor, worked from home and Nancy seldom saw him. When a batch of edits was left on her desk, she took them over to the Hotel Navarro. Once she got Jacqueline's responses, she retyped that section of the manuscript, then it would go back and forth until all parties were happy. If there were loads of scribbles and crossings-out, Nancy would have to type up another clean copy for the typesetter. By then she reckoned she would know the whole book by heart—and hopefully her typing speed would have improved.

Watching the way Don edited was a fascinating introduction to the craft. She noted how he drafted a clear introduction to each character on first appearance: who they were, what they looked like, and what their "goal" was. He didn't seem to like what he called "back story" and was forever asking Jacqueline to cut it so it didn't slow the action. He also wanted her to cut lengthy descriptions of setting for the same reason. Every chapter, every page, had to move the story forward. Nancy felt privileged to learn from such an experienced teacher.

She took it upon herself to check the spellings of drug names, after finding a mistake in one of them. A public library down the street proved invaluable for checking all kinds of facts. She was determined to keep up with the flow of work so they didn't miss the six-week deadline Bernie had imposed, so she stayed in the office each evening until she had caught up with the day's retyping. Sometimes she didn't get back to Barbara's until midnight, and she was often forced to skip meals because she couldn't afford the pizza and burger joints near the office.

As Nancy typed up Jacqueline's revisions one day, she realized a plot strand about Neely was still not making sense. Nancy checked and rechecked the notes before daring to mention it to Jacqueline.

"I wondered if it might be useful to explain why Neely had lost her voice when she came back from Europe?" she ventured. "You imply it was because of psychological trauma but perhaps it would strengthen the characterization to use the medical term, 'aphonia'—which means 'a loss of voice brought on by emotional stress.'"

"Sure, we can mention that," Jacqueline said.

"Sufferers find it impossible to raise their voice above a hoarse whisper, and the voice they hear in their head sounds strange to them, which must be devastating for a singer." Nancy had read a research paper about it in the library. "Perhaps you could expand on Neely's anxiety about this, and her fear that she will never sing again."

"Great idea," Jacqueline said. "Good work, Nancy! Don't be afraid to come to me with any further suggestions."

It was that easy? Nancy was brimming with pride as she typed up her very first editorial correction.

* * *

A GIRL WITH waist-length sun-kissed hair, a white crocheted blouse, and an eye-popping short orange skirt stopped by Nancy's desk and introduced herself as Brandi, saying she was an assistant in the publicity department. She wanted to know if any pages of Jacqueline's novel were available to tantalize journalists, so Nancy gave her the first batch that she was sure had been approved.

"The great thing about Jacqueline Susann," Brandi told her, perching on the edge of her desk, her unbelievably long legs crossed at the ankles, "is that she treats publishing like a business and is prepared to go to any lengths to publicize her books. That's what we like. The bad thing about her is that there is no end to her demands." She smiled at Nancy. "I hear you're getting on well with her. We wondered if you might continue to deal with her once the campaign starts? She needs one-on-one attention, but one of our team is pregnant and we have dozens of authors to manage. Bernie says it will be good for you to learn a different side of the business."

Mesmerized by this confident, stunning young woman, Nancy didn't hesitate: "Of course. What will I have to do?"

"We're planning a nationwide book tour," Brandi said. "Jacqueline's idea. She's the first author ever to do this, but she and Irving have great media contacts so I'm sure she'll make it work. She needs someone to reserve flights, limo drivers, and hotel rooms, arrange for books to be delivered to the locations of her appearances—plus whatever else she wants wherever she happens to be. I've put together a folder of useful numbers."

Nancy glanced inside the folder. She'd never booked a flight or a hotel room before, but it all sounded wildly exciting. "Were you here when *Sex and the Single Girl* was published?" she asked Brandi. It was a bestselling advice book by Helen Gurley Brown that Bernie Geis had published in 1962. Nancy had read it cover to cover twice. "What was she like?"

"Helen's a dear," Brandi said, "so it all went swimmingly. Jacqueline, on the other hand . . . well, bless you, you'll find out in due course."

"What does that mean?" Nancy asked. She was puzzled that so many people at Bernard Geis Associates described Jacqueline as difficult. So far, she'd been nothing but charming toward her.

Brandi slid off the desk with a slight eye roll, and said, "I'm sure you'll be fine," before gliding away toward the stairs. Nancy hoped Bernie wouldn't ever make her slide down the pole in that skirt; it would be positively obscene.

* * *

JACQUELINE HAD STRONG views about the editing of what she called "her baby." Nancy soon got to know the words she preferred. She liked "tit" and "boobs" but hated "nipples" ("too bestial"). Homosexuals were "fags" to her, and she preferred the terms "humping" or "fucking" to "making love." If any of these had been changed, they had to be switched straight back again. A sentence had been cut from the first page—"New York was an angry concrete animal that day"—that she insisted point-blank should be reinstated.

Don had asked her to write a few new scenes he felt were necessary, such as Anne losing her virginity to Lyon in a seedy hotel room, and Neely and Helen fighting in a washroom. Nancy worried that she would object to this, but when she visited a week later, the new scenes were ready and waiting. There was no denying Jacqueline was a hard worker.

After she dropped off some pages one morning, Nancy was astonished when Jacqueline invited her to lunch at the Plaza Hotel.

"Have you ever been?" Jacqueline asked. "It's very chichi. Irving?" she hollered. "Call and book our usual table." She turned back to Nancy. "I bought something for you. I saw it on a rack at Saks and thought it was made for you, with your fabulous slim figure." She retrieved a red Saks carrier bag from beneath her desk and handed it over.

Nancy blushed. "I don't know if I'm allowed to accept gifts," she said.

"Sure you are! It's a token of my appreciation for all your hard work on my novel. Have a look!"

Nancy reached inside and pulled out a black silk evening dress with rhinestone straps. She could feel the quality of the fabric. The design was simple, stopping just above the knee, and it had built-in bust support so you didn't need to wear a bra.

"Try it on!" Jacqueline suggested, gesturing toward a bedroom. "Over there."

Nancy didn't recognize herself in the full-length mirror. The dress gave curves to her boyish, straight-up-and-down figure, making her look chic and sophisticated. She had never seen herself in that light.

"Perfect for cocktail parties," Jacqueline said approvingly when Nancy went back in to show her. "This will wow the men in your life."

"I can't thank you enough. I've never owned anything like this . . ."

Irving interrupted, coming into the room to say he had a table in ten minutes' time, then he stopped dead and wolf-whistled his appreciation. "Look at you," he said. "Whadda dame!"

Nancy suppressed a grin. He sounded like a hustler from *Guys and Dolls* with his Noo Yoick accent. She went to get changed while Jacqueline crouched to say goodbye to Josephine, feeding her some slivers of ham. The dog was sweet, Nancy thought, but grossly overweight and clearly spoiled rotten.

They walked the couple of blocks to the Plaza, where they

were led into the Palm Court, with real palm trees stretching toward an Art Deco glass ceiling. Nancy was overawed by the grandeur of the décor and felt underdressed in her corduroy skirt and polo-neck sweater. When she opened the menu, it was full of dishes she didn't recognize, like Consommé Sultan and Timbale, Renaissance.

"Shall I order for you?" Irving asked. "I can recommend the lamb with mint sauce."

Nancy was grateful for his help. She glanced around at the other diners: ladies with fur stoles and tight perms, and besuited gentlemen with oil-slick hair. Were they looking down their noses at her? Or didn't they notice her at all?

Jacqueline asked if her cousin Louise had shown up yet, and Nancy replied, "No, it's a mystery. I hope she's alright."

"Something must have come up to make her forget the invitation," Jacqueline mused. "Maybe she's having a wild love affair."

Nancy hoped that was true, but couldn't help worrying about her sophisticated older cousin. They had grown up on opposite sides of the country and there was a twelve-year age gap, but Louise used to visit them in Ossipee every summer. They shared a bedroom and spent their days sunbathing at the lakeside, where Louise flirted with the local boys. She seemed worldly and daring, with her talk of which ones were good kissers and what it felt like when you smoked marijuana. She fell in and out of love with giddy speed, and Nancy listened with awe to this glimpse into an adult world.

"How's your roomie, Barbara?" Jacqueline asked, interrupting her thoughts. "Has she washed a dish yet?"

Nancy was astonished Jacqueline remembered these details. "Not to my knowledge," she replied. "I'm saving up for an apartment of my own because it's difficult sharing with someone who has such different standards of hygiene." Jacqueline made a face of disgust when she described pulling hanks of Barbara's decomposing hair out of the bath drain.

Next Jacqueline began to quiz her about her mother's death and her relationship with her stepfather.

As she answered, Nancy's thoughts returned to the phone call that had shattered her life in a split second. She'd been in the public booth in her halls at college when her stepfather told her that her mother had dropped dead of a heart attack in the kitchen just a few hours earlier. "It was so fast she won't have felt a thing," he said, as if that should be a comfort. Nancy slid down the wall to sit on the floor and stayed there after the call ended, still clutching the receiver. She couldn't think what to do. *Where should she go? Who should she tell? How could she carry on?*

At the funeral, her stepdad told her to come home when she finished college so they could "pull together as a family," but Nancy couldn't face Ossipee. He'd married her mom only seven years earlier, and for three of those Nancy had been away at college. While he was a good man, truth be told he didn't feel like family. If she didn't go back to the house, part of her could imagine that her mom was still there, baking apple cake, painting watercolor sunsets, and tending her precious roses.

"I always planned to try and get a publishing job and Mom encouraged me," she told Jacqueline. "So I started applying straight after graduation."

"If she could see you now, she would be very proud," Jacqueline said. "And I firmly believe she can."

Nancy decided not to take the bait and ask her views on the afterlife. She had a feeling they would be there all day.

Jacqueline's inquisition continued throughout the meal, as if she wanted to find out every last detail about Nancy. Did she have a boyfriend? she asked. Nancy said no, since she'd arrived in New York she'd been too busy working, and she hadn't had college boyfriends because Smith was an all-female college.

"Perhaps I'll find one for you," Jacqueline said. "I'll have a little cocktail party and introduce you. You can wear your new dress."

Irving smiled indulgently. "Matchmaking is one of her hobbies," he said.

Nancy couldn't imagine that Jacqueline would be able to predict her taste in men. She didn't know what it was herself. Her heroes tended to be dead literary ones, like Yeats and Shakespeare and Hemingway, and she'd never had fantasies about kissing them.

Over coffee, Jacqueline asked questions about the progress on *Valley of the Dolls*. Had Nancy seen any designs for the cover? She said she hadn't—she wasn't included in the production meeting on Tuesdays where covers were discussed.

"You'll let me know as soon as you see it, won't you?" Jacqueline asked. "With *Josephine*, their designer headed off in *completely* the wrong direction and I had to make him start from scratch."

Nancy promised she would. She volunteered that Brandi had asked if she would help making arrangements for the book tour, and Jacqueline frowned.

"Who's Brandi?" she asked, and Nancy told her. "Well, I hope she isn't trying to shirk her responsibilities."

"Not at all," Nancy hurried to assure her. "In fact, she has taken some pages already. She said she's going to tantalize journalists with them."

The change in Jacqueline's expression was immediate. "You let her take pages? Which ones? I haven't signed off on them yet." Her tone was furious. "She must be stopped. I'll call right away." She stood up, her coffee sloshing in its saucer, then whirled back to Nancy with a fierce hiss. "Don't *ever* let anyone in the company take a single page of the novel until you have express consent from me. Understood?"

Nancy was shocked. "I won't," she insisted. "I promise."

Jacqueline disappeared. Irving gave her a kindly smile. "It's something she feels very strongly about. Don't worry, you weren't to know. Perhaps you should leave now—I'll deal with her when she gets back."

Nancy hadn't drunk her coffee but she took the hint and stood up, thanking him for the lunch. She felt guilty picking up the bag containing her new dress. Did they still mean her to have it? Irving nodded and waved her away with a smile, as if this happened all the time. She got the impression Jacqueline was the boss in their marriage. Somehow Irving didn't seem as shrewd, and he certainly didn't have her drive, but she guessed he knew how to handle her.

As she walked through the lobby to the front door, she couldn't see Jacqueline but could hear her voice booming out from a phone booth nearby: "What do you mean you can't find her? Well, get me Bernie himself. . . . Interrupt his meeting. . . . This is *vitally* important. I'm not taking no for an answer."

Nancy slipped through the revolving door and out into the street. She walked half a block, then broke into a run, worrying that she might have ruined everything.

CHAPTER 8

Jacqueline
Hotel Navarro, 1965

Jacqueline opened the package of galley pages Nancy had sent around. The typeface was fine, but when she read the first paragraph, her favorite sentence, "New York was an angry concrete animal that day," was missing. Her first thought was that they might have accidentally typeset an old version of the manuscript, so she picked up the phone to quiz Nancy.

"No, it's definitely the right version," Nancy replied, "but I'm afraid Don took that sentence out. I guess he thinks the metaphor gives the wrong kind of signal about the book."

"Well, you can tell him that I'm going to keep putting it right back in," Jacqueline said. "Which of my other instructions have been ignored? I'll have to read the whole damn thing again." She'd planned to reread it anyway. She'd heard Harold Robbins didn't bother about edits, but she was a perfectionist when it came to her own words.

"I'm sorry I gave Brandi those pages," Nancy said. "She promises she hasn't shared them with anyone."

Jacqueline had forgotten she'd been upset about that last time they saw each other. "Don't worry, I spoke to Letty about it." Letty was the head of publicity and had worked with Jacqueline before, so she understood.

"Did you see the cover mock-up I slipped inside the package?" Nancy asked. "It's not been approved yet but I promised I'd show you. . . ."

Jacqueline flicked to the back of the set of pages and screamed out loud when she saw it: three doll-like women in cocktail frocks, standing by a swimming pool. "You have *got* to be kidding me." She hung up the phone abruptly and called through to the bedroom: "Irving? Arrange a meeting with Bernie for this afternoon."

She looked again at the cover mock-up. The only decent thing about it was that they'd used her title. Bernie appeared to have caved in on that. But if they were trying to market *Dolls* as a women's romance novel, they had another think coming.

* * *

"WHERE THE HELL did you get that?" Bernie asked when she thrust the cover design at him. "You weren't meant to see it yet."

"It doesn't matter where I got it, so long as we're clear that you will use this cover *over my dead body*," Jacqueline told him. She pulled up a chair and sat down. Irving did the same.

"Look, Jacqueline . . ." Bernie launched into a well-worn spiel about publishers knowing the market best—*yadda, yadda*—but she had come prepared. Before he finished speaking, she motioned to Irving to open a suitcase of books they'd purchased on the way and began thumping them down one by one on Bernie's desk.

"*Herzog, The Magus, God Bless You, Mr. Rosewater*—all recent bestsellers, and all with strong graphic covers."

"Yes, but not appealing to the females," Bernie argued.

The females! Jacqueline thought to herself. *Who on earth says that?* She produced another book: *Up the Down Staircase*, by Bel Kaufman. "This is surely appealing to 'the females,' Bernie, and it hasn't left the *New York Times* bestseller list in a year," she said. "And look—interesting typography and not a woman in sight."

"Well, yes, but—"

Jacqueline dumped an armful of paperbacks on his desk, all with illustrations of pretty women on the covers. "Harlequin romances. Is that what you want my book to resemble? As if the 'dolls' in my title means 'girls'? Because if so, you can forget it right now."

"No, I don't think that's what we were aiming for . . ."

"Good. Because I won't have pictures of women on my cover. Full stop. I have an idea for you." She pulled out a sketch she had worked on that morning: some multicolored pills falling onto a white background, with her name and the title in stark black letters. "This gets across the concept of dolls being another name for pills. You did realize that was the meaning of the title, didn't you, Bernie? It's easily as striking as any man's book on the market. We can double potential sales by appealing to both sexes—the males and the females."

He cleared his throat. "I'll show this to the sales team and get an opinion." He wouldn't meet her eye.

Shifty toad, she thought. *He'd double-cross his mother if there was a buck to be made.*

"Why does this have to be a battle?" she demanded. "We all want the same thing—to sell lots of books. But I see from the galleys that I've been overruled on several crucial matters and I *insist* they are corrected before you print. I won't pay correction charges either. They're your team's changes."

Bernie sighed. "I'll supervise your galley corrections myself."

"No," she said, "let Nancy do it. The girl's got a good eye and I trust her."

"Fine," he agreed with a shrug. "Now, while you're here, why don't we go through the promotional plans? Letty has some terrific ideas." He picked up the office telephone.

Jacqueline liked Letty. She was sharp and modern and good at her job, but she was always busy, busy, busy, and so it proved that morning. She was out, Bernie was told, but one of her assistants would come to the office with the plans.

Jacqueline's promotional tour for *Josephine* had had to be scaled right back when President Kennedy was assassinated the week after publication—*such a pain!* For *Dolls*, she was determined to have a major nationwide tour with coverage in all the print media, and plenty of television and radio interviews too.

A girl who introduced herself as Brandi breezed in wearing a purple miniskirt and a pink blouse, and looking like a million dollars. She saw Irving check out her impossibly long legs, then turn away quickly as if he didn't trust himself.

Brandi handed her a sheet of paper designed to look like a doctor's prescription. "Letty's plan is that we mail these to booksellers and reviewers," she said.

Jacqueline skimmed the words: "Take three yellow dolls before bedtime for a broken love affair; take two red dolls and a shot of scotch for a shattered career; take *Valley of the Dolls* in heavy doses for the truth about the glamour set on the pill kick."

"Brilliant!" she exclaimed, and passed it to Irving.

"A follow-up mailing will include imitation 'dolls' taped to the pages," Brandi continued. "Don't worry—they'll just be sugar candies."

Jacqueline loved the ingenuity of this approach. At least something was being done right.

Brandi told them the tour would kick off with an interview with Johnny Carson on *The Tonight Show*. The schedule was still being finalized, but there would be TV and radio, meet-the-press parties, and bookshop events every step of the way. "This is just a preliminary itinerary."

Jacqueline nodded approval. It was countrywide and she would be busy, busy, busy from February through the end of June. At one stage they had ten city-stops in ten days. "I hope the book will be stocked at every single bookstore along the way," she said. During the *Josephine* fiasco, she had called Bernie from LA at three a.m. New York time to berate him about the lack of stock in stores, so she hoped he had learned his lesson.

Irving was reading the itinerary and he chimed in: "Hey, when you're in Atlanta, why don't we arrange for a car to bump into you at the exact spot where Margaret Mitchell, the *Gone With the Wind* author, was killed? That would make a great news item."

It was an idea in such bad taste that Jacqueline was embarrassed for him. "You're not getting rid of me that easily," she quipped, tapping him on the knee.

Bernie said he had a piece of good news to share. "Twentieth Century-Fox is inquiring about film rights. They won't commit till they see the final pages, but I hope we'll be able to cut a deal. Irving, you and I need to discuss."

Irving said he would give him a call, and Jacqueline narrowed her eyes. They weren't excluding her from *that* conversation. She was desperate for a movie. She'd written the novel picturing the way each scene would work on-screen and already had some casting ideas. She wanted script approval at the very least.

When they left, she was exhausted. At least they had made progress, even though it had only been achieved by backing Bernie into a corner. She knew he found her difficult, but she didn't give a damn. He was a big boy. Besides, she was doing it for her son, and for his sake she didn't care who she pissed off.

On the way out, she spotted Nancy at the drinking fountain and waved.

"I was going to telephone but you've saved me the trouble," she called across the room. "Cocktails at ours on Saturday evening, seven p.m. Wear the dress! I may have a boyfriend for you."

Jacqueline was amused that the girl seemed embarrassed. She was such a funny, old-fashioned creature!

In the taxi home, Irving asked Jacqueline who she was lining up for Nancy, and she replied, "George."

He gasped. "Why would you do that to her? He'll only break her heart."

George was a television director friend of theirs, a charismatic guy with oodles of sex appeal but an unfortunate habit of breaking up with women if they got serious. Jacqueline had been left comforting more than one of his castoffs, who thought they'd found a future husband and father for their children and couldn't understand what they'd done wrong when he disappeared over the horizon. But George lived in the present and put his career first, his friends second, and his women much lower down his priority list.

"I have a hunch about those two," she said. She could see qualities in Nancy that she thought might appeal to George: her ambition and smartness, combined with an innocence and optimism that would contrast with his jaded outlook. He would provide stability for her, while she could puncture his cynicism and make him open his heart again. At least, that was the plan.

Irving didn't approve: "You're treating her like a character in one of your novels," he said. "She's too young and inexperienced to be thrown in at the deep end."

"I think she's tougher than we realize," Jackie said. "There's a core of steel in that girl."

She adored George. If she were twenty years younger, she would have been tempted to have a fling with him herself, but not now, she couldn't now. At least if he and Nancy became an item, and Nancy told her all the details, she could enjoy their romance vicariously. She nodded to herself. It might work.

CHAPTER 9

Jackie

London, 1962

Jackie was feeding Tracy mashed banana for breakfast when the telephone rang. She reached out to grab it with her left hand, still holding a spoonful of banana in her right.

"It's Elsa," her dad said. "I'm afraid she passed away in the night."

Jackie dropped the spoon and it clattered onto the kitchen linoleum. "What happened? Were you with her?"

Jackie had seen her mother the previous afternoon and had sensed she was weaker than ever. She'd been in bed, propped against the pillows, her lips blue-gray and her eyes sunken. Her appearance was alarming, but it never occurred to Jackie that that would be the last time they spoke, the last time she kissed her. If only she'd known.

"She died in her sleep," Joe told her. "I've called the undertaker."

"When will the funeral be?" Jackie asked, already wondering how she would get through it without collapsing. Her heart was fluttering in her chest.

"Soon," he said. "I'll let you know."

Jackie hung up the phone and stared at it. Wallace had only just left for the office and wouldn't be there yet, but she didn't feel like telling him anyway. Sympathy wasn't his strong suit.

She lifted Tracy out of her high chair and squeezed her hard. "It's you and me now, kid," she whispered, a tight pain like a fist inside her rib cage making it hard to breathe.

* * *

WALLACE GOT HOME late that evening after Tracy was in bed. When Jackie told him the news, he hugged her and said, "Poor baby! I'm here. You're not alone in this."

She served the casserole she'd kept warm in the oven, but couldn't face eating a morsel herself. It felt as though her throat had closed and it would be impossible to swallow. When he'd finished eating, Wallace got up and put on an Elvis record, "Return to Sender," and started swiveling his pelvis and miming to it.

"Wallace!" she rebuked. "Mum's not been dead twenty-four hours."

"Oh yeah, sorry," he said, scratching the needle across the vinyl. "What do you want to do then?"

She looked at him and knew he was going to be useless at comforting her. She was teetering on the verge of panic, terrified of living in a world without her mum in it, already missing her more than she could bear, while Wallace was behaving as if it were a normal evening.

That's how it was in the following weeks. He wanted them to entertain friends, go dancing, and make love as if nothing had changed. When Jackie reminded him she was in mourning, he became loving and affectionate for a while—but he had a very short memory.

"You're no fun anymore," he complained one evening. "What's wrong with you?"

"My mum just died," she replied. "Remember?"

She could sense him calculating how long he would have to tiptoe around her. When would he get his wife back? She couldn't answer the question. It took all her strength to look after Tracy, put meals on the table, and get through the day. She felt heavy, dull, and slow.

Elsa had been a proper motherly mother, and without her the

world didn't feel as safe. Her dad certainly wasn't a safe haven, with his brashness and irascibility. Over the ensuing weeks, Wallace's behavior became increasingly erratic, as if Jackie being fragile had made him unbalanced too.

Jackie had plenty of close women friends, and talking to them helped, although she had to swallow her jealousy that they still had their mums and she didn't. She missed telling Elsa about Tracy's achievements: new foods she tried, her first haircut, baby words she gabbled. No one else cared; she was just another baby to them. Wallace barely remembered to kiss their daughter when he left for work in the morning.

One day, Jackie was folding away laundry and opened Wallace's closet to hang up some shirts. A shoebox on the top shelf caught her eye. Had he been buying new shoes? Money was still tight and she was wary, because extravagance was often a sign that he was about to have a manic episode.

She lifted the box down, put it on the bed, and opened it, then struggled to process what she saw inside: dozens of oblong white pills in a blister pack; a syringe and some brown rubber tubing; a silver foil package containing white powder; and a lump of a sticky substance with a sweet herbal smell—could it be marijuana? She'd had the occasional toke of a joint if someone was passing one around at a party but hadn't much liked it.

She sat, contemplating the box: these were illegal street drugs, a cornucopia of them. Had Wallace been taking these? That would explain his volatile moods. Goddamn him, he couldn't do this!

Once Tracy was in bed, she placed the box in the middle of the kitchen table, lid off, where he would see it as soon as he got home.

"Well?" she asked, arms crossed. "When did you get these?"

"I've had them for ages," he replied, as if it were no big deal. "Occasionally I take a little something to manage my moods. Uppers for the down times, and downers when I can't sleep. I've never injected anything, I swear." He put the lid back on the box.

"You didn't think to tell me?" She was horrified. "They're illegal, expensive, and dangerous. I can't have you keeping drugs in the flat. What if Tracy got hold of some and swallowed them?"

"That's why I keep them on the top shelf of my closet," he said, opening the fridge and pulling out a can of beer. "I'm not a complete imbecile."

"It was a huge secret to keep from your wife," she replied. "What else are you not telling me?"

"There's no talking to you nowadays," he said. "Always moping around, bursting into tears at the slightest thing. I'm scared to open my mouth in case it brings on the waterworks."

Jackie's temper snapped. She grabbed the box, ran to the toilet, and threw the brown substance and the silver package down the bowl, flushing just before Wallace got there to stop her.

"You stupid cow!" he shouted, wrestling the box away from her. "Do you have any idea how much these cost?"

She punched him on the back, over and over. "I need a husband, not a drug addict. If you don't pull yourself together, I'm going to leave you, Wallace. I've had enough."

That same old threat came out: "If you leave me, I'll kill myself and it will be all your fault."

Jackie wanted to gouge his stupid face with her nails. In that moment, she truly hated him. How had the love that had felt so indestructible when they got married become poisoned? What had happened to them? She had never felt so alone.

* * *

THE END OF the marriage came more than a year after her mother's funeral. Wallace arrived home from work waving some tickets.

"Fancy a trip to Paris, darling?" he said in a mock Cockney accent. "It'll be just what the doctor ordered."

Jackie took the tickets and read them. They were for the boat train to Paris, leaving at seven a.m. Friday morning and returning on the overnight train on Sunday.

"My friend Marie-Jean is having a party for her twenty-fifth birthday," he said. "She's got room to put us up. It'll be like a second honeymoon in the city of romance."

A half-empty whiskey bottle was clutched under his arm and she could tell he'd been drinking already—or possibly taking drugs, or both, because there was a dangerous energy about him.

"What about Tracy?" Jackie asked, examining the tickets. They were just for two adults. "Do children travel free?"

"Adults only. You'll have to find a babysitter." He lifted a glass from the cupboard and opened the whiskey.

"I'm not leaving her with a babysitter for an entire weekend," Jackie said. She had never been separated from her daughter overnight and wasn't about to start. "Either she comes or I don't."

Without warning, Wallace hurled the bottle at her head. "You boring *bitch*!" he yelled. She had just enough time to swerve so that it glanced off her shoulder. It struck the corner of the table and smashed, showering shards of glass and sloshing whiskey in all directions.

"Jesus Christ, Wallace!" she screamed. Her dress was soaked, her shoulder hurt, and when she looked down, she saw her legs were bleeding.

She rushed to the bathroom, and tears filled her eyes as she peeled off her stockings. *He's crossed a line*, a voice in her brain said. *If that bottle had hit me on the head, it could have killed me.* Tiny splinters of glass were embedded in her legs and she pulled them out with tweezers before rinsing off the blood in the bath. The voice echoed in her head: *He could have killed me.*

In the sitting room, she could hear Wallace crashing around, then the sound of the television news turned up loud. Her heart felt as if it was beating too fast, too hard.

She removed her dress and rinsed off the whiskey, then hung it to dry over the bathtub. Next, she went to the bedroom and put on some jeans and a sweater. She packed a shoulder bag full of baby clothes, nappies, and a few of Tracy's favorite toys, before filling a weekend bag with her own essentials. She tested to see if she could carry both bags, one on each shoulder, and found she could manage, just about. Where would they go? Not back to her dad's; he didn't approve of women leaving their husbands. She would try her friend Stella first and if Stella was out, they'd go to Babs's. She had plenty of friends who would help.

When she emerged from the bedroom with a sleeping Tracy in her arms, Wallace was slumped in front of the TV with a beer in his hand. She saw him notice the bags. Without a word, she lowered Tracy into the pram and pulled on her coat.

"Don't leave me, Jackie," he pleaded. "I'll kill myself if you do. You know it's not my fault I do these things."

She didn't reply, just fastened her coat buttons and opened the door. She had to protect her daughter and herself. She couldn't stay.

He turned his head the other way as she maneuvered the pram into the corridor, then out to the street, where she stood in the drizzly rain waiting for a black taxi with a yellow light to come by.

CHAPTER 10

Nancy

Hotel Navarro, 1965

Jacqueline and Irving's cocktail party was held in a banquet hall downstairs from their apartment at the Navarro, with waiters in bow ties bearing trays of clinking glasses and a buffet table laden with delicacies. When Nancy entered the room, self-conscious in her slinky black dress, it was already thronged. Jacqueline swept across to hand her a cocktail and introduced her to a woman called June, who she said was her best friend in the world.

"Jacqueline is best friend to most of the women in this room," June confided. "She's the most generous soul you're ever likely to meet. We all rely on her."

Nancy told her that Jacqueline had given her the dress she was wearing and June admired it, then introduced her to Beatrice Cole, with whom she said Jacqueline had cowritten a play. Bea introduced her to Helen Gurley Brown, the *Sex and the Single Girl* author, who was so smart and sophisticated in her zebra-print dress and tousled bob that Nancy was awestruck. She wanted to say how much she loved the book but worried she'd sound like a toady, and in the end she scarcely managed to squeeze two words out.

Irving came to freshen her drink and announced that they were celebrating because they'd signed a deal with Twentieth Century-Fox.

"When will the movie come out?" Nancy asked. "I guess they'll try to coincide with the paperback. I heard about the deal."

Irving frowned and tipped his head to one side. "What deal?"

Nancy felt her cheeks color. Had she put her foot in it again? "I heard Bernie sold paperback rights for one hundred and twenty-five thousand dollars." She backtracked: "But I might have gotten that wrong. Please don't quote me."

Without another word, Irving dashed across the room to Jacqueline's side and whispered in her ear, then they both hurried back to quiz her. When did she hear about the deal? Was it signed? Who was it with?

Nancy bit her tongue. What had she unleashed? Bernie was going to kill her. He'd been cross when she leaked the cover design and had made her slide down the fireman's pole in penance. What would he do about this new indiscretion?

"Maybe it's still being negotiated and he's waiting to tell you once the ink is dry." She tried to remember the exact wording she'd seen in the minutes of the editorial meeting.

"Bernie's a goddamn swindler," Jacqueline growled. "I've a good mind to call him at home right now." She glanced at her watch.

"Later. After the party," Irving urged, placing a hand on her arm. "We have guests to look after."

Nancy chewed her lip. "I shouldn't have said anything."

"Of course you should," Jacqueline assured her. "Don't worry. I won't let slip that you told me. I'll say I heard it through the grapevine. Oh look!"—she glanced toward the door, narrowing her eyes—"Here's someone I want you to meet."

She gripped Nancy's elbow and guided her across the room toward a man with unruly dark hair, a tanned, lived-in face, and a lopsided smile. He wasn't movie-star handsome but he looked intriguing, as if he might have tales to tell. Jacqueline threw her arms around him and hugged him close, before they kissed on both cheeks. She was tall but he was a full head and shoulders taller. They seemed very close, Nancy thought. There was an easiness between them.

"George has joined us straight off a plane from London, so it must be—what?—two in the morning his time. Forgive him if he is less than coherent." She grinned at him, then turned. "And Nancy is my newest friend, who's doing an incredible job working on my novel."

As they shook hands, George regarded her with curiosity. "Congratulations," he said. "Jacqueline has high standards so you must be good."

Nancy wondered if this was the man Jacqueline intended to matchmake her with. From the creases at the corners of his eyes and the streaks of gray at his temples, he must be in his thirties at least, which was too old for her.

"How do you know Jacqueline?" she asked, once their hostess had disappeared into the crowd.

"Do you remember her as the Schiffli girl on TV?" He smiled at her blank look. "No, you're far too young. She used to have her own slot every night, where she talked live to a camera, without a script, promoting Schiffli lace products. She was a total professional from the word go. A TV natural."

"I can believe that," Nancy said. "Do you work in television too?" He was wearing a white open-necked shirt under a slate-gray blazer, an outfit that could place him anywhere in the pecking order between artist and CEO.

"I do," he said. "I write and direct a documentary series for CBS. They give me a budget to fly round the world covering stories of interest. For me, it's the dream job."

"Oh my! What kind of stories?" she asked, thinking that the people at this party were by far the most glamorous and interesting she'd ever met.

He ticked them off on his fingers. "Mao's Long March in

China. The funeral of Winston Churchill. The Watts riots. Life in Cuba under Castro. I love travel and I'm allergic to boredom."

"Did you film in Cuba?" Nancy asked. "I read that Castro's brand of communism is in some ways stricter than that in the Soviet Union, but, of course, the American press is biased on the subject."

"I did get into the country, via Mexico," he said. "You should watch my documentary. It's out next week."

"I would if I had a television set," she said. "But sadly my publishing salary doesn't stretch to such luxuries."

He swiped a fresh cocktail from the tray of a passing waiter and handed it to her, then took her empty glass. "Might as well make the most of the free drinks if money is tight," he said.

"Thank you." She took a sip, with no idea what she was drinking, except that it tasted fruity and alcoholic. "When I arrived in Manhattan six months ago, I had vague dreams of renting a penthouse with a river view. I didn't realize the city is so ludicrously expensive that a secretary in publishing has to endure Dickensian squalor if she wants a roof over her head." Her tongue already loosened by alcohol, Nancy told him about sleeping in the corridor outside Louise's apartment for her first six days in the city because she couldn't afford a hotel.

He seemed part amused, part horrified. "Anything could have happened! What a darn fool thing to do! But I guess it shows you're ballsy. Has the missing Louise turned up yet?"

Nancy shook her head. "She's a singer, so I suppose she got a job somewhere and our arrangement slipped her mind." It still stung that she had been so easily forgotten, as if it had just been a throwaway comment when Louise offered to help her find her feet in New York.

"What kind of singer?" he asked. "Classical? Cabaret? Pop?"

"She writes her own songs and sings in nightclubs," Nancy

told him. "She had a hit a couple of years ago with the song 'My After Midnight Man.' Do you know it?" She hummed a bar.

He froze with his drink halfway to his lips and stared at her. "Louise Cardena? *She's* your cousin?"

"Yes," Nancy said. "Well, kind of a half cousin. We've got a fractured, dislocated sort of family."

"I know exactly where Louise is," George said. "I heard her sing at the Ad Lib club in London two weeks ago."

Nancy was stunned by the coincidence. "Are you sure? Long blond hair, blue eyes, curvy figure."

"Come to think of it, she looks a bit like you," George said, scrutinizing her. "There's something about the shape of your face. . . . Yes, I see the likeness now, although you're taller and slimmer."

Nancy's first reaction was relief that Louise was safe, quickly followed by irritation. What was she doing in London? "Do you know how long she's staying there?" she asked.

He shook his head. "I think she has a regular slot at the Ad Lib. Tell you what . . . I know the manager, Johnny Gold. Why don't I call and get him to ask Louise if you can use her apartment while she's away? It seems the least she can do."

"Would you?" Nancy asked. "That would be amazing! This morning I was greeted by a rat in the kitchen of the slum where I'm staying. A rather cocky rat, who didn't seem too bothered by my presence and who had tunneled right through my loaf of bread." She was making light of it, but had been shaken to realize the rat could easily have scampered over her while she slept, because her bed was a mattress on the floor.

"This sounds like an emergency," George said. "I'll get on the case." He paused, as if considering. "Let's meet Wednesday evening. I should have news by then."

She gave him a quick look. Was he hitting on her? He didn't appear to be.

"I'm going to leave now before the jet lag bites," he said. "Jacqueline insisted I put in an appearance, but I reckon I've done my duty. How are you getting home to your rat-infested slum?"

"I'll take the subway," she said.

"At night? Wearing that dress? Are you *serious?*" When he frowned, a groove appeared between his brows.

"I often take the subway. There are a few kookie types and a load of drunks, but I've never had a problem I couldn't handle." She didn't add that she'd soon be down and out if she started taking cabs on her paltry salary.

He shook his head firmly. "Uh-uh. Not on my watch, you don't. My car's outside. Let's say our farewells to the divine Jacqueline."

Jacqueline's face lit up when she heard they were leaving together, and she glanced from one to the other with a knowing smile. Nancy guessed this must have been the man she intended to matchmake her with. She clearly hadn't told George her intentions because he spent most of the journey lecturing her about the dangers of the subway at night, and warning her to take better care of herself.

"I'm sure you're right," she replied in a long-suffering tone, like a kid being told off by a parent.

He dropped her at the entrance to her block, grimacing at the overflowing trash cans on the sidewalk and the broken handrail. She had to admit, it looked very dilapidated.

"Can you find Toots Shor's on Wednesday?" he asked. "I'll be there at six."

"I can and I will," she replied. She'd never heard of it, but someone at work would know.

He walked her to the street door. Just as she unlocked it, he stretched out his arm and Nancy got the momentary impression he was planning to kiss her. She tilted her face toward his, then realized he was only holding the door. *Silly girl!* She blushed and hurried inside. What was she thinking? He was far too old and far too sophisticated for her.

So much for Jacqueline's matchmaking! She may be good at it for other people, but she'd gotten it wrong this time.

CHAPTER 11

Jacqueline

Hotel Navarro, 1965

As soon as the last party guest had left, Jacqueline rushed upstairs to their apartment, unclipped her right earring and dialed Bernie's number from the bedroom telephone. She glanced at the clock: two thirty. It took several rings before he picked up, but as soon as he did, she launched into an attack: "What's this I hear about a paperback deal for *Dolls*, Bernie? When were you planning to tell me?"

"Where the hell . . . ?"

"A hundred and twenty-five thousand, I was told. That means you owe us sixty-two thousand five hundred. When were you thinking of paying up?" Josephine shuffled into the bedroom, and Jacqueline bent to stroke her head.

"Good god, you wakened me at home for this? I'm not contractually obliged to pay you till next year." She heard Darlene's voice asking who it was. "Jacqueline," he replied, and there was a prolonged "Oh" sound.

"I bet the money's already in your account. How can I trust that you won't spend it?" That was her biggest fear. Bernie's operation was small and if he went bust, her share would be lost. That money was for her son's care. The bills she footed every month were huge and growing.

"Publishers need cash flow," he said, with the tone of exaggerated patience he often used with her. "I have to cover printing costs and staff wages long before we sell a single copy. But I will have your money for you next year on the exact day it is due."

"I'm not a gambler, Bernie. I need more security than that."
She lit a Lucky Strike and inhaled deeply.

"I'll put it in writing for you first thing Monday morning. How
about that?"

She wasn't satisfied, but Irving would get their lawyer to
check the contract and see if there was a legal way to force him
to pay sooner.

She hung up without saying goodbye. It was a great deal, but
she couldn't afford to take the pressure off Bernie Geis, not for
one second.

The next morning, she couldn't resist giving George a quick
call to see if her matchmaking had been successful. "What did
you think of my new protégé?" she asked.

"Nancy? She's a bright girl," he replied. "Wet behind the ears
but I like her."

"Did you seduce her? Is she there now?"

He laughed out loud. "What do you take me for? No, Jacqueline, I did not seduce her."

"Why not? You must be losing your touch," she teased. "You
have to admit she's beautiful, with the kind of natural style you
tend to go for."

He was still laughing. "I don't know where you got this impression of me as the perennial womanizer. Truth is, I spend
most of my time traveling and working, and when we're done,
my cameraman and I are lucky if we manage a beer in a hotel
bar."

"You forget that I've met several of your exes," she replied.
"Plus, I have my novelist's powers of intuition. So are you going
to see Nancy again or was it a complete washout?"

"We're meeting Wednesday . . ." he began, and Jacqueline
hooted, "Ha! I knew it!" He continued: ". . . but only because I

happen to know where her cousin is. I met her in London, and I'm going to put them back in touch."

"That's good. Poor kid needs some family," Jacqueline said. "Her mother died earlier this year and she's pretty cut up about it."

"I'm not sure Louise will be much help—but I'll see what I can do."

"I'm trusting you to look out for her while I'm away on the book tour. Don't let me down." She listened down the line while he considered the request.

"Sure, I can do that," he said at last.

She smiled to herself. She was responsible for matchmaking several couples of her acquaintance. Sometimes they needed a nudge before they realized what was good for them, but fortunately she had sharp elbows.

* * *

JACQUELINE WAS DETERMINED to lose fifteen pounds before the book tour started. TV cameras added pounds so it was best to be as skinny as possible. She'd tried various diets over the years—the grapefruit diet, the cabbage soup diet, Sego meal replacements, and Helen Gurley Brown's favorite, the wine-and-egg diet. Jacqueline had developed her own version of Helen's diet: caviar—which was eggs, after all—and vodka, either drunk on the rocks or with grapefruit juice. That's virtually all she ate and drank for an entire month. Every morning she did a workout in the gym at the Navarro, then weighed herself on her bathroom scale. The pounds were dropping off, but it was slow going. She carried around a pack of mints to quell hunger pangs—and also because her breath smelled rank from all the fish eggs.

Another part of the pre-tour planning involved shopping. Pucci dresses and pantsuits traveled well: she could just roll them up in a suitcase and they came out looking good as new. She loved the vibrant new season colors of pink, yellow, and orange, and the floral patterns that twined around the body like grapevines, but she also chose some solid colors that would work on the big screen, where patterns could give a moiré effect.

After that she stocked up on beauty essentials: Revlon pan-stick makeup, loads of eyelashes and eyelash glue, blue and green eyeshadows, black liquid eyeliner, a range of lipsticks and nail varnishes to match her new outfits, Elnett hair spray, Elizabeth Arden Eight Hour Cream—she ticked them off from a master list. She would take her own wigs and falls, and her favorite pieces of jewelry.

To be in top form, she needed a carapace to hide her inner self behind, the self with secrets she would never share with the world. Secrets like the fact she had a son in his late teens who lived in an institution. What if reporters dug that up? She couldn't bear it if they wrote about him and called her a refrigerator mom.

"You've been in the public eye before," Irving reassured her, "and no one has ever asked if you have children. If it's not mentioned, people assume you don't."

He was right. She'd been the Schiffli girl on TV, and she'd been profiled in the press when *Every Night, Josephine!* came out. She'd be fine. Her secret was safe. How sad it had to be a secret, though. The grief over her son's diagnosis never left her; it was part of her, a wound that reopened from time to time when something reminded her of all she had lost as a mother.

Before flying to LA to start the tour, Jacqueline and Irving went to visit him. She could tell he recognized them when they arrived, but there was never an enthusiastic welcome. Despite the best care money could buy, he still didn't speak, didn't make eye contact, and wasn't comfortable being touched. He was much more demonstrative with the staff than he was with her, and that was heartbreaking, but she told herself it was inevitable since the staff saw him day in, day out, and knew him better than she did. The most important thing was that, as far as she could tell, he seemed content.

She couldn't stop a few tears leaking out when they left, but she quickly pulled herself together. Next stop LA: it was time to face the public and push, push, push them to buy *Valley of the Dolls*. No one could know, but she'd be doing it for her beautiful, silent son.

CHAPTER 12

Jackie

London, 1963

For the first week after leaving Wallace, Jackie stayed with her friend Stella. She missed him so badly, it was as if a limb had been amputated. Tears were never far away, but each time she pictured that bottle hurtling toward her head and the fragments of glass embedded in her leg, she knew she couldn't return until he got help.

Clearly he wasn't going to change overnight, so she answered an advert in a newsagent's window and rented a one-bedroom flat with a tiny garden, using her mother's nest egg to pay the deposit. It was dark and poky, with a smell like boiled cabbage in the hallway, but she spruced it up with some colorful cushions and throws. One afternoon, Stella made an anonymous phone call to check that Wallace was in his office, then drove her back to the old apartment to pick up Tracy's cot, more clothes, and other essentials.

Jackie had tried several times to phone him but each time, as she dialed the number, her nerve failed. He'd been ringing all her friends, demanding where she was, but those who knew wouldn't tell him. Finally, on a Saturday morning ten days after she'd left, she rang him from a telephone box while Tracy slept in the pram outside, her tiny fists curled on top of the blanket.

His voice sounded slow and slurred when he answered: "Hello, who is it?"

"It's me," she said. "Are you alright?"

"No, I'm bloody well not alright because my wife has disappeared into thin air and I didn't know if I should be calling the police to report a missing person. You've made your point. When are you coming back?" He was angry. That wasn't a good sign.

"I can't come back until you've got the manic depression under control," she said. "Tracy and I aren't safe around you."

"Of course you're safe! I would never hurt you," he insisted. "Never."

She noticed that he didn't ask how they were. It didn't occur to him. "You sound stoned, Wallace, and it's not even noon. That's not the voice of a responsible husband and father."

"It's your fault! I've been taking the meds, just like you wanted, and they turn me into a zombie."

"See your doctor again," she urged. "Explain the problem. There must be something else you can try."

"Will you make an appointment for me, Jackie? I'll go if you do it."

She considered for a moment. She'd been organizing his life since long before they got married and the habit was ingrained, but it was important he learned to look after himself. "You do it," she said. "You're the one who has to change if I'm ever going to come back. I'll call this time next week to see what the doctor said."

"But I need you, Jackie. I love you. I can't live without you."

He sounded so sad, she started crying, but forced herself to hang up the phone. How easy it would be to forgive him and go home again. Everything would be dreamy and romantic at first—until the next time he lost his temper.

* * *

JACKIE RANG WALLACE the following Saturday, then the one after, and she got a different man every time: maudlin, obstreperous, quiet, demanding, sometimes all four in the same call. She borrowed a book on manic depression from the public library and read that Freud thought it could be caused by childhood trauma, and that psychoanalysis could help. When she suggested that to Wallace, he was withering, saying she was the one who needed a shrink, not him. A few moments later, he told her he couldn't live without her and pleaded with her to come back.

"If you want to prove you're a changed man and we would be safe living with you, you're going the wrong way about it," she told him.

She was still weighed down by the pain of missing him, but the further she got from the relationship, the more she realized that although she loved him, she couldn't save him. She could never risk leaving Tracy on her own with him because he wasn't trustworthy. He wouldn't deliberately harm her, she was sure of that, but he wasn't in control of his actions, and if he was still dabbling in street drugs, he would only get worse.

Months passed without Wallace making any progress. Jackie began to go out for the odd evening, leaving Tracy with a baby-sitter. Johnny Gold had become the manager of a nightclub called the Ad Lib, and he welcomed her there; "On the house, sweetheart," he'd say every time she tried to pay for drinks. Jackie loved to dance, and listen to the live musicians, and chat, and people-watch. The first time a man asked her out, she automatically replied, "I'm married." He asked, "Where's your husband then?" Jackie glanced around, guiltily. Johnny had promised to warn her if Wallace showed up, but it seemed he was frequenting other clubs these days.

The Beatles sometimes came to Ad Lib, and Jackie was there one night when John Lennon and George Harrison burst out of the lift screaming that the place was on fire. There was mass panic because the club was on the fourth floor and there was only one lift and a narrow set of emergency stairs. Johnny stood on a chair and yelled, "False alarm! There's no fire! Nothing to worry about."

"They're on LSD," he told Jackie later. "They claim their drinks were spiked. I told them to pull the other one."

She laughed. George and John were sprawling in a booth now, both wearing sunglasses, their heads bobbing as they watched the colored lights bouncing around the walls, reflected off a giant mirror ball. A curvy blond woman was singing her heart out on the tiny stage and gazing in their direction as if desperate to attract their attention, but they were too stoned to notice. Between numbers she riffed a few bars of "Love Me Do" but they still didn't look up.

"Poor Louise," Johnny said with a sigh. Jackie made a point of clapping when Louise's set finished, but no one else did, and she slunk offstage, shoulders slumped. She was beautiful, with a rich melodious voice, but singers like her were ten a penny in clubland.

One night a famous actor came to the club—a friend of Marlon Brando's—and Jackie asked him how Marlon was. They had a couple of drinks together and he was very flirtatious, complimenting what he called the "gravity-defying curve" of her bum. When he invited her back to his hotel, a switch clicked in her head. Why not? She had no illusions that she would ever see him again, but she was only twenty-six years old and she deserved a bit of fun.

It was odd making love with another man. The unfamiliar shape of his body, the strange scent of him, the way he kissed, all made her miss Wallace so badly she had to fight back tears. As soon as the actor fell asleep, she slipped away and took a cab home to relieve her babysitter.

After that, she was chatted up most nights she went to Ad Lib. It was as if an "Available" sign had lit up on her forehead, like the yellow "For Hire" sign on taxis. It was fun to flirt, but she realized many of the men in the club were married. She could spot them a mile off: their wives made sure they were well fed and groomed, but they still wanted a taste of novelty in their bed.

The next morning, an idea came to her: maybe she could write a novel about married men who had affairs. Why they did it, and how it worked out. She wondered if Wallace had slept with another woman yet. He was still begging her to go back, but she wouldn't be surprised if he'd had female company in the marital bed since she'd left. His ego required regular stroking, as did his penis.

* * *

"I'M LEAVING AD Lib," Johnny told her one night. "Our American investor, Oscar Lerman, wants me to manage a new club called Dolly's, on Jermyn Street. And he wants to meet you."

"Me?" Jackie was baffled. "How has he even heard of me?" She looked around. "Is he here?"

"No, he's in New York. He saw a picture of you in Hollywood years ago and was bowled over by your beauty. He said he's been dying to meet you ever since. He asked if I knew you and I said as a matter of fact you were one of my closest friends."

"Are you sure it was me he saw?" Jackie asked. "Not Joan?" She had never felt beautiful; she was tall and angular, and couldn't bear to look at herself in a mirror without full makeup.

"Nope, it's definitely you he wants to meet. Oscar's a good guy—a Broadway producer who also invests in nightclubs. I think you'll get on. He'll be in town next Saturday. Want me to set you up?"

She shrugged. "If you can vouch for him, why not?"

Oscar was only an inch taller than her, with dark hair in a side parting, but he was much older, easily in his forties. What was Johnny thinking of, hooking her up with someone so ancient? He seemed very mature and his manners were old-school, opening doors for her and slipping around to walk on the outside of the pavement. Who did that anymore?

He took her for dinner at Mirabelle, a classy French restaurant, and asked questions about her life. She found herself telling him that she used to act in B movies when she was in her late teens, and she'd had bit parts in the TV series *The Saint* and *Danger Man*, but that work had dried up. Her ambition had always been to write novels. She explained that she needed to earn a living somehow, since her estranged husband was refusing to support her.

"If you've decided not to go back to your husband, you should get a lawyer and finalize it," he advised. "The man has to take responsibility."

She laughed. "That word is not in Wallace's vocabulary."

She didn't tell Oscar that she was getting desperate, as her mother's nest egg was disappearing fast. She had even swallowed her pride and called her father to ask if he could lend her some money until she found her feet, but he yelled expletives at her, telling her to be a good girl and go back to her bloody husband because she wasn't getting a penny out of him.

She couldn't go on like this. She was fed up with scraping by and not being able to afford new clothes and toys for Tracy. Maybe Oscar was right. Maybe it was time to hire a lawyer.

She had started writing a novel about married men while Tracy had her daily nap, but soon hit the same old problem: whenever she read back the pages they sounded trite and amateur. Was she too self-critical or was she simply not good enough? Who was she kidding that she could ever be a writer? But how else could she support herself and her little girl?

Oscar took her home in a taxi after dinner, and leapt out to open the door for her. He'd been good company. He'd made her talk about herself more than she usually did because he was a good listener who asked the right questions. She thanked him for the date, but she didn't invite him in or even give him a peck on the cheek. He was too grown-up, too straitlaced for her.

CHAPTER 13

Nancy

Toots Shor's, 1965

Nancy walked through the front door of Toots Shor's into a dimly lit cavern, with a circular wooden bar lined by barstools in the center. A few drooping garlands of shiny paper represented a nod to Christmas décor. Most of the clientele were men in suits who looked as if they'd dropped by straight from the office. In fact, gazing around she couldn't see another woman. The bar stank of stale cigarettes and beer, and she was surprised George didn't frequent a classier type of joint. She found him sitting at a corner table reading some documents, a half-drunk martini in front of him.

"I used this as my office today to get some work done without anyone being able to find me," he said, sweeping the papers into a folder. "Now, before you start swilling cocktails I'm going to order you a steak and salad. You look as if you need vitamins. Want a baked potato to go with it?"

"Yes, please," she said. She was famished because she hadn't had lunch. She'd tried keeping food in the fridge at the apartment to make a bag lunch, but Barbara usually ate it.

"What will you have to drink?" he asked, and she said, "Whatever you're having," embarrassed to admit she didn't know the names of many cocktails.

George called a waiter and placed her order. "First time here?" he asked, and she nodded, gazing around. "You wouldn't think to look at it but all the celebrities come here: Frank Sinatra, Dean Martin, Jackie Gleason. . . . That's the owner, the eponymous Toots." He pointed at a rotund character with receding hair who was smoking a fat cigar and gesticulating furiously with it at the man he was in conversation with. Nancy scanned the room but couldn't see any celebrities. She was more of a books than a movies kind of girl so perhaps she didn't recognize them.

George sipped his martini and watched, looking amused, as she wolfed down a forkful of steak. It was tender and juicy, the potato oozing butter, and the salad coated with tangy dressing. "Aren't you eating?" she asked, her mouth full.

"Too early for me," he said, and she wondered if he was meeting someone else for dinner later. A girlfriend perhaps? It seemed presumptuous to ask.

When she had put down her knife and fork and was dabbing her mouth with a napkin, he reached inside his jacket pocket and placed a bunch of keys on the table. There was a plastic Statue of Liberty charm attached.

"These are the keys to Louise's apartment," he said.

"But how . . . ?" Nancy blinked.

"I called my friend Johnny in London. He spoke to Louise and she said of course you can stay. There's a message for you." He handed over a note that had been scribbled on the back of a nightclub flyer.

"How did you get these so quickly?" she asked. The advertisement on the front of the flyer was for the Ad Lib club, showing a silhouette of a curvaceous singer against a background of blurred multicolored lights.

"A friend of mine is a Pan Am air hostess. She brought them over on a flight yesterday."

Nancy searched his face, wondering if the air hostess was a girlfriend, but he was giving nothing away. She turned over the flyer and read the note: *"Hey, Nancy, Hope you're enjoying Manhattan! Sorry I wasn't there to greet you but I got this great job in London and couldn't turn it down. My apartment is rent controlled at only forty dollars a week and it would be amazing if you could pay it. Please take a check to this office"*—she gave an address—*"and deal with any bills that come in the mail. I'll let you know when I'm heading back. Love from London!"*

Was that all? A brief "sorry"? No indication how long she might be away? Nothing personal, just a casual list of terms. It didn't sound like the affectionate cousin she used to spend summers with, but it was great news about the apartment. She would only have thirty dollars a week left to live on, but she'd manage if she was careful. She thanked George for all the trouble he'd gone to, and added, "Please thank your air hostess friend too."

She took a sip of the martini and shuddered. It tasted like pure ethanol. She took another sip and felt it burn its way down her throat, the heat radiating outward.

"We could pick up your things this evening if you like," George said. "I'll drive, and come up to Louise's apartment to make sure the utilities are switched on."

Nancy hesitated. The offer was tempting but, according to Helen Gurley Brown, inviting a man into your apartment could be seen as an invitation for him to seduce you. Did he know that Jacqueline was attempting to matchmake them?

He read her expression and laughed. "Are you worried I'll pounce once we're alone? That's not how I operate."

"So how *do* you operate?" she asked, with what she hoped was a sassy air, then took another sip of martini.

"I like women," he said. "I have a lot of female friends, but I'm not looking for a wife. Anyone I date knows the score—that I travel a lot and don't want to be tied down."

"Why do they agree to those terms?" she asked. "If they like you, I imagine they will want to tie you down."

His lips twitched with a suppressed smile and he looked her

straight in the eyes. "You're very innocent, Nancy. Have you had many boyfriends?"

"Not yet." She blushed. "I was at an all-women college so . . ."

"Wow! So you've not even jumped on the dating merry-go-round yet." He looked amused. "Well, you're a pretty girl, and you're going to be pursued by all kinds of men once you put yourself out there. Dating is a jungle full of perils."

The way he was looking at her, Nancy felt like a specimen in a zoo rather than a jungle. "I'm sure I'll manage," she replied.

"Are you really? Would you know how to spot a con man at twenty paces, or will you fall into bed with the first guy who buys you a few drinks and says you have beautiful eyes?"

Nancy was annoyed. "You must think I'm dumb as they come."

"No, I don't think you're dumb, but I don't want to see you getting hurt. Broken hearts are painful and they can make you defensive so it's harder to recognize true love when it comes along." There was a faraway look in his eyes that made her wonder if he was speaking from experience. "That's why it's important to choose your first lover carefully. Make sure he's one of the good guys, someone who genuinely cares about you."

Nancy felt patronized. "Have you decided to become my honorary New York father? Because I really don't need one."

"You don't? Are you sure?" From his tone, it didn't sound as if he was joking anymore. "So you know what can happen if a guy is too rough in bed, do you? If he just takes his own pleasure rather than looking after you? If he lies when he tells you he's wearing a condom?"

"I thought romance involved champagne and flowers," Nancy protested, "but you make it sound clinical, like a trip to the gynecologist."

That groove appeared between his brows. He rose abruptly,

saying, "Wait a second," then walked over to Toots Shor and said something that made him turn to check her out. Next they both walked out the bar's street door. What was going on?

Nancy realized the martini had gone straight to her head. She opened her compact mirror and saw there was a speck of potato under her lower lip. She wiped it off, then drained her glass, wondering what George was up to.

When he reappeared a minute or so later he was holding a flute glass and a straggly fistful of red carnations.

"How's that for enterprise?" he asked, putting them on the table in front of her. "Toots stole the flowers for me from the lobby of the hotel across the road."

"Very impressive," she said, picking them up and sniffing them. "I like a man of action. But why bother if you're not planning on seducing me?"

"I wanted you to see how easy it is to produce champagne and flowers, Nancy." He spoke seriously now. "I want you to realize you're worth more than a bunch of sweet talk and empty gestures. Use your critical judgment before leaping into bed with anyone. You deserve the real deal."

She took a sip of champagne. The bubbles tingled on her tongue like sherbet, and she liked the subtle fruity taste. "How am I supposed to know the difference? I mean, is this real or fake champagne? I've never had it before so I can't tell."

"It's real," he said, watching her take another sip with a distant look in his eyes again. "It's refreshing to meet a girl who's not pretending to be something she's not."

Nancy wasn't sure she understood what he meant. What would she pretend to be?

"Let's be friends, shall we?" he said. "Maybe you can restore my faith in human nature. Now, shall we go and help you move home?"

"Not till I finish this champagne," she told him. "I want to savor every sip. I think it has just become my new favorite drink."

* * *

ON THE DRIVE to Barbara's apartment, Nancy asked George how he chose his documentary subjects, and he explained that he had a long list of topics, which he cleared with senior management. He tried to keep his pieces topical and respond quickly to current events so the schedule could change overnight.

She asked what his next subject was, and he said he was off to film migrant fruit pickers in California, who worked long hours and survived well below the poverty line.

"Will you interview Cesar Chavez?" Nancy asked. The labor leader had recently organized a strike among grape pickers in California. "He seems to speak a lot of sense."

George gave her a quick look. "He's on the list. Do you always follow the news?"

She shrugged. "I like to keep up to date." She couldn't afford to buy her own newspaper but read one in the library during her lunch hour, or borrowed Bernie's from his desk. "How long will you be away?"

"Around three weeks. I have to find people to interview, decide the footage we need, film it, check we have enough material, then fly back to New York to edit. I'm away from home more than I'm here," he said, "but that suits me. I've always lived out of a suitcase."

Nancy thought she wouldn't like sleeping in hotels and continually having to find her way around new places. She still got lost on the New York subway, traveling uptown rather than downtown, or accidentally getting an express service that took her all the way to Brooklyn before she could change trains and head back.

George waited in the car while Nancy went into the apartment to tell Barbara she was moving out.

"Thanks for leaving me in the lurch," Barbara said snarkily.

"I'll pay next month's rent to give you time to find someone else," Nancy promised. It would leave her flat broke once she'd paid Louise's rent too, but it seemed only fair.

It didn't take long to pack. All her belongings fit into the same scuffed suitcase she'd arrived with. George drove her to Chelsea and parked outside Louise's building. As she turned the key in the street door, Nancy thought of all the evenings she had hovered there, waiting anxiously for one of the other occupants to let her in. Thank goodness they always had or she'd have been sleeping on a park bench.

When she opened the door to number 4B, she gasped at the spacious room inside. One wall had floor-to-ceiling windows looking out toward the opaque windows of the building opposite. There were polished wooden boards underfoot, a brown leather couch, and framed art posters on the walls. She opened a set of double doors and found the kitchen was crammed inside a cupboard-like space. Another door led to a windowless bedroom that was only big enough for a double bed and a closet, and beyond it was a tiny washroom. It was neat and clean and modern and perfect.

George walked around trying the lights, the gas cooker, the heating, and hot water. He pronounced all were working and he couldn't detect any evidence of rodents.

"I'll leave you to settle in," he said, then gripped her shoulders firmly and kissed her on both cheeks, European-style, as she'd seen him do with Jacqueline. He smelled faintly of a citrusy cologne. "And I'll give you a call when I get back from California. Judging by the speed with which you demolished that steak tonight, I reckon you'll need feeding again."

After he left, Nancy wandered around, exploring the apartment. Looking out the windows she could see cars and passersby in the street below and a grocery store down the block. She unpacked her clothes and hung them in a closet, which contained a few dresses of Louise's and loads of swinging metal hangers. The refrigerator was empty, but the cupboards held three cans of Campbell's soup and two boxes of crackers. She felt as if she were trespassing, but this was going to be her home for a while at least.

"Home." She said the word out loud, testing the feel of it.

As she lay in Louise's bed later, she placed a hand between her legs and squeezed her thighs tight, imagining the sexual pleasure George had described. She admitted to herself that she was attracted to him, despite the age gap. He was interesting and unpredictable, but he hadn't given any sign that he found her attractive, so maybe she wasn't his type. Besides, he'd been clear that all his relationships were temporary.

Would she consider having a short-lived affair with him, were he to try and seduce her? Helen Gurley Brown recommended "sex without strings" in *Sex and the Single Girl*—but only as a stopgap while you were waiting for the right man. Nancy wondered again if that air hostess friend who'd brought George the keys was one of his conquests. Were there many women in his life?

She was aware she was late to the dating scene for her generation and couldn't wait to start. She thought of a scene in *Valley of the Dolls* where Neely's husband and a showgirl have sex in a swimming pool and decided she wanted to try that one day. She was filled with a sense of wonder about all that lay ahead of her: passion, lust, adventure, then finding her one true love.

It would have to wait till after the *Valley of the Dolls* PR tour finished, though. Publication date was February tenth and she would be working around the clock to keep Jacqueline happy and make sure it ran smoothly. After that? Who knew?

CHAPTER 14

Jacqueline

Beverly Hills Hotel, Los Angeles, 1966

When their limo turned into the driveway of the sunset-pink, palm-tree-fringed Beverly Hills Hotel, Jacqueline reflected that it had become her second home. She knew all the staff by name and they knew her. She and Irving always took the same suite, with sliding glass doors leading out to a red-tiled patio that bordered the yellow-and-white cabanas by the swimming pool. While in residence, she fed a family of cats that lived under a hedge at the back of the grounds, and she was eager to visit them and see how many kittens they'd had since her last visit.

But there was no time for cats now. She was being picked up in an hour to go to a television studio for her *Tonight Show* interview with Johnny Carson. They would touch up her hair and makeup, but she always did the fundamentals herself: she'd never met a makeup artist who could do the black eyeliner flicks out to the side as well as she did. She chose an orangy-pink pantsuit, which warmed her complexion and flattered her figure, and accompanied it with dangly silver Mayan earrings and a matching necklace.

She wasn't nervous about the show, even though it was live. Irving had known Johnny for years and they considered him a friend, so it shouldn't be a challenging interview. She knew the routine on arrival: a quick stop in the makeup chair, a chat about timing with a production assistant, last dab of powder to take away shine, then the wait till Johnny introduced her and she walked out onto the famous set. He rose to greet her and out of the corner of her eye she checked the camera positions. It was force of habit after all these years. She sat slightly at a slant in her seat so they caught her best angle, and waved hello to the studio audience.

Johnny held up her book and began. "I know lots of readers love your novel, but it must be disheartening to have received such terrible press reviews." Jacqueline kept the smile pinned to her face as he read some from his crib sheet. "'Poorly written' said *Publishers Weekly*; 'As if it was written by a slightly bashful fan of Harold Robbins' said the *New York Times*; 'Dirty book of the month' said *Time* magazine. Tell me—how would you respond to those critics?"

Jacqueline widened her smile before replying. "Way back in the sixteenth century, they probably didn't think Shakespeare was that great a writer—but time has a habit of showing the books readers actually want to read. By the way, those reviews you quoted were all written by men. I'm guessing they resent a woman writing about sex. Harold Robbins doesn't get this treatment, but how dare *I*, a mere female, venture into this territory?" She hammed it up, turning to the studio audience for affirmation, and they cheered their support. "Let me tell you, Johnny, the more rocks they throw at me, the more copies I will sell."

"You cover some pretty heavy themes in your book." He counted them on his fingers: "Abortion, suicide, plastic surgery, and drug addiction. Do you feel any sense of responsibility not to glamorize them or encourage readers to try them?"

"Absolutely," she replied. "But I'm writing about reality in *Valley of the Dolls.*" *Keep repeating the title*, she reminded herself. "I have worked with actors and actresses for decades and I am telling the truth about the pressure they're under and the ways some of them deal with it. Dolls—that's what I call uppers and downers—are easily available in Hollywood and New York, wherever showbiz folk hang out, because the stress of that job is immense."

Next, he asked her about the speculation that her characters were based on real people. Was Helen Lawson really Ethel Merman? Was Neely Judy Garland? Jacqueline knew she had to tiptoe around this question to avoid getting sued.

"My characters are composites of different actresses I've known over the years, and situations I've faced myself, plus a huge dollop of imagination. It's called fiction," she said. "Do you read novels, Johnny? You should try it sometime." That got another cheer from the audience. She turned and waved at them.

The time passed quickly, as it always did on television, and soon she was in the greenroom with Irving hugging her.

"So much for an easy ride!" she exclaimed to Johnny when he joined them.

"I knew you could take it," he said. "You were great. Women all over the country will be rushing to bookstores to buy your book."

"Men too, I hope," she said. "Have *you* read it, Johnny?"

He winked. "Not yet . . ."

"You might learn something," she teased. "Your wife might thank me."

It was late, but before they headed back to the hotel, she made a point of thanking the entire team, from cameramen through to the most junior assistants. From her previous television experience, she knew they could be promoted to positions of power in no time, and they might soon be the ones making decisions about which guests to invite.

First stop the following day was at Chevalier's Books, a favorite store of Jacqueline's. She greeted the staff by name, chatting with them, asking after their families, and finding some quality on which to compliment each individual, whether it was a new haircut, a piece of jewelry, or an item of clothing. It was a trick she'd learned from Dale Carnegie's book *How to Win Friends and Influence People*: make others feel noticed. She was keen to get bookstore staff on her side because these were the people who could recommend her book to readers.

She was delighted to see a queue stretching down one side of the store, all of them women clutching copies of her book. She sat at a desk and began signing, taking time to chat with each customer. When she asked what they liked to read she was amazed how many said they didn't normally read books, but they'd heard about *Valley of the Dolls* and wanted to see what the fuss was about. If she probed, some admitted they were curious to read a woman's view of sex, because they imagined it would be quite different from men's. Jacqueline grinned and agreed it certainly was.

From Chevalier's, she was whisked across town to an event organized by *Cosmopolitan* magazine. Irving had brought a jar of caviar, and she ate a few spoonfuls in the limo, then touched up her lipstick. Gay Geranium was today's shade, matching her fingernail polish and a close-enough match to her swirly-patterned pantsuit. At the event, she sat on a gilt throne and answered questions from the female audience, before signing yet more books until her wrist seized up. Irving hovered by her side, fetching drinks and pens as required, and when he saw she was flagging, he leaned over and whispered that it was time to go.

"You need to save yourself," he said. "We're having dinner at Chasen's, then there's a radio show at seven tomorrow, so the alarm call is set for five and the limo is booked for six thirty."

Jacqueline worried that might not be enough time. Even though it was radio, not TV, she wouldn't dream of going to the studio without full makeup and one of her wigs or falls. She'd lay everything out before going to bed.

Back in their hotel suite, she ran a bath, tipping in some of her favorite jasmine bath salts. Her gut had been cramping all day. She had a spastic colon that caused pain and bloating, even when she was on her caviar diet. Her joints ached as if she were ninety-seven years old, not forty-seven, and she had a tension headache like a steel band around her temples. But the day had gone well. She was pleased with her performance.

Lying back in the hot water, she gently massaged her swollen abdomen. Then her fingers slid upward and ran lightly along the ridge of scar tissue where her left breast used to be. She'd never get used to that loss, although it had been more than three years since the operation. She lay back, eyes closed, thinking of the deal she'd made with God after the op. She'd kept her side, and now she was counting on him to keep his.

* * *

IN DECEMBER 1962, Jacqueline had been in Japan on vacation with her mother. She was showering one morning in a Tokyo hotel when she felt a tiny hard lump in her breast, like a frozen pea trapped under the skin. She rubbed it back and forward, and decided it was probably another cyst. She'd had them before, and her doctor simply aspirated the fluid, then they collapsed and disappeared. On the telephone later, she asked Irving to make an appointment for her return, then thought no more of it.

As the doctor examined the lump in his surgery, she felt a twinge of anxiety, but told herself it was bound to be benign. There was no cancer in the family; her mother was the picture of health in her seventies.

"I think I'd like to get this one biopsied," he decided. He called the office of a surgeon he recommended, explained the situation, then reported back: "The first available appointment is Christmas Day."

"Oh joy!" she said sarcastically. "Merry Christmas to you too!"

Before the operation, the surgeon came to her bedside and told her they would remove the lump and test it while she was still under anesthetic. He asked her to sign a release form permitting him to do a mastectomy then and there if it turned out to be malignant.

"Absolutely not," she replied. "If it's malignant, I want to be wakened and have all the options explained to me."

Privately, she was convinced it was benign, so she was doubly shocked when she came around to be told that the lump was a "malignant infiltrating ductile carcinoma"—a loathsome phrase. At least her lymph nodes were clear, so it hadn't spread, the surgeon assured her, but a mastectomy as soon as possible was his recommendation.

She lay back in the hospital bed and closed her eyes. The area around the biopsy site was bandaged, but she stroked the contours of the breast they wanted to remove, feeling stunned. She had great boobs—shapely and pert, not too big and not too small. "A perfect handful," Irving called them. This had all happened at breakneck speed and she hadn't been given any choices—it was basically surgery or die of cancer.

George usually spent Christmas with them, and he arrived at the hospital that afternoon, wearing a Santa hat and carrying a bag of gifts, but his face fell when he saw the grim expressions on their faces.

Jacqueline asked Irving if she could talk to George on her own, so he stepped outside.

"They want to cut off my tit," she told him, and explained the diagnosis. "But it's part of me, part of my identity as a woman. I'm worried Irving won't find me attractive with only one tit. I won't be sexy anymore."

"That's ridiculous," George told her. "I've never known a man so passionately in love with anyone as Irving is with you. He would still find you attractive if it was your nose they were cutting off. You've got to do it, Jacqueline."

The mastectomy was performed the day after Christmas.

As she recovered at home afterward, Jacqueline had space to reflect. It was the first time she'd come face-to-face with her own mortality. She was only forty-four years old. She couldn't die in her forties! She'd assumed she would have at least thirty more years on this earth. There was far too much she still wanted to do. And what about her son? Would Irving earn enough to keep paying the fees for his care?

That's when she decided she needed to make so much money that his future would be secured. She'd tried acting, television presenting, and writing plays, as well as her little book about Josephine, but they didn't bring in seriously big money. She'd long wanted to write a novel and had an idea kicking around in her brain. Now was the time.

As soon as she was allowed out of bed following the op, she took Josephine for a walk in Central Park. Just across the road from their apartment there was a small grassy mound, a place she called the Wishing Hill. The grass was crisp with frost and the freezing air stung her nostrils as she stood making a pact with God.

"Give me ten more years to become a bestselling author," she implored. "If you choose to take me after that I won't complain. Just let me make enough money for my boy's care."

There was no answer, no sound apart from the muffled hum of traffic and that quality of stillness peculiar to winter days.

Three weeks after the mastectomy she sat down at her type-writer to start writing *Dolls*. And now, three years later, it was time to make it sell, sell, sell and keep selling. She would accept nothing less than number one on the *New York Times* bestseller list.

She decided not to tell anyone about her brush with cancer. She didn't tell her own mother, and the only friend who knew was George. She didn't want sympathy, didn't want anyone looking at her differently or whispering about it behind her back. She stuffed a foam prosthetic in her bra, threw out her low-cut dresses and swimsuits, and carried on as normal. The follow-up checks were every three months at first, then every six months, and all had shown her to be in remission.

Her energy levels never returned to where they'd been before the operation, and her periods became erratic because the surgery, or the drugs they gave her afterward, had hastened menopause. Her hair had always been thin but now it got thinner, and that's when she started wearing wigs or falls. Her skin had aged and her jawline sagged but she'd had a facelift at forty and it was too soon for another. Helen Gurley Brown recommended an electric stimulation machine she could use to give herself mini facials. Little rollers delivered electric currents that tightened up the muscles: "Like a gym workout for the face," she said. Jacqueline bought one and tried it but wasn't sure it made a difference.

It felt as if her youth had been stolen by the cancer. But that was OK, she would accept it so long as God kept his side of the bargain.

* * *

ON MARCH THIRD, less than a month after publication, while Jacqueline and Irving were in Cincinnati, Bernie rang to say that *Dolls* had leapt onto the *New York Times* list at number five.

"What's number one?" Jacqueline asked, and he told her it was James Michener's *The Source*. That's who she had to beat.

Irving had somehow managed to get hold of a list of the 125 bookstores that reported their sales figures to the *Times*, and he sat down to call all their friends who lived near those stores. He asked each one to go in and buy twenty copies, promising to reimburse them. It would cost a packet but was cheap at the price if it worked.

Everywhere they went, Jacqueline visited bookstores, chatted with staff, and checked they had plenty of copies of *Dolls* on display. If not, she got straight on the telephone to Bernie. One store manager asked if she would sign a copy he had bought with his own money and that gave her an idea: wherever they went she started buying copies of her own book and signing them as gifts for the bookstore staff. It proved a popular gesture.

After they left each store, she scribbled notes about the booksellers she had met so that next time she could ask after their wives, kids, elderly parents, and dogs by name. When the scrappy bits of paper grew too chaotic, she bought a Rolodex in which to file them alphabetically. Dale Carnegie, eat your heart out!

Finally, eight weeks after publication, came the call she'd been hoping and praying for.

"You've done it, Jacqueline," Bernie said. "*Dolls* is number one on the list coming out tomorrow. Congratulations!"

Jacqueline screamed and dropped the receiver in her excitement. "We did it, Irving!" she yelled and he came rushing into the room. "We're number one."

He took the phone to talk to Bernie while she collapsed in a chair, momentarily overcome. God had done as she asked. She closed her eyes, feeling goose bumps on her arms and tears welling.

As a teenager she had been voted Queen of Philadelphia in a beauty contest, and that had felt good. She'd gotten several acting parts she'd auditioned for, and that was exciting too. But none of those triumphs even came close to the feeling of writing the country's most popular novel. She wished she could send all the reviewers who'd been vile about *Dolls* a framed print of this list with her name right at the very top.

CHAPTER 15

Jackie

London, 1965

A few weeks after Jackie's damp squib of a dinner date with Oscar Lerman, he telephoned her out of the blue.

"I've got two tickets for a Supremes concert on Friday," he said, "at the Flamingo Club on Wardour Street. Would you like to come?"

Jackie hadn't planned on dating him again because she didn't think they had a spark, but she loved the Motown sound emerging from the States, and especially the silky-smooth voice of Diana Ross. "I'll see if I can get a babysitter," she replied, hedging her bets. Two hours later, she called him back and said, "Sure, I'd love to." What harm could it do?

The Flamingo was in a basement, accessed down a dark, precarious flight of stairs. A dozen or so tables were arranged in front of the stage, but most people were wandering around chatting. No alcohol was served, but there was a pungent whiff of marijuana. Jackie wondered if Oscar knew what it was. Did his generation smoke weed?

The Supremes strutted out in tight-fitting candy-pink cocktail dresses and launched straight into "Where Did Our Love Go?" Their voices were true and perfectly harmonized, their dance moves completely in sync. Jackie started swaying to the music and, to her surprise, Oscar did too. He was a good dancer, with jazz-style slouchy shoulders and perfect rhythm. She grinned at him.

"Baby Love" came next and the crowd roared and whooped. The whole set lasted about ninety minutes and Jackie and Oscar danced nonstop, then yelled themselves hoarse begging for a finale. After a minute or so, the Supremes reemerged from behind a curtain and belted out "Stop! In the Name of Love," looking as fresh and lively as when they first stepped out on stage.

"I don't know about you but I could murder a drink," Oscar said as he helped her on with her coat.

He took her to the French House pub farther down Wardour Street. It was thronged with customers, but they managed to grab a pair of barstools. Gaston, the twirly-moustached proprietor, poured them tequila shots and placed a saucer with slices of lemon and a dish of salt in front of them. The next morning Jackie wouldn't remember whose idea it was to drink tequila or how many shots they'd had, because the first one went straight to her head. They were pressed up against each other, ducking to one side or the other as customers leaned across to pay for drinks, and Jackie got increasingly giggly. Why did they start telling each other dirty jokes? That was another thing she wouldn't remember the following day.

The whole date was hilarious. She had a blast. She even considered inviting him in at the end of the evening, but knew she was too drunk to enjoy sex. Besides, Tracy would be awake in a few hours.

"Can we go out again soon?" he asked, slinging his arms around her and kissing her cheek.

"Definitely!" she replied, turning her head to kiss him on the lips.

* * *

OSCAR AND JACKIE began dating whenever he was in town. After the Supremes, he dropped his polite reserve and they often went dancing, or tried out some of the different types of ethnic restaurants that were springing up across town. She slept with him on the third date, and the sex was sensual and imaginative. It was nice to have a man in her bed again, but in the back of her mind she worried about Wallace finding out. They were still married and she knew he would not be happy to hear that she was being unfaithful.

She still called him every weekend, but he was showing no sign of controlling his manic depression. Sometimes he berated her on the phone, calling her selfish and unfeeling for leaving him; other times he sobbed. He maintained that he couldn't afford to pay a penny of alimony and seemed incredulous that he should have to support her and Tracy when he didn't even see them.

"You have a legal responsibility for us," Jackie tried to explain, but he clearly wasn't going to budge on that point unless she forced him, so, with a heavy heart, she consulted a divorce lawyer. The legal fees would wipe out the very last of her mum's nest egg, so she hoped the case would be settled quickly.

"Let me help," Oscar offered when she confided in him.

She shook her head and said, "It's not fair that you should support another man's child." He always paid when they went out together, and that was fine, but if she accepted a monthly allowance she'd feel like his kept mistress.

"Marry me then," he said, to her complete astonishment, when they had only been dating for three months. "I mean it," he urged. "I want you to be my wife. I love you, Jackie. I'm willing to wait for an answer if you think there's an ounce of hope that one day you might say yes."

Jackie was knocked sideways by the proposal. It was the last thing she'd expected, especially since she was still married to someone else. She'd assumed she'd be on her own for a few years, dating lots of candidates and testing the water. But would she meet anyone better suited to her than Oscar? Would she be a fool to let him slip away? She'd found out he was eighteen years older than her, forty-five to her twenty-seven. Did that matter? Did he have any dark secrets she hadn't yet discovered? That's what worried her most.

Wallace had been diagnosed as manic depressive soon after their wedding and, looking back, she wondered if he had already known and had hidden it from her in case she changed her mind. It made her wary of trusting another man in case he also had something to hide.

She asked advice from her friends. Johnny Gold said Oscar was a true gent and would always treat her well. Her female friends seemed to like him, and he was generous to little Tracy.

But Jackie was perverse: the fact that Oscar was so smitten made her wonder what was wrong with him. She'd grown up with a father who called her an ugly duckling, and who belittled her at every opportunity. Now that she'd found a man who seemed to adore her, she kept waiting for the catch. Was he too much in love? Was he in love with the *idea* of her rather than the actual person? Jackie mulled it over, then told him she wouldn't make any decisions until her divorce came through.

The day the decree nisi was delivered in the post, Wallace telephoned her sounding distraught. "I can't live without you," he sobbed. "Everything has gone wrong since you left. I'll do whatever you ask, but please, Jackie, please come home and be my wife again."

She felt as if a giant hand was twisting her heart. She loved Wallace but it was too late for reconciliation. That ship had sailed.

"Please can I see you?" he begged. "We can meet anywhere you choose. I'll behave myself, I promise, I just need to talk to you face-to-face."

"I can't," she said. "I'm sorry, but I can't." She didn't trust herself. The sight of him might make her weaken, and it would muddle her brain just as her feelings for Oscar were growing.

Oscar bought a house in St. John's Wood, a proper family home with a garden, and invited her and Tracy to move in. Still Jackie had doubts. She couldn't let herself become reliant on a man again; it would make her too vulnerable if it all fell apart.

"If I marry you, I want to earn my own money and have my own bank account," she told him.

"Of course you can," he agreed.

"I don't want Tracy getting confused about why she has two different fathers. It's not fair on her."

"I've thought about that," he said. "If Wallace agrees, I'd like to adopt her and raise her as my own."

That would be ideal, Jackie thought. Wallace was too absorbed in his illness to show any interest in his daughter. And then she told him her final condition: "If you ever raise a hand to me, I will leave you immediately, no matter what. I want you to know that from the outset."

Oscar shook his head with sadness in his eyes. "I would never hit you," he assured her. "I couldn't hit a woman. I'm not Wallace."

They set the wedding date for June fifteenth. The day before the ceremony Jackie telephoned Wallace to let him know. She felt she owed him that. He took the news quietly, but the next day he turned up at the Marylebone register office, shouting and swinging punches in the air, clearly off his head on booze or drugs or both. The security guards had to restrain him and escort him out to the street. Jackie felt humiliated for him, and sad that she had hurt him, but she tried to force the image from her head. This was her wedding day. She should be ecstatic.

They had a party for a few friends and Jackie socialized and drank champagne, but all the while she watched Oscar and wondered if she had done the right thing. He seemed very much in love, but could she really trust him or would he let her down, just as Wallace had? She supposed only time would tell.

* * *

A FEW MONTHS after the wedding, Oscar arrived back from a trip to New York bringing her a copy of a book that was topping the bestseller list there: *Valley of the Dolls*. It was a chunky book, its black-and-white cover dotted with bright-colored pills.

Jackie started reading that evening and was hooked straight away. It was similar to the kind of novel she wanted to write— set in the showbiz world, real gritty truths mixed with glamour and heartache. She finished it in two days flat.

"I think I could do this," she told Oscar. To herself, she thought: *Maybe I could even do it better.* She had started and discarded umpteen novels by that stage, but the success of *Valley of the Dolls* demonstrated there was a market for what she was trying to achieve. Maybe she just had to choose a story and force herself to finish it this time.

She let Oscar read the first few pages of the novel she'd started to write about married men and he said he loved it.

"Write the rest," he challenged. "I dare you!"

Jackie bought a few reams of paper and got down to work the very next day. Tracy was at nursery in the mornings so that would be her writing time. She decided to write from three points of view: a married man who was having an affair, his wife, and his mistress. She could feel it would work, with the three stories merging neatly and a twist at the end. It would have a more compact time frame than *Valley of the Dolls*, but she would include drugs, wild parties, and kinky sex—all the elements that had made *Dolls* such a hit. And this time, she vowed she would get to the end without letting self-doubt stop her. It might turn out to be rubbish, but she would force herself to reach the finish line.

Wallace rang one morning while she was busy writing. His voice was so quiet it was barely audible and she knew straight away he was in one of his "lows."

"Can you ask a friend round to keep you company?" she asked. "How about Johnny?"

He said he didn't want to. "You're the only person who can help when it's this bad. Won't you come over, Jackie? I'm begging you."

"I can't," she said, biting her lip. "We can talk on the phone, but I can't rush round every time you feel blue."

"I need you so badly," he said, his voice scarcely more than a whisper. She could hear the heaviness weighing him down and knew he wouldn't be able to eat, wash himself, or get dressed, never mind go to work. The depression stole his energy.

"Why not go for a walk and get some fresh air?" she suggested. "That's helped you in the past. Then call someone and arrange to meet for a pint later. Remember, you've sunk this low before but you always bounce back. There are loads of people who care about you, Wallace. You're a wonderful man."

"Not wonderful enough for you," he muttered, and she had no answer for that.

After he hung up, she was worried. She called back a few hours later, but there was no reply. She tried again that evening, then the following morning, but the phone rang out. She hoped he had taken her advice and called a friend.

Late that evening, when she was getting ready for bed, Johnny Gold called with devastating news: "Wallace is dead," he said.

"What? *How?*" She dropped to her knees on the hall floor.

"He was found by some hikers in the New Forest. I hear there was a whiskey bottle and an empty pill bottle by his side. No note has been found but . . ."

Jackie knew it was suicide. He'd finally carried out his threat.

"He begged me to go round yesterday. If only I'd gone, he'd still be alive," she told Johnny, her throat tight with shock.

"You can't think that way," Johnny told her firmly. "He was ill. His mind was disturbed. It was always going to end like this, no matter what any of us did."

But Jackie remembered the spontaneous, fun-loving man she had married and knew that, while she could tuck it away in the back of her mind, she would always feel responsible for his death. She could have stopped him. He'd been her first love, the father of her child, and she'd let him down.

CHAPTER 16

Nancy
Manhattan, 1967

Part of Nancy's job was to forward press reviews to Jacqueline, but she decided to hold back the most vicious ones. Why did critics feel entitled to attack her personally? It reminded Nancy of the editorial meeting soon after she started at Bernard Geis Associates when the men had ridiculed Jacqueline's hair, eyelashes, teeth, and clothes. Did they feel threatened by her? she wondered.

Long after the official tour ended, Jacqueline was still accepting invitations to be interviewed on radio and TV shows or attend bookstore signings, and at many of them she was challenged over the "taboo" subjects she wrote about. A religious nut phoned in to one talk show telling her that God would judge her and she would burn in hell. Some women's libbers staged a protest outside a television station, claiming she was setting back the cause of women's rights with lines like "A man must feel he runs things, but as long as you control yourself, you control him." Nancy could see their point, but, as far as she was concerned, *Dolls* was about liberated women making their own choices, and the fact that the world punished them for it was hard reality. Jacqueline always had an articulate answer for critics, but Nancy imagined it must be exhausting to be constantly alert, like a prizefighter who has to defend herself from all comers.

One evening, Nancy was about to leave the office when she got a call from a bookstore in Connecticut where Jacqueline was due to appear at lunchtime the following day. It seemed a truck bringing their copies had been in a collision and the cargo had been damaged. There were only three books left at the store.

"Don't worry—I'll get more to you," Nancy promised. She hung up and dialed the nearest warehouse, in upper New York state, but it was after six p.m. and the number rang out. She couldn't even get through to the nightwatchman. It would be too late by the time they opened in the morning, and Jacqueline would go berserk if there were no copies for her to sign.

Her chest tight with panic, Nancy pored over the list of emergency phone numbers in her folder but couldn't see anyone who could help. What should she do? Bernie had left long ago. In fact, the entire editorial floor was deserted.

She climbed the stairs to the floor above and saw a light under the door in Steven Bailey's office. He'd always been friendly toward her. She knocked and he called, "Come in!"

Nancy explained the problem, a tremor in her voice. Steven nodded as he listened, then said, "Don't worry. I'll call Tony, the Connecticut rep, at home." He gestured for Nancy to sit down as he dialed.

It sounded as if Tony was in the middle of his evening meal, but he agreed straight away that he would round up sufficient stock the following morning.

"Borrow some from other stores in the area and tell them we'll replace them," Steven suggested. "Aim to get at least a hundred copies there by noon."

Nancy was so relieved, she could feel tears prickling her eyelids.

"Hey, hey," Steven soothed. "Has the Jacqueline monster been terrorizing you? Don't let it get you down. I guess you drew the short straw when you volunteered to work with her."

"It's been fine up to now," Nancy said. "I'm very fond of her, but I don't want to get on her bad side." She thought back to the time Jacqueline had snapped at her in the Plaza Hotel; that had been scary enough.

"You must have had a tough year," Steven said, then looked at his watch. "It's almost seven o'clock, time we both packed up for the evening. Let me buy you a burger."

Nancy still had a pile of work on her desk, but she calculated there was nothing that couldn't wait till the next morning. "That would be cool," she said. "Thanks!" She'd only had an apple for lunch and her stomach was growling.

They went to a nearby diner and slid into opposite sides of a booth. After they'd ordered, Steven began telling her about difficult authors he'd worked with.

"One who shall remain nameless used to call me every single morning wanting updated sales figures, as if I had a universal cash register in my head." Nancy laughed. "And another kept calling bookstores directly and berating them for not stocking his book—which is one sure way of *not* getting stocked anywhere."

While they ate, Steven asked about her ambitions and she told him she was desperate to be an editor. It was the job she had dreamed of since she first learned to read.

"You're certainly smart enough," he said. "You should ask Bernie to let you dip into the slush pile." When she looked blank, he explained: "That's what we call the mountains of un-solicited manuscripts that turn up at the office. Most are bilge, but occasionally you discover a pot of gold."

"I'd love to do that," Nancy said, deciding she would ask Bernie the very next day, although the term "slush pile" was off-putting. Was it really so bad?

They had been drinking beers with their burgers and when they finished, Steven ordered a couple more. The alcohol blurred the edges and helped Nancy forget about the work on her desk she hadn't had time to finish. Her typing was faster now, but she never reached the bottom of her in-tray before someone dumped a heap more work in it.

Steven's car was nearby and he offered her a lift home. On the way, she found herself telling him about the week she spent sleeping in the corridor because her cousin Louise had accepted a singing job in London without telling her. She turned it into a humorous anecdote.

"Aren't you the plucky one!" he exclaimed, glancing around as if reappraising her. When he parked his car outside the apartment, he said, "Now I have to come up and see this famous corridor."

Nancy hesitated. He wasn't her boss at the office but he was definitely her superior. Still, he was behaving like a friend and it was out of office hours, so what harm could it do?

They rode up in the elevator and she showed him the spot where she had slept, then it seemed only polite to invite him in for coffee. He wandered around the apartment looking at the posters while she rushed to the washroom to gather up some panties that were drying on a rack.

"How long have you worked at Bernie Geis?" she asked as they drank their coffee side by side on the couch.

"I've been there right from the start," he said. "It was founded in 1959. Did you know Groucho Marx was one of the backers? He's much more businesslike than you would expect from the public persona." He wiggled his eyebrows Groucho-style, and she giggled at the accuracy of the impersonation.

They were sitting close in a way that felt relaxed and companionable when he leaned in and kissed her on the mouth, very quickly, very softly. She was too surprised to react. He put his hand behind her head and she felt a thrill ripple through her as he kissed her again, more purposefully. What was he doing?

She pulled back. "Wait! We shouldn't. What about work?"

He stroked her hair, his face so close she could see there was a darker brown rim around the hazel of his irises. "I wasn't planning on rushing to announce it in the office tomorrow morning," he replied. "I don't think it's anyone's business but ours."

He kissed her again, insistently, and his fingers brushed across her nipples, whether by accident or design she wasn't sure. He had a woody scent that she liked. Her brain was muddled. She was grateful to him for rescuing her over the stock problem and for buying her a burger. He'd always been kind, and her body was responding to his touch with a tug of lust deep inside. Did he expect to have sex with her now? Right here? Was she going to do this?

She should tell him to stop kissing her, stop touching her, but it felt too delicious. His kisses were more determined now and his hands were sliding all over her body, bringing it alive in ways she had never experienced, ways that made any remaining willpower dissipate into thin air.

She remembered what George had said about how important it was to choose your first lover carefully, and whispered, "I'm a virgin."

He pulled back, his expression tender. "I'll be very careful," he said. "You have nothing to worry about." He stroked her back in long sensual movements and spoke between kisses. "I've wanted you since the first time I saw you. You're so pretty and smart. You're a very special girl, Nancy."

His hand slid up her skirt and his fingers rubbed lightly on the outside of her panties, driving her crazy. She had been fantasizing about losing her virginity since the conversation with George, and Steven seemed smitten with her. Were the beers she'd drunk clouding her judgment? She didn't think so. She liked him. She wanted him. It was the nineteen sixties and no one expected girls to be virgins anymore.

He unfastened her skirt and slid it over her hips, then pulled off her panties too, and he was inside her before she had properly decided. She felt a momentary discomfort, then a glorious sensation of fullness. This was it—she was having sex!

It didn't last long. He pulled out a few minutes later and she reached for him, unsure why he had stopped, aching for more.

"Hang on," he whispered. "I think I have a condom somewhere. Why don't we go to bed and get comfortable?"

He fumbled in his wallet and took out a small foil packet, then pulled her to her feet. She half stumbled to the bedroom, leaning against him, intensely aware of the throbbing sensation between her legs. Once on the bed he undressed her completely, exclaiming how beautiful she was, stroking and kissing her breasts in a way that made her whole body tingle. Before long he had pushed inside her again and this time she sensed how to move her hips to meet his strokes.

"You're a fast learner," he whispered, and she was pleased. It seemed important to be good at sex.

After he finished with a grunt, she dozed in his arms, feeling warm and comfortable and full of bliss. Her head fitted neatly in the dip beneath his shoulder, her thigh straddled his, and even their breathing was synchronized, in and out, like two identical organisms.

When pink-and-orange dawn streaked the sky outside, he slipped inside her again and they made love a third time, drowsily. He was tender and loving, and it brought tears to her eyes. It had been so long since she'd felt a loving touch—since the last time she saw her mother.

Afterward, she lay with her head on Steven's chest, her heart pounding. Did this mean he was her boyfriend now? Would people in the office be able to tell she had lost her virginity?

Yesterday she'd been a hardworking spinster, but now she was a daring, modern career girl.

"I suppose I'd better go home and change into fresh clothes," he said, sitting up.

"So you don't go to the office smelling of sex?" she asked, with a coy smile, breathing in the musky scent of the sheets.

"Exactly." He rolled out of bed. "You should try and get another hour or two's sleep or you'll be exhausted later."

She was very tired, she realized. That was a good idea. "Where do you live?" she murmured.

"New Jersey," he said. "Just the other side of the Holland Tunnel."

"I thought it was only married couples with kids who lived over there," she said drowsily, because that's what she'd heard. Everyone said the cool young people stayed in Manhattan, despite the expense.

"Yeah, pretty much," he admitted. "Jeanette and I moved there after we got married because there are good schools."

Suddenly she was wide awake. There was a ringing sound in her ears. She sat bolt upright, clutching the sheet to her chest. "You're *married*?" she whispered in horror.

"You didn't know?" he asked. "Oh Nancy, I'm sorry. It's common knowledge in the office. How could you not know?"

"I didn't," she insisted. She didn't explain that she never stood gossiping with the other secretaries in the kitchen. She got the impression they saw her as standoffish because she took her work so seriously.

"Please don't worry about it," he said. "Jeanette and I sleep in separate bedrooms and lead separate lives. She has a lover and we agreed that I can take one too, but till now I've never met anyone I wanted." He kissed her forehead and stroked her hair.

"We decided we would stay together for the sake of our son, Darren, but we're not a couple. Oh, please don't look so sad, Nancy. It's only a bit of paper."

She hadn't realized she looked sad; she just felt stunned. He had a son too!

"This needn't make any difference to us," he told her. "Pretend you don't even know. We're like any new couple starting out and this boy is very, *very* keen on the girl."

He zipped his trousers. "Can I take you on a date Thursday? I'll find somewhere wonderful and surprise you."

"Alright," she said, her voice flat. What else could she say to the man who'd just taken her virginity, a man who worked for the same company? *No, I never want to see you again?*

He slipped away after more lingering kisses, leaving Nancy exhausted but wide awake, mulling over all that had happened. She wasn't a virgin anymore. It ached between her legs, but in a pleasurable way. It didn't feel as if he had been too rough, as George had warned.

How was she to feel about the fact that Steven had a wife? He should have told her before. If he had, she wouldn't have had sex with him. But now the deed was done, her body was already craving more. Was that immoral of her? Could she carry on treating him like a boyfriend—a lover—and try not to think about Jeanette and Darren?

She wished there was someone she could confide in, but most of the people she knew in New York worked at Bernard Geis, and she couldn't risk the news spreading there. She certainly didn't feel she could tell Jacqueline. And she was pretty sure George would tell her she'd been a prize idiot for falling into bed with someone on the first date without checking his marital status first. She definitely couldn't let George find out.

Oh god, what had she done?

CHAPTER 17

Jacqueline

Manhattan, 1967

The *Valley of the Dolls* hardback stayed at number one on the bestseller list for twenty-eight weeks, and Jacqueline was determined that the paperback would do even better. She launched herself into yet another countrywide tour, this one including stops at truck depots in the middle of the night to take trays of Danish pastries to the drivers who were transporting huge pallets of copies around the country. Always she'd make sure a photographer was on hand. Her efforts paid off when *Dolls* leapt straight onto the paperback bestseller list at number one and wouldn't budge.

She and Irving were quick to grab with both hands any publicity opportunities that came their way. When they heard a Chicago bookstore was refusing to put *Dolls* on display but kept it under the counter because it was a "dirty book," Irving brought a lawsuit against them, and made sure it got loads of press coverage.

"Every time someone calls it a 'dirty book' I hear the ker-ching of cash registers!" Jacqueline told reporters.

The downside was the critics. You'd think she'd get used to them, but she found that, if anything, she got more sensitive to their jibes as time went on. She knew Irving tried to keep the worst of the barrage from her, and she appreciated that. She was especially hurt when she spotted a review by feminist journalist Gloria Steinem, a woman she had a lot of respect for. Steinem wrote that *Dolls* was "for the reader who has put away comic books but isn't yet ready for editorials in the *Daily News*."

Jacqueline could just about deal with the men who attacked her because they were uncomfortable with women talking about sex, but when she was attacked by other women it cut to the bone.

"Isn't that slander?" she asked Irving, but he said everyone was entitled to an opinion and there were no grounds to sue. Instead, she called her friend Long John Nebel, who had a late-night talk show on the radio in New York, and asked him to invite her on air so she could answer her critics.

"I'd be lying if I didn't admit the negative reviews wear me down," she told him. "I'm a woman with strong religious beliefs who wouldn't harm a fly—or any other animal, great or small— but the critics don't hesitate to take personal potshots at me. What did I do to deserve this? Are they jealous because my books sell more than theirs?"

The late hour relaxed her and she spoke freely, almost forgetting anyone was listening.

"Have you taken dolls yourself?" John asked.

"Sure, I take sleeping pills," she said. "Who doesn't? I've also got some dexies in case I need a bit of pep in the morning, but I don't take them regularly. They're all supplied by my doctor on prescription, by the way. I've had some vitamin injections from the famous Dr. Max Jacobson, which feel amazing. But I've never taken LSD or marijuana or any illegal drugs. I care too much for my health to risk it."

That was the truth. She didn't add that she'd had breast cancer and lived in fear of it returning, so wouldn't take any pill unless it was okayed by her doctor. She had cut down to ten cigarettes and two cocktails a day, which was positively abstemious as far as she was concerned, and she exercised in the gym at the Navarro most mornings before she started work. She was forty-eight years old and could feel in her bones that she needed to take better care of herself than she had in her younger days. She couldn't count entirely on her deal with God.

* * *

AT THE END of the paperback campaign, Jacqueline bought Nancy an extravagant gift to thank her for her help with *Dolls*— a brown suede coat lined with white rabbit fur around the hood and the hem.

"I can't accept this," Nancy protested. "I was only doing my job."

"Of course you can!" Jacqueline guided her into the bedroom so she could check her appearance in the full-length mirror, and overruled her objections. "You look like Julie Christie in *Dr. Zhivago*. I insist you have it." She liked shopping for the girl. Someone needed to do something about her appalling taste in clothes, and it was fun spoiling her.

Irving had mixed cocktails and called them back into the living room to clink glasses. As soon as Nancy sat down, Josephine jumped on her lap, as she always did. Jacqueline's friend Bea had been looking after her during the book tour and she was much more svelte as a result.

"You've been in Manhattan for two years now, haven't you?" Jacqueline asked Nancy. "Does it feel like home yet?"

"I guess so," she replied, hesitantly.

"Have you made many friends?"

Nancy wrinkled her nose. "Not really. New Yorkers all seem to lead busy lives. Besides, I often work late. And while I love the apartment I'm staying in, it's not truly mine."

"Any word from Louise recently?"

"No, nothing."

Jacqueline wasn't sure she liked the sound of this Louise. She seemed selfish. She kept her opinion to herself, though.

"I heard your next novel is to be called *The Love Machine*," Nancy said. "Bernie told us it's about a womanizing television executive."

Jacqueline bit back her annoyance that Bernie had mentioned it. The idea was confidential because Irving hadn't finished negotiating the deal. But then she remembered Nancy took minutes at the editorial meetings so she would have heard about it there.

"How's it going?" Nancy persisted. "I can't wait to read it."

Jacqueline gave a big sigh. "Bernie has sent me a long list of revisions he wants to make to the outline. He's a very unimaginative man. He doesn't seem to believe it's possible to have an orgy on an airplane, and he questioned all my women having plastic surgery—but you know what? I understand that world better than he ever will."

"Bernie will be Bernie," Nancy said. "He means well, but he's not very tactful."

"Let's just say I doubt any woman will ever offer to fuck *him* on a plane," Jacqueline said with a defiant toss of the head.

"I wondered if your television executive might be based on George?" Nancy asked. "It seems quite the coincidence that your hero works in TV and travels a lot. But is George a womanizer?"

"Women certainly like him," Jacqueline replied with a teasing smile. It was true: George had been very much on her mind while she was writing, but there were some clear differences between him and her character, Robin Stone. "Do you see him often?"

"Every couple of months," Nancy admitted. "He buys me dinner at Toots Shor's when he's in the city on a stopover."

"I'm glad he's wining and dining you," Jacqueline said. "He's a very special friend of mine so I'm happy you two get along."

"We do," Nancy replied, "but perhaps not the way you intended. He's like a protective big brother."

"Give it time," Jacqueline urged, then was surprised to see Nancy's cheeks color. "Unless . . ." She looked hard. There was something different about the girl. She seemed glowing. "You haven't met someone else, have you?"

Nancy lifted her glass in front of her face as if trying to hide behind it. "There is someone," she answered at last. "But it's too soon to tell if anything will come of it."

"You clearly like him." Jacqueline was intrigued. "Who is he?" She thrived on gossip from her girlfriends. She spent hours every week on the telephone keeping up with the complexities of their love lives, and considered herself the unofficial advice guru for her set.

"His name's Steven," Nancy said. "But really, there's nothing to tell."

"Where did you meet?" Jacqueline persevered, folding her legs beneath her and leaning forward eagerly. "Was it love at first sight?"

"I met him through work," Nancy said. "He's in the book trade."

She was being frustratingly reticent. "What age is he?" Jacqueline asked. "Where does he come from?"

"I haven't asked these questions yet," Nancy said. "Truly, I hardly know him."

She was definitely sleeping with him, Jacqueline decided. That would account for the blushing. "Is he tall or short? Dark or fair?"

"Medium height, with short sandy-blond hair, hazel eyes." She drained her cocktail.

"Good kisser?" Jacqueline asked, and the pink of the girl's cheeks deepened again. Why wouldn't she share more details? Women in love usually wanted to talk endlessly about their beloved. "Will you bring him to our next party?" she persevered.

"I'll try," Nancy said. "I'm not sure if he's the party type."

It seemed an odd answer. Who didn't like parties? Was this guy giving her the runaround already? Surely if he was a stand-up guy, he would want to meet Nancy's famous novelist friend? She hoped her poor little protégé wasn't going to have her heart broken by her very first boyfriend, but there was nothing she could do if Nancy wouldn't share the details. She'd have to wait. Shame it wasn't George . . .

Seeing Nancy always made Jacqueline think about her son. After the girl left, she called the institution to chat with one of the nurses. She rang regularly, to hear what he'd been doing, whether he was eating properly, and how he was feeling, as far as they could tell. No matter how much they told her, it wasn't enough. If only he could come on the line and talk to her himself—but of course he never would.

* * *

JACQUELINE SIGNED A new two-book deal with Bernard Geis Associates and immersed herself in work on *The Love Machine*. Every morning she was at her desk by ten and she usually stayed there till five, going through her color-coded sequence of drafts.

She was interrupted one morning by a call from Helen Gurley Brown.

"I've just seen the new edition of *McCall's* magazine and thought you should know there's an article that mentions you," Helen said.

"Oh yeah?" Jacqueline replied, only half focusing.

"It's called 'The Truth About the Bestseller List.' The author, Walter Goodman, interviewed Bernie Geis about his experiences publishing *Dolls*."

She had Jacqueline's full attention now. "And?"

"I'm sorry to say, but he seems to be implying that they were the ones responsible for its success. He says his editor virtually rewrote it. I think you should have a look."

"He said *what?*"

"Also," Helen continued, "I don't know about you, but he is way behind on paying me the royalties he owes. I get a feeling the firm might be in trouble."

Jacqueline sent Irving to buy a copy of *McCall's* and read the article, her fury mounting. It claimed that Bernie and his editors had "put their taste at Miss Susann's service" as they "guided her in cutting, inserting a new scene and bringing her characters into sharper focus." They were already helping to do the same for her new novel, *The Love Machine*, it read.

First, she felt like crying, but soon fury took over. How dare they? Bernie had made a small fortune on the back of her success. She was sick to death of patronizing men undermining her achievement. It hadn't been easy to write a huge bestseller. She was a natural storyteller with great insight into character and no one gave her credit for that.

Irving was reading the *McCall's* article now.

"Will you call Bernie?" she asked. "I'm so furious, I might say something I'd regret."

She hovered in the doorway listening as Irving made the call. At first Bernie tried to claim he'd been misquoted, then said it wasn't so bad anyway. All publicity was good publicity, yadda, yadda, yadda.

Irving asked him when they would receive their share of paperback royalties and Bernie didn't answer directly. Irving pressed again and Bernie said there might be a slight delay. He couldn't pay all that was owed for the paperback of *Dolls* until he sold rights to the paperback of *Love Machine*. Jacqueline's heart sank. Helen was right. The company was struggling.

By the time Irving came off the phone, she'd made up her

mind. "How can I put my career and livelihood in the hands of a man who is happy to belittle me in print and who can't pay his debts?" she demanded. "It's time we started shopping for a new publisher."

"It'll be tricky," Irving cautioned. "We've just signed a two-book deal."

"We have to get out of it," she said. "Whatever it takes."

Bernie Geis was small-fry. If he went bankrupt, her son would lose his inheritance. They should sign with one of the big, well-established publishing houses next time—preferably the highest bidder. With a record-breaking bestseller under her belt, she was in a great position to negotiate.

But how to get out of the deal with Bernie? After Irving consulted their lawyers, they decided to launch a lawsuit charging him with fraud. Attack was the best form of defense.

She telephoned George to have a rant about Bernie, and at the end of the call she mentioned Nancy's new boyfriend. "She didn't tell me much about him," she said, "but she seems smitten."

George didn't respond for a couple of beats. "I hope he's good to her," he said at last, and Jacqueline was convinced from his tone that he was jealous.

CHAPTER 18

Jackie
London, 1966

The inquest into Wallace's death ruled that he had poisoned himself with barbiturates while the balance of his mind was disturbed. Jackie had given a statement to the police about their last telephone call and about his manic depression, and was grateful when she was told she didn't need to attend the hearing in person.

She went to his funeral, accompanied by Johnny Gold. Several hundred people turned up to pay their respects to a man who had been the life and soul of swinging London parties for the last decade. Jackie had just found out she was pregnant, and she was feeling fragile and emotional as she sat in a front pew looking at the coffin containing his body. Tears rolled down her cheeks as friend after friend stood up to share anecdotes about Wallace's generosity, his creative flair, and his capacity for fun. It was true, every bit of it; if only he hadn't had a dark side as well.

The wake turned into a raucous party with free-flowing booze, just as Wallace would have wanted. She wished he could see how well he had been loved.

Johnny called her a taxi just after nine and when she got home, Oscar was waiting.

"How was it, darling?" he asked, putting his arms around her.

"Sad," she said, tears welling again. He hadn't argued when she asked him not to attend. Wallace wouldn't have wanted him there.

"Put your feet up and I'll make you a cup of tea," he said, leading her to the couch.

It was early days—she was only ten weeks' pregnant—but he was thrilled that he was going to be a father. They'd applied for him to adopt Tracy, so by the end of the year, all being well, they'd be a family of four. A nuclear family, they called it, in a phrase she always found chilling.

Jackie had never wanted Tracy to be an only child; she loved babies. She should have been ecstatic about the pregnancy, but part of her was still watching and waiting for Oscar to make a wrong step. Every time he flew to New York on business, she worried that he had another woman there. He telephoned each day and she never caught a hint of anyone else in the background, but who was he spending his evenings with? She didn't want to subject him to an inquisition, but the suspicions niggled. He always left his mail lying around and sometimes she glanced through it, glad to see that he paid bills on time, unlike Wallace. He hadn't once lost his temper with her—in fact, they'd never had a proper argument. He seemed too perfect to be true, but she didn't believe in perfect. Perfect was only in fairy tales.

She was making good headway with her novel about a cheating married man. Maybe that's what was making her cynical about men in general. They weren't all deceitful, self-centered hypocrites like David Cooper, her protagonist, but in her experience plenty were. Her dad certainly was.

The story poured out onto the pages and she was still only halfway through the pregnancy when she wrote the words "The End." She went back to read it from the beginning, and the amazing thing was that she didn't hate it. Some bits made her cringe, but others were really punchy. She'd done it!

Oscar hired a woman to type it for her. She still needed a title and played around with several options. "The Affair" was boring. "The Truth About Marriage" sounded like a textbook. And then it came to her—"The World Is Full of Married Men." She got the typist to put that on the front page, then when the typed version came back, she gave it to Oscar to read.

She hovered in the doorway, trying to interpret his facial expressions, until he shooed her off to bed. Next morning, he gave his verdict: "It's completely and utterly brilliant! I've never read anything like it. You're a natural."

Jackie knew it wasn't great literature, but she secretly thought it was better than Jacqueline Susann's *Valley of the Dolls*, which was sprawling and unwieldy in places. Her plot knitted together neatly, and her sex was more raunchy and real.

Her dad was friends with an editor called Robert Armstrong who worked at W. H. Allen publishers. She had never expected any favors from Joe, and certainly didn't want him to read her work—he would hate it—but she called and asked if he could mention it to Mr. Armstrong. Word came back that he'd be happy to read it, so, full of trepidation, Jackie parceled it up with a handwritten note.

Then the wait began. She didn't want to allow herself to hope, because then she'd be let down. She very much doubted the first novel she ever finished would be good enough for publication, but perhaps the editor would give her some pointers. It had been fun to write and she was proud of herself for getting to the end, but that was all.

And yet, a tiny capsule of excitement fizzed inside her brain. Maybe, just maybe, W. H. Allen would agree to publish it.

CHAPTER 19

Nancy

Manhattan, 1967

Nancy wondered how Steven would let her know where to meet for their first proper date. Her desk was close to the other secretaries' and anything he said to her would be overheard and gossiped about. He got around the problem by walking up with a polite smile and handing her a note.

"Here's the information you wanted, Miss White," he said. His words were businesslike but accompanied by a wink so subtle no one else could have detected it.

Cafe Au Go Go, 152 Bleecker Street, 7 p.m., the note read. *See you outside. Can't wait.*

"I understand," she told him, equally formal. "Thank you."

She was in two minds about letting herself get involved any further with Steven. The moral course would be to tell him that sleeping together had been a mistake and couldn't happen again; but if Jeanette had a lover, wasn't he entitled to one too? Besides, she yearned to have sex with him again. The very thought made her giddy with lust.

It was comedy night at the Cafe Au Go Go and the basement club was already thronged with customers when they arrived. Steven gripped her hand tightly and wove through the tables to an empty one near the back.

"It's gotten busier since Lenny Bruce was arrested for obscenity," he said. "I hear they plant undercover cops in the audience to pounce at the least hint of a swear word."

Nancy looked around but none of the audience seemed like

police to her. Steven ordered some drinks, then the first act came on stage. It was a young man joking about his work in a car show-room.

"A customer nearly died in front of me today," he said, deadpan. "But I counted to ten and put the scissors back in the drawer." Nancy laughed so hard her stomach hurt.

Steven kept his fingers laced through hers during the show. She worried about someone from the office spotting them, or a friend of his wife's perhaps, but he didn't seem concerned.

Afterward they went to an Italian trattoria and he ordered a bottle of Valpolicella to accompany their prawn linguine. Nancy took the opportunity to ask questions about his marriage that had been burning inside her. How many years had he and Jeanette been together? Eleven, he said; they'd met in college. His son, Darren, was seven. Nancy did the math: that made him around thirty, she guessed, maybe just over.

"Do you and Jeanette plan to stay together forever? Living in the same house but taking other lovers?" She sipped the wine. It was the first time she'd tried red wine and she wasn't sure about the taste but it made her feel nicely mellow. She took another sip.

"Of course not," he insisted straight away. "Just till Darren is a bit older. He started a new school recently and needs stability at home."

"How much older?" she asked. It might sound pushy but she had a right to know what she was getting into so she could decide whether to back out.

"It's hard to choose an exact age, but recent developments might force my hand." He gave her a meaningful look. "I haven't been able to stop thinking about you since the other night. It's excruciating to see you in the office and not be able to touch you and hold you."

"I don't know how to treat this," Nancy admitted. "I don't want to be your mistress, but I suppose that's what they call women who sleep with married men."

He shook his head. "I wish you would treat me like any new boyfriend."

"I've never had a boyfriend before so I don't know how to do that," she told him.

"Never?" He was surprised. "OK, I guess we should be discreet in the office, but we can be ourselves on nights out. You can call me at home if you want—I'll give you the number. And we can see each other at least twice a week, I'll make sure of it. Will that do to start with?"

Nancy's mind felt foggy. It was reassuring she could call him at home, but at the same time this wasn't normal, was it? She drank more of the wine, trying to work out how she felt. "Jacqueline Susann guessed I have a new boyfriend and she wants to meet you. I don't know what to tell her."

He pulled a face. "That's awkward," he said. "I met Jacqueline a couple of times in the office and I'm sure she knows I'm married. Can you keep her at bay for now?"

Nancy sighed. None of this was going to be straightforward. Why couldn't he have been single?

"Tell me about *your* family," he asked. "You mentioned your mom died not long ago. Were you close?"

Nancy took a deep breath and did her best to describe the strength of the bond she'd had with her mom. As an only child she had been the sole recipient of her unconditional love, and after her father died, they'd been joined at the hip. Even after she went to college they talked every day, about friends, about books, about everything. The loss was so immense that it was easier for Nancy not to think about it or she got a sense of vertigo, as if she were falling from a great height into a dark void.

"The thing about love like that is you never lose it," Steven said. "You still have all the love your mom gave you, tucked away inside, making you the person you are. It was a gift for life, even if you can't pick up the telephone and chat with her anymore."

Nancy felt tearful, and took another gulp of wine. What would her mother think of her dating a married man? She had only ever wanted her happiness, but Nancy knew she'd be concerned.

"Are you close to your stepfather and stepbrothers?" Steven asked.

"Not really," Nancy admitted. "My stepfather, Joe, is a good man, but I haven't felt like going home to Ossipee since Mom died. It's silly but I can't face seeing the house without her in it. He's brought the boys to New York to visit me a few times, and that was nice." She knew she should see more of them. It's what her mother would have wanted.

"I've noticed you don't go for lunch with the other girls in the office," he continued. "You work right through, and I've seen little evidence of a social life. Now you tell me you don't have a close family either. Isn't that very lonely?"

She shrugged, but a lump in her throat made her too choked to reply.

He touched her cheek, gently. "Do you know what I think?" he said. "I think it might do you good to go back to Ossipee and confront all the memories of your mother there. You might find they bring you comfort and at the same time help you get closer to your remaining family."

It made sense, but suddenly everything was too overwhelming. Nancy scraped her chair back and excused herself to go to the restroom, where she splashed her face with cold water. When she returned to the table, Steven had paid the bill and was holding her coat.

"Let's go back to yours," he said in a low, throaty voice, and she nodded.

Their lovemaking was so intense and passionate that Nancy felt as if every nerve ending was alive to the touch of him, while her head was stuffed with cotton wool. For the first time since she arrived in New York she felt connected to another person, someone who saw who she was and cared about her. Suddenly she wasn't alone anymore.

CHAPTER 20

Jacqueline

Manhattan, 1967

T he legal battles with Bernie Geis commenced. It was in the hands of the lawyers and Jacqueline left it to Irving to get updates because it made her too stressed. She was incensed when Irving explained there wasn't enough evidence to make a fraud case stick and that they would have to buy their way out of the contract with Bernie.

"But he tried to cheat us!" she complained. "He's a grade-A hustler."

"Unfortunately, the lawyers don't agree," Irving explained. "He's counterclaiming for loss of the earnings he would have made from this and your subsequent novel. He wants four hundred grand."

That took her breath away. "Seriously?" She felt a crushing weight on her chest.

He pursed his lips and gave a slight nod. "We'll make sure we cover it with the advance from your next publisher."

Jacqueline stormed into the bedroom and threw herself on the bed, burying her face in a pillow. Bernie was cheating her son out of money that should be his! The thought made her sick to her stomach. She was convinced he had double-crossed her. He owed Helen back royalties. They had to cut ties with him. Bernard Geis Associates was a sinking ship and Bernie was a rat.

Irving came into the room to see if she was OK.

"What about future earnings from Bernie?" she asked. "Can we have a cast-iron guarantee that he will pay royalties promptly?"

"We'll get one," Irving assured her.

"And can you ask for a clause saying that Helen Gurley Brown's royalties are guaranteed too?"

He leaned over to kiss her. "I love that you care so much for your friends," he said. "I'll see it's done."

* * *

JACQUELINE FELT SHE was suffocating under a black cloud of worries that left her anxious and out of sorts. It was hard to carry on writing *Love Machine* when her mind was constantly whirring over her problems. Among them, the *Valley of the Dolls* movie premiere was coming up and she was dreading it.

"No novelists like the movie versions of their books," George told her over dinner, "but they love the effect they have on their sales. Grin and bear it."

"They asked my opinion on casting, then completely ignored it," she complained. "Why did I waste my breath?" She had wanted Bette Davis to play Helen Lawson, but they said she was too old. She didn't like Patty Duke in the role of Neely. Sharon Tate was perfect as Jennifer and she liked Barbara Parkins well enough as Anne, but she had a bad feeling about it.

As they watched the premiere, her concern grew, and the upbeat ending they'd imposed, where Anne walks off through a snowy wood, left her incandescent. All the carefully wrought nuances of her characters had been lost.

"It's a disaster," she whispered to Irving as the credits rolled. "A piece of shit." She waved and smiled at reporters gathered outside the movie theater but refused to answer questions about the movie because there was nothing good to say.

The next day, the press coverage was predictably dire. Many reviewers used it as a chance to rehash their old criticisms of the book: "badly written," "obscene," "vulgar." She skimmed a few, then hurled the papers across the room. She hated the way she had lost control of her creation once the movie people stepped in. They had trashed her work and she didn't even get a say.

A week later, Jacqueline drove past a movie theater that was screening *Dolls* and saw a line stretching down the block. She slowed the car and realized it was a motley assortment of folk: several were clearly transvestites, with magnificent wigs and gaudy frocks, and a whole heap were scantily clad girls who looked for all the world like hookers. Were they her people? Good for them! She considered getting out of the car to introduce herself, but the drivers behind started honking and she had to drive on.

The reviews might have been dreadful, but initial figures showed the movie was a huge success, setting box office records for its opening weekend, and it became the number one movie in the US for the next seven weeks.

"At least we'll make some decent money from that pile-of-shit movie," Jacqueline commented to Irving, and he mumbled something incoherent. "What was that?" she asked.

"It's a shame our contract is based on net profits rather than gross," he said. "The producers get to deduct their expenses before paying us."

"How did that happen?" Jacqueline demanded, sharply. "Is that normal?"

Irving muttered that he'd thought it was standard practice.

"Why didn't you get more advice?" Jacqueline felt her temper snap. "We pay umpteen agents and lawyers and God knows who else, and you're telling me you all made a rookie error in my first-ever movie contract?"

Irving said he would see it didn't happen next time.

"Damn right you will," Jacqueline retorted. She picked up an ice bucket from the dining table and tipped the ice and freezing water over Irving's head. He realized her intention at the last minute and held up his arms to protect himself but still got a soaking. Josephine started barking, alarmed by the furor, but Jacqueline ignored her and strode to her office, slamming the door hard.

Everything Irving did was irritating her at the moment. Everyone else was too, but she blamed him most of all. He was supposed to have her back. She needed to be able to trust him, but in this case she clearly shouldn't have.

Their marriage had gone through phases like this before and she knew they would come out the other side, but she felt very alone in dealing with the carnage created by book reviewers, publishers, and movie producers. She was their hen that laid the golden eggs and she deserved a darn sight more respect from all these effing men than she was currently getting.

CHAPTER 21

Jackie

London, 1967

While Oscar was in the States on business, Jackie sometimes dined out with friends. One night, when she was eight months' pregnant, a group of them went to Dolly's nightclub. They secured a table tucked in the corner and Jackie ordered a tonic water. There was a rowdy bunch crowded around a table in the middle of the room and Jan de Souza, a Mary Quant model who was Johnny's latest squeeze, whispered that she thought they were friends of the Krays, the notorious East End gangsters.

Jackie turned to look. Their dark suits and narrow ties, greased-back hair, and shiny two-tone shoes were very different from the fashionable hippy style of the rest of the clientele. One of them eyed her up and down in lascivious fashion, despite her obvious pregnancy, and she shivered.

When Johnny dropped by their table, he confirmed that they were indeed associates of the Krays.

"What are they doing here?" Jackie asked, sure that Oscar wouldn't approve.

"Being a right royal pain in the arse, that's what," Johnny said, his mouth tight.

"Can't you throw them out?" Jan asked.

He made a face. "Sometimes you have to deal with their sort in the nightclub trade. Don't worry—I've got my eye on them."

The group carried on with their conversation. Jackie had her back to the men, but she could hear the noise level rising steadily, then there was a loud shout. She swiveled to see one of them standing on the table and leaping up to catch hold of a chandelier. For two precarious seconds he swung from it, before the molding detached from the ceiling and crashed down, the chandelier landing on top of him. Jackie screamed and clutched her belly as Jan de Souza jumped in front of her to shield her from flying glass.

Johnny was on the scene in seconds, closely followed by two of his bouncers. The culprit was dragged to his feet and led off, his forehead gushing blood. A waiter scurried out with a brush and dustpan while Johnny remonstrated with two of the remaining gangsters. Voices were raised. Jackie couldn't make out the words, but she could tell they were giving him lip. She shivered at the ugly expressions and the thought crossed her mind that they could be armed.

"Johnny knows what he's doing," Jan assured her. "He can handle himself."

Jackie felt the baby shift inside, as if it had been wakened by the fray. "I want to go home, but not till these men are gone."

"I'll take you out the back way," Jan said. "My car's parked one street over."

Jackie didn't feel safe until they were in the car and on their way. She decided this would be her last night out until after the baby was born. Her bump made her too vulnerable.

A few days later, she took Oscar's car to the supermarket to stock up. On the way home, she wound down her window to catch the breeze.

She stopped at a red signal at Euston Road, vaguely aware of another car pulling up alongside. It felt too close, as if it might bump her side-view mirror. She turned and saw a man in a dark suit with a sneering expression sitting in the passenger seat and pointing something at her. She'd never seen a gun up close and it took a few seconds to register that's what it was.

"Give us your purse, lady," he said in an accent that was East End and rough. "Hand it over and you won't get hurt."

She glanced around but there were no passersby close enough to help. She was petrified but had the presence of mind to say, "I've just been shopping. There's nothing left in my purse."

"In that case, I'll follow you to the bank and you can get some from your old man's account."

Did he mean Oscar? Or her dad? "Which old man?" she asked, trying to control the tremble in her voice.

"Your lovely husband needs to learn the way things work round here. He's being a bit slow on the uptake. Now there's a Barclay's a block to the left. When the lights change, drive straight there and don't forget I'm right behind you."

Jackie looked at the gun again. The round black hole where the bullet would emerge was obscene. She had to pick up her daughter from school soon. She couldn't be late.

Sheer instinct took over. The light was still red but in one swift movement she released the handbrake, raised the clutch, and pressed her foot down hard on the accelerator. The car shot straight across the road, swerving in front of an oncoming bus. The gangster's driver was slow to take off and had to wait for the bus to trundle past, by which time she had darted left through a council estate. She took an immediate right, then another left, zigzagging and checking her mirror for a good ten minutes until she was positive she had lost them.

She pulled into a secluded mews and it was only then she realized her entire body was trembling. She had five minutes to calm down before she had to collect Tracy. Might the gangsters know which school she attended?

She parked at the caretaker's entrance behind the school, slipped in the back door, grabbed her daughter from the infant classroom, and hurried back to the car.

What now? Could they risk going home? No, they probably knew where she lived and might be waiting for her. They must have been watching the house; how else did they figure out she was Oscar's wife? She cast her mind back to the crowd at Dolly's, trying to remember if the gangster was one of them, but she hadn't seen their faces clearly.

Jackie drove around for a while, trying to think. Checking the nearest street sign, she realized she wasn't far from Jan de Souza's apartment, so she parked there and hammered frantically on the door, praying she wasn't out on a modeling assignment.

When Jan answered, Jackie said, "Can I use your phone to call Oscar in the States? It's urgent. I'll pay you back."

"Course you can."

While Jackie placed the international call, Jan made her a cup of tea and gave Tracy some juice.

Jackie told Oscar what had happened and he swore out loud, using words she had never heard him utter before. "Johnny and I have been negotiating with them over protection money. I guess they're trying to force my hand by threatening you, but they have no idea who they're dealing with."

Jackie felt goose bumps prick her arms. "Who exactly are they dealing with, Oscar? Perhaps you should tell me first." Was he a gangster? Is this the kind of life she could expect? She'd been waiting to discover the downside of marriage to him, and now it had been dramatically demonstrated.

He ignored the question. "I'll call Johnny right after we hang up and tell him to sort this. You'll be safe to go home within the hour."

"No way! I'm staying with Jan tonight," she said, glancing at Jan, who nodded immediately. "I've got two children to protect, Oscar. That doesn't seem to have occurred to you."

"OK, you stay there," he said. "I'll fly home overnight and collect you in the morning."

She hung up without saying goodbye, so furious she didn't trust herself to speak. How could he have put her in that position? He couldn't play tough with gangsters while leaving his heavily pregnant wife unprotected! Was he uncaring or stupid? Either way, she wasn't putting up with it. She'd already divorced one irresponsible husband and she still had the lawyer's number.

Oscar arrived in a taxi the next morning, fresh off the red-eye. They dropped Tracy at school, then Jackie berated him all the way home. He was clearly upset about the attempted holdup, and desperately sorry, but she told him he should have been able to predict they would target her. It was inexcusable. She'd been waiting for him to let her down, and now he had.

When they got back, she pushed open the front door and picked up the post lying on the mat, flicking through it. One letter had the W. H. Allen colophon and her heart beat a little faster. She ripped it open standing in the hallway and scanned the words: Robert Armstrong liked her novel very much and wanted her to come for a meeting at the earliest opportunity.

She burst into tears. The horror of the previous twenty-four hours, followed by such incredible news, was all too much. Oscar tried to hug her, but she shoved him away. He wasn't going to be forgiven that easily.

CHAPTER 22

Nancy

Hotel Navarro, 1967

Jacqueline called and asked Nancy to stop by after work. Her tone was breezy and upbeat, but it sounded as if she had an agenda. Nancy hoped she wasn't going to be interrogated further about her new love affair. Steven filled her thoughts so completely it would be hard not to blurt out the truth. If only she could; she was dying to tell someone.

When Irving opened the door, Nancy bent to pet Josephine, then looked up to see Jacqueline waving from the couch, wearing a startling lime-green, black-and-white geometric-patterned dress. A bottle of champagne stood in an ice bucket with three flutes alongside.

"Are you celebrating?" she asked.

"In a way, yes," Jacqueline replied. "Irving, be a dear and open that before we all die of thirst." She turned to Nancy. "I'm leaving Bernie Geis. I've had enough of the way they treat me like a laughingstock. Don't think I'm unaware of all the snide little put-downs that go on in that office. Well, the joke is on him now."

Nancy sat down and Josephine immediately climbed onto her lap. She felt stunned. She didn't feel special loyalty to Bernie, but she knew he had high hopes for *The Love Machine*. Steven had told her they were relying on the cash it would bring in. "When will you tell him?" she asked.

"He knows," Jacqueline replied. "He's fighting it, but *Love Machine* is getting a lot of interest from other publishers and a new deal will be announced soon. We thought we should warn you because it could get awkward in the office."

There was a dull pop as Irving opened the bottle and poured. Champagne surged over the rim of the first glass and Jacqueline dipped her finger into the puddle on the table and sucked it. Irving handed Nancy a glass.

"In the meantime, we're relying on your discretion," Irving said. "Just till it's signed off."

"Of course," Nancy said quickly, although she decided she would warn Steven. Why were they telling her? What did they want from her? She looked questioningly at Jacqueline.

Jacqueline lifted her glass and clinked it against Nancy's. "We wondered if it might be time for you to move up the career ladder a rung or two. You say you want to be an editor, but, from what you tell me, Bernie's not giving you any chances."

Irving joined in. "I got our agent to ask around and find out if anyone is hiring editorial assistants, and it seems Heywood & Bradshaw is interviewing because one of their girls is getting married. With a single call, I can get you a meeting."

Jacqueline nodded encouragement. "And I've written you a reference, saying how much editorial help you gave on *Dolls*. I can't imagine Bernie giving you your due. They'll be petulant about me leaving and they might take it out on you."

Would Bernie punish her for Jacqueline's defection? Would he make her slide down that stupid fireman's pole? Nancy didn't want to be trapped in her current job much longer. She knew Heywood & Bradshaw had a decent list, ranging from histories and biographies to modern fiction. Was she good enough to get a job there?

Irving smiled. "Wouldn't do any harm to meet them, would it? Shall I make the call?"

Nancy hesitated.

"Go on!" Jacqueline urged. "Take the plunge."

She shrugged. "OK. So long as Bernie doesn't find out."

Irving got up and went to his office to make the call.

Jacqueline grinned at Nancy. "We've got our fingers crossed that you'll be able to hand in your notice soon. In a worst-case scenario, if we end up in court, he might try to get you to testify against us, even lie about us. Much better if you're out of the way, don't you think?"

"No one could make me lie in court," Nancy said, feeling uneasy about the turn this conversation was taking.

"No, of course not," Jacqueline said quickly. "But still."

Nancy could hear Irving on the phone in his office. "Tomorrow at two alright?" he called through the doorway.

"OK," Nancy replied. She would take a late lunch. If anyone asked, she would say she had a dentist appointment.

"You have to phone straight after and tell me how it goes," Jacqueline insisted. "I bought you something to wear. Irving, can you hand me that bag?"

He picked up an Yves Saint Laurent carrier bag from the dining table and brought it to Nancy. She looked inside and saw a navy-blue pantsuit in an expensive silky fabric, with the exclusive YSL label.

"I thought this was your style," Jacqueline said. "*Très sexy, très cool.* Try it on when you get home. My reference is in the bag, so you can hand it over tomorrow."

The thought crossed Nancy's mind that they were trying to buy her. Just how vitriolic was it likely to be with Bernie? It was an awkward situation, having to choose between her loyalty to Bernie Geis and her loyalty to Jacqueline, but if the chips were down, she already knew which one she trusted more.

* * *

ON HER WAY home, Nancy stopped to use the phone booth in a diner. Her stomach was twisted with nerves as she dialed Steven's number, not least because it was the first time she'd called him at home.

It took her aback when a woman answered and asked, "Who's speaking?"

"It's Nancy, from the office," she said, her voice shaky.

"Hi, Nancy, I'll just get him." Jeanette sounded pleasant, Nancy thought. Friendly. Would she be so friendly if she knew Nancy was sleeping with her husband?

Steven's voice came on the line: "Hey, you!" he said, his voice tender. "What's up?"

"You have to promise not to say anything at work yet," she told him, before divulging the news about Jacqueline.

"Goddamn it!" he swore. "It's that darned article in *McCall's*. Bernie needs to learn to zip his lips."

Next, Nancy told him about her job interview at Heywood & Bradshaw.

"I hope you get it," he said straight away. "They're a solid company, and Bernard Geis Associates will be in trouble without *Love Machine*. I'm going to start job hunting myself."

It occurred to Nancy that it would make life easier if they worked for different companies. At least they wouldn't have to tiptoe around each other in the office.

"It would be a good career move for you," he continued. "And they'd be lucky to have you."

"Thank you," she said. It was strange talking to him in his home. What was the room he was standing in like? She wondered if Jeanette and Darren could hear his side of the conversation.

"Good luck, honey!" he said at the end, his tone warm. "You can do it."

When she hung up, she stood for a few moments gathering her thoughts. It must be true that he and Jeanette had an "arrangement." How did his wife feel about it, though? Was it really as amicable as it seemed?

* * *

THE FOLLOWING AFTERNOON she made her way to Heywood & Bradshaw's Midtown office, wearing the navy-blue suit. This time there was no typing test, but she was asked to read a couple of galley pages of a novel and mark any errors she spotted.

She focused hard. There were some glaring spelling mistakes, and she was glad she knew the correct proofreading symbols to mark them. A whole sentence was repeated at one point, and elsewhere the tense slipped from past to present for no good reason. A character's name was given as Ethan on one page, Ethen on the next, so she marked that. She just had time to reread her work quickly before she was called into director Bill Heywood's office.

He was unusual-looking: bald, with a salt-and-pepper beard, and eyes too close together, like a cartoon character. He took the pages from her and read through them while she waited. She couldn't judge from his expression whether he approved of her work or not.

"Why do you want this job?" he asked, putting the pages down.

"It's been my ambition to be an editor since I learned to read," she said, "long before I knew what the job entailed."

"You reckon you know now, do you?"

She explained her role in the editing of *Valley of the Dolls*, saying, "I was excited to be able to include some of my own ideas in the finished novel." She handed over Jacqueline's reference, which she hadn't read herself because the envelope was sealed.

He chuckled as he read it, and that increased her curiosity.

"What age are you?" he asked abruptly, putting the reference down.

"Twenty-four," she replied.

"Do you have a boyfriend?" he asked. "Fiancé?" He glanced at her left hand.

How should she answer that? "No one serious," she said, and he nodded slowly as if he didn't believe her.

"You will, though. You're at that age where we'll train you for a couple of years, then you'll disappear off to have babies and our investment will be wasted." He stared at her, challenging her to contradict him.

Nancy took a deep breath. "I can't guarantee that I won't have children at some point in my life, but I fully intend to continue working. I'm extremely ambitious and would very much like a chance to develop my own list of authors, especially authors who appeal to women readers."

"You mean romances?" he asked, with an almost imperceptible gesture of dismissal.

"No. The success of *Valley of the Dolls* shows there is a market for gritty books about romances that don't have happy endings—and for glamour too. Women like stories that transport them out of their everyday lives."

"Uh-huh," he said, and leaned his chin on his fist, his elbow on the desk.

Nancy wondered if she was overstepping the mark, telling him what to publish. "Of course, I know I wouldn't be commissioning books for a while, but I'd love to help read your slush pile and see if I can discover a bestseller or two. I'm a hard worker and I'll do whatever it takes. I worked late most evenings when Jacqueline was doing her book tour for *Dolls*, especially when she was on the West Coast."

"That tour was something else," he agreed. He picked up Jacqueline's letter again. "She says here that you contributed more to the success of *Valley of the Dolls* than anyone else at Bernard Geis Associates. That's quite a recommendation."

"She did?" Nancy couldn't suppress a grin.

"I'm guessing it wasn't a walk in the park," he said. "She's got a fearsome reputation." He sat up. "Tell you what, the job's yours if you want it. And responsibility for the slush pile can be part of the package."

Nancy blinked. "Are you sure?"

"Yeah, you're the last of the candidates and I didn't warm to any of the others. How's a hundred a week sound?"

That was thirty dollars more than she got from Bernie. Nancy asked a few more questions about practicalities such as office hours and vacation time, which all sounded fine.

"I guess we have a deal," he said, glancing at his watch and standing up. "Let me know how much notice Bernie wants you to work. The sooner you can start, the better."

That was it. After all the trouble getting her first job, Nancy couldn't believe how easy the second one was. It was all down to Jacqueline's wonderful reference. She stopped in a drugstore to call her from a public phone, and had to hold the receiver away from her ear when there was a deafening shriek.

"I knew it!" Jacqueline screamed. "I'm so proud of you."

As soon as Nancy got back to the office, she took a deep breath and knocked on Bernie's door to tell him she was handing in her notice.

"Is this because I didn't get back to you about the slush pile?" he asked. "Of course you can read it. I just need to explain what we're looking for first."

"No," she said. "I'm very grateful to you for giving me my first publishing job, but it feels like the right time to move on."

When she admitted she had been offered a job at Heywood & Bradshaw, and that they were paying more, his attitude turned to fury. "In that case, you can clear your desk and leave the premises immediately. I don't want you spying and taking confidential company information to the opposition. Who would have thought you'd turn out to be a traitor, after all I've done for you!"

It was a shame to leave on a sour note, Nancy thought, but on the bright side, she would never have to slide down that fireman's pole again.

CHAPTER 23

Jacqueline

London, 1968

A couple of weeks after New Year's, Jacqueline and Irving
flew to London to meet her British editor, Adam Cosgrove,
who worked at W. H. Allen. They'd gotten off to a bad
start the previous year when he sent a telegram asking if they
could replace the word "fuck" with "f—k" throughout the novel.
She had cabled back "F—k you!" But when the first finished
copies came in the mail, she saw that's exactly what they had
done.

She arrived at their office prepared to do battle but found
Adam very convivial and welcoming.

"I apologize wholeheartedly for the blanked-out swear words,"
he said. "We wouldn't have got your books into South Africa or
Australia otherwise, and I think you'll find they're both lucrative
markets. In the UK too, there are straitlaced types who would
boycott the book simply because of the swear words."

"I thought attitudes had changed after the *Lady Chatterley's
Lover* trial," Jacqueline said. The prosecution had argued that
D. H. Lawrence's book should be banned for the sexual content and obscenities it contained, but Penguin Books's lawyers
had successfully counterargued that it had literary value. Their
stance back in 1960 had opened the door for other UK publishers
to bring out books with more liberal approaches to sexuality.

"Times are changing, of course," Adam agreed, "but we took
a decision in this instance that we wanted to sell the maximum
number of copies for you, and that this was the best way."

She couldn't argue with that, she supposed.

He carried on: "My publicity team have organized a tour so you can do some book signings in London, Birmingham, Manchester, and Liverpool. That's all we had time for, given your schedule, but I hear you're quite the star in bookshops so we couldn't resist the chance to show you off."

That was music to Jacqueline's ears. She adored meeting "her people" and there seemed to be plenty of them in Britain. As in the US, she gave signed copies of her book to the staff at each store she visited, and added their personal details to her Rolodex.

Sharon Tate, the actress who'd played Jennifer in *Dolls*, had invited them to her wedding in London, to a Polish film director called Roman Polanski. Jacqueline was in two minds about going. She was in Liverpool the day before and was enjoying meeting British readers so much that she considered asking Adam Cosgrove to extend the tour across the north of England, maybe even into Scotland. Irving thought they should go to the wedding, though. He said they could make some useful connections in the movie business, to help them have more control when *The Love Machine* was filmed.

Jacqueline had forgiven him over the *Dolls* movie contract. Their rows never lasted long. Perhaps he was right: she could come back to tour England and Scotland another time.

The ceremony was in a tiny register office in Chelsea. Sharon was luminous in an ivory silk minidress she had designed herself, with a garland of ivory flowers in her hair. Roman was in Edwardian-style finery, with an ivory silk ruff at his neck. The party moved to the Playboy Club in Mayfair, where champagne was served by waitresses wearing black miniskirts, bunny ears, and fluffy tails. As Irving had predicted, there were many stars Jacqueline recognized, among them Candice Bergen and Michael Caine.

Jacqueline got into conversation with a glamorous young

woman called Jackie Collins, who was wearing a pale-yellow minidress and sporting a beehive hairdo. They discovered they had both worked as B movie actresses and compared notes.

"I was always cast as the Secretary or the Girl Next Door," Jackie told her. "Directors couldn't wait to get me into a bikini, but mostly my characters didn't even have names, never mind any lines."

Jacqueline laughed. "I think I was strangled, shot, or bludgeoned to death in all my movie roles," she said. "I guess they wanted rid of me."

"Congratulations on getting out of that world and into literary stardom instead," Jackie said. "I adored *Valley of the Dolls*. Who's your British publisher?"

"W. H. Allen," Jacqueline told her. "We got off to a bad start when they replaced all the swear words in my book with dashes, but we're friends again now."

"I'm meeting an editor there next week," Jackie said. "I'm hoping they might publish a novel I've written. It's my first."

"Good luck with that," Jacqueline said. "Writing has its challenges but there's no question it's a giant step up from B movie acting."

An older man came to drag Jackie onto the dance floor, where guests were twisting and writhing to psychedelic-sounding music Jacqueline didn't recognize.

"I'm tired," she told Irving, turning his arm so she could read his watch. "Can we go soon?"

He fetched her coat and they slipped out to a taxi. There were more books to sign in W. H. Allen's office the following day, then they were flying back to New York—and her beloved Josephine. In a world where Jacqueline felt she could trust no one—at times, not even her own husband—Josephine always greeted her with genuine uncomplicated adoration.

CHAPTER 24

Jackie

London, January 1968

J ackie was knotted with nerves about her meeting at W. H. Allen, which had been postponed till the new year to give her time to recover from the birth of her second daughter, Tiffany. She didn't want to get her hopes up, but couldn't help fantasizing that they would offer to publish her book. Why else would the editor invite her for a meeting?

The big decision was what to wear. Oscar was useless. He always said she looked wonderful, even when she was in slacks and an old sweater. Her stomach wasn't quite flat yet, so she opted for a loose brown minismock, cream pantyhose, and long brown boots. She took extra care over her makeup, with carefully drawn eyeliner, pale pink lipstick, and fluffed-up hair.

As she sat in reception before the meeting, she watched staff bustling around. There was an elderly lady answering the telephone and putting calls through on a switchboard; a skinny young man wheeling postal deliveries on a trolley, who looked her up and down, then seemed embarrassed when she caught his eye; a fashionably dressed woman about her own age who bustled in, asked the receptionist if there were any messages for her, and gave Jackie a curious glance. Were these people going to be her publishers? She smiled at them all, unable to contain her excitement.

Robert Armstrong came to collect her. He was young and bookish-looking, with round spectacles and baggy cords. She was conscious her palms were slightly damp when they shook hands. Damn, she hoped she wasn't going to make an idiot of herself.

"I love your novel," he began. "Is it really your debut?" She nodded, biting her lip. "It doesn't read like one. You've woven the stories together very skillfully."

"I've been trying to write novels for years and abandoned loads," she said. "This is the first one I managed to finish." She crossed her legs carefully. The minidress could reveal too much if she wasn't careful how she sat.

"I'm very glad you did," he said, "because we would like to publish it. Do you have an agent I should speak to about the financial offer?"

"No, no agent," she said. She couldn't believe her ears. Did he mean it?

"Good for you!" he exclaimed. "You get to keep the ten percent. I can offer you four hundred pounds' advance for world rights. You'll get royalties on every copy sold, and once those royalties have paid back the advance, you'll start getting checks every six months. Sound OK?"

She agreed, clasping her hands together to stop them shaking. She felt like jumping up and down and cheering out loud, but that wouldn't be cool.

Robert said he wanted to make a few minor editorial changes—no big rewrites, he said, but he added, apologetically, that they would want to take out the four-letter words and replace them with dashes. "It's so that South Africa and Australia don't ban the book," he explained.

She already knew that, of course, and said it was fine. In her opinion, the dashes drew attention and gave the words more impact, not less.

"I'm glad to see you are suitably glamorous," he said, glancing at her outfit. "We're hoping that you'll give press interviews on publication."

"Of course," she agreed. "I heard about Jacqueline Susann's approach to publicity in the States and I'm determined to put in as much energy as she does. I'll be an obedient author and do whatever you ask of me." She smiled, still nervous that he might change his mind if she gave a wrong answer.

"What we want is for you to write another novel just as soon as you possibly can," he said. "Think you can deliver another one next year? Same kind of subject matter?"

"I've already started another," she was able to tell him. "It's about a womanizing nightclub manager." She had based the character loosely on Johnny Gold.

"Perfect! I look forward to reading it," he said, with warmth. He couldn't have been further from the philandering type himself. Jackie liked him instinctively, and not just because he was publishing her novel.

She walked out of the building into wintry sunshine and stood for a moment breathing the cold air. It was ages since she had earned any money and she had begun to feel she wasn't good for anything except child-rearing. To have a professional editor at a respected company think her writing was worth publishing— it was the most exciting thing that had ever happened to her.

* * *

JACKIE'S LIFE OVER the next few months was split into separate compartments. During the day, she was mum to seven-year-old Tracy and baby Tiffany. She did school runs, cooked meals, cleaned house, and got down on the floor to play with them. Mothering always came at the top of her list of priorities.

When she could grab an hour or two alone, she worked on her next book, which she called *The Stud*. She told Johnny about the character she was writing and he thought it was hilarious.

"I hope you'll hire me to play Tony Blake in the movie," he said, and she promised to put in a word for him if anyone bought film rights. *If only!*

"Don't tell Jan you're making me a womanizer, though," he said. "We seem to be going through a peaceful patch, touch wood."

Jackie knew that it was only peaceful because Jan had stopped pressuring him to settle down. The moment she did, he bolted like a spooked horse.

"You really should make an honest woman of her before you lose her for good," Jackie told him. "You're punching way above your weight there."

"I know you're right," he said, "but I've got this phobia about the old marital shackles. The very thought brings me out in hives."

At least he's honest about it, Jackie thought, unlike all the married men who had come on to her over the years with their hackneyed lines: "My wife likes to stay at home; it suits us both." Or, "She's not interested in sex and encourages me to get it elsewhere."

Once a week she and Oscar hired a babysitter and went out for dinner before heading to Dolly's around eleven o'clock. It attracted a glitzy crowd, and Oscar and Johnny seemed to know them all: the Beatles, the Stones, David Bailey, Michael Caine, Twiggy—everyone stopped by their table to say hello.

Jackie was a good listener and if she found herself sitting next to someone interesting, she would coax confessions from them with leading questions. "Who would you go to bed with if you could have anyone in the world for one night?" she asked. Or, "What would you do if you were king of the world for a day?"

Sometimes she stepped back and marveled at the direction her life had taken. She had a wide circle of friends, a comfortable home, two beautiful daughters, a loving husband, and now she had a book coming out. If only her mum were still around. She pictured how proud Elsa would have been.

Oscar was happy for her, of course he was, but he praised everything she did or said or cooked or wore. She walked on water, as far as he was concerned.

She knew she shouldn't knock it. Being adored by your husband had a lot to recommend it, but sometimes she missed the fun and unpredictability of life with Wallace. If only he could have lived to see her book published, he would have been every bit as thrilled as she was. She considered dedicating her first book to his memory but decided that wouldn't be fair to Oscar. In the end, she left the dedication page blank so she wouldn't have to choose between them.

CHAPTER 25

Nancy

Manhattan, 1967

N ancy started work at Heywood & Bradshaw a week after leaving Bernard Geis. Bill Heywood's secretary, a prim, unsmiling brunette called Alice, led her to a desk in an alcove on the second floor. It wasn't quite an office of her own, as it only had three walls and no window, but she was separated from the typing pool and that seemed symbolic. Bill strode out to welcome her, clutching a manuscript in his arms.

"Your first challenge," he said, dumping the pages in front of her. "This one just needs a cleanup. Correct the spellings and punctuation, cross-check facts, and list queries. Be aware the author doesn't like being edited so you may need to justify any changes. It might be an idea to take him for lunch or dinner to get acquainted. Alice will explain the expenses system."

Alice remained stony-faced.

"You've got a couple of weeks till the deadline," Bill continued. "And the slush pile you were so keen to dive into is in that cabinet." He pointed to a set of double doors. "Fill out a submission form for each, with a three-line summary and your recommendations. No more than three lines. Be pithy!"

He disappeared into his office again, and Nancy blinked. She had loads of questions. Maybe Alice would be able to answer some of them—but she had also turned to go back to her own desk. Nancy opened the cabinet and her heart sank: it was stuffed full of manuscripts, some of them covered in a patina of dust as if they had been there for months on end, trails of gray fluff exploding from the lining of the envelopes. Each one represented an author's hopes and dreams; she imagined them all watching the mail for responses, with no idea their masterworks had been abandoned in this graveyard.

Farther up the corridor she could see a kitchen and decided to make herself a coffee before starting work. As she stood waiting for the kettle to boil, a young man popped his head around the door, said, "Three coffees for the boardroom, sweetheart. Cream and sugar," then pinched her bottom, hard, and hurried off.

Nancy jumped and nearly dropped her cup. The pinch had hurt! She looked around but no one else had seen. Her job didn't involve making coffee, did it? She walked back to Alice's desk and said, "Someone just asked me to take three coffees to the boardroom. What should I do?"

"You'd better take them, hadn't you?" Alice replied, not even pausing in her typing.

Nancy wondered if Alice had applied for her job and been passed over, or if she was just unfriendly. So be it. She made the coffees, asked a passerby where the boardroom was, and delivered the tray.

She'd hoped to make friends in the company, but on her first day not a soul stopped by her desk to say welcome or even to ask her name. She started reading the novel Bill Heywood had left, making notes as she went. It was well written, but in her opinion it could use a little more pace. She could see ways to inject some, but would the author agree if he didn't like being edited?

Before she left that evening, she pulled a manuscript from the top shelf of the slush cabinet and put it in her bag. There were around fifty at a rough estimate; if she read three a week, she might catch up in four months, depending on how many new ones arrived in the meantime.

* * *

ABE WALKER, THE author whose manuscript she was editing, said he would like to discuss it over cocktails at the Waldorf Astoria, so they made a date. Nancy arrived first and gave her name to the maître d', then sat, reading through her notes and planning how she would persuade him of the changes she wanted to make.

Abe swayed in ten minutes late, with a pink face, a sheen of perspiration on his top lip, and bourbon breath. He spoke slowly, as if she were an imbecile who wouldn't understand him otherwise.

Nancy began to explain her impression that the novel needed more pace in the middle chapters, and told him her idea that it could be achieved by making one of the characters untrustworthy, even treacherous.

He was watching her closely as she spoke, and she thought he was listening, but when she finished, he slid his hand onto her thigh and sighed: "God, you're sexy. What's a beautiful girl like you doing in a dreary job like this? You should be in the movies."

She picked up his hand and guided it back to his lap. "What do you think of my suggestions?" she asked. "Can I go ahead?"

"Sure, yeah," he said, grabbing her left breast and squeezing hard. "But only if you'll come upstairs to a hotel room with me right now."

Nancy had encountered plenty of lecherous men—she was no longer as green as when she'd arrived in the city—but this was the first author whose book she had edited all by herself and she'd been hoping to impress him. She hesitated, trying to decide how to handle the situation. Jacqueline would have thrown a cocktail in his face, but that didn't seem professional. And then she wondered what her mother would have done, and the answer came to her.

"Mr. Walker," she said in her best schoolmarm tone. "Please would you remove your hand from my breast. I am not the kind of girl you seem to think I am, and I certainly haven't given you any cause to presume that I might be."

"Look, sweetheart, I could get you fired . . ." he said, but he looked uncertain and removed his hand all the same.

"How? By telling Bill Heywood that I refused to go to bed with you?" She pretended to consider this. "You could do that, and maybe he would fire me, although that would be grossly unfair. Alternatively, you and I could start this meeting again, calling each other Miss White and Mr. Walker, and I will tell you how to make your very good novel into an even better one that could have a decent crack at the bestseller lists. The choice is yours."

She held her breath.

He sighed, crossed his legs, and lit a cigarette. "Alright, *Miss* White. Could you run through those points again? Please?"

Steven was enraged when Nancy told him about Abe Walker's behavior, but in fact it worked out fine. Abe agreed to most of her edits, didn't attempt to grab her body parts again, and reported to Bill that he thought she'd done a terrific job.

* * *

OVER THE FOLLOWING months, she progressed rapidly through the slush cabinet. In most cases, she could tell from the first page whether a manuscript was going to be publishable or not, but she forced herself to read at least fifty pages before giving up. The majority of submissions stood no chance. A few started with promise and trailed off midway, losing her interest.

She began to read the trade magazines that came into the office, including the British magazine *The Bookseller.* One day her attention was caught by a brief article entitled "The British Jacqueline Susann?" It was announcing a debut novel by an actress named Jackie Collins that had just been bought by W. H. Allen, and the title intrigued her: *The World Is Full of Married Men*. She knew Bernie had sometimes spotted books there and written to the UK publishers requesting a proof for consideration, and Nancy decided to do the same. What harm could it do?

One way or another she was determined to impress her new boss by discovering books that became bestsellers. One submission leapt out at her: *Miss Craig's 21-Day Shape-Up Program for Men and Women*. The author was a director of exercise at Elizabeth Arden's salon in the city, and the exercise and diet tips she described were simple to follow and sounded effective.

Nancy wrote a three-line report saying she thought this book would have wide appeal, and she recommended that Heywood & Bradshaw publish it.

She delivered her reports to Bill every Tuesday afternoon because the editorial meetings were on Wednesday mornings. She'd been disappointed but not surprised to learn she wasn't allowed to attend them herself, but that Bill would present her ideas for her.

After the meeting, Bill stopped by her desk to say the team had decided against Miss Craig because they didn't think anyone wanted a book to nag at them. "They've got wives for that," he said. "Write a standard letter saying it's not for us."

Steven whistled when Nancy told him that evening. "They're making a mistake. That one will sell."

He was still working at Bernard Geis and desperate to find another job. Jacqueline's settlement had bailed out the company in the short term, but they didn't have any bestsellers in the pipeline and there was an air of desperation at the top. Bernie was irritable and more forgetful than ever. Listening to Steven, Nancy was relieved she'd gotten out when she did.

* * *

"ARE YOU FREE next weekend?" Steven asked one evening in early spring. "And can you take next Friday off work?"

"Why? What did you have in mind?" She was mystified by his expression—part mischievous, part tender.

"Jeanette and Darren are going to her parents' for a few days so I'm a free man. I wondered if you might like to invite me to Ossipee? It seems about time I met your family."

Nancy had several reactions all at once: excitement at the thought of spending a whole weekend with Steven; delight that he wanted to meet her stepfather and the boys; trepidation at the thought of asking Bill for a day off when they were so busy at the office; and, most of all, nerves at the prospect of going back to the house where she used to live with her mother, which she still hadn't visited since her death.

"It's too far to drive," she protested.

"I checked, and it should take around six hours each way if I hit the gas," Steven said. "We can manage if we leave early Friday morning and head back Sunday afternoon."

"I'll have to ask my stepfather . . ."

"No more excuses. Just say yes," Steven said, and gave her a lingering kiss that led to the bedroom, precluding any further discussion.

* * *

NANCY HAD BEEN in Steven's car before but not in daylight. It was clearly a family car, with a tattered baseball glove on the backseat and a gold lipstick tube rolling around the seat well. She was trying not to think about what it would be like to be in her mom's house. She'd created a mental block around it, but Steven was probably right that it would be good for her. It had been three years since her mom died and the acuteness of the pain had ebbed into a dull ache of missing her.

On the drive up, Steven asked about her childhood and she told him she had been on her school's swim team—she loved swimming—and that they had spent a lot of time outdoors as a family. "Hiking, fishing, and swimming are popular in Ossipee," she said. "I'm guessing Darren is a baseball fan?" She inclined her head toward the backseat.

"Actually, basketball is more his thing," he said. "He's obsessive about it. We both support the Knicks and watch their games on TV, always with our team pennants, cans of root beer, and a bowl of popcorn."

He talked for a while about his son, whom he clearly adored, and Nancy listened, feeling uncomfortable. Maybe Darren would hate her one day if he got the impression she had broken up his parents' marriage. Her stepfather, Joe, had waited a respectful year after her father's death before proposing to her mom, so there had been no stepping on toes. Nancy hadn't minded at all. He'd been a friend of the family beforehand and he came into their lives with tact and sensitivity, never getting between her and her mom. Maybe she could manage that transition with Darren, if Steven decided to leave his marriage for her, but it would be tougher with Jeanette still around.

When Steven turned his car into the drive of the house late Friday afternoon, Nancy got goose bumps all over. It wasn't a grand place—white clapboard, with a covered porch and a rope swing dangling from an apple tree out front—but it was home. Joe strode out to greet them, shaking hands with Steven, and hugging Nancy.

Everything was unchanged inside, from her mom's watercolors in the hall to the shepherdess ornaments in a cabinet in the sitting room. Steven wandered over to a dresser covered in framed photos and Joe talked him through them: three-year-old Nancy in a Hawaiian grass skirt at the beach; her father in the yard before he got ill; her cousin Louise singing in a school show; and her mom wearing a paper hat on Christmas Day a couple of months before she died.

"Can I go up to Mom's room?" Nancy asked, feeling a sudden need to be alone.

"You don't have to ask," Joe said. "This is your home too."

And it was. It felt like home. Her mother's clothes still hung in her closet. Her jewelry and makeup still sat on the dressing table. The same flowered curtains were draped in the windows. When Nancy pulled a sweater from a drawer and held it to her face, she was sure she could smell her mom's jasmine scent lingering in the soft wool. She opened a lipstick and smiled at the way her mom's lips had worn it to a point. She turned over a silver-backed hairbrush and saw a few strands of her mom's silvery-blond hair. She'd imagined this experience would be unbearable but instead it was comforting.

"It feels as if she's still around, doesn't it?" Joe asked from the doorway, echoing her thoughts. "I left everything as it was so you can take whatever you want."

"Thank you," Nancy said. "That was thoughtful." She looked over his shoulder. "Where's Steven?"

"He's helping your brothers build a model Spitfire. I offered to rescue him but he seems to be enjoying himself."

Nancy thought it was no wonder he was good with young boys since he had one himself, but they'd decided not to tell Joe that—or that he was married.

"I've put him in the pulldown bed in the office. You're in your old room. Is that alright?" Joe looked embarrassed. "It's up to you what you do, of course. You're all grown up now."

"No, that's perfect." She got up and hugged him. "Thank you for letting me bring him. It means a lot."

"He must be keen on you to drive all this way," Joe said.

"Proves he has good taste." They stood, with arms around each other. He felt solid, Nancy thought. Dependable. She should call him more often.

The whole weekend was relaxed and easy. Nancy told Joe about her job, and he told her how proud her mom would have been. She spent a couple of hours picking out clothes and jewelry, and some paintings she was fond of. When they left after a late brunch on Sunday, there were hugs and promises not to leave it so long next time.

Nancy was contemplative on the drive home. By meeting her stepdad, Steven seemed to be showing that he took their relationship seriously. According to Helen Gurley Brown's book, it was a momentous step for a couple.

"I've loved this weekend," Steven said. "Seeing you in your family home, I could picture you as a little girl, with your straight A's and your swimming medals."

Nancy smiled. "I was always competitive," she agreed.

"It's helped me to make a decision," he said, glancing around and placing a hand on her knee. "I love you, Nancy. It's clear it's you I should be with. If you want me to, I'll leave Jeanette so we can get a place together."

"Of course I do," Nancy said quickly, her heart pounding and her mouth dry. He'd never said he loved her before.

He squeezed her leg. "So now I need to find a way to manage this that will do the least harm to Darren. Will you give me time to figure it out?"

"Of course," she said, feeling dazed. It's what she'd dreamed of, but the reality was overwhelming. She was in no rush.

After this momentous conversation, and a weekend of sleeping in separate beds, she couldn't wait to get back to her apartment so they could make love. But when he pulled up outside, Steven announced he had to head back to New Jersey so he could drive Darren to school in the morning.

She couldn't hide her disappointment. "I was hoping you'd stay."

"Sorry, it's not possible. Let's go out Wednesday. Why don't you choose a movie?"

She knew it was wrong, but part of her felt jealous of Darren. How come he got to have Steven tonight and she didn't? But it would fall into place once they lived together, she told herself.

"Don't forget I love you," Steven whispered before he left.

She loved him too. When she was with him, she felt understood, as if he saw the real person inside, but when his car drove off down the street and turned out of sight, she felt lonelier than ever. She should have been happy about the decision he'd made. He wanted to be with her. That was good, wasn't it?

She rode the elevator up to 4B, leaned the paintings against the wall inside, laid out her mother's clothes on the bed, then sat in front of a mirror to try on her mother's rings and necklaces. Without warning, tears came and she started sobbing so hard her chest ached. In that moment, she missed her mom terribly. She would have known what to do about the emotional muddle Nancy had gotten herself into. They would have talked it through and figured it out together—but she was gone and no one could ever ask her advice again.

CHAPTER 26

Jacqueline

Philadelphia, 1968

W hen *Valley of the Dolls* was first published, Jacqueline had sent her mother a copy and braced herself for an avalanche of invective: "no daughter of mine" . . . "public humiliation"—she feared the worst. Instead, Rose telephoned after reading it, gushing with praise.

"I always knew you were a natural storyteller," she said. "You used to write such lovely stories at school. Remember you got that prize when you were twelve?"

Rose was proud as proud could be. She made a scrapbook of press cuttings, and got Jacqueline to send signed copies of *Dolls* for her to give her friends. One night she rang with a special request.

"A group of us have been chatting about you with our local bookstore owner, and we wondered if you might meet with us next time you're in town. The ladies have some questions they'd like to ask."

Jacqueline wrinkled her nose, fearing the worst about the kind of questions she might get from her mother's conservative friends. "How many of you?" she asked.

"At least twenty," Rose said. "I'm sure it will be more if the store owner advertises. Please say you'll come."

Jacqueline delayed the trip, claiming pressures of work, but after she delivered *The Love Machine* to her new publisher, she had time for a break.

"I'd better get it over with," she told Irving, and he booked them train tickets to Philly.

Rose scheduled the bookstore chat for the morning after her arrival. She was buzzing with importance, as if she had acquired a veneer of celebrity from her association with *Dolls*. She dressed in a smart dove-gray suit and wore the three-stranded Akoya pearls she kept for special occasions.

"No men allowed," she said, holding out a hand to restrain Irving when she saw him reach for his coat. "Women only."

Jacqueline shrugged and grinned at him. "Guess I'll see you later, hon."

The bookstore was full of women, who cheered and clapped when she walked in. Around twenty were seated in four huddled rows of fold-out chairs, but more were crowded into the aisles. Jacqueline sat on the high stool provided and surveyed the audience. There wasn't anyone under the age of fifty, she guessed, and that surprised her. She'd thought her book mainly appealed to a younger generation.

She began by thanking them for coming, using her theatrical training to ensure her voice carried to the back of the room. She talked about her teenage years in Philly, and the love of reading instilled by her high-school teachers. She said the success of *Dolls* had taken her completely by surprise, but she couldn't be more delighted, and gave a plug for *Love Machine*, which would be out the following year.

"My mother tells me you have some questions, so please fire away," she said.

A dozen hands shot up, as if they were eager eight-year-olds. Jacqueline pointed at one woman.

"I wondered how your husband feels about the sexual content of your book?" she asked. "Was he upset by you sharing your bedroom secrets?"

Jacqueline laughed out loud. "If he was, he didn't say. But it wasn't necessarily *our* bedroom secrets I shared in *Dolls*. I'm a novelist, and I make things up. Imagination is a wonderful tool, both in writing and in sex. I'm sure you all know what I mean." She gave a slow wink.

As audience members turned to whisper to their neighbors, Jacqueline picked another questioner, a woman with gunmetal permed curls, tortoiseshell spectacles, and a twinset.

"I *do* know what you mean, Miss Susann," she agreed, "but how would you deal with a husband who has gone about sex in exactly the same way once a week for the last forty-four years? He comes out of the washroom, tells me I'm looking real nice, then gets on top of me and it's over in two minutes." She faked a yawn. "He's not a bad husband in other ways, but imagination doesn't come into our sex life."

Jacqueline was so astonished she couldn't answer straight away. Many audience members were nodding in recognition, and looking to her for guidance. She took a deep breath. "What's your name?" she asked.

"Ida," came the reply.

"Well, Ida," she said, "you deserve a medal for putting up with that for forty-four years. I'm sure a lot of women whose husbands are boring lovers keep finding excuses not to have sex until eventually they stop trying. But I'm guessing you must be a sexual woman, if you're still letting him have his way." She was thinking out loud. "It's hard to start a conversation after all that time, but you could try reading sexy books together. Take some on vacation and read out passages when you're in a new bed. Or seduce him on the couch instead of in the bedroom. Or over the kitchen table. Even in the backyard."

There was laughter, and someone shouted, "Yeah, the neighbors would love that."

Another woman joined in. "My husband's too rough in bed. He mounts me like I'm a steer and he's in a rodeo."

"Yeah, mine too," someone else agreed. "But if I criticize him, he sulks. It's not that I don't want to make love, but I want him to be gentler. How do you get that across?"

Wow, Jacqueline thought. *Somehow she'd become a sex guru. Who would have thought it?* "Reward good behavior," she suggested. "Respond with enthusiasm when you like what he's doing, but shift away if you don't. And be more active yourself, so he's not always the one in charge. Get on top, girls!"

They cheered. It was only then that Jacqueline remembered her mother was in the room. She glanced around to see that Rose was cheering along with them.

At the end of the hour, the women queued to get their copies of *Dolls* signed, and Jacqueline took the opportunity to ask them how much they read and what kind of books they liked.

"I'm afraid I read romances," one woman said. "I just love the escapism."

"Don't apologize," Jacqueline replied. "I don't approve of women's books being patronized by the literary establishment. We should all read whatever we want, without shame."

Another woman asked a question in a low voice as Jacqueline was signing her copy. "I don't want to divorce my husband, but I'm not attracted to him anymore. Should I forget about having a sex life?"

Jacqueline lowered her own voice to match her level: "I'm sure all of us in long marriages close our eyes and pretend we're with someone else. Personally, I often have sex with Burt Lancaster."

The woman laughed. "I'll try that—maybe with Cary Grant. Thank you, Miss Susann."

"How did it go?" Irving asked when they got home.

"Fascinating literary chat," Jacqueline told him. "It was very enlightening."

Rose snorted loudly and gave her a conspiratorial smile.

CHAPTER 27

Jackie

London, 1968

Publication day for *The World Is Full of Married Men* came around fast. Jackie was thrilled to hold a copy in her hand, to feel the weight of it, smell the faint almond scent of the paper, and flick through the pages that contained her words. It was going out into the world and she prayed it would find readers who enjoyed it.

Jackie's publicist had arranged for a journalist called Jean Rook to interview her at home, around eleven in the morning, when Tiffany would be having a nap. Bang on eleven the doorbell rang and Jackie opened it to find a brassy blonde in a beige trench coat with a satchel over one shoulder, who looked slightly older than her—maybe late thirties. She knew Miss Rook already had a formidable reputation in Fleet Street, and was determined to make a good impression.

"Would you like tea? Some cake?" she asked, taking the woman's coat and leading her into the sitting room. Suddenly she saw it through a stranger's eyes—the abandoned toys, the red wine stain on the rug, the mismatching cushions.

"Tea and an ashtray," Jean Rook replied in a raspy voice, looking around, as if taking mental notes.

Jackie left her in the sitting room while she made the tea, and when she came back found her examining the photographs on the piano.

"That's your dad, isn't it?" Jean asked, pointing to one. "Joe Collins, theatrical agent. How do you get on with him?"

Jackie was taken aback. "Fine," she said hesitantly. "I don't see as much of him as I'd like."

Jean sat down, opened a red-and-gold pack of Dunhill International, pulled out a cigarette, and tapped it thoughtfully on the arm of the chair. "I called and asked him if he'd read your book, and he said it was so disgusting he couldn't get past the first page." She cackled. "Fathers, eh?"

It sounded like something Joe might say, but Jackie wouldn't let it get to her. "He's clearly not opened it because the first sex scene isn't till page twenty-eight," she replied.

Jean scribbled her answer in a ring-bound notebook, then lit her cigarette, drawing the smoke deep into her lungs. "Were you worried how people would react to your sex scenes? Or do you consider yourself an expert on sex?"

Jackie raised her eyebrows. "I don't plan on handing you a list of my sexual partners, if that's what you're angling for, but let's just say I've done my fair share of research." She smiled, waiting for Jean to finish scribbling her words before she continued: "I hope I'm speaking for my generation of women who enjoy sex and aren't ashamed to be open about it."

"You started young, didn't you? I heard you were expelled from school for befriending the local flasher." Jean took a long drag and narrowed her kohl-rimmed eyes to slits. "What was that about?"

Jackie wondered where on earth she had heard about the flasher, a homeless chap called Trevor. Had she gotten access to school records? No, more likely her dad had told her. "He was a sad, lonely man and I felt sorry for him," she explained. "I was just being friendly and didn't mean any harm. The school took a dim view, though. It was rather a snobbish place."

Jean smoothed back a lock of hair using the hand that held the cigarette and a half-inch column of ash toppled onto the arm of the chair. She didn't notice and Jackie didn't mention it.

"I heard your first husband committed suicide. Do you think your getting remarried drove him to it?" She gave Jackie a hard stare.

Jackie took a deep breath to steady herself before replying. She hadn't expected Wallace to come up, and still found it difficult to talk about him. "My husband was ill," she said. "I loved him very much, but I couldn't save him. No one could." How much more of this did she have to put up with? The questions were intrusive, and Jean's manner was downright rude—but it was her first book and she needed the publicity. "He was a wonderful man. Please put that in if you're mentioning him at all, although I don't see how he is relevant to my novel."

"Do you consider yourself a feminist?" Jean Rook asked, still scribbling away.

"Absolutely, yes," Jackie replied. "In my book I'm trying to make the point that there's a double standard in our society. If a man plays around, he's seen as a bit of a lad, and everyone nods approval, but if a woman plays around, she's a slut, a tramp, an evil whore. For me, feminism should mean total equality of the sexes. And from where I'm sitting, that still feels a long way off." She made a play to try and win Miss Rook over. "I mean, it's impressive that you've earned such a great reputation in journalism, but I bet you've had to put up with a load of sexist nonsense from male colleagues to get where you are today."

Jean gave her a quick smile. "And the rest," she said, with a world-weary sigh.

The atmosphere lightened. They chatted for another half hour about the symbolism of Playboy bunnies, the draftiness of miniskirts, the misogyny inherent in the Free Love movement, and the unfairness of Harold Robbins being allowed to say "fuck" in his novels while Jackie could only say "f—k."

There was a brief cry from upstairs, indicating that Tiffany had wakened. Jackie went to fetch her, expecting Jean to cluck and coo the way women did about each other's babies, but she clearly had no interest. She packed her notebook and ciggies into her satchel and stood up without so much as asking the baby's name.

"Our photographer will pop round same time tomorrow," she said, "and the article comes out the day after. Good luck with the book. I enjoyed it!"

When her feature came out on publication day, the headline read "Joan Collins's Sister Writes Dirty Book," which was annoying. Still in Joan's shadow, after all these years! The rest of it was fair, Jackie thought. She came across well and the photograph they used was flattering.

The press reviews were damning, though. "The most disgusting book ever written," one read. Another was simply titled "Ugh!" A member of parliament for a London constituency took out an ad in the *Sunday People* to protest about it. Each new piece felt to Jackie like a slap across the face. These people didn't know her. How could they direct such vitriol against her just for writing a book?

"It's all good publicity," Robert Armstrong told her when she rang him, distressed by the coverage.

Then came news that the book had been banned in South Africa, Australia, and New Zealand anyway, despite her taking out the swear words.

"Don't worry," Robert told her. "I find there's nothing like a book ban to whip up demand."

Everyone was upbeat. Early sales were promising, they said.

Within a week it had tipped onto the bestseller list at number nineteen and they were sure it would rise higher. An American publisher was considering it, and they hoped there might be an offer.

"Can I go on a book tour, the way Jacqueline Susann does?" Jackie asked.

Her publicity girl screwed up her face. "You're not well enough known yet. I don't want you sitting in bookshops like a lemon when only two people show up. That happens, you know."

"Can I go on television? Or radio?" she persevered. How else could she sell her book?

"I've got some local radio lined up, but no tele, not yet."

"Just write the next novel," Robert told her. "Leave us to sell this one. It's doing fine."

"Fine" wasn't good enough, Jackie thought. Jacqueline Susann wouldn't put up with "fine." But she couldn't think what else to do, so she went back to writing *The Stud*. It was fun describing Tony Blake, her womanizing nightclub manager, and the dilemma he faced when the owner's wife insisted that he "serviced" her.

A letter arrived one morning in a plain white envelope with the address written in childish block capitals. Tiffany was straddled on her hip as she walked into the hall to pick it up, then tore it open. A grayish-yellow rubber object fell to the floor. Frowning, she bent to retrieve it, still clutching the baby. On closer examination it was a condom with a gobbet of semen inside and a knot tied in the top. She shuddered. How vile!

There was a note inside the envelope, which read: *I'd be better than any man you've ever had. Why not let me show you what I can do?*

What kind of person would write that? And how had he gotten her home address? The envelope had a London postmark. Might he turn up at her house one day?

Jackie hesitated, wondering if she should report it to the police, but decided it was probably a one-off. This guy had read her book and worked up a schoolboy fantasy, but he'd no doubt find someone new to fixate on before long. She threw the note and the condom into the kitchen bin and washed her hands under the tap, still clutching Tiffany on her hip.

She was pleased her book had been published, of course she was. She just wished she hadn't been so naïve as to think writing a sexy book would come without a price tag.

CHAPTER 28

Nancy

Manhattan, 1969

Nancy and Steven got back to her apartment late one evening, both of them giggly after drinking too much red wine at a folk club in the Village. She turned the key in the lock and, as the door opened, she frowned to see that the lights were on. She stepped inside and there, sitting on the couch in a red satin dressing gown, was her cousin Louise.

"Oh!" Nancy jumped. "You gave me a fright!"

It had been so long since Louise disappeared to London that Nancy had come to think of the apartment as her own. She paid the rent, but the lease was still in Louise's name.

"The caretaker let me in," Louise explained. "I see you've taken good care of the place for me. Who's this?" Steven was hovering behind.

Nancy made the introductions. Steven shook Louise's hand, then said, "I hope we can meet properly before long, but I'm going to head off now and let you two catch up."

Nancy didn't want him to leave, but she could hardly invite him to stay over with Louise there and only one bedroom.

"Your boyfriend?" Louise asked as the door closed behind him. "He seems very grown-up. Isn't he quite a bit older than you?"

"Nine years," Nancy replied. "But we have so much in common, we don't really notice."

"Why the military haircut?" Louise asked.

"He likes it neat. He's not a fan of long hair on men."

She sat down beside Louise and looked at her properly. Her cousin was thinner than she'd ever seen her. Her cheekbones were more pronounced, and the biggest shock was that her blond hair had been cut short, giving her a gamine look, like Mia Farrow in *Rosemary's Baby*. She was beautiful as ever but she looked tired.

"Tell me about London," she said. "You must have loved it to stay so long."

"It's a cool city," Louise replied. "I met everyone who's anyone—the Beatles, the Stones, The Who. And Twiggy, David Bailey, Jean Shrimpton—they came to the Ad Lib, and I got to sing for them."

Nancy didn't recognize all the names, but they sounded impressive. "You've been away ages. Was there a man involved? Did you fall in love in swinging London?"

Louise shrugged and wouldn't meet her eyes. "Sure, loads of men. Why confine yourself to one when there's so much choice?"

That didn't sound like the Louise Nancy used to know, who read romance novels and dreamed of finding true love with her ideal guy. She let it pass. "Why did you come back," she asked, "if you were having so much fun?"

Again, Louise wouldn't make eye contact. She was very fidgety. "The work dried up, sadly. I'll need to look for a job here, but if you can help with the rent till then, that would be great." She picked at her fingernails. "Sorry I wasn't around when you arrived. I was so excited to get the London offer that it completely slipped my mind you were coming. I heard I was going on a Thursday and flew out on a Saturday so there was no time to breathe."

At last, an apology. It sounded offhand, like an afterthought, but Nancy decided to let it go. She didn't mention having had to sleep in the corridor because she didn't want Louise to feel bad. "It was quite a coincidence that my friend George saw you performing in London," she said. "But I'm glad he did, because I was worried about you."

"George Carter? Is he a friend of yours? What a louse!" Louise exclaimed. "Don't you just hate guys who lead you on, then never call?"

Nancy was stunned. George had admitted he liked women, but she hadn't seen him with any yet. Somehow she couldn't imagine Louise would be his type. Had he gone to bed with her? She didn't like that idea one bit.

"I was working with the novelist Jacqueline Susann," she explained, "and she introduced me to George at a party. He treats me like his kid sister, buying me dinners every few months when he's in town because he thinks I'm not getting enough vitamins. I'm seeing him in a couple of weeks so I'll tell him you're back."

"Why don't I join you?" Louise asked, a glint of mischief in her eyes. "Don't warn him—I'll surprise him."

Nancy felt uncomfortable about this, but couldn't think of an excuse to say no. She loved her evenings with George and didn't want to share him, but until she found somewhere else to stay, Louise was going to be her live-in landlady.

* * *

NANCY BEGAN VIEWING apartments during her lunch hour, but her budget was so limited she soon realized she wouldn't find anything halfway decent. She asked Steven if he might help with the rent somewhere, a place that could be theirs one day, but he was adamant he couldn't incur any expense.

"Jeanette doesn't mind me seeing you, but she gets very cross if I spend money on you."

That made her feel awkward, but she supposed his family's needs came first—of course they did.

"I miss making love with you," she told him. "It's frustrating saying goodnight on the doorstep, like high-school sweethearts who live with their parents."

"We could always sneak into my office once everyone's gone home," Steven suggested. "I'd get a kick out of making love to you on my desk."

Nancy hated that idea. She would feel cheap, and she'd be nervous the whole time that Bernie would walk in on them. The very thought made her shudder, and she was hurt that Steven would consider it. She missed the intimacy of lying in bed together after sex almost more than she missed the act itself. They chatted on the telephone most days and always he told her he loved her. They still saw each other twice a week, but the old loneliness began to creep back, making her feel low.

It didn't help that Louise was behaving erratically. She seemed different from the sweet older cousin who used to spend summers in Ossipee. Now she was touchy and volatile, so Nancy never knew which Louise she'd come home to. Fortunately their schedules didn't overlap much because Nancy was at work during the day and often stayed at the office late, while Louise went out most evenings, dressed to the nines in sexy frocks and heels. "You never know—I might get lucky!" she quipped one night when Nancy asked if it was a special occasion.

Louise particularly loved the black-and-rhinestone dress Jacqueline had given Nancy, and often borrowed it without asking. Nancy didn't want to lend it, but it seemed churlish to say so.

One evening she was making soup in the kitchen while Louise was getting ready to go out. She was edgy and Nancy wondered if she was nervous about a date.

"Is he cute?" she asked. "Where did you two meet?"

"He's nothing special," Louise replied dismissively. "It's not serious."

She was wandering around the apartment, checking shelves and opening drawers as if looking for something. "Have you seen my cherry-red nail polish?" she asked. "I'm sure I left it on the table."

"It's in the washroom," Nancy replied. "I tried it on my toe-nails last night."

"You did *what*? Without asking?" Louise's tone was aggressive, and Nancy whirled around in surprise. "Don't. Touch. My. Stuff." She jabbed the table with her finger as she spat out each word.

Nancy stared, open-mouthed. She looked like the old Louise, she had the same voice, but it was as if she had transformed into an entirely different person. What had happened to her in London?

Louise rushed into the washroom and slammed the door, then left soon afterward without apologizing for her outburst.

I've got to get out of here, Nancy thought to herself. *The sooner, the better.*

* * *

TWO WEEKS LATER, Nancy went straight from work to meet George at Toots Shor's. His hair was longer than usual, curling over his shirt collar, and he was sporting a short, stubbly beard, which made him look rugged and sexy, she thought.

"Sorry I didn't have time to shave," he said. "I flew in from Jordan and"—he checked his watch—"it's the middle of the night there."

"What were you doing in Jordan?" she asked.

"There are always interesting stories in the Middle East," he said. "We've filmed enough material for three documentaries. Tomorrow I have the tricky task of persuading the powers that be that American viewers will be interested in them. Shall I order you a glass of champagne?"

"Yes, please," she said. It was sweet that he always remembered her favorite.

"How's the job?" he asked, after calling a waiter to place her order.

"It's OK," she said, "but it's going to be tough getting promoted to an editor's role because I'm not included in the decision-making." It was difficult to learn how commercial calculations were made—advances paid, print runs ordered—without being present at the editorial meeting. "Meanwhile, I'm apartment hunting again because Louise suddenly arrived back from London."

"She did?" George looked surprised, then concerned. "Is she OK?"

Nancy paused. She considered telling him that Louise had come back as a selfish, short-tempered version of her former self, but decided against it. "I guess so," she said at last. "But I need to move out, and the rental market hasn't gotten any cheaper." She pulled a face. "You wouldn't believe some of the dives I've viewed."

"Why don't you move in with that boyfriend of yours?" George asked, his tone gruff.

Nancy was surprised. He'd never asked her about Steven, although she knew Jacqueline had told him she was dating. "We're not ready to take that step," she said, choosing her words with care.

He picked up a cocktail menu and twiddled it between his fingers for a few moments before seeming to come to a decision. "If you're stuck, you could use the spare room at my place. I'm going to Asia the day after tomorrow and I'll be away more often than not over the next six months."

"Are you serious?" Nancy asked. "I couldn't possibly . . ."

"It feels irresponsible to leave Manhattan real estate lying empty, and I'd be grateful to know you were keeping an eye on it." He fumbled in his pocket, pulled out a set of keys, detached two, and handed them to her, then scribbled the address on the back of a business card. "I'll tell the doorman to expect you.

The spare room is first door on the left down the hall. I trust you not to have any wild drug-taking orgies."

She looked at the card. It was a very swanky address on the Upper East Side. "I can't afford to pay the kind of rent you could charge there," she said.

"I'm not looking for rent. Save your money to get a place of your own."

"But why . . . ?" *Why would you do that for me?* she wanted to ask. *You hardly know me.* The waiter brought her drink and she took a sip, trying to gather her thoughts.

"Just say yes." He grinned. "It's not forever. I want it back in six months."

The bar door opened and Nancy looked up to see Louise walking toward them, wearing a white minidress and open-toed white sandals, with a white fake-fur stole around her shoulders.

"George, darling!" Louise exclaimed and leaned over to kiss him on the lips. Nancy saw him flinch.

Louise looked at the glass in Nancy's hand. "I see you two started without me." She raised her arm in the air and called, "Waiter! Over here!"

Nancy was embarrassed. It was George's table and Louise should have let him order. Was she drunk? Or was she acting up in front of George?

Louise pulled up a chair alongside his, and demanded that the waiter bring her a Manhattan, then turned her attention to George. "How have you been since I saw you in London? It was sweet that you remembered my song. Nancy told me that's how you figured out I was her cousin."

"I was glad to be able to help *Nancy*," he said, emphasizing her name, and there was no mistaking the coolness of his tone. "What brings you back to New York?"

"Oh, you know, pastures new." She waved a hand in the air. "I did love London clubland, and Johnny Gold is a darling man, but when the Ad Lib closed, I couldn't get a regular slot anywhere else. Just a week here, a few Saturday nights there—you know how it goes, George. It's hard to make a living that way."

"At least you always had plenty of men looking out for you," George remarked tartly, and Nancy wondered what he was implying.

Louise turned to Nancy. "It's true," she said. "I was pursued by everyone from aristocrats to politicians to gangsters. Such fun!" She turned to George, leaning close, and whispered, "But you're the one who got away, darling. I was sorry we weren't able to *connect*." Then, to Nancy's horror, she placed her hand over his crotch and gave it a squeeze.

"Louise!" Nancy exclaimed. She'd never seen her behave like that, and was humiliated on her behalf. She should have warned George Louise was coming; it seemed there was complicated history between them.

George removed her hand and spoke icily. "I don't mind girls who are promiscuous; I don't mind girls who can't hold their liquor; but I draw the line at ones who shoot up in my bathroom."

Nancy's eyes widened in surprise. What could he mean?

Louise made a tutting sound. "It was a vitamin shot. Don't be such an old prude. All the girls use them because we work late hours and don't get regular meals."

"But you're not working tonight," George said, "and I can tell you had a shot recently. Your pupils are huge black holes, and you can't sit still."

Nancy looked into Louise's eyes and saw that her pupils were enormous, while her foot was tapping manically under the table. Could it be true? Was her cousin a drug addict?

"Screw you!" Louise shouted. In a sudden flare of temper, she picked up Nancy's champagne and hurled it at George. "I don't have to listen to this."

Her aim was poor and most of it sloshed over his shoulder onto the floor behind, but some caught his cheek. He mopped it with a napkin, then scraped his chair back and stood up. "Neither do I," he said, picking up his briefcase.

Nancy couldn't believe what was happening. "Please don't go, George. Louise, apologize immediately."

"I'll pay Toots for your drink on the way out, Nancy," he said, looking at her. "My offer about the apartment still stands. I think you should get out of your current environment for your own safety." He walked off before she could respond.

Nancy turned to Louise, who was quaffing the remainder of George's martini.

"Isn't he rude?" Louise asked. "I thought that was uncalled for."

Nancy shook her head in disbelief. "Is it true you're on drugs? What are you thinking of? And why were you so awful to George?"

"God, you're a square," Louise said. "Everyone takes vitamin shots—even your beloved Jacqueline Susann, I hear. So don't come over all high and mighty with me, my sweet little country cousin. Welcome to the real world."

Nancy decided then and there to take George up on his offer. She would still see Louise, but she couldn't live with her. Not when she was like this.

* * *

THE NEXT MORNING, Nancy telephoned Steven to tell him she was moving into the spare room at George's apartment. She suggested they could meet there the following evening, by which time George would have left the country. At last they could spend some time alone.

He hesitated. "To be honest, I'm not sure how I feel about you staying in another man's apartment. You realize this is probably a ruse on his part to get you into bed."

Nancy chuckled. "When you meet him, you'll realize that couldn't be further from the truth. He treats me like a scrappy kid who can't look after herself. Anyway, it's just a stopgap till I save enough for a place of my own."

"Don't get me wrong. I can't wait to see you," Steven said. "But not tomorrow evening because Jeanette's going out and I have to babysit. The day after?"

Nancy was disappointed. It had been weeks since they were able to share a bed, and without physical intimacy she was more aware of the emotional distance between them. It felt as if they were drifting inexorably apart and the only thing that could stop it would be for him to get a move on and leave Jeanette. That wasn't a conversation for the telephone, though.

Louise didn't come home that evening, and Nancy took the opportunity to pack. She'd amassed several boxloads of books and more clothes than would fit in the single suitcase she'd arrived in New York with, then there were her mother's paintings as well.

Straight after work the following day, she went back to collect her belongings, and her heart sank when she found Louise sitting on the couch, a magazine in her lap.

"Please don't leave," Louise begged straight away. "I know I've been difficult to live with these past couple of weeks, but I need you, Nancy." She sounded sad. "What can I do to make you stay?"

Nancy was torn. "We can still see each other," she said. "We can go to the movies or for cocktails."

Louise shook her head and her lip quivered as if she was about to cry. "I'm not safe on my own," she said, but refused to explain why. Was it because of the vitamin injections? Or the type of clubs she went to?

"You lived on your own before," Nancy said. "And you've got my work phone number. Call anytime and I'll come over," she promised, wondering if she would regret that offer.

"How will I pay the rent without you?" Louise asked, and started to cry.

Is that what it was about? Nancy wondered. *Or was she being cynical?* "I've already paid this month," she said. "If you don't get a job soon, could your mom and pop help?"

Louise sobbed even louder. "They don't want to know me."

Nancy knew they'd both remarried since their divorce but couldn't believe they wouldn't help their own daughter. "Contact them," she urged. "I'm sure they won't let you become homeless."

"I don't even know where Pop lives, and Mom doesn't care." Louise blew her nose loudly. "I was the black sheep at school— always in trouble for skipping lessons and necking boys behind the running track."

Nancy remembered her mom once describing Louise as "boy crazy" but surely that wasn't the worst crime in the world? She comforted her until she had stopped crying, then she heated some soup and served bowls for them both. She kept her eye on the clock, though, and when it reached nine, she announced she had to go. She felt guilty leaving Louise in a distressed state, but every time she remembered her grabbing George's crotch, then throwing a drink at him, she knew it was for the best.

She took a taxi to George's address, with her suitcase and paintings. The doorman helped her to carry everything into the elevator. She turned the key in the lock and looked inside to find a hallway opening into a stunning living room, decorated in ethnic style. It was a total surprise. She had expected an unadorned masculine décor, but this was full of beaten silver mirrors and mosaic lampshades, rugs of rich jewel hues, and piles of lavishly embroidered cushions. It was so far from what she had imagined that she stood for a few moments taking it in.

In the corner of the living room there was a dark-wood cocktail bar and she noticed a sheet of paper lying on it—the only thing out of place in the room. She walked over and found it was a note from George. *Please make yourself at home. Help yourself to any food and drink I've left. I'll give you plenty of warning when I'm coming back. The only thing I ask is that you don't use my bedroom and private bathroom. Oh, and please don't bring Louise here. I guess you'll understand why. George.*

She wandered out into the hallway, which was decorated with a set of antique prints of elephants, tigers, and monkeys. The kitchen had an old wooden table with carved serpents climbing the legs, and a cabinet displaying vivid painted ceramics. The first door on the left in the hall was the spare bedroom, he'd said. Like the rest of the apartment, it was decorated with a mixture of colorful elements: a throw on the bed that looked South American; paper lampshades in Japanese style; an Islamic patterned rug. She opened the next door to find a luxurious bathroom with a clawfoot tub and ferns trailing from hanging baskets. The final door led to a larger bedroom with a king-size bed: she glanced inside, then closed the door, to respect George's privacy.

The whole apartment was worthy of a design magazine feature. He must have picked up these artifacts on his travels. She was impressed that he had such a good eye for putting them together. What a privilege to stay there! She vowed to take excellent care of it.

Nancy unpacked her clothes, then poured herself a vodka and Coke from the corner bar and sat on the couch with a copy of *The World Is Full of Married Men*, which she had received in the mail from the British publisher, W. H. Allen. The cover had a curious illustration of five men and a blond woman crammed together in a double bed.

She started reading. An advertising executive called David Cooper was having an affair with a model called Claudia, and when his wife, Linda, discovered it, she threw him out. He moved in with Claudia, but she soon grew sick of him, and the plot played out with cleverly interlinked stories about Linda, Claudia, David, and his mousy secretary. Nancy was riveted. It was only two hundred pages long and she finished it just after midnight, then went to bed and lay awake mulling it over.

The story didn't exactly reflect her situation with Steven—she was sure she would never get fed up with him the way Claudia did with David—but it made her focus on the fact that the end of his marriage was likely to be painful. He'd told her he would let Jeanette have custody of Darren during the week but hoped Darren could come to them on weekends so he and his son could watch sports together, then he'd take him back Sunday night. That sounded fair, but Darren's little world would still be shattered and Nancy felt bad that she would be partly responsible. Sadly, it was the only way if she and Steven were to be together. She lay awake pondering different scenarios, but in none of them was there a happy ending for all concerned.

The next morning, Nancy wrote a report on the novel for Bill Heywood, summarizing the plot and strongly recommending that Heywood & Bradshaw make an offer. It had the same pacy glamour and gritty sex scenes as *Valley of the Dolls* and she thought American readers would love it despite the British setting.

Bill took her report to the editorial meeting and, when he emerged, he said: "Mixed feelings, Nancy. We're not convinced it would work here."

"It's a bestseller in Britain," she told him, "and I strongly suspect she could be the next Jacqueline Susann."

He frowned. "You've not had enough experience to judge what will or won't work. Launching a British author in our market is a tough call."

"Remember I was right about *Miss Craig's 21-Day Shape-Up Program*," she argued. It had sat in the top ten for three months, vindicating her recommendation. "Are you sure you don't want to read Jackie Collins's book yourself before turning it down?"

"God, no!" He paused. "I suppose you could give it to Michael Loveday for a second opinion." He was the one who had pinched Nancy's bottom on her first day there. "Don't get your hopes up, though. He's very choosy."

Bill patted her on the head before disappearing into his office. She reflected that it was almost more patronizing than having her bottom pinched.

CHAPTER 29

Jacqueline

Manhattan, 1969

Jacqueline was pleased when Nancy rang one morning saying she needed advice. It had to be in person, she insisted; she couldn't explain on the telephone.

"Meet me for lunch at Sardi's," Jacqueline suggested. "It's not far from your office and their cannelloni is the best in New York City."

What could it be about? Was Nancy finally going to confide in her about the mystery boyfriend? By her estimate they had been dating for almost two years but she still hadn't met him. Maybe he had proposed and Nancy was deciding whether to accept? Jacqueline had strong views on the choice of husbands. She'd advised many a girlfriend on that score, and she had never been wrong.

Jacqueline got there first and watched Nancy arrive and glance around at the caricatures of celebrities that lined the walls. Her clothes were still old-fashioned but slightly more presentable than they'd been when she had arrived in the city. Today she was wearing a cute navy-blue dress with a white Peter Pan collar and cuffs, but she'd styled it with schoolgirl-style T-bar sandals. *Ugh!* She must take her shoe shopping one weekend.

As Nancy sat down, she commented on the caricatures. "Who did these? They're wonderful!"

"Most are by a Russian émigré called Alex Gard, who drew them in exchange for free meals," Jacqueline told her. "I like the tradition of restaurant owners supporting artists."

"He should do a cartoon of you," Nancy suggested, but Jacqueline wasn't sure she liked that idea. Cartoons were never flattering.

They ordered, then Jacqueline cut to the chase. "What did you want my advice about? I'm all ears."

"It's my cousin Louise," Nancy replied.

Jacqueline was crestfallen. Not the boyfriend then. "What about her?"

"She's been behaving erratically since she came back, and doesn't seem her old self at all. George says she's a drug addict, but Louise denies it and says she just gives herself vitamin shots for energy when she's working nights." Nancy paused. "I wondered if you knew anything about vitamin shots and whether or not they're addictive?"

"For sure they are," Jacqueline said straight away. "They contain amphetamines, which are highly addictive. I've used them as a pick-me-up from time to time, but I always got the shots from a doctor, who does a full medical before administering them. There's no way Louise should be injecting herself."

"I thought as much." Nancy looked worried. "I think she got hooked on them in London. George says he caught her injecting herself in his hotel room."

Jacqueline nodded. George had told her. "I gather she was involved with a shady crowd there."

"Was she? How come George knows shady people?" Nancy asked.

Jacqueline hesitated. "He was making a documentary about London clubland when he met Louise. He mixes with all sorts when he's making his films."

"I'd like to watch that," Nancy said. "I haven't seen any of George's shows, but I'm staying in his spare room now and there's a television in the living room so maybe I'll catch one."

George had told Jacqueline about Nancy moving in. She'd

thought it a curiously generous gesture on his part and had interrogated him about his motives. First, he said he wanted to get
Nancy out of Louise's orbit since she was a bad influence. Then
he claimed he was getting a sense that the mystery boyfriend
wasn't treating her very well and he didn't want Nancy to be
dependent on him for a roof over her head. Reading between
the lines, she sensed George's feelings for Nancy were growing.
"He's falling in love, you mark my words," she told Irving, who
responded by rolling his eyes.

"Won't you mind if Steven stays over at your place?" Jacqueline had asked George. "What if you walk in on them in bed
together?"

He grimaced and said, "I will make one hundred percent sure
not to do that."

Jacqueline masked a smile. He clearly didn't like the fact that
Nancy had a boyfriend. Moving her into his apartment struck her
as being somewhat like a stag staking its territory and warning
off the competition.

"Has Louise found any work in New York?" she asked Nancy
over their lunch.

"Not yet," Nancy said. "I think money is tight."

"That's good in one sense, because it means she won't be able
to afford the shots much longer," Jacqueline said. "They cost
twenty dollars a pop. She might feel lousy for a couple of weeks
when she comes off them, but then she should be good as new."

"I feel guilty for abandoning her," Nancy said. "But her apartment isn't big enough for two and . . ."

"And she was behaving erratically. You did the right thing."
Jacqueline mulled it over for a few moments. She didn't want to
get involved, but Nancy seemed troubled, and it was a subject
she knew a lot about. "If you're still worried about her in a week
or so, you're welcome to bring her to meet me. I can explain all

I know about the injections and advise her on how to get off them."

"Would you?" Nancy asked. "I'd be ever so grateful. I don't know what else to do."

Their food arrived and they began to eat. Jacqueline summoned the waiter to ask for extra parmesan. She loved cheese. She should be cutting back because she had the *Love Machine* book tour coming up, but a little sprinkle couldn't hurt. She'd start the diet tomorrow.

"When you called, I thought you might want to talk about Steven," she said, giving Nancy a probing look. "Any hint of wedding bells?"

Nancy shook her head and stared at her lap, as if struggling to keep her emotions in check. "Not yet," she said.

"I'm worried about you. It's not a good sign that he doesn't want to meet your friends."

Nancy pursed her lips. "He's met my stepfather, and Louise too."

"So it's just me he's avoiding?" Jacqueline challenged. "Am I so scary?"

"It's not that. He's very busy."

She said it as if she was trying to convince herself, Jacqueline thought. Women deluded themselves about men all the time. It was an age-old story.

"Are you sure he's being faithful? No other women on the side?"

"He's not that type," Nancy said firmly.

How did she know? Jacqueline thought. They didn't all come wearing a "Philanderer" badge. Many years ago, she'd had her heart broken by a singer called Eddie Cantor, with whom she'd had an affair while Irving was at war. She had fallen for Eddie with all her heart and soul, but he was married and not planning to leave. Jacqueline wasn't used to rejection, so when Eddie finally dropped her, the pain was unbearable. Worst of all, she'd been humiliated.

"I wish you would introduce me to Steven," she said. "I'm a great judge of character, and I'm good at winkling out information. I could tell you his intentions after one teeny cocktail."

Nancy forced a laugh. "I don't doubt it for a moment," she said, but still wouldn't commit to a day when she would bring him over to the Navarro.

Jacqueline couldn't help feeling hurt. Presumably Nancy would have introduced Steven to her mom, if she were still alive, and she considered herself *in loco parentis*.

When she discussed it with Irving later, he suggested Nancy might be worried that she would be too forthright. "You have a habit of interrogating people," he said. "Perhaps Nancy is worried about how he would cope."

"That's nonsense," she snapped. "I can be as tactful as the next person. What's he got to hide? That's what I want to know."

Irving gave an irritating little smile, as if he believed she had proved his point.

* * *

THE LOVE MACHINE was to be published on May fourteenth, and Jacqueline was busy discussing ideas with her new publicist. After meeting the women in her mother's local bookstore, she had decided she wanted plenty of events where she could meet the public directly and thus bypass the reliance on book reviewers, whom she expected would be just as bitchy this time around as they had been over *Dolls*. She still wanted to woo booksellers, though, so she persuaded her publicist that she could host a banquet for them at the American Booksellers Association annual convention in Washington, DC.

Jacqueline oversaw the arrangements herself. Nat Miles, her favorite barman at Danny's Hideaway, invented a *Love Machine* cocktail for the event, a deceptively lethal concoction with vodka, Pernod, crème de cacao, and fruit, served over crushed ice. She had a huge *Love Machine* cake made with two clasped hands on top, mirroring the book's cover. She commissioned a *Love Machine* theme song and hired a professional singer to perform—she tried for Tony Bennett but his agent said he was otherwise engaged. And she invited two hundred booksellers to attend, all of whom would be given a copy of *Love Machine* personally signed by her.

The tables in the hotel banquet suite seated ten and a space was left at each for her to sit down, sign her books, and chat with everyone. Many of the booksellers she knew already from the *Dolls* tour, and the rest she intended to know by the end of the evening.

It was a lively event from the start. The booksellers had been stuck in a conference hall all day and when they were handed a potent cocktail, many of them gulped it down and went back for seconds. Jacqueline realized when she started chatting that some of them were already the worse for wear, but what the heck? She was glad they felt able to relax.

Dinner was served, but Jacqueline didn't have time to eat. She spent around ten minutes at each table, chatting, asking after the booksellers' wives, children, grandchildren, and pets by name, and telling them about *Love Machine*'s womanizing television executive, Robin Stone. She hinted that the character was based on a friend of hers who would remain nameless.

"What do you think of Jackie Collins's novel, *The World Is Full of Married Men*?" one bookseller asked.

Jacqueline remembered the name; that was the woman she'd met in London at Sharon Tate's wedding. "I know her. Has her book been published?" she asked.

"It just got a US deal, and trade reviewers are comparing it to *Valley of the Dolls*," he replied. He pulled a copy of *Publishers Weekly* from his briefcase and flicked to a page, then handed it over. "More Sex Than Susann," the headline read.

She laughed out loud. "Any more sex than *Dolls* and it belongs in a sex shop, not a bookstore. I must get hold of a copy. Have any of you read it?" She looked around the table. There were a few nods.

"It's certainly racy," one said, with a grin.

She checked the article and saw that the book was published by Heywood & Bradshaw. Why hadn't Nancy mentioned it over lunch? Jacqueline was piqued to learn that she had a competitor. Had Jackie Collins copied her?

The cake was brought in, the hired singer sang the theme song, and all night long Jacqueline chatted and smiled and talked about her book, but a hard little seed of irritation was niggling her.

First thing the following morning, she got Irving to call Bill Heywood and ask him to send over a copy of *The World Is Full of Married Men*. She sat on their hotel balcony in the spring sunshine, with a pack of cigarettes and a coffee, and began to read.

There was a lot of copulation, as if Jackie Collins felt the need to insert a sex scene every few pages. Some of it was more raw and graphic than the sex in her novels, so perhaps that's why the review had been titled "More Sex Than Susann." There was a horrendous scene at a film producer's house where a young girl who wanted to be an actress was tricked into having sex with loads of lecherous old men. The ending with the mousy secretary was grim too, but at least the wife came out on top.

Jacqueline had smoked almost an entire pack of Lucky Strike before reaching the end. It was much shorter than *Dolls*, and it lacked the psychological complexity of her novel, but it was definitely aiming at the same readership. *Her* readership. She had created it. She knew from chatting to her readers that many of them didn't normally read books, but they bought hers to read in the subway on the way to work or in the waiting room at the dentist. They wanted to escape the mundanity of everyday life and imagine the glamour of the showbiz world she described. Now someone else was muscling in on her territory and she wasn't happy about it.

Irving laughed at her. "You can write one book a year if you push yourself, and your readers finish it in one or two days. What are they supposed to do for the other three hundred and sixty-three? You won't sell one less copy because of her. If anything, she'll expand the market for this kind of novel."

Jacqueline read the biography on the jacket. "It says here she is a 'glamorous and attractive actress,' but she told me she only ever got bit parts. Have you come across her?"

"No," he replied, "but I know her husband, Oscar Lerman. He's a Broadway producer. Nice guy."

She felt irrationally cross with Irving, as if by liking Jackie's husband he was being disloyal to her. At least their books hadn't gone head-to-head; *Love Machine* wasn't coming out till May.

"Maybe you should befriend her," Irving suggested, raising an eyebrow.

"You think?" Jacqueline growled. She considered throwing the book at him but changed her mind. Instead, she picked up the hotel telephone and called her son's institution to ask what he had been doing that day. The routine was always the same, but she liked hearing it anyway.

CHAPTER 30

Jackie

London, 1969

Jackie got her first royalty statement from her UK publishers, in a business-like brown envelope with a transparent address window. Robert Armstrong had explained that they had to recoup the advance before any royalties were payable, but she had assumed that since *The World Is Full of Married Men* had gotten onto the bestseller list, the sales must be decent. She peered inside the envelope but there was no check, just a statement covered in columns of figures.

She sat down to try and make sense of the disappointing totals and realized they only covered sales up to six months previously. It would be October before she got royalties on subsequent sales, along with her share of the advance for the American deal. She was never going to make a living this way. How did any authors survive on four hundred pounds for what amounted to two years' work?

It had been exciting to get an offer from an American publisher. She'd received a very enthusiastic letter from her US editor, Michael Loveday at Heywood & Bradshaw. He invited her to the States to help publicize *The World Is Full of Married Men*, but that would have to wait till the autumn because Jackie was heavily pregnant with her third child.

When *The Stud* came out in the UK, Oscar threw a launch party at Dolly's. Jackie sat regally in a velvet armchair, her huge bump—bigger than the previous two—covered in a white embroidered smock. She gave interviews to a handful of women's magazines and to the London *Evening News*, feeling more confident now about the message she wanted to put across. Women came out on top in her books, she said; her heroines were powerful and self-determining, they looked great, and, yes, they loved sex.

The reviews were damning as always, but she'd expected that. One magazine sent a copy to romance novelist Barbara Cartland and she responded with a quote that made Jackie and Oscar double over with laughter: "Filthy, disgusting and unnecessary," Miss Cartland said. It became their favorite catchphrase for the next few months, applied to everything from a sinkful of dirty dishes to the state of the girls' clothes after they'd been playing in the muddy garden.

After the UK release of *The Stud*, another letter containing a used condom arrived in the post. The accompanying note read in block capitals: *I'm more of a stud than Tony Blake. When are you going to try me out?* So the condom creep hadn't given up? Jackie dropped it on the floor in disgust. At least he hadn't turned up at the house, or tried to make his charming offer in person, but what kind of person did that?

She sat down in a kitchen chair to think about it. If she told Oscar, he would probably call the police and make a big deal out of it. But surely if this guy was planning to attack her, he would have done so by now? Maybe he was a harmless pervert, like Trevor, the flasher she'd befriended at school. The letters contained pathetic, childish boasting rather than threats.

She decided to ignore them for now. Any response would only serve to feed the creep's sense of self-importance. She picked up the latest condom and note with the tips of her fingers and threw them in the bin, thinking to herself, "Filthy, disgusting and unnecessary."

* * *

JACKIE'S THIRD DAUGHTER, Rory, was born at home. Throughout the pregnancy she had felt certain the baby was another girl
and was glad to have three daughters. They could borrow one
another's clothes and makeup, and look out for each other. She
asked Oscar if he was disappointed not to have a son, and tears
sprang to his eyes.

"Not even remotely," he said, with a croak in his voice. "Our
girls are perfect and I couldn't love them any more than I do."

One evening, when Rory was two weeks old, he told Jackie he
needed to have a word with her when the girls were in bed. His
tone sounded so serious that a chill ran through her. What could
it be? Had he met someone else and wanted a divorce? Was his
business going bankrupt? Disaster scenarios filled her head as
she tucked the girls in, then came downstairs. He'd mixed them
both gin and tonics and handed her one.

"I didn't want to worry you before," he said, "but I haven't
been seeing eye to eye with Malcolm lately."

Jackie vaguely remembered him mentioning a couple of dis-
agreements with his main partner in Dolly's, but she hadn't
paid much attention. Squabbles seemed par for the course when
several investors co-owned a business.

"So we decided to settle our differences on the toss of a coin."
He gulped his drink. "Whoever lost the toss had to sell their
share in the club to the other."

"And?" Jackie held her breath.

"And I lost the toss, so I'm selling out."

She opened her mouth to protest: "No!"

He held up his hand. "Wait a moment! Johnny Gold is leaving
as well. The two of us have cooked up an idea for a new venture
of our own."

"What kind of venture?" Jackie's voice was little more than
a whisper. How could he risk their family's security on a coin

toss? It was the kind of irresponsible gamble Wallace might have taken, but she'd thought Oscar was more steady.

"The lease is available for the old Society Club on Jermyn Street, and Johnny and I have an idea to turn it into the ultimate hangout for the rich and famous—like we did at Dolly's but more so." He was grinning, clearly excited by their plan. "It will be strictly members only, with no press or photographers allowed. A totally discreet environment where stars can let their hair down and know that no matter what they do, it won't make the tabloids."

"How is that different from other clubs, like Annabel's?" A new venture would be risky, she thought. London clubs came and went all the time, subject to the unpredictable whims of fashion.

"Annabel's is for the super-wealthy and aristocratic. Last time I went it was full of oil sheikhs. I want ours to be cooler than that: pop stars, movie stars, and models, all mingling on the dance floor. Johnny and I have the connections, and I managed to raise the money with a couple of phone calls because investors know I have form." He came to sit beside her and took her hand. "We've been talking about it for weeks. We've planned the décor, the cocktails, the food . . . we've even hired the DJ we want."

"That was a big secret to keep from me," she said, with a tinge of foreboding. She remembered all the secrets Wallace had kept during their marriage: his use of illegal drugs, for starters.

"I didn't want to worry you when you were in the late stages of pregnancy, before I knew it was definitely happening." He tucked a strand of hair behind her ear and kissed her temple.

She tried to think of objections: "If it works, you'll have the whole of Fleet Street camped outside photographing the celebrities coming and going, so it won't be that discreet."

"I know, but they won't get inside."

"Did you think of a name for this club?" she asked.

He grinned. "Johnny came up with a name. We're going to call it Tramp." She frowned, not following him. "He got the idea when watching a Charlie Chaplin movie in which Chaplin was described as 'the greatest tramp of all.' I like the different meanings of the word: it could be a down-and-out, a promiscuous woman, or the sound of marching. *Tramp*."

"Tramp." Jackie tried it out. The vowel sounded completely different in her British accent to his American one. "Why not?"

After their discussion, Jackie brooded on Oscar's decision. He seemed to have thought it through, but she was anxious that if it failed, her family could lose their home. Tramp wouldn't open till December that year and in the meantime, Oscar wouldn't have an income.

He should have discussed it with her, pregnancy or no pregnancy. She was alarmed that he had kept such a huge secret from her, when it must have been filling his thoughts for weeks. It was his career, but it affected her too. If Tramp went bust, she might have to become the family's main breadwinner and, based on the earnings from her first novel, that would be tough. It brought back all the anxiety she'd felt after leaving Wallace, when she had to live hand to mouth. She had no one to fall back on now, and her mum's nest egg was long gone.

Jackie decided she would have to put all her energy into promoting her books, both in the UK and the US, and to write a third novel as soon as possible. She couldn't leave her family's financial stability in the hands of a man who rubbed shoulders with gangsters, who kept secrets from her, and who was prepared to gamble his family's security on a coin toss. She had to make all the money she could in the only way she knew how.

CHAPTER 31

Nancy

Manhattan, 1969

Nancy's stepfather called to say he was bringing her step-brothers to New York to celebrate her twenty-sixth birth-day. They would buy her dinner and take her to a show. She assumed Steven would be busy with his family, since it was a weekend, but when she mentioned the visit, he insisted that he wanted to join them.

"Is George away?" he checked first, as he always did.

"Yes, in Indonesia," she replied. "There's some controversy over a vote they held to take over the state of West Papua so he flew out with his cameraman."

"In that case, why don't I stay the whole weekend and we can make your birthday extra-special," he suggested.

She hugged herself, wondering what plans he might have. The thought crossed her mind that maybe he would propose to her this weekend—but that was silly. How could he propose when he was still married?

On her birthday morning, Steven made a heap of pancakes and bacon, served with orange juice and coffee, and brought her a tray in bed. Beside the pancake plate, there was a black jewelry box tied with a green ribbon and she looked from it to him. "For me?"

"Of course." He smiled.

The box was too big for a ring, but Nancy still held her breath as she untied the ribbon and opened it. Inside there was a neck-lace: a heart-shaped emerald surrounded by marcasite dangling from a silver chain. She didn't wear much jewelry apart from a few pieces of her mom's, but this looked expensive. She wondered what Jeanette would make of the cost?

"Emerald's your birthstone since your star sign is Taurus," he said, sounding unsure, "so I thought . . ."

"I love it!" she exclaimed, fastening it around her neck. The heart sat just between the tops of her breasts. "It's beautiful. I'll have to wear something to match it today."

She looped her arms around his neck and kissed him, wondering how he had chosen it. She imagined an assistant in the shop had helped because he didn't seem the kind of man who would be an expert in jewelry. Then her thoughts strayed. . . . Had he often bought jewelry for Jeanette? Would this necklace be to her taste? What had their relationship been like in the early years, before it went sour? She shook herself.

Once breakfast had been devoured, they made love, slowly and languorously.

"Why don't we shower together in George's shower?" he suggested afterward. On a previous visit, he had peeked in George's room and noticed that his private bathroom had a walk-in shower, big enough for two. "He'll never find out."

"No, I promised I wouldn't," Nancy insisted. It would feel weird. How many women had George made love to in that king-size bed and spacious shower? She didn't like to think about it.

* * *

OUT ON THE sidewalk, there was springlike warmth, with prisms of sunlight slanting through the gaps between buildings and pale green leaf buds unfurling on trees. As they walked hand in hand to Penn Station to meet Joe and her stepbrothers, Nancy was filled with optimism. She was with the man she loved, meeting her family, whom she also loved, and spring was here.

The boys, now aged ten, were excited to be in the city and

Steven was the perfect tour guide, able to tell them facts about the height of the Empire State Building and the number of people who died during the construction of the Brooklyn Bridge—why did boys love numbers so much?—while Nancy walked behind with her stepfather.

When she was sure the boys weren't listening, she confided to Joe how worried she was about Louise. She'd met her for a cocktail two evenings before and, within minutes of arriving, Louise had picked a fight. "I don't know what you see in Steven," she'd said. "He's not that attractive. Why don't you find some-one your own age?" Nancy replied that she loved him, and the age difference didn't matter. "Why aren't you living with him, then, instead of camping in George's spare room, which is weird and unnatural," Louise challenged. Her toe was tapping and her pupils were huge. Nancy knew there was no point in talking rationally to her when she was like that. She tried to shift the conversation to other topics, but Louise was edgy and aggressive, so after the first drink, Nancy had made her excuses and left.

She told Joe that she believed Louise's unpredictable moods were caused by the vitamin shots she was self-administering, which contained amphetamines, and asked if he knew anyone on her side of the family who might be able to intervene.

Joe shook his head. "I've never met Louise's mom or dad, and I can't think of anyone else." He hesitated. "You haven't tried these injections yourself, have you?"

Nancy punched his arm playfully. "Course not. My only vice is champagne," she said, and saw relief flash across his eyes.

"I know lots of young people experiment with drugs these days," he explained. "I'm not such a fuddy-duddy that I would read you the riot act if you smoked a bit of marijuana, but I've always thought you had a sensible head on your shoulders. Lou-ise, on the other hand . . . she seems more . . ." He sought the right word. "Fragile, I suppose. Vulnerable. As if she has the word 'victim' stamped on her forehead, like a sign inviting men to take advantage of her."

Nancy had never thought of Louise that way. To her, she'd seemed cool and worldly because she was older and lived in the city and wore fashionable clothes. Teenagers were so shallow. She remembered believing her entire life would work out if only she could get a pair of Capri-style jeans like Louise's. Then her mom bought her some for Christmas that year, and of course they made no difference at all.

Everyone loved the show Nancy had chosen, a musical called *1776*, about the Declaration of Independence. When she glanced around, she saw that the boys were every bit as engrossed as the adults. During the intermission they asked loads of questions: Was it true that John Adams had to persuade the thirteen colonies to sign a declaration, and that Thomas Jefferson wrote it, and was that really how it all started?

Joe had booked an Italian restaurant for dinner, and before Nancy could open the menu, he ordered a bottle of champagne. A waiter brought it and popped the cork with a flourish. She grinned, touched by the extravagance. Joe was normally careful with money, so it meant all the more when he splurged.

Over dinner, Nancy got a chance to talk to her stepbrothers, asking them about school, their friends, their favorite sports, and what shows they liked to watch on television. She didn't know any boys their age but found them easy to talk to, easy to love. Like her, they were keen swimmers and she challenged them to a race that summer in the lake near their home.

"I used to be fast," she warned. "You'd better get in shape."

Joe was quiet as they ate, and Nancy saw him watching Steven out of the corner of his eye, as if trying to make him out. She guessed he was concerned for her and wondering about Steven's intentions. She wished she could confide in him but didn't want him to think badly of her, or of Steven.

After dinner, they walked up Broadway, through the surging crowds of theatergoers, and the boys begged to see virtually every show they passed. Nancy could tell they were happy. It had been four years since their mother died and she guessed they scarcely remembered her. She was lucky to have twenty-one years' worth of memories, and the benefit of all the wisdom and love her mother had crammed into that time. If Joe was right in thinking she had a sensible head on her shoulders, that was why.

She felt pensive as they reached the station. The boys insisted she come to see their sleeper car, wanting to show her the fold-out bunk beds and the tiny sink in the corner. They were lovely kids. She had enjoyed their company, relished the feeling that she was still part of a family even without her mom. She had tears in her eyes as the train pulled out, and Steven wrapped his arms around her from behind.

* * *

THE FOLLOWING MORNING, Nancy woke to the sound of his voice talking on the telephone. She got up to use the bathroom and couldn't help overhearing snatches.

"Did you notice that Willis Reed was limping when he came out, but he still got the first two baskets? . . . Yeah, me too. They're definitely the best defensive team in the league."

He must be talking to his son about the previous day's game. He'd watched the highlights on George's TV when they got in. She smiled to herself. When she emerged from the bathroom, the basketball talk was continuing.

"Red Holzman has definitely made a difference. He knows

how to nurture the younger players because he used to be a scout. . . . I'll be home for the next game," he said. "See you at dinner, buddy. Can you put your mom on the line?"

Nancy knew she shouldn't listen but something made her hesitate.

"Hi," he said, his voice deeper, more businesslike. "Yeah, I was in Chicago yesterday, Detroit today, but I'll be home at five-ish."

Nancy covered her mouth with her hand in shock at the glibness of the lie. He didn't stumble.

"It's been a long slog—all work and no play—but worth it for the contacts I've made," he told her. "Are you OK, hon? What's up?"

Nancy noted the casual endearment. Stomach churning, she tiptoed back to the bedroom and slid under the covers. She'd assumed he told Jeanette the truth when he was spending time with her. Why wouldn't he if they had an arrangement? But he'd lied to her about working this weekend. Would he lie to her about the money he'd spent on Nancy's birthday present?

Nancy considered confronting him about what she'd overheard, but decided she didn't want to spoil what had otherwise been a happy weekend. Besides, she could imagine his reply: best to keep the peace at home for their son's sake. She understood that. What shocked her most was that he was capable of lying so fluently. Might he be lying to her too?

"Jeanette's not feeling well," he said when he came into the bedroom five minutes later. "So I need to head off. Sorry I can't spend the day with you." He lay down on top of her, kissing the tip of her nose.

"What's wrong?" Nancy asked.

"Woman trouble," he said, making a face. He rose and began to get dressed.

Nancy wondered if Jeanette got "woman trouble" every month but didn't ask. She didn't want to know any intimate details.

"That was a perfect weekend," Steven said before he left. "What more could a man ask for? A beautiful girl, a great night out on the town, and then the news that the Knicks won."

"At least I got top billing on that list," Nancy said, quietly.

"You've got top billing on all my lists," he said in a jovial tone and kissed her on the lips.

"Really?" she asked, drawing back to look into his eyes, but he wouldn't meet her gaze.

CHAPTER 32

Jacqueline

Hotel Navarro, 1969

The *Love Machine* tour kicked off in New York, and Jacqueline mentally switched on her "public face." She had her usual carapace: plenty of new Pucci dresses and pantsuits, wigs and falls, and dozens of sets of her trademark false eyelashes. She also had a supply of sleeping pills and dexies to regulate her energy but decided not to have any more vitamin shots. Aside from their including amphetamines, her oncologist had warned her they contained estrogen, which could trigger a return of the breast cancer.

Her publicist gave her a list of the appearances she'd booked and Jacqueline read it, nodding her head in agreement until she got to a television talk show scheduled for fall, where they wanted her to appear alongside Jackie Collins. *So she was coming to promote her book in the States, was she?*

"Who organized this?" she demanded, pointing to the page. Appearing with Miss Collins would be akin to endorsing her novels and inviting readers to compare them, and she refused to do that. Apart from anything else, Jackie was about twenty years younger and would look much better on camera.

"It's not a bad idea, is it?" the publicist faltered. "I've read her book and it's a terrific story." Her face fell at Jacqueline's expression. "I mean, nothing compared to yours, but . . ."

"Get this show canceled," Jacqueline ordered. "No way will I appear with that woman."

"Of course," the publicist agreed, making a note on a lengthy list.

* * *

JACQUELINE LAUNCHED INTO the usual round of radio and television talk shows. She had requested some bookstore signings so she could talk to "her people" but the first two were spoiled by creeps. One revolting middle-aged man with camel lips asked if she wanted to join his swingers' club and pressed her for her personal telephone number, refusing to take no for an answer until Irving threatened to call the cops. Another guy handed her a plastic dildo and suggested they might try it together, whereupon she hurled it at his head and screamed at him to get lost.

"Maybe you've gotten too famous for personal appearances without security," her publicist suggested.

It was a shame but she might be right, Jacqueline thought. Why did a couple of perverts have to ruin it for everyone else?

Just three weeks after publication, *The Love Machine* hit number one on the bestseller list and Jacqueline felt vindicated. The critics were offensive as usual, but she was at the top again. Film rights sold for a whopping $1.25 million, and the book stayed at number one right into the summer. The fund for her son was growing rapidly, and she had already covered the losses incurred in the settlement with Bernie Geis. She should have been on top of the world, but her mood was anxious. Always there were the downsides, reminders of the price women paid for being in the public eye.

On July twenty-third, Irving's birthday, Jacqueline was booked to appear on *The David Frost Show*, along with her friends Rex Reed and Nora Ephron, and a journalist called Jimmy Breslin. It should have been a lively, informal chat, but at the last minute, while they were already on set and the makeup girl was giving Jacqueline a final dab of powder, the producer came to say that Breslin had got stuck in traffic and they were bringing in a literary critic called John Simon to take his place. Jacqueline had never heard of John Simon, but she was an old hand at these shows, so she wasn't concerned.

The first half was fun. Rex and Nora teased Jacqueline with speculation about the real-life people who had inspired her characters in *The Love Machine* and she gracefully sidestepped the questioning. David Frost pointed out the way Jacqueline had revolutionized book promotion with her round-the-country tours, and she explained that since reviewers were generally snooty about her books, it forced her to reach out directly to readers. Her art wasn't the kind that appealed to literary critics, but, as the bestseller lists showed, it did appeal to vast swathes of the public.

John Simon had been largely silent up to this point, but suddenly he challenged her. "Do you really believe your writing is art?" he asked. "Shouldn't you be honest and admit that you are writing trash to make money?"

Jacqueline caught her breath and turned to him. "Who even *are* you?" she asked. "I've never heard of you."

"I'm one of those critics you're talking about," he replied.

"And have you read my books?" she challenged.

"I forced myself through the first forty pages of *Valley of the Dolls*," he said, "then had to give up before I lost the will to live."

Jacqueline was incensed. "How can you call yourself a critic when you only read one-tenth of the bestselling book of 1966 and 1967?"

He folded his arms. "How can you call yourself a writer when you churn out pages of cardboard characters in predictable situations, with no style whatsoever, and call it a novel?"

"*Little* man," Jacqueline retaliated. "I am a storyteller. Are you not satisfied by that? It sounds as if you need to learn about the book industry before you open your mouth and vomit bile."

David Frost interrupted to guide them back to safer territory, asking if there was to be a film of *The Love Machine*, and Jacqueline told him there most certainly was, and she looked forward to helping cast the role of Robin Stone, the man women couldn't resist. "Why don't you audition, David?" she quipped, and he smoothed his hair and puffed out his chest, saying, tongue in cheek, that he just might.

When the show finished, Jacqueline refused to go to the greenroom if John Simon was going to be there. She was furious that she had been subjected to such rudeness on air, and complained to her publicist.

"It wasn't her fault," Irving intervened. "Let's go straight to dinner. I've booked a table at Danny's Hideaway and he won't mind if we're early."

Jacqueline waved goodbye to Nora and Rex, and they hurried out to catch a taxi across town. Loads of television stars hung out at Danny's, from Ed Sullivan to Jack Carter, and the eponymous owner, Danny Stradella, wandered around, topping up glasses and chatting with his clientele. They served a fabulous filet mignon, and Jacqueline felt the need to get her teeth into some red meat to work off her fury.

After dinner and a few cocktails they went home and watched television in bed. Irving soon fell asleep, but Jacqueline was still riled about the show and didn't feel sleepy. She flicked over to the Johnny Carson show and saw he was interviewing Truman Capote about his book *In Cold Blood*. Jacqueline didn't like Capote, and didn't approve of the fact that he had written a fictionalized account of the real murders of a Texas family just seven years earlier. She felt it was in extremely bad taste. Capote was a poisonous little man with no scruples, in her opinion, and she couldn't understand why anyone took him seriously.

Suddenly she heard her name being mentioned and she sat up in bed.

"Jacqueline Susann?" Capote said. "With her sleazy gowns and wigs, she looks like a truck driver in drag."

She screamed in rage and shook Irving awake. "Guess what Truman Capote just said about me on live television?" She repeated it, trembling with anger. "How dare he! I'm going to sue. I'm not putting up with that."

Irving rubbed his eyes. "I know his agent, Swifty Lazar," he murmured. "Let me call him in the morning and ask for an apology."

"That's not enough," she insisted. "I want damages. I want him financially ruined."

Irving went back to sleep, but Jacqueline lay awake, brooding over the insult and plotting her revenge. She never attacked other writers in public; she respected their craft, even if their work wasn't to her taste. She knew the laws of libel and defamation and was sure she could prove Truman's personal insults would cause her "reputational harm," by bringing her into "ridicule," which could negatively affect her professional occupation. She rehearsed the words in her head and couldn't wait till nine the following morning when she would get Irving to call their solicitor.

The lawyer was frustratingly negative about her chances of winning a lawsuit. "It would be hard to prove defamation, and would be costly for all concerned," he advised. "Meanwhile, Mr. Capote's comments would reach a wider audience through the trial. And both of your private lives would be raked through in court."

Jacqueline felt sick from lack of sleep combined with the dexy she had swallowed half an hour earlier. What if Truman somehow found out about her son? Would he use that against her? She wouldn't put it past the loathsome little man. She'd heard him use the term "refrigerator moms" in an interview about his book, *In Cold Blood*, and she could imagine his glee if he found out he had grounds to hurl the insult at her.

"Get back to me when you've found a way to make him suffer," she told the lawyer, "because I am *not* letting this matter drop."

When it was nine a.m. LA time, she made Irving call Swifty Lazar, and sat beside him eavesdropping on the conversation.

"You'd better warn Truman that he should brace himself for a massive suit," Irving said. "What the hell was he thinking of?"

"I haven't spoken to him yet this morning," Swifty replied, "but my advice to him will be that if you launch a suit, he should countersue because I heard Jacqueline mimicking his accent on a radio show not long ago and saying he was 'a homosexual who was jealous of her productivity.'"

Irving covered the receiver and asked her, "Did you say that?"

"I only spoke the truth," she snapped.

Irving talked to Swifty again. "You and I don't want to turn this into an ongoing slanging match that will be damaging for both. See if you can get Truman to apologize, won't you?"

Jacqueline punched him on the leg. "I still want to sue," she insisted.

"Let's wait and see," Irving cautioned.

She felt he wasn't taking her distress seriously enough, so she called George, but he gave her the same advice. "Don't sue, Jacqueline. You'll make yourself a laughingstock. Take the high ground."

She calmed down a little; she almost always listened to George. But a few days later, Truman gave an interview to *After Dark* magazine in which he said that all his attorney would have to do to win the case against Jacqueline Susann would be to bring in a dozen truck drivers, dress them in drag, and get them to parade in front of the jury. Point proven!

Jacqueline got straight on the phone to her lawyer again and this time he agreed to write to Mr. Capote, warning him that his reply to their letter would dictate whether they took action or not.

When he replied, Truman was conciliatory, claiming his comments had been "bitchy perhaps, but not malicious."

"Pah!" Jacqueline spat. The fire had gone out of her initial rage, and she was beginning to realize a spat that kept her name in the gossip columns was no bad thing while she was publicizing a book. Everyone knew Truman was a grade-A bitch and most women would sympathize with her.

Irving had a word with Johnny Carson about the feud, and Johnny invited Jacqueline on *The Tonight Show* to give her response. She accepted, and spent most of the interview promoting *The Love Machine*, until Mr. Carson asked: "Now, why don't you tell us what you think of Truman?"

"I think he was one of our best presidents," she replied, and turned to wink at the studio audience. She had come out on top—but the memory of Truman's insult still stung.

* * *

ON AUGUST EIGHTH, Jacqueline and Irving landed in LA for the West Coast leg of the book tour. A limo took them to the Beverly Hills Hotel and, before unpacking, Jacqueline rushed out to visit the cat family in the back hedge. Five new kittens, who looked less than a week old, were scrabbling for their mom's teats, so tiny their eyes were still closed. "You've been busy," she cooed, offering chicken scraps to the nursing mom. She was too worn out to eat but managed to lift her head and lap some water from a saucer. "It will get easier," Jacqueline promised—but maybe it wouldn't. The chances of her keeping all five of her babies alive were slim, with coyotes and possibly even mountain lions in the vicinity.

As she wandered back into the hotel, she was remembering her son as a newborn: how sweet and perfect he had been, with no sign of anything wrong, and how fierce her compulsion to protect him. A receptionist interrupted her thoughts by handing her a message: Sharon Tate was having a few people over for a party that evening and wondered if she and Irving would like to come? Jacqueline had a full round of media appearances the following day, but she knew Sharon was heavily pregnant so it wouldn't be a late night and it would be fun to see her. In their room, she told Irving about the invitation and laid out a psychedelic jumpsuit to change into.

Just then there was a call to say that Rex Reed was in reception. Jacqueline rushed out to greet him and they ordered cocktails to drink by the pool. They laughed about the David Frost show debacle with John Simon, and Rex did a sidesplitting impersonation of Truman Capote. Jacqueline relaxed and allowed herself to order a second cocktail. Being around friends, especially a friend with a great sense of humor, was the best therapy after the stress of the last month.

A third round of drinks arrived—she wasn't sure who ordered them—and the sun set with a pinky-orange glow behind the palm trees that lined the pool. The water lapped against the side with a delicate sound that reminded her of the mother cat lapping from the saucer.

"We should be going," Irving said, checking his watch.

Jacqueline downed the rest of her drink, stood up from her chair, and swayed, unsteady on her feet. Rex caught her elbow.

"I feel a little tipsy," she giggled. "Oops-a-daisy!"

Up in their suite, she lay down on the bed and realized she was more than just a little drunk. "I don't think I can make it to Sharon's," she told Irving. "You go without me."

"Of course I'm not going without you," he said. "I'll call and make our excuses."

Before he finished the call, she was asleep.

Next morning, she was wakened by the ringing of the phone. It was Rex Reed. "Have you heard the news?" he asked. "Sharon Tate and her guests were murdered last night."

"What?" Jacqueline mumbled, foggy with sleep.

"It's on all the radio stations," he continued. "They weren't just killed, they were butchered. The killers wrote insults in blood on the walls."

Jacqueline dropped the phone and shook Irving awake, then they turned on the radio to listen. It was true. There was speculation it had been carried out by religious fanatics. How could they slaughter a pregnant woman?

She burst into tears and couldn't stop crying. For the first time in her professional career, she asked her publicist to cancel her events for the day. She knew she would be too devastated to speak. Had it not been for Rex turning up at the hotel, then her drinking a couple too many cocktails, she would have been there, among the dead.

Why Sharon? Was it something to do with Roman's films? Or was it simply the price of fame? She knew her publisher received sacksful of letters addressed to her from religious nuts, telling her she'd burn in the fires of hell. The staff tried to weed them out before forwarding correspondence to her, but a couple had snuck through and the naked hatred in them had been shocking and terrifying.

Then there were those perverts in the bookstores. . . . Might one of them decide to kill her, just as Sharon had been killed? Was she safe in public, or could some maniac wielding a knife or a gun attack her, in the belief that slaughtering her guaranteed his passage to heaven?

She spent the day locked in their suite, crying and chain-smoking and calling friends, trying to make sense of a world in which such an atrocity could happen.

CHAPTER 33

Jackie

Manhattan, 1969

Jackie flew to New York alone to meet her US publishers. Oscar had given her the keys to an apartment he rented just off Broadway and she took a taxi there from JFK. There were three flights of stone steps to climb, then a complicated lock to grapple with before she swung open the door and dragged her suitcase into a sunny room with a wooden floor and brick walls. It was functional and unadorned: table, chairs, couch, bed, and a basic kitchen and bathroom.

It felt strange to be in a place where her husband spent time without her and she snooped around, checking inside drawers and cupboards. She'd been suspicious that he might entertain other women here, but this was no love nest. The toiletries in the bathroom were strictly masculine and there wasn't a stray hair clip or nail file to indicate a female presence. Damn her father! It was Joe Collins who had given her such a cynical view of men.

Someone knocked on the door, startling her.

"I live opposite," an elderly woman told her. "I took in this box that was delivered for you yesterday. It was sitting in the hall, just waiting for someone to steal it."

"Thank you *so much*," Jackie gushed. "That's very kind. I'm *so* grateful."

"Of course," she said, backing away and looking slightly baffled, as if unused to the excessive nature of British politeness.

Jackie had asked Robert Armstrong to send over a box with twenty copies of *The Stud* so she could hand out previews to US booksellers without weighing down her luggage. There they were, nestled together, their black covers adorned with a striking photograph of women's legs. She would take some with her to the meeting with her publisher tomorrow. Meanwhile, jet lag was kicking in and she needed to sleep.

The next morning, she had a bath and dressed carefully for her meeting. She applied her makeup, stuck on false lashes, fluffed out her hair, and sprayed on a sticky cloud of lacquer. "I'm an author going to meet my American publisher," she whispered to her reflection in the mirror. Who would have thought it? If only her mum had been alive. And Wallace; poor Wallace—he'd have been so excited, he'd have insisted on coming with her.

She didn't fancy trying her luck on the subway in case she got lost, but, according to a creased street map she found in the apartment, the Heywood & Bradshaw office was only a few blocks away. She set off, carrying ten of the books in a bulky shoulder bag, high heels clicking on the pavement.

The blocks were longer than they looked on the map, she soon discovered, and the sun was strong, so she was hot and bedraggled by the time she got there.

She was met in reception by her editor, Michael Loveday, a man who looked to be in his thirties, with a fleshy face and strawlike blond hair. He led her to the elevator, asking about her flight, and she told him it had passed quickly as she'd been reading *The Godfather* by Mario Puzo.

"We're very jealous of that book," he said. "The editor, William Targ, bought it based on the idea alone, without seeing a single word on the page, and his hunch paid off because its success has been phenomenal. That's what we're looking for—big ideas. And we believe you're an author who can deliver them."

He guided her into his office and asked a girl sitting outside to bring them coffee.

"What are you working on next?" he asked. "I mean, after *The Stud*—which I am planning to read soon."

"I don't have a title yet," she told him, "but I'm working on a novel set in Hollywood. It's about the way actresses are treated on film sets, with all the crew crowding round like voyeurs whenever there are nude scenes. It's partly based on my observations when I spent time there in my teens."

"Brilliant!" he exclaimed. "Serve it up with lots of sex and glamour and we'll be happy to publish it." He glanced at his watch, just as a pretty girl with long dark hair, wearing a burnt-orange minidress and white vinyl Courrèges-style boots came in. "And right on cue, here's your publicist," he said. "Melanie—meet Jackie Collins."

Melanie looked fresh out of college, but the schedule she handed Jackie was impressively full, and she had all the sparkle of a successful PR person.

"We're meeting some booksellers for drinks at the Colony at five this afternoon," she said, "then tomorrow there are interviews with women's magazines. *Cosmopolitan* wants to photograph you in some fabulous clothes they're bringing. . . ."

Jackie pulled a face. "Really?" She still wasn't confident about her looks, even in full makeup. When photographers caught her at odd angles, her eyes seemed too small and her chin too square, her shoulders broad and mannish.

"Don't worry! You're so beautiful, everything will look amazing," Melanie insisted, and Jackie got the impression things were often "beautiful" and "fabulous" and "amazing" in Melanie's world. "After that I have some radio lined up. We're going to keep you busy."

Jackie liked the sound of that. "I wonder if you could also introduce me to the team here?" she asked. "I particularly wanted to meet Nancy White. She was the editor who discovered my book, wasn't she?"

"Nancy's not an editor," Michael replied. "Just an assistant." His tone was a little short and Jackie wondered if she had committed a faux pas.

"Shall I give her the guided tour?" Melanie asked quickly, and, when he consented, she led Jackie out to the corridor, chatting brightly, scarcely pausing for breath.

She introduced Jackie to the boss, Bill Heywood, the production team, the designers, and some of the sales team. As they approached an alcove where a blond girl was bent over a manuscript, Melanie said: "Now here's Nancy."

Nancy stood up and Melanie made the introductions.

Jackie clutched her hand. "I'm so grateful to you for recommending my book. Getting an American deal has meant the world to me. Thank you."

Nancy's cheeks colored. "I've just read a proof of *The Stud* and I adored it as well. I read it in one sitting, then went back to reread it the following day."

Jackie delved into her shoulder bag and pulled out a copy of *The Stud*. "Let me sign a finished one for you," she said, and leaned over the desk to write: *To Nancy, with warmest thanks for your support! Jackie Collins x.*

"I love the way you reverse the gender roles in your novels," Nancy said, "with your strong women and hapless men. In some ways they remind me of Jane Austen. She was also merciless toward her male characters."

"I love it!" Jackie laughed. "Jane Austen but with sex. We should put that on the front cover." She wanted to carry on chatting, but Melanie was hopping from foot to foot and glancing at her watch.

"Are you coming to the Colony with us later?" Jackie asked

Nancy. "I do hope so. It's because of you that I'm published here, so I should buy you a drink at the very least."

Nancy glanced at Melanie, who smiled encouragement and exclaimed, "Yes, do come. Fabulous!"

* * *

A LARGE ROUND table had been reserved in the middle of the Colony and Jackie sat down, greeting the booksellers, a dozen or so of them, all men. Melanie ordered drinks, then asked Jackie to say a few words to introduce *The Stud*. She was nervous but took a deep breath, pretending she was an actress giving a performance.

"The main character in *The Stud* is based on Johnny Gold, a business partner of my husband's—but the real Johnny is much nicer," she began. "As a woman, I'm fascinated by what motivates men to treat sexual conquest as a competitive sport, with the winner being the one who gets the most notches on his bedpost. I wonder . . ." She looked around the table, catching eyes with one after the other. "Which of you is the most successful stud of the New York book world?"

Names were called out, with jostling and banter, and one youngish, bearded man was nominated by the others.

"Do you see yourself as a stud?" Jackie asked him, in a teasing tone.

"I enjoy women's company, certainly," he said, meeting her gaze directly, and she thought to herself: *Yup, he's a player.*

"It's not so much their company as their . . ." another quipped, using his hands to draw a curvaceous female shape in the air.

Jackie glanced at Melanie and Nancy, hoping they weren't embarrassed by the ribaldry.

"Have you read Jacqueline Susann's *The Love Machine*?" another bookseller asked her. "It features a stud too."

"I *adore* Robin Stone," Jackie said straight away. "I'm a huge fan of Miss Susann's work."

"Robin is based on a TV director friend of hers," Nancy told them. "And I believe he knows Johnny Gold, your muse. I heard they met in London."

"That's quite a coincidence!" Jackie exclaimed. "We should ask if they keep scoresheets so we can judge who's the greatest stud of all."

A fresh round of drinks was ordered while Jackie was still sipping her first. They talked about readers' reactions to *The World Is Full of Married Men*, then one bookseller asked her, "Do you think it ever works out when men leave their wives for their mistresses?"

Jackie laughed. "Are you asking for yourself?" she responded. "Or for a friend?"

"Definitely a friend," he said quickly, his face turning beet red.

"Here's what I know," Jackie said. "Mistresses save more marriages than any marriage counselor. The husband feels good about himself because another woman finds him desirable. It puts him in a better mood at home and that has knock-on effects. He'll argue less with his wife. He'll take care of himself so he might begin to seem more attractive to her, and sooner or later their romance is rekindled—all thanks to the mistress."

"Surely some men leave their wives to marry their mistresses?" another bookseller asked.

"Not often," Jackie replied. "In ninety percent of cases it's the wife who leaves the marriage. Trust me on that!" She had done her research. "And if a man leaves, he hardly ever ends up with the original mistress—he finds someone else. The mistress role is terminated as her services are no longer required—until he gets bored with his new wife and looks for the next mistress."

"So why do women bother having affairs with married men?" someone else asked. "What's in it for them?"

Jackie considered: "I suppose they assume he will have experience so he won't be a total dunce in the bedroom." They laughed and she noticed a couple of them exchanging glances.

Nancy frowned and piped up: "Some men don't tell you they're married when they hit on you. What would you say about them?"

Jackie caught a flicker in her expression and wondered if she was talking from personal experience. "There are plenty of dishonest men out there, and the problem for us girls is that men don't wear wedding rings. I always look for little signs: a well-pressed shirt either says he's rich enough to use a laundry service or he has a wife." They laughed. "Married men look at their watches a lot as the evening progresses. Most of all, a refusal to give you his home number is a dead giveaway."

Nancy nodded and took a gulp of her drink. Suddenly Melanie nudged Nancy and whispered something to her, then they both swiveled toward the restaurant door. Nancy scraped back her chair and hurried across to greet a couple who had just walked in and were hovering, as if waiting to be seated. Jackie watched as Nancy spoke to them. Suddenly the woman broke away and advanced toward their table.

When she got close, Jackie recognized the distinctive raven hair and toothy smile of her fellow author, Jacqueline Susann. She strode up to them.

"My goodness, this looks like fun. How are you, Eric? Pete?" She greeted the booksellers by name, then turned to Jackie, who rose to shake her hand.

Nancy made a hurried introduction: "Jacqueline, this is Jackie Collins." She turned to Jackie: "Meet Jacqueline Susann."

"Welcome to New York!" Jacqueline said, with a broad smile.

"How wonderful to see you again!" Jackie exclaimed. She felt intimidated by the apparent ambush but determined not to show it. "Please, won't you join us?"

"I'd love to gate-crash your party—you and I have so much to talk about—but I'm afraid my husband and I are meeting friends. Why don't you give me a call in the morning and perhaps we can have coffee?" Jacqueline scrabbled in her silver evening bag and pulled out a business card, then wrote a number on the back. "Not before ten," she said. "But definitely before twelve."

Jackie blinked at the bossiness of the tone, but she was intrigued. "I surely will," she said.

As Jacqueline walked away, Jackie heard Melanie hiss to Nancy: "How did she know we were here?"

"She says she called me at the office and someone told her," Nancy replied. "Sorry!"

"Is she going to eat me alive?" Jackie asked Nancy, keeping her voice low.

Nancy smiled. "She's definitely checking you out . . . but I'm sure you two will get along like a house on fire."

* * *

JACKIE WASN'T ENTIRELY reassured by Nancy's response, but the next morning she dialed Jacqueline's number just after ten, as she'd been instructed. Irving answered and told her Jacqueline was working but suggested she come to their apartment at five for cocktails, and gave the address. Jackie felt nervous. She'd met plenty of famous actors through her dad's work, but being entertained by a multimillion-copy-selling author was daunting.

Next, Melanie arrived in a taxi to take her to the *Cosmopolitan* photo shoot, at the publisher's West Fifty-Seventh Street office. Jackie succumbed to the ministrations of the magazine's hairstylist and makeup artist and slipped into the outfits they supplied. One she particularly liked was a knee-length leopard-print coat teamed with white calf-high boots. Oscar had given her an envelope containing a few hundred dollars, instructing her to "spoil herself," so she asked the stylist if she might buy the coat. The stylist called the designer and came back to say she could have it at half price, for two hundred dollars. Jackie nearly fainted. She had never spent that much on a coat. But she loved it, and she had the cash in her bag. . . . It was an investment in her career, she decided, one that would help to boost her confidence.

Irving greeted her at the door of the Navarro apartment and led her through to the sitting room, where Jacqueline looked as glamorous as a Golden Age movie star in a pair of pink silk lounging pajamas and high-heeled marabou slippers.

"I love your coat," Jacqueline said straight away, reaching out to stroke the fabric. "Take a seat and name your poison."

"Would it be too boring to ask for tea?" Jackie asked. "I'm still on UK time and I'll fall asleep if I drink alcohol." Irving went to the kitchen. "What a lovely apartment!" she said, taking off her coat and smoothing it carefully over the back of the couch.

"We've always lived in hotel apartments," Jacqueline replied. "I don't do housework."

"I like you already." Jackie laughed. An obese black poodle climbed onto the couch beside her and thrust its nose in her crotch, having a good sniff. She crossed her legs and patted its head, whereupon it rolled onto its back, legs spread, and demanded a tummy rub.

"How are you coping with the media madness?" Jacqueline asked. "I mean, the questions about your morality and whether you are causing the nation's children to become depraved."

Jackie exhaled loudly. "It's exhausting. I know you handle this brilliantly, but I'm still figuring out how to cope. It feels as if I have to stay on the ball because they're trying to trick me into saying something scandalous they can throw back at me."

"You bet they are," Jacqueline agreed. "Don't let your guard down for one second. Have you done any TV yet?"

"My publicist says I'm not famous enough for tele," Jackie said, and noticed Jacqueline and Irving exchanging glances.

"How's your book doing in the States?" Jacqueline asked.

"I haven't asked about sales figures," Jackie replied. "I'm too nervous!"

"Oh, but you must!" Jacqueline insisted. "Keep your publishers on their toes or they'll take their feet off the gas pedal."

"I haven't made the *New York Times* list at any rate, not like you," Jackie said.

"That's easy," Jacqueline replied. "Irving, do you have a copy of that list?" Irving disappeared into a side room. "A hundred and twenty-five bookshops provide the data from which the bestseller list is compiled. Get your American friends to buy lots of books from those stores and—hey presto!" She snapped her fingers.

Irving brought her a copy of the list and Jackie thanked him before folding it into her handbag, wondering how on earth she would find a hundred and twenty-five American friends to buy books at all those locations.

Irving served her tea next. He'd put milk in and she usually took lemon, but she didn't mention it.

"Why did you start writing novels?" Jacqueline asked. "Did the acting work dry up?"

Jackie smiled to herself. Usually she was the one who asked the questions. Jacqueline was stealing her tactics!

"After my first marriage ended, I was a single mother and

needed to earn a living, but B movie schedules don't tend to accommodate babies." She shrugged. "I've remarried now, but I still feel more secure making my own money rather than relying on my husband's."

Jacqueline nodded approval. "Your new husband is a producer and nightclub owner, I heard?"

"He is. He's currently setting up a new private members club in London, which is going to be called Tramp—after the Charlie Chaplin persona."

"So he's not short of money?" Jacqueline asked, and Jackie was taken aback. In England no one would ask such a question, but either Americans were brasher than Brits or this woman was a particularly forthright type. Jacqueline continued without waiting for an answer. "Still, I hope Heywood & Bradshaw is paying you enough. Who's your agent, and is he a shark?"

"I don't have an agent," Jackie confessed, and they looked horrified. "I got my UK deal through a friend of my father's, then I was picked up by Heywood & Bradshaw because Nancy White wrote requesting a copy of my novel from my UK publisher. I think you know her? She was there yesterday at the Colony."

"Nancy discovered it, did she?" Irving said. He and Jacqueline looked at each other and Jackie couldn't interpret their expressions. What was the story there?

"You must get an agent so they don't rip you off," Jacqueline advised, and she and Irving started tossing names between themselves. "Paul Gitlin perhaps? She needs to sell movie rights."

"She definitely wants someone with West Coast connections," Irving said.

Jackie smiled: they were talking about her as if she weren't there, as if boosting her sales in America was their new pet project. She found them quirky characters. Jacqueline seemed to be the boss, while Irving hovered around obeying orders, but she knew surface impressions could be misleading.

Before she left, she invited them to the London opening of Tramp in December, and they promised to be there.

"Cheerio!" she called on her way out, and Jacqueline laughed at the British word.

"*Cheerio*—you mean like the breakfast cereal?" she called. "You Brits are weird." Jackie could still hear her chuckling as she walked down the hallway to the elevator.

She decided she liked them. Jacqueline might be bossy but she seemed well meaning, and there was certainly no one better placed to give her advice on how to become a bestselling author.

CHAPTER 34

Nancy

Manhattan, 1969

The day after Jackie Collins visited the office, Nancy was at her desk, bent over a novel she was editing, when the receptionist called to say that a Mrs. Jeanette Bailey was in reception and wanted to talk to her. Nancy's heart skipped a beat. What was Jeanette doing there? Her first thought was that Steven might have been in an accident. *Please no!*

She sat for a few moments, deathly still, trying to compose herself. A host of possible explanations flitted through her mind. Perhaps Steven had told Jeanette he wanted a divorce and she'd come to decide if Nancy was a suitable stepmom? Golly, she hoped it wasn't that! Maybe she wanted them to be friends?

When she reached the lobby, she saw an auburn-haired woman in a black trench coat sitting opposite reception, and beside her was a young boy reading a comic book. The woman spotted her and stood. Nancy stepped forward and held out her hand.

"I'm Nancy White," she introduced herself, then turned: "And this must be Darren." He was the spitting image of Steven, even down to the military haircut. He grinned at her and her heart turned over; she knew that grin.

"We wondered if you'd care to join us for a soda?" Jeanette asked. "I spotted a soda parlor across the street." Nancy couldn't read her tone: it was polite but not especially warm.

Darren tugged her arm. "You said ice cream, Mom."

"You can have ice cream," she agreed, ruffling his hair.

Nancy followed them to the soda parlor, and they shuffled into a booth and scanned the laminated menu. Nancy asked for a Coke, while Jeanette ordered a coffee, and she let Darren request a banana split.

Once the order had been taken, Jeanette said, "You're probably wondering why we came to visit you today."

Nancy nodded, chewing the inside of her lip.

"It's because we're worried that Steven has been working so much *overtime*." She emphasized the word "overtime," her eyes signaling to Nancy that it was code. "I know he works with you a couple of evenings a week, sometimes even on weekends, and Darren and I wondered if you could please tell him to stop working so hard so he can spend more time with his family."

"Goodness!" Nancy exclaimed, taken aback, her cheeks hot. "I don't force Steven to work overtime. You should probably talk to him about it."

Jeanette's smile didn't reach her eyes. "Darren, tell Nancy about all the things your pop has missed because he was busy working."

Darren's lip quivered. "He didn't come to the Harvest Festival at school when I made a speech. And he didn't see me playing basketball for the school team."

Jeanette's tone was cool now. "He's often not there to help with math homework, and I'm hopeless at math. It's become a problem for our family."

Nancy was thrown for a loop. She wondered if Steven knew about this visit, but guessed not or he would have warned her. "Steven told me he had an arrangement with you regarding his overtime and that you didn't mind," she said, choosing her words with care so that Darren wouldn't guess the real subject of the conversation.

Jeanette held her gaze. "You're younger than I expected," she said, "but surely you can't be that naïve?"

Darren opened his comic book, *A Boy Named Charlie Brown*,

and pored over the pages. Nancy watched his little face as his eyes flicked from one frame to the next, totally absorbed. He was a very sweet kid.

"I'm sorry," she said. "Perhaps I misunderstood." She could feel tears behind her eyelids and blinked hard. "I thought he loved *working overtime*." She used Jeanette's code.

"I expect he does," Jeanette said, and now there was maybe a trace of sympathy. "But he has responsibilities to his family. I—"

She was interrupted when the waiter brought their order. Darren was overjoyed by his banana split, which had two scoops of vanilla ice cream inside a halved banana, with a squiggle of pink syrup and a glacé cherry on top.

"We wanted another, you know," Jeanette said, looking at Darren, who was too engrossed in his dessert to pay attention. "But I kept miscarrying. I think Steven has found that very hard to deal with. Perhaps that's why he has sought escape in *overtime*."

"I'm sorry," Nancy said. Why had Steven never told her that? She'd thought they were honest with each other, but that was a huge omission.

"The last one was in April this year, when Steven was away for the weekend. I had to ask a neighbor to look after him"— Jeanette nodded toward Darren—"while I went to the hospital because I had no way of getting in touch with his father."

Nancy felt cold from head to foot. The last miscarriage must have been over her birthday weekend—she remembered Steven saying that Jeanette had "woman trouble." But that meant they must have slept together earlier this year. She felt sick to her stomach. "I thought . . ." she began, then stopped. She had never questioned Steven's assertion that he and his wife slept in separate bedrooms. If they were still sleeping together, that changed everything.

"I know. He doesn't come across as a playboy," Jeanette said.

Darren glanced up at the word, then continued eating. He had an ice cream moustache.

"He's sensitive and caring. He listens to women and treats them as equals," Jeanette said. "These are the qualities I fell for. But he is also capable of deception. There are two sides to the man."

"He told me that you were working overtime too," Nancy said. "Was that not true?"

"No, I don't have a job," Jeanette replied, with a firm shake of her head.

Nancy believed her instinctively. It meant that everything she thought she knew about Steven during their entire relationship had been based on a lie. She remembered the condom in his wallet that first night: Why did he carry a condom if he and Jeanette were trying for a baby? Had there been other women before her?

She swallowed hard. "I obviously got the wrong impression," she said. "I'm very sorry. I'll make sure Steven doesn't work overtime with me anymore." She could feel tears coming. "I can't believe . . ." She shivered.

Jeanette reached across the table and put her hand on Nancy's. "I know the man," she said. "I can see how it could have happened and I don't blame you."

"Do you mind if I go now?" Nancy said, standing up. She fumbled in her purse for some change, but Jeanette raised a hand to stop her and said, "I'll pay."

"Nice to meet you, Darren," Nancy told him, before she hurried toward the door. The last words she heard were Darren asking, "Mom, what's a playboy?"

The tears came as soon as Nancy reached the street. They streamed down her face and she gulped back a sob. She couldn't possibly return to the office. Instead, she broke into a run and sprinted three blocks to the nearest subway station, then jumped on a train to George's apartment, trying to hold her emotions in check until she was behind closed doors.

She unlocked the door, poured herself a vodka and Coke from his bar, then sat on the couch, curled in a ball, and cried so hard that her chest ached and her breathing came in ragged gasps. It was all gone. Everything. And she was alone again.

CHAPTER 35

Jacqueline
Manhattan, 1969

Jacqueline rang Nancy, intending to ask why she hadn't mentioned that she was the one who had recommended that Heywood & Bradshaw publish Jackie Collins's novel. But as soon as Nancy answered, Jacqueline could hear from the wobbliness of her voice that she'd been crying. "What's happened?" she asked, and it took hardly any nudging before Nancy confessed that Steven, the mystery boyfriend, was married. The story of his deception poured out in a long emotional stream, up to the meeting with his wife and son earlier that day.

Of course! Jacqueline thought. With anyone else, she would have suspected earlier, but she'd thought Nancy too straitlaced to date a married man. The poor kid sounded grief-stricken, humiliated, and furious, all at once.

"I thought he was honest," she finished. "I thought he really loved me. But I guess I was wrong."

"I'm sure he loves you," Jacqueline said, "but no man is entirely honest when he's trying to get a girl into the sack. Look, it could have been a lot worse. You know the truth now. You'll feel bruised for a while, but you'll come out of it with your dignity intact so long as you stop seeing him. Call him tomorrow morning and say that's it. No final meetings for old time's sake. *Finito!*"

"I can't face talking to him," Nancy said. "I couldn't bear to hear more of his lies. I thought I would mail back the necklace he gave me for my birthday with a note telling him not to contact me ever again."

"Good girl!" Jacqueline said. "He'll keep trying for a while, but you stand firm." She had a couple of girlfriends who were never able to leave men. They kept going back for more, no matter how badly they were treated.

"You know him," Nancy continued. "Steven Bailey. He works at Bernie Geis."

"*Him!*" Jacqueline remembered a polite man, good at his job, pleasant-looking without being anything to write home about. "He didn't seem the Casanova type. I guess it's always the quiet ones who surprise you."

"I hope you don't think less of me," Nancy said, her voice cracking.

"On the contrary," Jacqueline assured her, "I think you're being very brave. Everyone should have their heart broken at least once. It's part of being human. But I hope that your turn's over, and your next boyfriend will be adorable."

"I'm not going to date again for a very long time," Nancy insisted.

"Keep an open mind," Jacqueline told her. "You never know what might be right around the corner." She still hoped Nancy and George would fall in love one day. She knew he cared about her; he often mentioned her with a tenderness in his tone, but she worried that being "roomies" could have gotten them too used to each other and ruined any chance of passion sparking.

Before they hung up, Jacqueline asked after Louise, and Nancy replied that she was rude and unpleasant whenever they met, so she guessed she was still injecting the vitamin shots.

"Bring her to the Navarro for a cocktail and a chat," Jacqueline suggested. "The Friday after next perhaps?"

She didn't bring up the initial purpose of her call, to have a word about Nancy's discovering Jackie Collins's novel. The girl had to do her best to impress in her new job, and Irving was right that Jackie's novels wouldn't damage her own sales. Anyway, Miss Collins seemed naïve about the publishing business, and the American market was tough to crack.

When the call was over, she felt sad for poor Nancy. Her mom and dad were dead, her first-ever boyfriend turned out to be a louse, and her cousin was a drug addict. If only she could protect her from the bad things in the world. She supposed parents felt this way when their children came to harm: you could protect them when they were at home, but you couldn't stop others treating them badly in the outside world. She worried constantly about her son. Was he safe around the other inmates at the institution, or were some of them capable of violence? Were all the staff kind to him? At least he would never have his heart broken, as Nancy had, because he would never know romantic love.

She decided she would go clothes shopping to buy Nancy a gift—a pretty dress, perhaps. She knew that no number of new outfits could make up for having your heart broken by your first love, but a dress might help a little.

CHAPTER 36

Jackie

Manhattan, 1969

Jackie's New York promotional trip was exhausting. She wasn't in the city long enough to adjust to New York time, so she kept awakening at four in the morning and felt tired by seven in the evening. Melanie accompanied her in taxis from one event to the next, and each time she had to dig out her snappiest repartee and widest smile. Jacqueline Susann seemed to revel in being a public persona, but Jackie found it draining and yearned to get home and curl up on the sofa with her girls. She vowed she wouldn't set foot outside the front door for at least a week.

On the final night, Melanie took her across town to a radio station, where she was to be interviewed by a presenter called Long John Nebel.

"What's he like?" Jackie asked. "Is it going to be a hostile interview?"

"You'll be fine if you're as honest and funny as you have been with everyone else," Melanie said. "Just be your amazing self."

Jackie thought that was all very well for her to say. People never guessed that beneath her smartly made-up exterior she was an introvert who worried endlessly about how she came across. That wasn't the "self" she wanted to project when publicizing her book. Jackie Collins the writer was supposed to be confident, witty, charming, and wise. She wrapped the two-hundred-dollar leopard-print coat around herself, like an invisibility cloak.

Long John Nebel was a bespectacled man with thinning hair and a mellifluous radio voice. "How would you answer those who claim *The World Is Full of Married Men* promotes promiscuity to young people?" he asked. "A lot of them will be learning about sex from your book. Does that worry you?"

Jackie had been asked versions of this question before and she had an answer ready. "On the contrary, I hope my book warns young people about the dangers of promiscuity. None of my characters who sleep around come out of the experience well. Those who are faithful to one partner are happiest in the end."

"I'm sure readers assume you have personally tried all the kinky things your characters do," he continued. "Do you get your husband to act them out as part of your research process?" He grinned cheekily over the top of his mic. She guessed this was the way the deal worked on both sides of the Atlantic: write a book with sex scenes in it and your own life becomes fair game.

Jackie laughed. "I would be flying home to divorce papers tomorrow if I talked about my sex life with my husband on air! What I can say is that I'm not ashamed of any sexual experimentation I've done. And if my ideas can help other couples to spice up their sex lives, that would make me very happy."

"Both you and Jacqueline Susann have written about womanizers in your latest novels," he said. "Was that coincidence, or was one of you copying the other?"

Was he calling her a plagiarist as well as a sexual deviant? "*The Stud* was delivered to my British publisher long before *The Love Machine* came out," Jackie replied, "so there was no copying involved. The books are set in different countries and our stories are quite different, but womanizing men are a worldwide phenomenon. I recommend you read them both, John!"

When she finished, one of the production guys told her that Melanie had had to leave because she'd gotten a call from her babysitter. Melanie had a child? Jackie was astonished! She didn't look old enough—and she was sure there had been no wedding ring on her finger, not that that mattered.

"I'll get you a taxi," the guy said. "Follow me."

He led her along dimly lit corridors toward the reception area. It was late and no one was about. Without warning, he turned and lunged at her, using his weight to pin her against the wall. His mouth pressed on hers before she could draw breath to scream, and his hands groped her breasts, then slid downward. Instinct took over and Jackie fought back, trying to knee him in the groin, but she was trapped. He smelled rank, as if he'd been wearing the same clothes for days.

His hand edged up beneath her coat and Jackie struggled with all her strength. She managed to free one arm and grabbed a handful of his shoulder-length hair, tugging hard.

"Ow!" he yelped and leapt back, rubbing his scalp. "I see you're all talk and no fun. There's a word for girls like you."

She shoved his chest, then straightened her clothes. "Yes, and there are several words for men like you."

"Frigid bitch!" he hissed.

"Oh grow up—and try bathing if you ever want to get a woman you don't have to force."

The whole incident took less than a minute, but she was trembling as she strode off in the direction of the door. She'd been dealing with men like that virtually her entire adult life. It was unpleasant, but the trick was not to let it get to you.

When she reached Oscar's apartment, there was a white envelope in the hall mailbox, addressed to her in block capitals. She frowned, recognizing the style.

When she got inside the apartment, she ripped it open and out fell a used condom. The note read: *When are you going to take me up on my offer and have the shag of your life?*

How the hell did the condom creep know where to reach her in New York? Was he following her? Across an ocean? Heart thumping, she rushed to double-lock the door from the inside.

She sank down on the unfamiliar couch, staring out at the anonymous windows on the other side of the street, and felt so homesick she was close to tears. There was a lump in her chest as if she'd swallowed a rock. She longed to cuddle her girls, but they were tucked up in bed thousands of miles away and many hours would pass before she could see them. They'd been apart less than a week, but she vowed she would never leave them for so long again.

CHAPTER 37

Nancy

Manhattan, 1969

Nancy dragged herself to the office the morning after meeting Steven's wife. She had written a letter to him describing Jeanette and Darren's visit and explaining that, given the circumstances, she didn't want to hear from him again. She packaged the necklace with the letter, admitting to herself that it had never been to her taste: it was too flashy, too obvious. She preferred her mom's quiet, tasteful jewelry.

At the office, she slipped the package into the mail tray, and told the receptionist that if Steven Bailey rang, he was on no account to be put through. It felt as painful as if she had been stabbed and the wound was gaping wide.

The telephone was ringing when she sat down at her desk and she answered warily, in case it was him.

"Nancy?" a British voice said. "It's Jackie Collins. My flight's not till this evening and I wondered if I might take you for lunch?"

Nancy hesitated. She didn't feel at all sociable.

"Please?" Jackie begged, and there was an edge to her voice as if she were upset about something.

"Of course," Nancy agreed quickly. "Do you like cannelloni?" She explained how to find Sardi's, then called to book a table for twelve thirty.

Jackie was already there when Nancy arrived, looking ultraglamorous in a belted camel jersey dress. "I'm sorry, I'm sure you're busy," she apologized as Nancy sat down, "but I had a horrible time last night and it made me feel really lonely." She told her about the radio assistant attacking her and then the condom arriving in the mail.

Nancy was horrified. "I'll get Melanie to complain to Long John Nebel in the strongest terms," she promised. "You say you've been getting condoms sent to you in the UK as well?"

Jackie nodded. "Since my first novel came out."

"Jacqueline Susann gets sent vile letters with all kinds of gross contents, but we filter them out in the office. We only call the police about the death threats." Jackie flinched and Nancy bit her tongue. Perhaps she shouldn't have mentioned those.

"It's the thought that the condom creep knows I'm here, in New York, that has freaked me out," Jackie said. "Is he following me? Could he be here now?" She looked around the room.

"I'm sure he's not," Nancy said, frowning. "Did you keep the envelopes and contents? If you take them to the police, they could assess where they were mailed from and take fingerprints."

Jackie shuddered. "I didn't think of that. I just threw them out straight away." The waiter came and they both ordered cannelloni, then Jackie asked for a gin and tonic.

"I didn't only call to burden you with my woes," she said after the waiter left. "I also wanted to ask why Michael Loveday is my editor and not you? You're the one who reached out to W. H. Allen to ask for my novel, and I didn't get the impression Michael had much interest in my work."

"I'm an editorial assistant, not an editor," Nancy explained. "I'm hoping to get promoted sometime, but first I have to pay my dues."

"Well, I would rather have you as my editor," Jackie said, "and I'm going to write to Bill Heywood and say as much. I'll tell him we have a connection." She smiled.

Nancy thanked her. It was flattering, although she worried how Michael would take it. Next, they talked about *The Stud*, and the new novel Jackie was working on, which didn't yet have a title. The food came and Jackie pronounced it delicious. Halfway through, she called the waiter and ordered another gin and tonic. "I'm on holiday," she said, gaily.

Nancy was doing her best to be good company, but thoughts of Steven kept creeping in, so she was startled when Jackie suddenly asked her an apposite question.

"I got the impression when I was talking at the Colony that you have had some experience with duplicitous married men. Was I wrong?"

Jackie's manner was so warm that Nancy found herself confiding in her about the relationship with Steven. "I wasted two years on him," she finished, "and I feel like a fool."

Jackie pursed her lips sympathetically. "First of all, don't think of it as a waste. At the very least, it was a learning experience. But secondly, I wonder if deep down you weren't looking for a husband?" She smiled at Nancy's expression of puzzlement. "I have a theory that women date married men because it's a way of keeping their independence. We don't all want the marriage-and-babies package straight away, especially an ambitious young girl like you. Maybe you prefer to have the freedom to advance your career, and a husband would hold you back."

Nancy frowned. Could she be right? "I wanted him to leave Jeanette, but I always had misgivings about it, especially because of the effect it would have had on their son."

"It sounds to me as if the right conclusion has been reached for all," Jackie said. "And a tip for the future: if a married man hasn't left his wife within three months of meeting you, he's never going to. Men are impulsive creatures, but if they realize they can have you and keep their home life as well, of course that's what they'll opt for."

"You sound very cynical about men!" Nancy commented.

"I have good reason to be," Jackie told her, "but we'll save those stories for another time."

So there was to be another time? Nancy was pleased. It felt as if this could be the beginning of a new friendship, although they lived on different continents.

"How did you get on with Jacqueline?" she asked.

Jackie snorted. "You were right, I got the third degree from her, but I liked them both. How do you find her?"

Nancy considered the question and answered honestly. "Generous, and a wonderful friend to have—so long as you *always* let her get her own way."

"That's exactly what I thought!" Jackie hooted with laughter.

On the way back to the office, Nancy felt her sadness over Steven had lifted a little. But when she got back to George's apartment that evening, a bouquet of flowers was waiting, along with a card from Steven saying that he loved her and needed her, and begging for a chance to explain. She put the flowers in water—it seemed wasteful to throw them out—but ripped up the card and threw it in the trash, then burst into tears.

* * *

OVER THE COMING days Nancy found it hard to stop thinking about Steven. Had he been sleeping with his wife the whole time? And trying for a baby too? What would he have done if Jeanette hadn't miscarried? Did he ever intend to leave his marriage, or had he just been leading her on? So many questions, but she wasn't sure she wanted to know the truth. It felt easier to cancel it out.

Steven didn't give up, of course. There was a letter next: he insisted he loved her and wanted to spend the rest of his life with her. He said he had tried many times to broach the subject of divorce with Jeanette, but when he looked at his son, he couldn't bear to think of the damage it would cause. *So there was an inherent contradiction there*, Nancy thought. He admitted he had slept with his wife "a few times" while he and Nancy were together, and he was aware that she wanted another baby, but claimed the only person he wanted to have a child with was Nancy. *So why sleep with his wife at all?* And he promised that if she would only have him back, he would take the plunge and leave his marriage. *It was too late for that. Far too late.*

When she didn't reply, more letters followed. The sentiments were passionate, and some of them made her cry, but Nancy was resolute. She hadn't realized it when they were together, but now she could see that he was a weak man. He had lied to her and he had lied to Jeanette, and she knew that no matter what transpired, she could never trust him again.

Nancy was lying awake in bed one evening, curled in a fetal position, her thoughts going around in circles, when she heard the sound of a key in the front door and remembered that George was due back for one of his flying visits.

"Are you awake?" he called softly.

She considered pretending to be asleep, because she dreaded having to tell George about Steven, but it had to be done sometime. She wrapped her dressing gown around her and walked out to the hall.

"Are you OK?" he asked straight away. "Jacqueline told me what happened."

"No, I'm not really OK." Nancy pulled a sad face, relieved that she didn't have to explain the whole story. "But I'll survive."

He kissed her on both cheeks, then he pulled her in for a hug as well. "You'd better not tell me too many details or I'll have to find this guy and punch his lights out."

"You'd do that?" she mumbled into his shoulder, surprised. George didn't seem the punching type. "But it's my fault too. I let it happen."

"He was your first boyfriend. You didn't know any better." His voice was gruff.

"I've read *Madame Bovary*," she replied. "I knew it was going to be tricky."

He released her, and she saw that groove between his eyebrows. "They should teach you girls at college to avoid married men. That would be far more useful than French verb declensions and analysis of Flaubert." He took his coat off and hung it on a hook. "Shall I make some cocoa?"

Nancy followed him to the kitchen and watched as he poured milk in a pot. "Where did you just fly in from?" she asked.

"Berlin," he replied. "We managed to get footage of the Wall from the east of the city, and interviewed some people helping those who want to escape to the west. We'll have to hide their identities, of course. It's extraordinary the risks they're taking to tunnel beneath no-man's-land. It'll make a great program."

"I sometimes think you look at the map and choose the most dangerous spot on earth to film," Nancy said. "I wanted to ask you about the documentary you made in London, the time when you met Louise. Jacqueline told me about it."

George looked at her, as if considering. "I've got a copy here," he said. "Want to watch? You might find it disturbing, but at least it will distract you from Lover Boy." He uttered the words with disdain.

"Sure," she said. "I'd love to see it."

George finished making the cocoa and handed her a mug, then he went to a closet off the hall. Inside, she saw a couple of dozen film canisters, each of them labeled with the name of a city or country and a date. He pulled out one named "London,

1965" and took it to the living room, then collected a projector in a leather case from the same closet. Nancy sat down, watching the assurance with which he set everything up, pulling a screen down over one wall and winding the roll of film onto the projector. Some grainy, flickering images appeared and George adjusted the dials until the images came into focus and the sound was audible.

The documentary began with atmospheric footage of London clubs: clientele huddled around tables laden with glasses, or dancing to pop music, the beat loud and the lights low. It showed waitresses in skimpy black skirts wielding drink trays, then it shifted to focus on the entertainers: girls singing backing vocals behind a male singer, burlesque dancers, and a few women solo singers, their faces blurred. Nancy peered at the screen, searching for Louise, but couldn't see her. The voiceover said that it was every young performer's dream to get a contract in London's West End, but those who accepted deals didn't always know what they were letting themselves in for.

A man identified as Johnny Gold appeared on screen, saying that as a London club manager he was concerned for the girls who were shipped in from overseas by criminal gangs. He said their passports were confiscated on arrival, and they were told it was for safekeeping, but if they asked for them back, they'd be offered all kinds of excuses why they couldn't have them. The girls were put up in crowded accommodations, often several to a room, and encouraged to take drugs to keep them fresh and lively through the long working nights. Once they were hooked on the drugs—usually amphetamines, or speed—they'd be told they had to entertain men in their hotel rooms or they wouldn't be given any more.

Nancy gasped and turned to George. "Surely Louise didn't do that?"

"I don't know," he said. "But when I met her in a club and said I wanted to talk to her in private, she came to my hotel room without question. I was planning to ask her if she needed help, without her minders watching, but instead she tried to seduce me. Then, as I told you before, I caught her shooting up in my bathroom."

Nancy couldn't believe that Louise would consider sleeping with a man she'd only just met—but then, she didn't feel she knew her cousin anymore.

"Louise insisted she was fine and didn't need help," George said, "but before I left I asked Johnny Gold to keep an eye on her. She was involved with a very dangerous crowd."

Nancy clutched her throat. How could Louise have gotten herself into such a mess? She watched the rest of the half-hour program as it followed the stories of two girls who were trying to extricate themselves from the control of the gangs. In the end, one of them succeeded and got home to her family in Canada, while the other was found dead of an overdose, which the British coroner judged to be self-inflicted. The program implied that it might not have been.

"Thank goodness Louise escaped," Nancy said at the end.

"I hope she's escaped," George said, "but it looks as though she has found a way to get drugs here in Manhattan."

"Jacqueline is going to try and talk sense into her," Nancy told him. "I don't know what else to do."

"Jacqueline will be persuasive," he said, "but Louise has to be ready to accept help. Otherwise there's nothing any of us can do."

They headed to their separate bedrooms and Nancy heard the sound of his shower gushing. It was odd to think of him naked just a few feet through the wall. He was slim—perhaps a little too thin—but she imagined he was in good shape.

Since she'd moved in, she had answered calls from several

women—Linda, Carol, Sharon, Judy, Hilary—who had sounded taken aback to hear a female voice. Were they work friends or romantic friends?

"Are you George's latest?" Carol had asked, with a hint of hostility, whereupon Nancy replied, "Just a friend!"

Whenever George called, she passed on any messages. When she told him what Carol had asked, he grunted but didn't comment. His private life was clearly off-limits. On balance, Nancy preferred it that way. She wouldn't like to cross paths with one of his lovers in the kitchen.

When Nancy visited Louise to invite her to Jacqueline's, she found her in a morose mood. She still hadn't found work, she said, and couldn't pay the bills. She perked up a little at the prospect of meeting a famous author. Nancy hoped she would behave herself, but there was no way of predicting.

Nancy found it hard to look at her without thinking about the girls in the documentary. Had Louise been coerced into prostitution? Their conversation was superficial and strained because there was so much being left unsaid. Louise didn't ask about Steven, so Nancy didn't tell her they had broken up. She and Louise had been close once, but it felt as though their friendship had been poisoned and it was hard to see how it could ever be the same again.

CHAPTER 38

Jacqueline

Manhattan, 1969

Every six months, in December and June, Jacqueline had a routine breast checkup with her oncologist. She'd been clear for six and a half years now, but still she felt tightly wound whenever she sat in his waiting room, clutching Irving's hand, looking at the same abstract painting with red, orange, and black swirls. She hated the angry, frenetic energy of that damn painting. Surely oncologists' waiting room paintings should be calm and serene! Every time she looked at it, she remembered finding that tiny, innocent-seeming lump, and then the moment a few weeks later when the doctor pronounced it to be a "malignant infiltrating ductile carcinoma."

Back then, she'd begged God for ten more years in order to become a bestselling author and secure her son's future. She'd used up more than half of these years, and she'd written two bestsellers, which had made a serious amount of money. If God took her literally, she only had three and a half years left, which wasn't nearly enough. In retrospect she should have asked for twenty! She hoped the Almighty would cut her some slack.

Inside the oncologist's office she took off her blouse and bra and let him do his poking and prodding, as well as his blood tests. He never smiled or chatted; this was a serious business. When his secretary telephoned with the results a week later, she was yet again pronounced to be in complete remission. "Thank you, God," she breathed, feeling the tension dissipate. Her cells were behaving themselves. She could get on with living.

That evening, Nancy was bringing her cousin Louise to meet

them and, with mortality very much on her mind, Jacqueline resolved to do her best to get through to the girl, for Nancy's sake. Their family seemed scattered, and from the sounds of things, no one else was looking out for Louise. Jacqueline prided herself on helping friends in need. She liked to be the first person they called with their problems and would go to great lengths to find solutions.

They arrived together: Nancy neat and bookish in a knee-length skirt and white blouse, Louise tarty in a skinny-rib button-up-the-front cardigan-dress and high-heeled boots. Her nipples poked through the knit fabric and, from the smooth lines, she didn't appear to be wearing underwear. Yin and yang with their outfits, they had the same shade of blond hair, pixie features, and sea-blue eyes, but Louise was clearly the elder. Hard lines were etched around her eyes and mouth, as if she had partied through too many decadent nights.

"I suspected you would be beautiful, because Nancy is," Jacqueline told Louise, shaking her hand warmly, "but I had no idea how stunning you were. And what a great figure you have!" She led her to a chair in front of the windows.

"Thank you!" Louise sat down, crossing her legs with a flash of bare thigh. "It's great to meet you. What a gorgeous home you have!" She gazed around. "I love your lamps! They're so original."

Nancy sat on the couch and Josephine made a beeline for her, as always. She had to be lifted onto her lap now because she'd gotten too old and arthritic to climb up. Irving asked what everyone was drinking and Louise requested bourbon on the rocks, while Nancy asked for a Coke.

"Are you still writing music?" Jacqueline asked Louise. "I hope so! 'My After Midnight Man' is one of my favorite songs and I was thrilled when Nancy told me her cousin wrote it."

"That's sweet of you," Louise said. "I haven't been writing for a while. I'm a bit rusty but I must get back to it."

"Have you found any singing work in New York since your return?" Jacqueline asked. She could detect a croakiness in Louise's voice, a sure sign she hadn't been practicing. Professional singers needed to sing every day to keep the vocal cords supple.

"I've been trying but there's nothing around at the moment." She shifted in her chair, recrossed her legs, then accepted her drink from Irving with a coy smile. "Thank you," she breathed, making eye contact with him.

"Irving knows loads of people in theater who might be able to help," Jacqueline said. "Don't you, darling? Maybe you could make some calls?"

"No problem," he said. "Send me your résumé and I'll ask around."

"I surely will. You two are the kindest people ever." Louise beamed, gulped her drink, then fixed her attention on Josephine. "What a cute dog! I adore dogs. I would love an English setter— the ones that are a gorgeous rust color with those silky ears. Aren't they just the best? Or maybe an Afghan: I always think they look like hippies with their long floppy hair. Of course, your dog is wonderful too."

She was high as a kite, Jacqueline decided. There was a nervous energy about her that wasn't just a result of meeting a famous author. She couldn't keep still, and her brain was ricocheting in a way Jacqueline recognized from her own experience. She asked more about Louise's career and smiled as she listened to the gushing replies. She always loved hearing other people's life stories.

When Louise finished, Jacqueline shifted her chair closer.

"I'm going to level with you about why I invited you today," she said. "I heard you are a devotee of the vitamin shots that are all the rage in some circles. I've had them too, and I know how much zip they can give you. I feel on top of the world for a few hours, but I'm sure you've already encountered the downsides: the anxiety, the shaking, the racing heart, and the sweats. You might even have found your hair falling out on the pillow, and your teeth rotting."

Louise was dismissive. "Oh no! I haven't had anything like that. Personally, I don't use them much at all."

Jacqueline continued as if she hadn't spoken. "I have a theory about amphetamines. Life is intense, exciting, and fast-paced when you're on them, but you are actually using up experiences from the future. It's a dangerous game, like dancing with the devil."

Louise drained her drink. "I'm fine, honestly," she said. "I only use the shots occasionally if I'm working late and need to stay fresh."

Jacqueline carried on: "Nancy tells me you actually inject yourself? I used to get them from a doctor, who always did careful heart and blood pressure tests first. If you are self-administering, you could be damaging your organs and causing all kinds of health problems. When did you last have a full medical exam?"

Louise waved her arms in airy denial. "I'm young," she said. "Only in my thirties. I'm absolutely fine."

Jacqueline nodded, assessing her. "So if I invited you to come and stay with us for a week, the only condition being that you aren't allowed to have any shots while you're here—would you be able to manage that?"

Louise giggled nervously. "Of course I would. But I'm very busy at the moment . . ."

Jacqueline decided to challenge her. "Let's choose a week when you're free and get it in the diary. Maybe in January, so you can start the New Year feeling tip-top. Irving, how are we placed for the first week of January?"

"Perfect," he said. "We're here all that week."

"Think of the money you'll save," Jacqueline said. "These injections don't come cheap. Tell me, out of interest, how much you pay per shot?"

There was a long pause. "I can't remember," Louise said at last.

"Go on, you must," Jacqueline urged. "How much did you pay for your last one?"

"I don't pay for them," Louise whispered.

There was a heavy silence. Jacqueline looked at Nancy and saw she was thinking the worst.

"There's always a price for drugs," she said. "I hope you're not paying too much in other ways."

"I have a friend who gives them to me free of charge," Louise said. She gazed into her empty glass as if hoping it would magically refill itself.

Jacqueline nodded, slowly. "Uh-huh, I see. And does this friend tell you which hotel rooms to go to so you can keep visiting businessmen company?"

Shock flashed across Louise's face. "I don't know what you mean. I'm not that kind of girl!"

Nancy looked dismayed. *Poor Nancy! She didn't need this worry on top of her recent heartache.*

"You can't keep doing this to yourself, Louise," Jacqueline told her. "It's too dangerous. Either the drugs will cause a heart attack or one of those men will hurt you. I've only just met you, but already I'm desperately worried about you. Please let us help."

Louise stood suddenly, swaying on her heels. "I thought I

was coming here to get acquainted with you and your husband. Nancy didn't warn me I was going to be accused of being a drug addict and a whore. Frankly, it's no one else's business how I live my life."

Jacqueline stood and grasped her forearms, looking her directly in the eyes: "Don't go! Stay and talk to us. Tell me how it happened."

"There's nothing to tell." Louise yanked her arms away. "You've got me all wrong. I'm getting out of here."

Jacqueline sighed. It had been too much to hope that she would confess all on the first meeting. "The invitation to stay is open. Come here and Irving and I will look after you. Here's my number." She handed her a card, with her number scribbled on the back. "Call anytime."

Louise shook her head quickly and tottered toward the door. "Thanks for the drink," she called over her shoulder before disappearing toward the elevator. "But you can shove your advice."

There was a stunned silence at her abrupt departure, then Nancy burst into tears. "I don't recognize her anymore. She's a completely different person. Do you really think she's going to men's hotel rooms?"

"I hope not, but why else would someone be giving her free shots?" Jacqueline sat beside her and put an arm around her. "Louise has gotten caught in an age-old trap, but we've offered her an escape route. Let's just hope she takes it."

She made a face at Irving over Nancy's head. From what she'd seen, she wasn't optimistic.

* * *

JACQUELINE AND IRVING flew to London in mid-December, planning to visit W. H. Allen, then attend the opening of Tramp on the eighteenth before flying back to New York for Christmas. Jacqueline loved a traditional Christmas, with exquisitely wrapped gifts under the tree, sparkly festive decorations, and carols playing on the radio. A couple of decades earlier she'd converted from Judaism to Catholicism and had adopted with relish all the rituals around Christmas and Easter, which her family hadn't celebrated when she was a child. She'd already done most of her gift shopping before they left New York, but if she got a chance to browse the London stores, she wouldn't pass it up.

They stayed in the Dorchester on Park Lane, which was only a fifteen-minute walk from Tramp. The evening was mild, and she and Irving enjoyed strolling through the Mayfair streets with their magnificent architecture, fantasizing about which grand town house they would buy if they ever needed a London base. There was so much history: all those distinguished families with aristocratic names living lives of luxury cocooned by teams of servants.

When they reached the club, the entrance was under siege by a bank of photographers, standing six deep, pointing cameras over the shoulders of the ones in front. Jackie gave them her most radiant smile as she pushed through, glad she'd worn her mink coat and had her hair styled that afternoon by Leonard of Mayfair.

A woman with a Jackie Kennedy hairdo and a smart black dress checked their names on a clipboard, then ushered them inside, down a flight of stairs with antique wood paneling and subtle lighting. Jacqueline checked her coat into the cloakroom, then they paused at the entrance to the bar, admiring the dramatic chandeliers shooting sparks of light around the room and a ceiling mural depicting the signs of the zodiac.

"Classy joint," Irving remarked in her ear.

Although it was still early, the room was thronged with guests and buzzing with chatter and the clink of glasses. Jacqueline could hear music drifting through from a dance floor bathed in multicolored spotlights, but no one was dancing yet.

A weathered blond man in a dinner suit approached them. "Jacqueline Susann—I'd recognize you anywhere." He grinned. "Welcome to Tramp! I'm Johnny Gold, one of the owners." He shook hands with her, then with Irving. "What do you think of our new venture? Maybe you can include it in one of your novels?"

Jacqueline smiled back. "If I do, does that get me a free drink?"

"All drinks are on the house tonight," he said. "Let me take you over to Jackie and Oscar's table."

As he led them through the crowd, Jacqueline spotted Peter Sellers, Natalie Wood, and Michael Caine chatting at the bar, and at a corner table she was pretty sure she could see John and Yoko, leaning so close their foreheads were almost touching. She elbowed Irving and saw he had noticed them too.

Jackie leapt to her feet when she spotted them. She looked sensational in a pink-and-gold minidress with gold gladiator sandals that laced up her calves. She flung her arms around Jacqueline's neck and kissed her cheek, then introduced her husband, Oscar, who looked much older than she was. He could almost have been her father, Jacqueline thought: not what she'd expected at all.

"May I offer you some champagne?" he asked, lifting a bottle of Cristal from an ice bucket.

"Great opening line," Jacqueline replied. "I can tell we're going to be friends."

They squeezed into the circular banquette, and Jacqueline made sure she was seated beside Jackie. Johnny had disappeared into the crowd, so she took the chance to ask about him. "Is he the one your 'Stud' was modeled on? He's very handsome."

Jackie laughed. "Loosely modeled on. He's a great friend, but he does have an eye for the ladies. He's currently dating a friend of mine, Jan de Souza, who is far more patient than he deserves."

"I saw him being interviewed in a documentary about London clubs made by my friend George. It claimed young girls are enticed over here on the promise of lucrative singing contracts, only for gangsters to get them hooked on drugs, then force them into prostitution. Have you come across that?" She sipped her champagne.

Jackie shivered. "I'm sure it goes on. Oscar and Johnny have to deal with some of the underworld types but only at arm's length. Why? Were you planning to write about them?"

Jacqueline hadn't thought of that, but maybe it wasn't a bad idea. *The Godfather* had been an instant bestseller, so readers clearly enjoyed reading about that world. Then again, she'd heard there was a price on Mario Puzo's head.

"On the whole, I'd rather not risk having a contract taken out on me," she replied. "No, I was asking because Nancy White's cousin, Louise Cardena, was one of those girls. She's back in New York now but still seems to be getting a supply of drugs and we're worried about what kind of hold they have over her."

"Nancy's cousin? Oh no!" Jackie seemed concerned to hear it. "Poor Nancy!"

"It's tough for her," Jacqueline agreed, "but there's not a lot we can do." She glanced around. "Clubs like this must be rich pickings for a novelist, with such exotic clientele, all with their own stories."

"Oh, I know!" Jackie agreed. "They don't realize when they tell me about their lives they run the risk of ending up in one of my novels. Anonymously, of course."

"How often do you visit your husband's clubs?" Jacqueline asked. "I thought you had youngsters at home?"

"I do, three of them, and the youngest is still breastfeeding. Oscar and I go out roughly once a week, but I never stay late because little Rory wakens for a night feed."

Jackie didn't look remotely sleep-deprived. Her complexion was fresh and her eyes bright, while her figure was trim and curvy. She leaned forward to reach her champagne glass, showing a glimpse of pert cleavage.

"I have a son," Jacqueline blurted, suddenly. "He's all grown up now. I didn't breastfeed him—we didn't in those days." She had no idea why she was telling Jackie about him. The words just slipped out. "I hired a nurse, who insisted on a strict routine when he was little. Looking back, I would do things differently, but I was cutting my teeth as a parent."

"Oh, we all muddle along, doing our best," Jackie said. "You haven't mentioned your son before. Does he live with you?"

"He lives in Texas," Jacqueline said, wishing she hadn't started this conversation. "Irving and I fly down to visit whenever we can and we vacation with him every year. But tell me more about your daughters. What ages are they, and what are their names?"

Jackie described them, her eyes sparkling with maternal pride, then pulled a photograph from her purse, showing the three of them in front of a Christmas tree that was dripping in tinsel and ornaments. They were beautiful girls, very well dressed, with natural smiles. Jacqueline felt tears prick her eyes. She would never regret having her son, because she loved him with all her heart, but she wished she'd been brave enough to risk having another baby. If she'd gotten pregnant after her son went into an institution, that child would be a teenager now.

The syncopated opening drum riff of the Rolling Stones hit "Honky Tonk Women" sounded from the dance floor and Jackie grabbed Jacqueline's arm. "I love this track. Will you dance with me?"

Irving and Oscar were deep in conversation. "Sure, why not?" Jacqueline replied.

They pushed through the crowd and found some space on the dance floor, which had filled as soon as the track came on. Jacqueline had studied modern dance as part of her drama training, but it had been a long time since she had danced anywhere except in her own sitting room and fashions had changed. She felt self-conscious: Was anyone watching?

Jackie had slipped into a sexy, sinuous, hip-swaying motion, her eyes closed. Jacqueline let herself feel the beat and start to move. It was a terrific song. Glancing around, she realized no one was looking and relaxed into the music. It felt wonderful.

She began to laugh and Jackie started laughing too and they danced and laughed together. They didn't know each other well, Jacqueline thought, but she liked her a lot. She hoped they could become closer. It felt as though they could be good for each other.

CHAPTER 39

Jackie

London, 1970

Jackie's telephone rang on the tenth of January, while she was reading a bedtime story to Tiffany. She hurried downstairs to the hall, thinking it was probably Oscar calling to say he'd be late. Instead, the operator told her it was an international call from New York. There were clicks and hisses down the line before Jacqueline's voice came on.

"I have terrible news," she said, sounding very far away. "Josephine died."

"I'm so sorry." Jackie frowned, racking her memory. Had Jacqueline mentioned a Josephine? Could it be her mother?

"She was off her food when we got back from London, and seemed very listless. I thought she was recovering, but when I went in this morning she was gone." Her voice wobbled with emotion. "She was cold and stiff in her bed."

"How awful for you," Jackie said, none the wiser.

"Irving has taken her to the vet's for cremation so we can keep her ashes close to us." She sobbed on the other end of the line.

Of course! Jackie remembered that fat, smelly poodle that had thrust its nose into her crotch. Who made a transatlantic call to someone she barely knew to tell her about a dog they'd only met once? Jacqueline was clearly a little eccentric.

"My condolences," she said out loud. "Pets are family members and I know it's heartbreaking to lose them."

"I have to go," Jacqueline said, sniffing loudly. "I have lots more people to share the news with. Josephine was a celebrity, you know." She hung up without saying goodbye.

At first Jackie wondered if she had offended her by not being effusive enough in her sympathy. When Nancy called that afternoon, she took the opportunity to ask if Jacqueline often hung up on people like that.

"Don't take it personally," Nancy said. "She's distraught about Josephine."

Bill had agreed Nancy could be Jackie's editor, and she'd called to discuss the title of Jackie's third novel. It was hard to find one as snappy as "The Stud" that also fit the storyline. They threw a few suggestions back and forth, and Nancy made a list for further consideration.

"I'm sorry to hear about your cousin," Jackie told her at the end of the call. "Jacqueline mentioned her problems. I wish there was something I could do to help."

"Thank you," Nancy replied. "But it's up to Louise, I guess."

After she hung up the phone, Jackie thought about it and wondered if there might be a way. She'd get Johnny Gold to make inquiries.

* * *

JACKIE WAS WORKING hard on the third novel, between school pickups, shopping, and meal preparation. Since the story was set in LA, she persuaded Oscar that the family should holiday there over Easter to take in the sights.

When she telephoned Jacqueline to tell her about the vacation, Jacqueline's voice sounded much brighter than the last time they spoke.

"You *must* stay at the Beverly Hills," she insisted. "The girls will love the pool. Can you ask them to feed the stray cats in the hedge out back? And if you're still there on the eighteenth of April, you can come to the *Love Machine* casting party." She explained that Columbia Pictures was holding a party on their lot, which would be full of the town's most glamorous actors and actresses, all vying for a role.

"I'll make sure I'm there," Jackie promised.

Remembering Jacqueline and Irving's advice, she telephoned a few literary agencies with LA offices and managed to schedule appointments while she was in town. Her sales were growing in the UK, but she still wasn't selling well in the States and she didn't know what to do about that.

Once they arrived in LA, she made a point of popping into bookstores wherever they went. Always Jacqueline's books were piled high on tables and arranged in special display stands, but Jackie was lucky if she could find a couple of copies of her books buried on the shelves. It was clear she needed more exposure. Perhaps an agent could help.

The first one she met was Swifty Lazar, a showbiz agent who knew her father, and who invited her for lunch at the Polo Lounge. Swifty was a short bald man in oversized bug-eye glasses and a Savile Row suit, who seemed to know everyone in town. From the moment they sat down, they were interrupted by a stream of passersby who stopped to greet him, then peered at Jackie, trying to decide whether she was someone to be reckoned with. Then they decided she wasn't and moved on.

"I've represented artists from across the worlds of music, litera-ture, and film," he told her. "Cole Porter, Nabokov, Noël Coward, Humphrey Bogart—they were all such dear friends. I miss Bogey to this day. He was the one who nicknamed me Swifty, you know. He once bet me I couldn't make three deals for him in a single day, and I did—hence the name."

Jackie sipped her ice water, musing that someone so well con-nected shouldn't feel the need to name-drop quite so blatantly.

"So you've written how many—two books? How's the third coming along?" Swifty asked, picking at a prawn salad.

"I've finished a draft," she said. "I brought a copy I can leave with you."

He shook his head quickly. "No, dear, I don't read. Pitch it to me."

She took a deep breath. "It's about an actress with a great body who is fed up being forced to do sex scenes in every movie while the crew ogle her from the sidelines. And it's about a chauffeur to the stars who sends anonymous lewd letters to the women he drives around." She'd developed this plot strand based on her own experience with the creep who sent her condoms in the post. "The general theme is how much more difficult it is for the rich and famous to find love than it is for the rest of us."

"I could get you fifty grand for that," Swifty said. He snapped his fingers. "With one phone call."

Jackie blinked. That was an astronomic sum. "I need someone who can sell film rights for this one, and my previous two novels as well."

"That goes without saying," he said. He polished off his salad and dabbed his lips with a linen napkin. "Publishers habitually underpay authors. They earn three to four times more from bestselling books than the people who write them, and I consider it my job to redress that balance." He glanced at his watch and called for a waiter to bring the check, even though Jackie had hardly touched her salad. They'd only been there half an hour. "So are we in business?" he asked.

"I have a couple more appointments with agents this week," she said. "Can I let you know after that?"

He shook his head. "That's not how I work, sweetheart. I need a fast decision. Is it yes or no?"

She laughed, feeling nervous. "You haven't even told me your terms of business. Could I have a look at a contract before deciding?"

He sounded impatient now: "Straight ten percent of every-thing, no contracts, a gentleman's agreement. Take it or leave it."

Jackie hesitated. She didn't want to turn him down in case she didn't get any other offers, but she refused to be pressured into a decision like this. "I'm hoping to find someone who will represent me for the rest of my career, so we need to be able to talk frankly to each other. Right now, I'd like to have a little time to consider your offer. Is that possible?"

He scraped his chair back and stood up. "Tell you what, discuss it with your husband and I'll call you tomorrow for an answer."

It was that last sentence that cost him the deal, Jackie thought as she sat alone finishing her salad. The implication that she needed her husband to help her make a decision about her career was sexist and insulting. Now she just had to cross her fingers she could find someone else to represent her.

That afternoon she met an elderly New York agent, who represented lots of high-brow male authors. When Jackie said that she admired Jacqueline Susann's ability to reach out to her readers, he replied that he feared the sensational vulgarity of Miss Susann's writing would corrupt the reading public by making them lazier and less discerning, and that could damage literature as a whole. Jackie was so astounded that she took out a pen and notebook and jotted down his words. She then told him that her aim was to corrupt the exact same readership, and their meeting wound up very quickly.

She finished the day at the office of Paul Gitlin, who was Harold Robbins's agent and famous for cutting five- and six-figure deals for his client. She mentioned that her books had gotten onto the UK bestseller list, she told him that her next novel was set in LA and that she would come to the States to publicize it. She hinted that she already had ideas for her fourth and fifth novels. He nodded and asked a few questions, but at one stage she saw him glance out the window, distracted by someone walking past, and she realized she was small-fry. If she signed with him, Harold Robbins would monopolize his attention and she would be an afterthought.

The following morning she had a meeting with a film agent, a woman, who told her apologetically that she only represented clients who had written screenplays. Feeling downhearted, Jackie said she might try that at some point, but was looking for someone to represent her books first. Maybe she would have to sign with Swifty Lazar after all, she thought gloomily, hoping he wouldn't have withdrawn his offer.

"You should talk to Mort Janklow," the film agent suggested. "He's a corporate lawyer, but he represents a few authors, and he's sharp as they come." She made a call to Mort's secretary and arranged a meeting for Jackie that afternoon.

Jackie felt weary as she arrived at Mort's office. She'd had no idea that finding an agent would prove so tortuous. He rose to greet her, looking unprepossessing in a plain brown suit and brown tie, but his manner was instantly sharp and businesslike.

"What's your deal with W. H. Allen?" he asked. "Do they have world rights? Have they made any foreign sales beyond the US one?"

He took notes as she answered. Jackie liked the fact that he didn't talk down to her but assumed she understood terms like "subsidiary rights" and "option clauses."

"So, what do you want from an agent?" he asked, sitting back in his chair.

"I want to sell millions of books worldwide," she told him, in all seriousness. "I want to reach the top of bestseller lists, and have films made out of my novels. And I want to make enough money that I can dictate my own terms."

He nodded. "I call it fuck-you money," he said. "To be honest,

I'm only interested in representing big authors in big deals, so if you had said to me your goal was to win a Pulitzer, I'd have told you to try someone else."

"I don't care about the Pulitzer," she said. "Do you think you can help me?" She crossed her fingers. She had already made up her mind that she wanted to work with him.

"When I call a publisher, I'm going into battle on behalf of my clients," he said. "And I will never accept defeat. Leave your latest manuscript with me and I'll call you with my answer when I've read it."

Jackie gave him her number in London, and mentioned that she would be staying at the Beverly Hills Hotel for another week. She was trembling when she left. *Please let him say yes!* Meanwhile, she was going to have to gamble on turning down Swifty Lazar and possibly ending up with no agent at all.

She needn't have worried. Mort called her the next morning and said, "Jackie Collins, it would be my honor to represent you. Let's get started!" And Swifty Lazar kept leaving messages at the hotel reception the rest of the time she was in LA.

* * *

BEFORE *THE LOVE Machine* casting party, Jackie bought herself a new outfit from a Sunset Boulevard boutique: a plunging gold lamé dress, split to the thigh, which she teamed with gold platform shoes. It was a dress for "Jackie Collins, author," not "Jackie, mum of three."

"We have to find my Robin Stone," Jacqueline explained when she met her at the entrance to the lot. "As we walk around and chat to the actors, I want you to nudge me if there are any you would jump straight into bed with, no questions asked."

Jackie glanced at the crowd and said, "I've spotted some already. Want me to make a list?"

Never had she seen so many beautiful people in one place. She knew that studios forced their actors and actresses to get plastic surgery and dental work until they were completely flawless. No moles or freckles, no excess flesh, no bumpy noses or double chins or gaps between teeth would ever appear on celluloid. It was the first time Jackie realized that the men were under almost as much pressure as the women: not a gray hair was in sight among the actors, nor a hint of five o'clock stubble, and they clearly lifted weights to give them such well-honed muscles.

Jacqueline stopped to chat with a few, introducing Jackie, and the conversations quickly turned flirtatious.

"Want to head off for a drink later?" one whispered to Jackie, his hand resting on her arm, his breath warm on her neck. "I know a little place . . ."

"Do you mean your apartment by any chance?" she teased.

"If that's what you want." His finger stroked the tender skin at the crease of her elbow.

She could almost smell the testosterone oozing from his pores, but wasn't tempted by such an obvious come-on. She thought back to the night she met Marlon Brando. What had attracted her was that he hadn't tried to seduce her, forcing her to do all the running. Being so cool that you didn't need to make an effort—that was genuinely sexy. She told Jacqueline about it as they wandered on to meet the next candidates.

"I wish you could talk Marlon into taking the part," Jacqueline sighed, but there wasn't a hope in hell. He was too big a name now, and Jackie wasn't sure he would remember their long-ago tryst.

They got into conversation with Brian Kelly, the actor who played a widowed father in the TV series *Flipper*. His image wasn't that of a Casanova type, but he had clean-cut, square-jawed dark good looks and a friendly nature.

Jackie nudged Jacqueline in the ribs. "Him," she whispered. "I definitely would."

"Yeah, me too," Jacqueline replied. "In a heartbeat."

"He's your Robin Stone." Jackie could tell he would bring warmth to the role, so Robin wasn't just a coldhearted serial shagger.

"I'll tell the producer our decision," Jacqueline said. "We make a good team: the two Jackies! Let me know when you're casting *The Stud* and I'll come and give my professional opinion."

She made the lewdest hand gesture Jackie had ever seen, and it reduced them both to schoolgirl giggles.

CHAPTER 40

Nancy

Manhattan, 1970

Nancy was editing a novel set in San Francisco during the summer of 1967, which everyone referred to as the "Summer of Love." Ironically, that was the summer when she and Steven had started their affair, and the novel kept reminding her of the music, the movies, and the news stories of the time. She wallowed in her sadness, almost relishing it in a strange way. She felt older and wiser since her heartbreak. As Jacqueline said, it was a rite of passage everyone went through.

She still hadn't told Louise about the breakup with Steven. She visited her roughly once a week out of a sense of duty, but her cousin was so self-absorbed it never occurred to her to ask about Nancy's life. Needless to say, Louise hadn't accepted Jacqueline's offer to stay with her and Irving for a week. She was still injecting herself, and she got thinner and more haggard as time went on. Hardly a visit went by without her begging to borrow money from Nancy, but Nancy resisted because she couldn't bear to think of it being used for drugs. Besides, she was hardly flush herself, even though she was living rent-free at George's; she hadn't had a pay raise since she started at Heywood & Bradshaw.

By now Nancy had discovered over a dozen books in the submissions pile that had been published to critical acclaim and decent sales, but she never got any credit because Bill passed them on to his established male editors. She acted as editor for her own little group of women authors, including Jackie Collins, but without having the official title or paycheck. What's worse, in June 1970, Dan Streather, fresh out of Yale, was parachuted into an editor's job despite not having any publishing experience. Nancy was incensed. She requested a meeting with Bill to discuss her role in the company and asked him straight out when she could hope to be promoted.

"We don't have any vacancies for an editor at the moment," he said, "but of course you can apply when we do."

"Dan didn't have to wait for a vacancy," she pointed out.

"He's a special case," Bill told her. "He's well connected in the literary world. Gabriel García Márquez, Saul Bellow, Philip Roth—Dan knows them all, *and* he graduated summa cum laude."

Dan's father was a distinguished literary critic so he was well connected via that route rather than his own merit. Nancy couldn't compete with him on that score, but she also graduated summa cum laude, and she told Bill so.

"You did?" He looked surprised. "But you're interested in women's novels rather than serious literature, aren't you?"

"I'm interested in publishing books that achieve far greater sales than most so-called literary authors do," Nancy argued. "Jacqueline Susann's *Valley of the Dolls* has sold sixteen million copies to date."

Bill clasped his hands on the desk, his index fingers forming a steeple. "If you can bring us the next Jacqueline Susann novel, I think a promotion might be in order."

Nancy sighed. Jacqueline would almost certainly take her next novel to the highest bidder, and Heywood & Bradshaw were cheapskates when it came to advances. "How about this for a compromise—can I start attending the editorial meetings so I can learn how you make publishing decisions? And when I find a book I think is worth publishing, can I pitch it myself?"

Bill considered this. "I suppose that would be okay, so long as you don't fall behind with your other work."

Nancy had been planning to ask him for a raise as well, but she decided to leave that for another day. Slowly but surely, inch by inch, she would fight for the promotion she longed for and knew she deserved.

* * *

THE SIX MONTHS George had offered to let Nancy stay in his apartment came to an end and he returned to live there. Nancy started apartment hunting, but, just as it had been last time she was searching, she found that most places in her price range were dingy, damp-smelling, and in areas where she would be nervous to walk at night.

"There's no rush," George insisted, but she felt self-conscious living in such close proximity with him. She got dressed in the bathroom straight after her shower and didn't feel comfortable wandering into the kitchen to make coffee wearing her robe. One day George returned from the gym in shorts and she couldn't help noticing he had particularly well-toned legs—then she glanced up and blushed to realize he had seen the direction of her gaze. She was hyper-aware of his movements and careful not to get in his way, and she sensed he felt the same unease around her.

It took several weeks before Nancy found a tiny fourth-floor walk-up to rent in the Theater District and agreed on terms with the landlord. It had been difficult to persuade a taxi driver to take all her belongings last time she moved, so she asked George if he would give her a lift.

"You didn't have to move out," he told her as he drove her across town. "I hope it's not because you've acquired another unsuitable boyfriend and want to keep him hidden from me." He glanced around at her.

"No, I just thought I should give you space for the hordes of women lining up to leap into your bed. I read about them in *The Love Machine*." She grinned at him.

George grunted, but didn't reply.

"Don't worry! From what I've observed, the only thing you and Robin Stone have in common is a career in television."

He didn't reply at first, then he said: "I finally read the book, and I'm cross with Jacqueline about it. We've had words." He pulled deftly into a parking spot across the street from her building.

"You have?" She waited for him to tell her why he was cross, but he got out of the car and opened the trunk to start unloading boxes.

"Did I mention my apartment's on the fourth floor?" Nancy asked as he picked up the first two boxes, testing the weight.

"I think you omitted that," he said. "No elevator, I assume?"

"Not on my pay grade."

As they heaved the boxes upstairs, Nancy tried to pick up the conversation about *The Love Machine*. "Robin Stone couldn't look at a woman without wanting to have sex with her, but you've been a positive saint while we've been roomies. Goodness, you never even tried to seduce me and I was right down the hall."

There was an awkward silence and she could have kicked herself. What a clumsy thing to say! George carried on climbing the stairs as if he hadn't heard. She'd hoped by now they were close enough friends to make fun of each other, but perhaps she had overstepped the mark.

When they reached the fourth floor, she unlocked the door, fumbling with the unfamiliar lock, then flung out her arms, exclaiming, "*Voilà!*"

George walked in, put the boxes down, and looked around. "This is the closet, right? Where's the actual apartment?"

She could see his point. It was a studio, about fifteen feet square, with a fold-down bed, a solitary armchair by the window, and a sink and hot plate squeezed behind the front door. The washroom didn't have a bath—just a narrow shower cubicle crammed beside a toilet.

"It will do until I make my fortune," she said. "I'll put up shelves."

"Do you know how to put up shelves?" George asked, looking skeptical.

She wrinkled her nose. "I'll figure it out." She felt a twinge of alarm at all that would need to be done to make the apartment habitable, but quelled it for another day.

They made six trips up and down the four flights of stairs before all of her bags and boxes were stowed in the apartment. They took up so much floor space that she couldn't imagine how she was going to pull the bed down later, but she would make it work somehow.

"Let me buy you a hot dog at the diner down the block," she offered. "It's the least I can do."

The diner wasn't promising: sticky Formica tabletops, tinny pop music, and a waitress who was chatting to a friend and seemed reluctant to take their order, but when the hot dogs came, they were surprisingly good.

"Are you going to tell me what you argued with Jacqueline about?" Nancy asked, squirting extra mustard onto hers.

He hesitated before replying. "She used the name Amanda— my wife's name—in *The Love Machine*."

"Your *what*?" Nancy gasped, stunned. "You're *married*?" Not another one! How could he have kept that from her?

"I *was* married," he said. "Amanda died almost ten years ago, just before our first anniversary." The words caught in his throat, as though they were still hard to say out loud.

Nancy put down her hot dog and cupped her hand over his. "I'm sorry," she whispered. "I had no idea."

"I wasn't sure if Jacqueline would have told you. It's not something I talk about," he said.

"What happened to Amanda? Do you mind me asking?" She hoped it wasn't leukemia. Amanda in the novel had died of leukemia.

He shook his head slowly, took a deep breath, and exhaled before beginning the story. "I had taught her to drive. She was a good driver, with very quick reactions. She was on her way to collect me from JFK when a truck skidded ahead of her. There were high winds gusting across an open stretch of highway and the driver lost control. Amanda managed to brake so she didn't crash into it, but the load on the truck came loose and . . ." His face crumpled, and he turned away.

"You don't have to tell me," Nancy said. She could see how much effort it took.

He breathed hard. "Her car was crushed by three steel girders. She didn't stand a chance." He took a sip of coffee and composed himself. "At the time I was working with Jacqueline on her Schiffli promotions, and she was incredible. She called me every single day, she turned up at the apartment with pizzas and bottles of vodka, and she sat up all night with me when I couldn't sleep. No one could have done more."

"And then she used Amanda's name for the girlfriend who died in *The Love Machine*. I can see why you're upset about that," Nancy said, biting her lower lip.

"When I called to challenge her, she apologized straight away and explained to me that authors have lots of fragments floating around in their brains when they're writing. Some make their way onto the page without them being fully aware where they came from." He twisted his mouth to one side. "She said she realized what she had done during the editing, and meant to change Amanda's name but there were so many versions going back and forth it slipped through."

"I can imagine how that could have happened," Nancy said. "She would never have done it deliberately."

"Of course not. Don't worry—I don't hold grudges." He shook himself. "It's not the end of the world. But you should be aware that Jacqueline uses her friends' lives. You might end up in one of her novels, and it may not be the way you would choose to be portrayed."

Nancy wondered if Jacqueline would write about her affair with Steven but guessed it wasn't dramatic enough for her purposes: just another gullible young girl tricked into an affair by a married man.

* * *

JACKIE MAILED NANCY the manuscript of her third novel, which she had decided to call *Sunday Simmons and Charlie Brick*, after the main characters. Nancy read it and sent back some notes suggesting ways it could be tightened up. Jackie rang from London shortly afterward.

"Thank you for your letter. I feel like you really understand what I'm trying to do," she said. "But that's not the reason I'm calling. I wanted to let you know that Johnny Gold found out who is supplying your cousin with drugs in New York."

"Who is it?" Nancy breathed.

"A man named Carl Johnson. He's English but lives in Manhattan, where he recruits female performers to work in London clubs. I can't tell you where he lives, but Oscar said he hangs out at the Picador club on Sixty-Fourth Street."

"Do you think I should report him to the police?" Nancy asked.

"Christ, no!" Jackie replied. "Don't even think about it. You'll only make things worse for Louise if you go to the police, and you'll put yourself in danger. Maybe Jacqueline or Irving will know someone in that world who might be able to have a chat. I haven't met him, but I can guarantee that appealing to his better nature won't work because he won't have one."

Nancy clutched her head in her hands after the call. How did Louise get involved with these people? And, more important, how could she get free of them?

"Johnny reminded me that I once saw your cousin perform at the Ad Lib," Jackie said. "She has a beautiful voice."

"Yes, she does." Nancy remembered Louise was always singing during the last summer she spent with them in Ossipee, back when her mom was still alive. They'd been so happy then.

That afternoon, Nancy attended her first Heywood & Bradshaw editorial meeting, and found it followed the same pattern as the ones at Bernard Geis. The editors were all men, most of them chain-smokers, and they crowded around the meeting-room table with knees spread wide, taking up as much space as possible. Nancy was crushed between Bill and Michael and had to balance her notes on her knee because there wasn't any room on the table.

She had brought along a proposal from a writer called Cheryl Runyan, who'd had a string of bestsellers in the early sixties, then had taken a few years out to have kids. Now she had written a new novel, which she was submitting to a handful of publishers, and Nancy thought it was sensational. When her turn came, she pitched it with enthusiasm.

"It's the story of a woman artist living in a remote seaside town, where she has two lovers who don't know about each other," she began.

On the other side of the table, the sales director faked a yawn and rolled his eyes at the man next to him. Nancy decided to ignore him and carry on.

"When a young girl's body washes up on the beach, the artist finds herself forced into giving an alibi to one of her lovers. . . ."

"Can I stop you there?" the sales director said. "I worked with Cheryl Runyan ten years ago and she's a nightmare. Her sense of entitlement is in inverse proportion to her talent. Frankly, a chimpanzee with a typewriter could write better books."

Nancy was astonished. "I don't agree," she said. "She's got gripping plots and characters women will empathize with. I think this has the potential to be huge."

"Woman artist, lovers, beach—it's not speaking to me," Dan Streather piped up.

"It's not aimed at you, Dan," she said, irritated. "It's about time publishers started focusing more on what women want to read, because they are a huge market. Did you know that eighty percent of all books in America are bought by women? How often do we ask them what they want?"

Eddie from production, who considered himself a wit, chipped in: "A good shag, then remembering their name afterward. Isn't that what women want?"

"That's vile," Nancy snapped.

"I think it's her time of the month," Eddie murmured to his neighbor, just loud enough to be overheard.

Nancy gasped and looked around the room for support but no one would meet her eye.

"I think that's a no," Bill said. "Sorry, Nancy. Who's next? Michael, what have you got for us?"

Nancy listened to the other proposals, too shocked to comment on any. She realized it wasn't just her; the general tone of the meeting was gladiatorial, with each editor determined to shoot down the others' ideas. In her opinion, it was a totally nonconstructive approach. She couldn't help thinking that women would at least have listened to one another and had reasonable discussions on the merits of each book. How any proposals were accepted in this bear pit was beyond her.

On the way back to her apartment later, she stopped by her neighborhood bookstore, the Gotham Book Mart. She liked to browse in bookstores and see which titles were getting attention. An elderly woman with a shock of white hair and a strong-boned face beckoned her over to the corner where she sat in a chair, watching the comings and goings on the shop floor.

"I'm Fanny Steloff," she introduced herself. "This used to be my store till I retired three years ago."

"Pleased to meet you," Nancy said. "It's a great store. Do you still work here?"

Fanny grinned. "I live in an apartment upstairs and come down most afternoons to help out—or interfere, as they might call it. I've seen you here a few times. You're clearly a book lover."

Nancy admitted she was, and told her about her job at Heywood & Bradshaw. "I'm trying to convince them to publish more novels aimed at women," she said, "but so far it's an uphill struggle."

"You should come to our women's poetry evenings," Fanny said. "You'd meet a lot of women writers there." She hoisted herself from her chair with difficulty and hobbled to a nearby shelf, selected a stapled pamphlet, and handed it to Nancy. "Some of them publish their own work because they can't get mainstream publishers interested."

Nancy flicked through the pamphlet. On the back it read: "Published by Shameless Hussy Press." "I love that name," she chuckled.

"Me too," Fanny said, lowering herself into the chair again. "I'm all for subverting stereotypes. The next poetry event is on the seventeenth, at seven o'clock. Come along."

"I'll surely try," Nancy promised.

Several weeks after moving in, she'd managed to cajole the New York Telephone Company to install a phone in her new apartment. Jacqueline rang later that evening to say Irving knew someone who was looking for a cruise ship singer and she wondered if Louise might be interested.

"That's a terrific idea," Nancy said. It would be a perfect way to get her out of Carl's reach and start her singing and earning a living again. "I'm seeing her over the weekend so I'll mention it." Louise still hadn't gotten a telephone so she couldn't call her. "By the way, do you know Fanny Steloff at the Gotham Book Mart? I met her this evening and thought you probably—"

"Oh, Fanny's adorable," Jacqueline interrupted. "And such an inspiration! Do give her my love and ask after Bluebell—that's her Siamese cat. She's champagne-colored with the bluest of blue eyes. Fanny feeds her on fresh salmon and heavy cream."

"Impressive!" Nancy commented. "You knew all that without consulting your Rolodex."

"Our Fanny is an original," Jacqueline said. "Once met, never forgotten."

CHAPTER 41

Jacqueline
Manhattan, 1971

Jacqueline finished the outline for her third novel, a father/daughter story that she called *Once Is Not Enough*, and she began writing her first draft. January Wayne was a naïve young girl who arrived in New York City without any experience of men or the ways of the world. Elements of her character were based on Nancy as she had been when Jacqueline first met her, with all her youthful optimism untarnished by betrayal and heartache. There was a handsome young man, whom everyone wanted January to marry, but who had a dark secret; an evil doctor; and a bossy magazine editor, who bore a few similarities to her dear friend Helen Gurley Brown.

From the start Jacqueline had planned that January would have to die by the end of the novel. How could someone so innocent survive in the modern world? But once she got to the final chapters, she couldn't bear to kill her. Instead, she slipped in a science-fiction-style ending stolen from a novel called *The Stars Scream* she had started and failed to complete a decade earlier. Would it satisfy "her people"? she wondered. She wasn't sure. She'd decide in a later draft.

Jacqueline stuck to her usual writing routine, but it wasn't the same without Josephine snoring at her feet. Friends urged her to get another dog, but only the ones who'd never had pets themselves. If Irving died, did they expect her to replace him within the year? She sighed, and stroked the engraved casket containing Josephine's ashes that she kept on the desk beside her.

One February morning, while she was hard at work, the doorman, Calder, buzzed on the intercom to say there was a woman asking to see her, who refused to give her name. Jacqueline hesitated. If Irving had been there, she would have sent him to deal with it, but he was out in meetings. She didn't like to interrupt the flow of her writing, but curiosity got the better of her. It must be someone she knew. They were careful not to reveal their address to strangers because of the death threats from puritanical maniacs.

"Send her up," she said.

"That's the problem," he replied. "She won't come into the foyer. She's outside in the street." He cleared his throat. "And she's not wearing shoes."

"Really?" Could it be a crazed fan who'd followed her home one night? "I'll come down," she told him. She'd be safe enough with Calder there.

She didn't take anything except the door keys, planning to have a quick chat and find out what the woman wanted.

"Where is she?" she asked, and Calder pointed through the glass doors. Crouched behind a planter on the sidewalk was a girl with short blond hair, wearing a sleeveless yellow summer dress, and, as he'd said, with bare feet.

When Jacqueline stepped outside, a wall of cold air hit her: winter hadn't yet loosened its grip on the city, and the low white sun wasn't providing any warmth. The girl turned her head and she saw it was Louise. She looked gaunt, with staring eyes, and she was shivering convulsively.

"For goodness' sake, come inside," Jacqueline urged. "You'll catch your death out here."

"They're after me," Louise said in a loud whisper. "They want to kill me."

Jacqueline felt a jolt of fear and glanced up and down the street. Who was? Her drug dealer? Or one of the other gangsters she had gotten herself mixed up with? She needed to get her indoors as fast as possible.

"They won't find you here," she said. "I'll call the police." She turned to ask Calder to dial 9-1-1, but Louise screamed, "No police!" Before Jacqueline could stop her, she sprang up and darted across Central Park South, causing traffic to swerve with a screech of brakes.

"Damn!" Jacqueline cursed. She'd have to run after her. She was only wearing a jersey dress with a long knitted cardigan, and the cold was seeping into her bones, but if she rushed upstairs for a coat, she would never find Louise again.

She hurried across the street, keeping her eyes focused on the sunshine-yellow fabric. Just past the Wishing Hill, Jacqueline lost sight of her and stood, scanning the horizon, until she spotted a glimpse of yellow behind a bench. As she drew closer, she saw Louise was crouched on the ground, rocking back and forth and muttering.

"Louise, it's Jacqueline," she said, keeping her voice low and calm. "Tell me what's happened and we'll find a solution."

"They're angry with me," Louise said, pressing her hands over her ears. "They're shouting."

"Who's shouting? Who's angry?"

Louise shook her head. "They say you mustn't ask questions or they'll get you too."

"Who does?" Jacqueline persisted.

"They're trying to brainwash me," Louise whispered. "They want to control me."

She had a wild look, her eyes darting from side to side as if she was genuinely terrified of something or someone. Her hair was matted and there was a streak of dried blood on her leg.

Jacqueline wrapped her arms around herself. She had the remnants of a winter cold and the chill air was making her wheezy.

"Please come inside and we'll work things out," she pleaded, but instead Louise stood abruptly and darted off in the direction of the boating pond.

Jacqueline followed more slowly, coughing with the effort. She was beginning to suspect Louise was experiencing a psychotic episode. She'd seen inmates with psychoses at the facilities where her son stayed, and she could understand why people in the Middle Ages used to believe they were being tormented by demons. Could Louise be dangerous? She considered looking for a policeman, but that would be petrifying for the girl in her current state.

When she caught up with her, Louise was hiding behind a bush, rocking back and forth. Jacqueline had to win her trust somehow.

"You must be freezing," she said. "Why don't you take my cardigan?" She peeled it off and held it out. Straight away, the cold penetrated to her bones. Irving would be furious with her for going out without a coat.

Louise reached for the cardigan.

"Put it on quickly, while it's still warm from my body," Jacqueline urged. "Wrap it tight around." Her teeth began to chatter. "Well done. I'm glad you came to me. You remembered that I'm your friend, didn't you?"

Louise nodded, her eyes round and childlike.

"I'm on your side," Jacqueline said. "I'm going to protect you from the bad people. You look very tired, as if you haven't slept for a long time."

"I didn't go to sleep in case the voices got me. I've been running away from them all night." Louise was poised, ready to bolt again, and Jacqueline knew she didn't have the energy to run after her.

"Wouldn't you like to get into a warm bed and have a rest? I'll watch over you and make sure no one can harm you."

Louise's eyes flickered. She was tempted. "But they might get me," she whispered.

"They can't," Jacqueline said firmly, as if soothing a child who'd had a nightmare. "They don't know where I live. I'll keep you safe. I promise I will."

Eventually she was able to persuade Louise to come back to the apartment. As they walked back arm in arm, Jacqueline was numb with cold and coughing like a walrus. She tucked Louise into her own bed, adding an extra blanket on top, then she pulled on her mink coat and curled in a chair at the bedside, holding her hand until she fell asleep.

Once she was sure Louise was out for the count, Jacqueline went through to the sitting room. Keeping her voice low, she telephoned her doctor's office and asked him to come as soon as possible. Next, she called Nancy.

She was still shivering as she stood in the kitchen in her mink coat, making coffee. She could imagine what Irving would say. Why had she gone to so much trouble for someone she'd only met once and hadn't even liked? But the way she saw it, she hadn't had a choice. Louise was too vulnerable. Anyone halfway decent would have done the same.

* * *

NANCY ARRIVED FIRST, out of breath after running all the way from her office. Jacqueline had explained on the phone that Louise appeared to have had a psychotic breakdown, which she suspected could have been brought on by the amphetamine shots.

"Oh, poor Louise," Nancy said, looking at her sleeping cousin. "I never did get a chance to tell her about the cruise ship vacancy. We were supposed to meet the day after tomorrow."

"I don't think it would have made a difference," Jacqueline

comforted her. "At least now I hope we can get her to accept help."

The doctor came just as Louise was beginning to stir. She huddled beneath the covers, clutching her hands over her ears, as if still hearing voices, but he took charge of the situation with calm authority. Louise allowed him to take her pulse, listen to her chest through his stethoscope, and then give her a tranquilizer.

While she rested, the doctor spoke to Jacqueline and Nancy in the kitchen. "I'm going to refer her to Pilgrim State for assessment. Perhaps one of you would go in the ambulance with her?"

"I will," Nancy volunteered.

"Will she recover?" Jacqueline asked.

"I'm sure she will," he said. "Psychosis is commonly associated with drug misuse, but there are very effective medications. She'll need to change her lifestyle, of course. If she goes back on the drugs, this will happen again and it could be more serious next time."

"If only we could stop whoever is supplying her," Jacqueline said to Nancy.

Nancy looked thoughtful. "Jackie Collins told me it's a guy called Carl Johnson who hangs out at the Picador club on Sixty-Fourth Street, but she warned me not to approach him. She suggested someone who knows that world might be able to talk to him."

"Interesting," Jacqueline said, her mind leaping ahead. "Leave it with me."

* * *

AFTER THE AMBULANCE left, Jacqueline poured herself a vodka on the rocks, even though it was only midafternoon. She felt shaken by the experience. Louise had been utterly convinced that voices were shouting at her and unnamed people were trying to brainwash and kill her. It was terrifying how the mind could turn against you and cause you to entirely lose touch with reality.

She picked up the telephone and dialed George's office number, waiting as a receptionist tried various extensions to find him. He sounded harassed when he came on the line, but his tone mellowed when he heard it was her. Relations between them had been strained after her stupid mistake in leaving Amanda's name in *The Love Machine* and she was glad of an excuse to talk to him about something else.

"Oh Christ," he exclaimed when he heard about Louise. "Poor girl!"

"Nancy told me the name of the guy who supplies her with shots, and I wondered if we could persuade him to stop?" She lit a cigarette, then told him who it was. "Let's go see him," she said. "Together."

"Absolutely not. I'll go alone," George said. "I don't want you getting on the radar of some lowlife."

Jacqueline gave a short laugh that turned into a cough. "All the years we've been friends, George Carter, and I still don't think you know me at all. I'm coming with you. End of discussion."

* * *

THE WALLS OF the club were nicotine-brown and damp, as if slick with sweat. The floor was uneven and Jacqueline stepped carefully because it was so dimly lit she couldn't see her feet. George led her through close-packed tables toward the bar. On stage, three girls were singing Supremes cover versions, at least one of them slightly off-key so all the harmonies were discordant.

They perched on barstools and George ordered drinks, then asked the barman if they could speak to Carl, and gave his name. The barman nodded, poker-faced, exactly like a character in a gangster movie.

George had made Jacqueline promise to let him do the talking, and that she would wear a blonde wig as a disguise. Looking around at the general sleaziness of the club, Jacqueline decided this would make excellent research for a future novel and tried to memorize a few telling details: the sour, yeasty smell, the dour barman, the sad-eyed daytime drinkers.

She turned her attention to the singers. They were older than they appeared at first glance and would never have been talented enough to make the big time. Why didn't they try something else instead of belting out tired songs day after day? Had Louise been working in a club like this when she was offered a glamorous London contract? It must have seemed a dream come true.

George looked miles away and she wondered what he was thinking. "You're not doing this for Louise, are you?" she asked. "It's for Nancy."

"Of course it is," he agreed.

"I know you're very fond of her." He didn't reply straight away and she continued to probe. "I'd say more than fond; I'd say you love her."

George gave her a quick, defensive look. "What if I do?"

"You should tell her before she finds some other guy and settles down. You'll beat yourself up if that happens." Jacqueline knew him so well. He'd let a few wonderful women slip through his fingers over the years because he hadn't gotten over the loss of Amanda. "Carry on like this and you'll end up a lonely old man, sitting in Toots Shor's boring anyone who'll listen about what might have been, back in the day."

"Thanks for that image," he said. "More than anyone else, you understand why I can't risk it. I only end up hurting the women I get involved with. Besides, I've never got so much as a hint that Nancy would be interested in me that way."

"I'm sure she would," Jacqueline said. "What have you got to lose?"

"A close friendship," he replied. "Keep your matchmaking for your novels, Jacqueline. Please don't interfere."

The singers left the stage and the club fell silent, then a slim young man emerged from behind a curtain and walked toward them.

"George Carter? How're you doing?" He shook hands, then turned to Jacqueline.

"Susan," she introduced herself, using the pseudonym she'd decided on, and he gave her a penetrating look. He was handsome, she'd give him that: shoulder-length dark-blond hair, and an engaging naughtiness about the eyes. A cravat tied around his neck gave him the louche air of a nineteenth-century dandy.

He turned back to George. "Are you the George Carter who made that film about London clubland?" George agreed he was. "Man, you skate on thin ice," Carl said. "You wanna watch your back if you ever visit London again." His accent was a curious hybrid of English and American vowels. "Anyway, what can I do for you?"

"It's about Louise Cardena," George said. "Name ring any bells?"

"Vaguely," Carl said. "What of her?"

"She's in the hospital after a bad reaction to some vitamin shots and I heard you supplied them."

"Me?" He shrugged with mock innocence. "I don't know anything about no vitamin shots, George. Did she tell you it was me? That was very naughty of her." His eyes were steely.

"It wasn't her," George said. "A contact in London gave me your name."

"You and I both know it's you who supplied her," Jacqueline butted in. "And we both know what's in these shots. What would your mother think if she knew, Carl? Do you think she'd be proud of you?" George tugged on her arm to try and shut her up, but this man's cockiness infuriated her.

"Ooh, feisty!" Carl mocked. "Are you threatening to tell Mummy I've been a naughty boy?"

"No, I'm threatening to tell the police," Jacqueline snapped, and George hissed at her to shut up.

"Truth be told, Louise has gotten a bit too unreliable lately. . . ." Carl was speaking to George now, man to man. "Not turning up for appointments, or, if she does, suddenly deciding she doesn't feel like working after all. I'm happy to take her off the books so long as you can guarantee she won't blab. You know what I'm saying."

"She's terrified of you, so I think you can relax on that score," George replied.

"Terrified of little old me!" He smiled at Jacqueline. "Can't think why . . . Miss *Susan*." He emphasized her name.

"I hope you're proud," Jacqueline said. "Couldn't you find a worthier career for yourself than exploiting young girls who dream of making it in showbiz?"

He grinned, and a gold tooth glinted. "My wife's a big fan of your novels, Miss *Susan*. I sincerely hope you manage to write more of them. Send me a signed copy of the next one, won't you?"

Jacqueline lost her temper and curled her fist to throw a punch at him, but George anticipated her, grabbing hold of her wrist. "Thanks for your understanding, Carl," he said. "We'll be off now."

Jacqueline glared at Carl before George dragged her out of the club. When she glanced back over her shoulder, he was still watching them, still with that insufferable grin. She would put him in a novel one day, she decided, and she'd give him an abnormally small penis.

CHAPTER 42

Jackie

London, 1971

Jackie never invited Oscar to read her work in progress. She was too sensitive to criticism at the early stages and didn't want to be influenced by anyone else's opinion apart from those of her UK and US editors. Besides, Oscar wasn't a big reader so she didn't think his judgment would be useful. After reading her first two novels, he'd offered nothing but unqualified praise, so when she gave him a proof copy of *Sunday Simmons and Charlie Brick*, she expected more of the same.

Jackie had taken the kids to the park that afternoon, then came home and was feeding them macaroni and cheese when Oscar walked into the kitchen.

"I finished it," he said.

She was puzzled by the flatness of his tone. "And? Don't you like it?"

He spoke hesitantly. "It's great storytelling, of course, but it's very anti-men."

"Charlie Brick isn't all bad, is he?" She wiped up some juice that had spilled on the table, disappointed at his lack of enthusiasm.

"That chauffeur who sent letters to actresses containing"—he glanced at Tracy, who understood a lot of adult words—"unwanted secretions. It's disgusting. What on earth gave you the idea?"

"I get letters like that," Jackie told him, rolling her eyes. "Charming, isn't it?"

"What?" Oscar looked horrified. "Are you serious?" He grabbed her by the elbow and pulled her out of the kitchen and into the

front room, speaking in a low voice. "You get letters with condoms in them? And you didn't think to tell me?" He sounded
furious. Jackie was surprised by the strength of his reaction.

"I think they're all from the same guy. He writes in block capitals and boasts about his sexual prowess, telling me how great it
would be if I slept with him." She shrugged. "It's unpleasant but
I don't think he means any harm."

"How long has this been going on?" he demanded.

"It started just after the publication of *Married Men*. I think
I'm providing a fantasy life for him and he likes to share it with
me." She glanced over her shoulder, wondering what the girls
were getting up to.

"He sounds like a lunatic! Of *course* he could be dangerous.
Normal men don't do things like that." His voice rose. "Are there
any other abusive perverts in your life you're failing to tell me
about?"

She got irritated then. "Do you want me to report every loser
who stands too close and rubs himself against me in a lift? Or
businessmen who think nothing of patting me on the bottom?
Women put up with this stuff all the time, Oscar. It's part of
life."

She decided not to tell him about the radio assistant in New
York who had molested her in a deserted corridor. When the publisher complained to his boss, he denied anything had happened,
and of course she had no way of proving it.

"In your novel, the letter writer kidnaps Sunday Simmons,"
he said, anger flashing in his eyes. "What if your letter writer
decides to kidnap you and make his fantasies come true? I'm
your husband and I need to be warned about men like this so I
can protect you."

Jackie's temper snapped at the assumption that she needed
looking after like some "little woman." "What would you do,

Oscar? Get one of your gangster friends to rough him up? I can look after myself, thank you."

Oscar's eyes were blazing. She'd never seen him so angry. "It's impossible being married to someone who shuts me out of her life. You don't talk to me about your writing, you don't tell me what happens on your book tours, you don't share any details of your career. I learn more about you from reading press interviews than I do in my own home. And now I hear some pervert has been sending you condoms and you didn't think to mention it. Don't you even *want* to be married, Jackie?"

She paused, trying to think of a way to defuse the tension without compromising. "I was very clear with you that, after what happened with Wallace, I didn't want another traditional marriage where my husband was 'in charge.' And I don't think I tell you any less about my career than you tell me about yours."

He wasn't appeased. "You told me you didn't want to know about the lowlifes I have to deal with in clubland, and that's fair enough. But I think any husband would be shocked to hear his wife has been receiving sleazy anonymous letters for—what?—two years now. Would you tell me if someone had raped you?"

"Now you're being sensationalist. No one has raped me."

"Not yet." His expression was cold.

Why had this gotten under his skin so badly? Perhaps he was embarrassed to have a wife who wrote so-called dirty books. She'd thought he was supportive, but maybe he secretly agreed with all the hypocrites and bigots who claimed her books were perverting the nation's youth. "Does it embarrass you that I write about sex?" she asked. "Is that what this is about?"

"If you want to know the truth, I don't love it," he admitted. "I get sarcastic comments from guys who ask if you make me act out all your sex scenes or if you have gigolos lined up for practice sessions."

"You shouldn't mix with such creeps," she snapped. She'd never considered before what it might be like to be Mr. Jackie Collins but, frankly, she didn't think he had much to complain about.

"I can take it, don't worry about me," he said. "I'm proud of you and I'll always support you. What I can't take is being excluded, so that I feel like a lodger who helps to pay the bills, who's handy for a bit of sex, but who doesn't get to share any of your thoughts and feelings."

Is that truly what he was upset about? "I'm busy, Oscar. I'm raising three daughters, writing novels, and keeping house. By the time you come home in the evening, forgive me if I don't have the mental energy for soul-searching conversations on the sofa."

"So you're happy for us to carry on living side by side but separate?" he asked, looking sad.

"Yes!" she exclaimed, exasperated. "That's the human condition. I don't know what more you expect from a wife."

"More than this," he said quietly, and walked out of the room. She heard him stomping upstairs to his study and stood for a moment, shaken. It was by far the worst argument they'd ever had.

Over the next few days, Jackie reran it in her head. Was she in the wrong? Did she shut him out? They'd been married almost six years—happily, she'd thought—but she certainly didn't involve him in her career the way Jacqueline did with Irving. She made professional decisions on her own, with Mort's help. Should she confide in Oscar more?

All her life she had seen evidence of marriages going bad: her father parading mistresses in front of her mother; and Wallace, poor dear Wallace, whom she still thought of with great sadness. Had that mistrust made her incapable of fully committing herself in her current marriage? Perhaps an analyst would say she couldn't accept that Oscar truly loved her because she didn't love herself enough.

Not long after the row, Jackie was bridesmaid to Jan de Souza at her wedding to Johnny Gold. Finally! They'd been together on and off for eight years, so it was a long time coming. In the speeches there were lots of jokes about Johnny burning his little black book. Jackie hoped that was true, but she was skeptical. There's no question that he loved Jan, and she was the perfect woman for him, but was any man capable of resisting temptation when he worked in a nightclub full of glamorous available women? Had Oscar been faithful since they got married? She believed he had been, but how far did anyone really know another person?

She got a little tipsy at the wedding party, looking around at their friends—those whose marriages seemed happy, those whose definitely weren't—and wondering what was the key to success. Then she looked at Oscar, so handsome in black tie, chatting animatedly with Johnny Gold, and she felt a rush of love for him. Maybe the secret to a long marriage was just hanging in there when the going got tough.

* * *

SUNDAY SIMMONS AND *Charlie Brick* was published to the usual scathing press reviews, but it sailed straight onto the UK bestseller list. W. H. Allen had arranged bookshop signings and talks in Manchester, Liverpool, Leeds, and London—a mini tour by Jacqueline Susann standards, but her publicist told her they were testing the water.

"We still don't want to risk you sitting at a table behind a pile of books and no one turning up," she repeated gaily.

Jackie wished she hadn't put that image in her head because

before every single event, she had anxiety dreams about being in an empty room with a pile of books no one wanted to buy. She needn't have worried, though: her readers turned out in droves, queuing patiently to get their copies signed. She made time for a quick chat with each one, and posed for photographs if they asked. She'd changed her lacquered sixties hairstyle to a long, straight one, and she often wore a pretty jeweled choker she'd found in a King's Road boutique, with a silky, figure-hugging dress and suede platform boots.

When Jackie signed books at Foyles in Charing Cross Road, a dozen women's libbers turned up with placards. She frowned as she read them on her way in: "Jackie Collins promotes sexual abuse of women!" "Traitor to the feminist cause!" One protestor spotted her and shouted, "There she is!" but Jackie slipped inside and a doorman barred them from following.

The shop manager came forward to greet her and she asked: "Could someone take out cups of tea for the protesters? It's a cold day for hanging around."

He said he would see to it.

When she reached the fiction floor of the vast book emporium, Jackie was delighted to see a line of women clutching copies of her book. The thrill that anyone wanted to read her words never faded. She greeted them with a cheery wave and called, "Hallo, ladies!" before sitting at a desk to start signing books.

Jacqueline had told her that readers asked her advice about their sex lives, but this crowd wanted to know where Jackie got her inspiration, how long it took to write a book, and what she was planning to write next.

"Hurry up!" one woman said. "You're my favorite author and I can't wait another year for your next one."

When she glanced up between customers, she noticed a long-haired youth loitering behind a display. Something about him seemed familiar but she couldn't think where she had seen him before. He ducked out of sight when he realized he'd been spotted and that struck her as odd, but the next customer was already in front of her.

The event was only supposed to last an hour, but when the time was up there were still lots of women waiting, so Jackie agreed to stay until she had signed every last copy. Between customers, whenever she looked up, she saw the young man watching her. He moved around the shop floor, but always he was there somewhere, watching. Where did she know him from? She racked her brains.

When the shop ran out of copies, they took the names and addresses of those still waiting and Jackie promised she would sign books for everyone and have them sent by post. She stood up and rubbed her neck, feeling stiff from sitting so long, then she glanced around, wondering if the young man had gone. A shadow flitted behind a shelving unit. She hurried around the other side of the stack to cut him off and came face-to-face with a thin, sallow youth, probably in his mid-twenties. He was slightly shorter than she was, with a scattering of acne on his cheeks.

Suddenly it came to her where she knew him from: "You work at W. H. Allen, don't you?" She'd seen him there when she visited the office. "I don't think we've been introduced. I'm Jackie Collins." She held out her hand.

He shook it, but hung his head and didn't say anything.

"What's your name?" she asked. "And what's your job there? Did they send you along to look after me today?"

"John Perkins," he said at last. "I work in the post room."

She was puzzled. "So why are you here, John?"

He shuffled his feet, staring at the floor. "I wanted to see you. I'm a big fan of yours."

Why was he so furtive? "You should have come over and

introduced yourself," she said, and he blushed a puce color. His behavior was strange and a little creepy. And then it dawned on her: "You must be the person who sent that box of books to New York for me," she said.

He gave a slight nod.

"That's how you knew the address," she continued. "Are you the one who's been writing me anonymous letters? I wondered how you knew my address but now I understand."

He took a step back and glanced around, as if poised to run away.

"No, don't go," Jackie said firmly. "We need to talk. The letters have to stop, John."

He looked up at her, his lip trembling as if he was about to cry. "I . . . I can't help it. I love you," he stammered.

Jackie felt sorry for him. Was this the kind of person she was accused by her critics of perverting? He seemed scared of his own shadow.

"You don't love me. You might feel as if you know me from reading my books, but you don't, not really." At thirty-four, she was probably only a decade older than he was, but he seemed much younger in terms of maturity. "I'm a happily married woman and nothing will ever happen between us."

"You put it in your new book, the bit about the condoms," he stammered. "I thought you were sending me a message."

"Yes, I was, in a way. If you remember, that character didn't turn out to be a very good person. He came to a bad end." She folded her arms. "I'm going to have to tell W. H. Allen what you've been doing, John. It will be up to them to decide if you can continue to work there."

He looked distraught. "But they'll sack me for sure. My mum needs me to pay rent for my room so she can cover the mortgage. We could lose our home. Please don't tell them."

Jackie paused to consider, but decided she had no choice. For all she knew, he could be sending similar letters to other authors, and goodness knows how he treated the pretty young girls in the office. "I have to," she said. "I suggest you promise them it will never happen again, and that you send me a written apology, which I will accept, then you might have a chance of keeping your job."

He stifled a sob and Jackie felt bad. But then she pictured him alone in his bedroom filling the condoms and writing the letters, and shuddered; she thought of the radio assistant who had denied assaulting her; she thought of all the men who abused women one way or another and the women who accepted it as if it were no big deal, and she knew she had to report him. She turned and walked away.

When she left the shop, the women's libbers were still there, but they'd put their placards down and were perched on the windowsill, chatting. One of them noticed her and jumped up: "Can we count on you to burn your bra, Miss Collins?" she called.

"Not on your life," Jackie replied. "It's a silk leopard print one my husband bought me. But good luck with the cause. I'm on your side!"

She considered stopping to debate her brand of feminism with them. Women always came out on top in her books: they earned their own money and made their own way in the world. But just then a black taxi with its light on juddered up Charing Cross Road and she decided she would rather go home and have a gin and tonic with her husband. She'd tell Oscar she had identified the condom creep, and that she was dealing with the situation all by herself.

CHAPTER 43

Nancy

Long Island, 1971

Nancy caught a train and a bus to Pilgrim State hospital to visit Louise. Her cousin seemed very frail but agreed to go for a walk around the snowy grounds, wearing oversized dark sunglasses because the medication she was on made her light-sensitive.

"I'm not hearing voices anymore," she said, in answer to Nancy's questioning, "but I feel kind of hollowed out, as if there's nothing left of me but skin and bone. Does that make sense?"

"Of course it does." Louise was painfully thin. Nancy took her arm, worried that if she slipped in the snow she might break a bone, because there was no flesh to cushion a fall. "I heard they have a music therapy group at the hospital. Have you been yet?"

"Singing makes me too sad," Louise said. "I don't think I'll ever sing again."

Her voice was so quiet Nancy had to lean in to hear. "I can understand your not wanting to sing in clubs anymore, but I hope you'll go back to writing music," she said. "You have too much talent to give up. Maybe you could teach singing. You'd be a great teacher."

"I'm not exactly a good role model." Louise sounded exhausted. "If I had a kid, I'd tell them to steer clear of the crazy lady."

"You're not crazy. You were lied to," Nancy said. "You thought the London contract was a dream come true and it's completely understandable that you snatched the opportunity."

"It was fun at first," Louise mused. "I met lots of famous

people, drank champagne, and dined out. The tips were astronomic!" She gazed toward the horizon.

"And then? When did it start to turn sour?"

Louise shivered. "There was no single occasion. I don't know what you believe, Nancy, but I was never a whore. We were told to be sociable to customers and if we wanted to make private arrangements, that was up to us. I had a few boyfriends—*man* friends, I suppose—and I slept with them if I liked them, but I never took money for sex. I wouldn't do that."

Nancy wanted to believe her, but several things didn't add up. Jacqueline had told her about Carl Johnson saying that Louise had become "too unreliable" at work. What "work" did he mean?

"I heard it was a man named Carl who gave you shots once you got back to New York. If only he hadn't done that, you could have made a fresh start," Nancy said, probing gently.

"Carl got the wrong impression about me," Louise replied. "I told him I would work as a hostess, but I meant that I would go on dates with men, that's all. He got cross when he heard I was refusing to have sex with them. He tried to force me by withholding the shots, then he'd give me some, then stop." She started crying, quietly. "My head was exploding."

Nancy waited but whatever memories Louise was wrestling with, whatever had happened between her and Carl, she clearly wanted to bury.

"Thank god it's over," she said, blowing her nose into a balled-up tissue. "I just wish I knew what to do next. I'm months behind on rent, I've got no work, and I can't sing anymore."

"I have a suggestion," Nancy said. She'd told her stepdad about Louise's situation and straight away Joe offered that she could go and stay with him and the boys in Ossipee while she recovered.

"I love that house," Louise said, thoughtfully. "Your mom made it so pretty."

"It's calm and quiet there, and Joe says you can stay as long as you want. He'll come and pick you up when you're ready. I'll get your things shipped from New York, and I'll visit when I can. As for rent—I'll just tell the landlord you're ill and have no way of paying."

Louise stopped and clasped her throat, as if something had just occurred to her. "I don't know how I'll pay the hospital fees. What will I do?"

"Jacqueline is taking care of them," Nancy told her.

"Jacqueline Susann?" Louise was stunned. "But I only met her once." She clearly had no memory of the Central Park episode. "How can people be so kind?"

"Some people just are," Nancy said. "And some not so much," she muttered under her breath, thinking of the obnoxious bunch of men she worked with.

* * *

As the months went by, the job at Heywood & Bradshaw became increasingly intolerable. Nancy came to dread the editorial meetings, at which Bill seemed determined to push her into a pigeonhole labeled "books for the ladies." He restricted her to working on romance novels with illustrations of "hot chicks" and "handsome hunks" on the covers, while Dan and Michael got to work on what he called the "big books." They all talked down to her in meetings and wouldn't let her pay more than minimal advances, so she had no chance of attracting any established authors. And still he wouldn't give her the title of editor.

On top of that, Michael had been obnoxious since she "stole" Jackie Collins from him. According to his simplistic mindset, anyone who held feminist views must be a lesbian man-hater and he joked that he was making it his mission to convert Nancy to heterosexuality. Many a time she had to wriggle away when he grabbed her bottom or breast in passing, or pinned her to the wall and tried to stick his fat tongue in her mouth. She shoved him off, calling him a jerk, but he treated it as a hilarious bit of office clowning and told her she had no sense of humor.

When Nancy spotted an advertisement in *Publishers Weekly* for an editor at St. David's Press, she leapt at the chance. It was everything she wanted in a job and would give her the opportunity to build her own fiction list at one of the top companies. She spent hours writing and rewriting her cover letter and résumé until she couldn't improve them any further. Before sticking them in the mail, she said a silent prayer and kissed the envelope for luck.

Only a week later she received a letter with the St. David's Press colophon on the envelope. She tore it open, heart pounding. The letter was short and concise: *Thank you for your application, but I'm afraid we are looking for someone with more editorial experience.*

She screamed in frustration. The ad had asked for two to three years' experience and in truth she had been doing an editor's job for almost seven years, but without having the job title to prove it. Could she write back and explain? But she didn't trust Bill Heywood to give her an honest appraisal if asked for a reference, and it was so long since she had worked on *Valley of the Dolls* that a reference from Jacqueline would be of limited value.

Nancy was crushed. How could she ever achieve her ambition? She would be stuck forever at Heywood & Bradshaw being molested by one colleague and patronized by the rest. She was going to turn twenty-nine in a few days and resolved that she would find a way to become an editor by her thirtieth birthday if it killed her.

She kept reading *Publishers Weekly* and from it she learned that Bernard Geis Associates had gone bust. That had been in the cards for a while. She wondered if Steven had managed to get another job but had no way of finding out. She didn't wish him ill and she certainly wouldn't want Darren to suffer, but she had no desire to set eyes on Steven ever again. Their affair felt as if it had happened a long time ago to a much younger, more naïve version of herself, one she hardly recognized.

* * *

WHEN NANCY FINALLY found time to go to a Gotham Book Mart poetry evening, everyone was friendly and welcoming. There was a striking black woman with dyed blond hair, a white woman with purple streaks in her silver hair, women in hippy gear with enormous hoop earrings, and women with oversized spectacles and bell-bottom jeans. They read poems about periods, about misogyny, about race, and about growing old in a youth-obsessed world. They talked in hippy slang: *Can you dig it? Groovy, babe. Down with the kids.* Fanny Steloff sat to one side, clapping and whistling enthusiastically, and Nancy guessed this event was her pet project.

She stopped to chat with Fanny afterward, and told her about her frustration over the St. David's Press job.

"I know I'm a good editor," she said. "I've discovered dozens of authors and edited loads of successful books. My authors like and trust me. But I work with men who talk over me in meetings, belittle my judgment, and override my decisions. Frankly, I'm not sure things would be any different if I moved to another publisher. Some companies have female editors, but they're all dominated by men at the top. You're lucky you were able to be your own boss."

"You could be your own boss too," Fanny said. "I heard in London, there's a group of women planning to start a publishing company for women's fiction—not just new novels but ones from the past that they think deserve more attention. It's called Virago Press. Why don't you try something similar here?"

Nancy laughed. "I think I may have given you a false impression of the extent of my experience."

"The bits you don't know, you would soon pick up," Fanny said, her eyes challenging. "I had only worked in a few bookstores when I started Gotham Book Mart. I knew what customers liked, but I knew nothing about the business side and had to learn from the ground up. Some days during the Great Depression I didn't sell a single book, but I still had to pay the rent and staff wages. Yet I got by. You need to be tough, ambitious, and single-minded. Do you think you've got those qualities?"

"I'm definitely ambitious," Nancy said, "but I've never thought of starting my own business. I don't have any savings, and no bank would lend money to someone as young and inexperienced as me."

"There are ways around everything," Fanny said, her chin thrust out, eyes sparkling.

"I know nothing about printing or distributing books, which you must admit is crucial," Nancy argued. "And why would any author want to be published by someone who is just starting out in business and could go bust within weeks?"

"You wouldn't do it all yourself," Fanny said. "Put together a team—an all-female team, like the London bunch. I know a lot of people in the industry who I'm sure would be willing to help, and I often hear what's going on behind the scenes."

"Yes, I bet you do," Nancy agreed.

"For example, that ex-boyfriend of yours, Steven Bailey—he's moved to North Carolina to work for a stationery company." Fanny laughed out loud at Nancy's astonished expression.

"How did you . . . ?" Nancy paused, trying to solve the puzzle.

"I saw you together one night in Cafe Au Go Go." Fanny chuckled. "I never forget a face. Nice guy, but definitely not right for you." She winked.

Nancy guessed Fanny must be in her eighties, but she had the playfulness of a teenager. What a life she must have led! Would she achieve a fraction as much with her own life? Based on current progress, it didn't look likely.

Jacqueline
Manhattan, 1972

One good thing came out of Louise's amphetamine addiction, as far as Jacqueline was concerned: it gave her the ending for her third novel. She made her main character, January, descend into drug addiction, using a few details inspired by Louise's condition. Her story about the naïve, unworldly daughter of a film producer was completely different from Louise's experience, so she didn't feel she was stepping on toes. She was simply using personal observations to give her story authenticity.

There was a fine line that shouldn't be crossed when using friends in your novels, Jacqueline realized. On the phone to Jackie, she confided in her about George's anger that she had accidentally used his late wife's name in *The Love Machine*. Jackie sympathized, and replied that one of Johnny Gold's ex-girlfriends had accused her of modeling an unsympathetic character in *The Stud* on her.

"To be honest, I hadn't been thinking about her at all," Jackie said, "but you never quite know where stories come from, do you? It's a mysterious process, as if you pluck a silver thread from the universe."

It was good to have an author friend to talk to. Jacqueline had plenty of American friends, of course, but none who understood the peculiar pressures of being a woman who wrote about gritty subjects and was publicly pilloried for it. That gave her and Jackie a unique bond. With Jackie, she could be honest about the nights she tossed and turned, arguing with critics in her sleep, then woke exhausted in the morning; the occasions when she spotted her name in the press and braced herself for more abuse.

"Do you read reviews?" she asked Jackie. "I try to avoid it, but they get thrust under my nose by radio and TV hosts, who hope I'll lose my cool and give them a dramatic show."

"I can't read them," Jackie replied. "I've got enough trouble with my inner critic, who sits on my shoulder telling me everything I write is rubbish."

"*Sunday Simmons* is your best yet," Jacqueline said. "I'm sure it's selling well." She had read a proof and given it a generous endorsement.

"Your quote really helped," Jackie replied. "My publishers were delighted."

"I'm glad. . . ." Jacqueline didn't mind helping her, now that it was clear that Jackie's books were no competition for hers in terms of sales. She still wouldn't appear on television alongside her; she was far too vain to let viewers compare her with someone so young and beautiful.

She looked up to see Irving pointing at his wristwatch, then drawing a finger across his throat. She laughed. "My husband is signaling rather graphically that I've been on the phone too long. I'd better go. Give my love to Oscar and the girls."

"Cheerio," Jackie called, as she always did, to Jacqueline's amusement.

In May, Jacqueline finally finished the edits on *Once Is Not Enough* and sent them back to her editor. It wasn't being published till March the following year, so she could afford to relax, but Jacqueline didn't do relaxation. She started making notes of ideas for the next four or five novels she planned to write, letting the essence of the stories marinate. She was physically worn out, but her brain kept on buzzing.

* * *

THE AMERICAN BOOKSELLERS Association convention was being held in Texas that year, not far from the institution where Jacqueline's son lived, so she decided to attend. She could wander around chatting to her bookseller friends, hand out teaser chapters of *Once Is Not Enough*, then visit her darling boy.

On the phone, she mentioned to Jackie that she was going, and Jackie replied that she was too shy to turn up on her own at events like that.

"I don't have your confidence," she said. "I can put on a brave front when I have to, but underneath I'm still an insecure teenager worried that people are laughing at me behind my back."

Jacqueline hesitated just a second before suggesting: "Come to Texas with me. We can wander around together. It'll be fun!"

"Are you sure? I'd love to."

Jacqueline wasn't entirely sure. The booksellers were "her people," with whom she had built up relationships over many years, and she didn't see why she should share her contacts. On the other hand, she calculated that introducing Jackie to them would enhance her reputation by making her look generous. She was still the one who had sold millions of copies, while Jackie hadn't had a sniff of a US bestseller list. Besides, they would have fun together at the ABA, and it was only for a couple of days.

The trip quickly became like a teenage sleepover, as they darted between their adjoining hotel rooms, trying on each other's makeup and perfume, and advising on clothing choices. At the convention, Jacqueline introduced Jackie to some of her favorite booksellers, and they became known to all as "the two Jackies." They signed books, had drinks and lunches, attended the main convention dinner, then both nights they finished off with a nightcap from the minibars in their rooms, and ended up chatting till the early hours.

"How did you meet Oscar?" Jacqueline asked one night. She was curious about the age gap between Jackie and her husband.

Jackie told her they'd been set up on a blind date by Johnny Gold. "I didn't fancy him at first. I thought he was too conventional for me, but boy was I being shortsighted!" Jackie made a lascivious face, as if to imply Oscar was the opposite of conventional between the sheets. Jacqueline laughed.

"How about you and Irving?" Jackie asked.

"I set my sights on him from the start and didn't let him escape," Jacqueline replied. It was true. She'd met him in Walgreen's on Broadway, a place where struggling actors used to hang out because they had payphones you could use to call about jobs. "I was only eighteen and wildly ambitious. Irving was a theater producer and publicist, so at first I thought to myself, 'He could be useful.' We started dating and he was the perfect gentleman, never trying his luck, always respectful. It was me who did all the running, right until I forced him to the altar."

No one had asked her about that for a while, and it made her reflect on her marriage of nearly thirty-four years. "I don't think outsiders understand our relationship," she said. "They see me as the brash, bossy one and think Irving trots along behind, carrying my bag and doing whatever I tell him. But he's been involved in the publicity campaigns for all my books and, before that, my TV career. I couldn't have done any of this without him. Emotionally, he keeps me steady."

"Same for me with Oscar," Jackie said. "I wouldn't have finished my first novel without him pushing me. I don't always give him the credit I should."

Jacqueline coughed. She had an annoying tickly cough, as if she'd irritated her throat lining.

"Is that hay fever?" Jackie asked. "I get it in May every year, like clockwork, and need to take antihistamines."

"I hate taking them because they make me drowsy," Jacqueline said. "I'm tired enough at the moment without adding to it, but I'll be fine when I get back to New York and can have a rest." Truth be told, she'd been popping dexies every morning on the trip to give her the energy to face the day.

When the conference was over, Jackie had to hang around waiting for a flight that left at eleven that night so she asked if Jacqueline wanted to do some sightseeing.

"I can't," Jacqueline told her. "I'm visiting my son. He lives near here."

"Can I come with you?" Jackie asked eagerly. "I'd love to meet him."

Jacqueline tried to put her off. "He's very shy, not good with strangers."

She saw confusion flicker across Jackie's face at the brush-off, and reconsidered. Could she trust her with her most precious secret? She was sure she could rely on her discretion. Her boy was a litmus test, with only her innermost friendship circle even knowing of his existence, but she was convinced Jackie wouldn't fail.

"Alright," she said with a nod. "Let's go."

When she told their taxi driver the address of the institution, Jackie gave her a quick, questioning look, but Jacqueline decided to let her find out the truth for herself.

The taxi pulled up the long driveway, then they climbed the steps. Jacqueline greeted the receptionist and signed them into the visitors' book.

"He's in the garden," a cheerful nurse told them, and pointed to a back door that opened onto a sprawling expanse of lawn. Jacqueline spotted him straight away, sitting on a bench under a tree.

"That's him," Jacqueline whispered, nodding in his direction. "That's my boy."

At that moment he raised his head and looked toward them.

He'd had a haircut since she last saw him, and was wearing a Jefferson Airplane T-shirt she'd sent for him.

"Oh my, he's so handsome," Jackie exclaimed straight away.

Jacqueline loved her for that. Most people couldn't see beyond his disability, but Jackie was right—he *was* handsome. She blinked away tears before walking across to greet him.

* * *

JACQUELINE FLEW BACK to New York to find that her publicist wanted to start making plans for the *Once Is Not Enough* tour. Already several television shows had invited her on; they knew she was entertaining and frequently controversial, which was good for ratings.

Hay fever season had long since passed, but she was still bothered by that tickly cough. It had grown so habitual she hardly noticed it herself, but Irving pointed out that she couldn't go on TV or radio with it, so at last she made an appointment with her doctor.

He listened to her chest through his stethoscope for a long time, instructing her to breathe in and out. He weighed her, and she was surprised but secretly pleased to see she was at the lowest weight she had been for years. That meant she wouldn't need to diet before the book tour.

"Have you been feeling tired recently?" he asked.

She laughed. "I'm always tired, but only because I'm so busy."

"I'm going to refer you for an X-ray," he said. "Just to be on the safe side."

Jacqueline was exasperated. She didn't have time for hospital appointments and, after all the years of breast cancer check-ups, she still hated the stress of sitting in doctors' waiting rooms staring at the execrable art on their walls.

Results usually took a week, so she was surprised to get a call from the hospital three days later, asking if she could come in that afternoon and bring her husband. A knot of fear formed in her gut. What now?

"I'm afraid the X-ray showed a mass in your right lung," the oncologist told them, with a grave expression. "We want to admit you straight away for a bronchoscopy and biopsy."

There was a buzzing sound in her ears, making it hard to think. Irving took her hand and gripped hard. Jacqueline told herself not to worry: her friend June had had a mass on her lungs and it turned out to be scarring from childhood tuberculosis. There were plenty of innocent explanations.

Six days later, the verdict came: the original breast cancer had metastasized in her right lung. The oncologist was a serious man, who probably prided himself on straight-talking with his patients. Jacqueline focused on the shiny bald patch on the crown of his head, then the wedding band on his left hand.

"Is it serious?" she asked—the clichéd question these doctors must hear every day. She wasn't even sure she wanted to know.

"Yes, I'm afraid it's serious," he said. "The cancer is advanced."

"How long have I got?" *Don't answer*, she wanted to scream, but the question was already out there, hanging in the air.

"We'll start treatment immediately," he said, "but, in a worst-case scenario, you may only have a few months to live."

She could hear Irving snuffling by her side, but Jacqueline didn't cry. She wondered if the doctor would go home and tell his wife that he'd delivered a death sentence on a famous author today. "I don't want this news to get out," she told him. "I have a book tour to do."

His expression was inscrutable as he said, "I'm bound by medical confidentiality, as with every other patient."

On the way out, Jacqueline remembered the date: it was January 1973, exactly ten years since she'd made her deal with God. It seemed he'd been listening all along.

CHAPTER 45

Jackie

London, 1973

Jackie was pleased to hear Jacqueline's voice on the telephone saying, "Hi, it's me," but quickly realized her tone sounded off.

"I've got bad news," she said. "That cough we thought was hay fever? Turns out it's cancer."

Jackie gave a little cry and clasped a hand to her mouth. *Not cancer.* "Oh God! I'm so sorry," she managed. "What are they going to do?"

"It's inoperable, but I'm getting state-of-the-art treatments." A coughing fit silenced her for a few moments and her voice was croaky when she spoke again. "It's a secondary cancer, from the breast cancer I had ten years ago. They're going to do chemotherapy first, then I'm having some newfangled treatment with cobalt radiation, which starts just before the publication of *Once Is Not Enough.* Can you believe it? Terrible timing!"

"Will you cancel the book tour?" Jackie asked, feeling shell-shocked.

"Of course not," Jacqueline wheezed. Even on a transatlantic phone line, Jackie could hear her straining to get air into her lungs.

"What can I do?" Jackie said. "Ask me anything."

"I do have a request," Jacqueline said. "I wondered if you will be my four a.m. friend?"

She coughed, painfully, and Jackie waited for her to explain.

"They've made me stop taking sleeping pills," she said, "and I always seem to be awake at four a.m. when Irving and my

American friends are sound asleep. But that's nine a.m. UK time and I think you're just back from dropping the girls at school. Can I call you then if I need to talk to someone?"

"Of course I'll be your four a.m. friend," Jackie said straight away. "Or any other time you want, day or night."

"I don't want anyone else to know," she said. "I couldn't bear people talking about me and pitying me. I suppose you can tell Oscar, but make sure he keeps it to himself."

When she came off the phone, Jackie sat down hard on the couch, filled with foreboding. Jacqueline had sounded pragmatic and unemotional but she must be scared. She was only in her early fifties. If anyone could beat cancer, Jacqueline Susann would, but it wasn't going to be easy.

Jackie thought back to her mother's slow decline from what she now knew had been cancer, although no one had used the word back then and she still wasn't sure what kind it had been. Elsa seemed to have accepted her prognosis without complaint, but perhaps she had shielded her children from the tough bits; perhaps she had done everything she could to survive. Jackie felt a pang of missing her. Grief never left you entirely; it took up residence deep inside and could be triggered at any time.

She rang Oscar at the club and told him the news about Jacqueline.

"Medical science has come on a lot in the years since your mother died," he said. "There have been loads of breakthroughs in the battle against cancer, and Jacqueline and Irving have the money to go to the top doctors."

Optimism was all very well, Jackie thought, but everyone knew the Big C was a killer. She asked a doctor friend of theirs and he told her that the five-year survival rate for secondary breast cancer was twenty-five percent, shockingly low. If she knew that, Jacqueline must be much more scared than she was letting on.

* * *

ALMOST TWO WEEKS went by before Jackie heard from Jacqueline again.

"Apologies, but my head has been inside a toilet bowl," she said. "The grapefruit diet might be all the rage, but the chemotherapy diet has it beat hands down for rapid weight loss."

"Oh poor you," Jackie said, her stomach churning in sympathy. "Are you at home or in hospital?"

"I get a cab to the hospital on the day of the treatment, then Irving picks me up after. He's being heroic."

"I knew he would be." Irving doted on Jacqueline. He wouldn't let her down when she needed him most.

"He took me across to the Wishing Hill the other day," Jacqueline said. "It's a place in Central Park where I made a deal with God ten years ago, when I first had cancer. I asked him to give me ten more years and let me become a bestselling author. Isn't it spooky that he gave me exactly what I asked for?"

Jackie frowned. "Do you really think it was God who gave you cancer? What kind of god would do that?"

"Good question. I guess he's a god who thinks a deal's a deal." She coughed, and took a while to recover enough to speak again. "Anyway, I went back to the hill and asked him if I could have another ten years please. I said I'll do whatever he wants: I'll work for charity, shave my head, give money to the poor—he just has to let me know. I feel I've got so much left to do."

"Do you truly believe in a god who makes decisions about what happens to each of the four billion individuals on the planet?" Jackie asked. "Even as a schoolgirl singing hymns in morning assembly, I was never able to get my head around that. I guess I'm a born atheist."

"I was raised a Jew," Jacqueline said. "My mom kept a kosher household and we followed Orthodox practices. But in my twenties a friend introduced me to Catholicism and I decided to convert. I guess I liked the matriarchal figure of the Virgin Mary, and the way you can do penance and have your sins wiped clean. That comes in handy." She chuckled.

"I can't believe you have any sins," Jackie said. "But I'm glad you're hedging your bets between religions. You should be fine on Judgment Day."

There was a silence on the other end, and she wondered if she'd gone too far in mocking Jacqueline's beliefs. She was about to apologize when Jacqueline said, "I wish I'd had grandchildren." She sounded wistful. "I would have loved some little ones to carry on my genes. My only legacy will be the books, and they'll go out of fashion before long."

"Are you kidding?" Jackie exclaimed. "You've changed the world of publishing. You're a phenomenon. *Dolls* is the best-selling novel of all time, and your books will live on for generations."

"I wish I could believe that." Jacqueline sighed. "I'm busy writing my fourth novel. Did I tell you? Just a short one about Jackie Kennedy that I started ages ago. I'm working on it whenever I can, so that I finish in time."

Jackie didn't ask what she meant by "in time." They both knew.

CHAPTER 46

Nancy

Manhattan, 1973

Fanny's suggestion that she start a women-only publishing company lodged in Nancy's brain. She had vowed to become an editor before her thirtieth birthday in April 1973, and it seemed that starting her own business might be the only way. But how could she, without money? Just for the hell of it, she bought a notebook and started jotting down ideas.

She liked the way Virago and Shameless Hussy Press had subverted terms used to denigrate women and, after some brainstorming, she came up with the name Harridan Press for her fantasy company. She started making a list of female authors from the past who she thought were due a revival: Willa Cather, Edith Wharton, George Eliot, Zora Neale Hurston. It would be cheaper if she chose authors whose work was out of copyright, but she wanted to have contemporary novels on the list too. Her dream was to discover and encourage new writers.

She started a list of the staff she would need, but soon gave up because it was too overwhelming. Accountant, lawyer, designer, typesetter, publicist, printer, sales team, more editors . . . Who was she kidding? This would never happen.

At a Gotham Book Mart poetry reading one snowy February evening, Fanny introduced her to a petite Korean woman with the delightful name of Lily Swan. Lily worked as a publicist for a small independent poetry press, and one of her authors was reading that evening. Nancy asked how she got press coverage for her poets and she admitted it was tough.

"I have to be creative, since we have zero budget," Lily told her. "For example, I always send out inexpensive but evocative gifts with review copies to catch attention."

"What kind of gifts?" Nancy asked.

"Like this." Lily dove into her oversized bag and pulled out a flat stone with a pretty painting of a kingfisher on it. "Homemade paperweights. Or I dye feathers to make multicolored quills, or I press flowers and laminate them into bookmarks."

"You do all this yourself?" Nancy raised an eyebrow.

Lily laughed. "It's a small press, so we all have lots of roles. I design the book covers and advertisements too."

The reading was about to start, so there was no time to talk further. Nancy pressed her business card into Lily's hand and whispered, "Can I buy you lunch sometime? I have an idea I'd love to discuss with you."

"Sure," Lily said. "I'll call you."

If she could use people capable of fulfilling two or even three roles each, she could keep staff costs down to start off with. Nancy liked the idea of everyone pulling together. Maybe they could all have a stake in the company?

* * *

WHEN NANCY EXPLAINED the idea behind Harridan Press over lunch, Lily was wildly enthusiastic. She offered her design services gratis if Nancy needed help in setting up the company, and she promised to introduce her to Elinor Drydale, an English friend who worked in the production department of a big publishing house, where she arranged for the typesetting and printing of their books. Elinor was unhappy with her bad-tempered, misogynist boss—a familiar story to Nancy, who was still fighting off Michael Loveday.

"Count me in," Elinor said, when Nancy told her about Harridan Press. "Definitely!"

"It's just a dream for now," Nancy cautioned. "I don't have any money, but if I figure out a way to make it happen, my first calls will be to you and Lily."

So far she hadn't mentioned her fantasy company to Jackie because she didn't want her to worry about her editor leaving when it probably wouldn't happen. She hadn't mentioned it to Jacqueline either because they hadn't seen each other for several months. Whenever she suggested meeting, Jacqueline claimed she was too busy planning her book tour. Nancy didn't want to blurt out her idea on the telephone in case Jacqueline got the impression she was begging her to invest in it. She didn't expect a cent, but she hoped Jacqueline might have some useful ideas and contacts.

The week before she knew the *Once Is Not Enough* book tour was starting, Nancy called again and this time she got Irving on the phone.

"She's resting right now," he said, "but I'll tell her you called."

Nancy hesitated. Irving was a businessman. Maybe it was worth talking it through with him. She explained her idea for Harridan Press, and finished by saying, "I know it's just a pipe dream but I thought I would mention it to you and Jacqueline in case you had any brainstorms about how I could raise funding."

"It's an all-women company, you say?" he replied. "In that case, ask George to introduce you to Hilary."

"Who's Hilary?" She was mystified.

"One of George's exes," he said. "Who also happens to be an investment banker."

* * *

NANCY HOPED THAT Jacqueline would call back after her rest, and she was hurt when no call came. Jacqueline had suffered more than most from the misogyny of the publishing industry, and Nancy had felt sure she would applaud a women-only company. In the back of her mind, she fantasized that she might even offer to let them publish one of her novels. A huge bestseller would set them up from the outset.

Why didn't she call? Had Irving forgotten to tell her? Was Jacqueline cross with her about something? She racked her brain but couldn't think what it might be.

She called George instead, and told him her idea for Harridan Press, hesitant at first in case he found it ridiculous.

"Brilliant!" he exclaimed straight away, with such enthusiasm that she grinned. "I know women's books are your passion, and I also know you're brave enough and smart enough to pull this off."

She glowed at the praise. His opinion meant more to her than anyone else's.

"Maybe I'll make a documentary about the company in a few years' time when it's a huge success." His tone was warm. "If you'll let me, that is."

"Of course," she said. "If you continue to flatter the founder, I'm sure that can be arranged. But before it can go any further, there's the small problem of financing. Irving suggested you might introduce me to your friend Hilary, and that maybe she could help me to raise money."

There was a long pause. She could hear his breathing at the end of the line.

"It doesn't matter if you don't want to, or you feel awkward about it," Nancy said. "Honestly, I do understand that it's a long shot."

"No, it's fine," he said at last. "You and Hilary will get along. I'll arrange a meeting and call you back."

Nancy was still trying to stop herself from getting too excited, because her chances of pulling it off were slim, but it was fun to daydream.

* * *

"DRINKS AT TOOTS Shor's next Thursday, six o'clock," George said when he called back. "I'll be there to make the introductions, but I'll scoot off if the conversation is too feminist for male ears."

Nancy laughed. "You don't have to do that," she said. "I'm not planning to overthrow the patriarchy—not yet, anyway."

Nancy wore her navy dress with the Peter Pan collar and some navy platform shoes that Jacqueline had bought her a while back. She wasn't a follower of fashion, but even she had noticed that her comfortable T-bar sandals were attracting derisive sniggers on the subway.

When she walked in and saw the chic style of the woman sitting alongside George at his usual corner table, she nearly turned and ran. Hilary had a sleek black shoulder-length bob and she was wearing an incredible white pantsuit with a waist-coat, fitted jacket, and—Nancy saw when she rose to shake hands—wide-legged trousers. There was a choker around her neck with a turquoise stone in the center that was almost the exact color of her eyes, and a large turquoise ring on one finger. The overall look was stylish, expensive, and ultra-glamorous, like Bianca Jagger but more so, and it made her feel as if she had just rolled out from under a haystack.

"I've heard a lot about you, Nancy," Hilary said. "It's a pleasure to meet you at last."

"Champagne?" George asked. "Why don't I get a bottle?"

He went to the bar and Hilary gave Nancy a warm smile. "George explained a bit, but why don't you describe your vision for the company, then I'll talk you through the options?"

As she spoke, Nancy tried to convey the passion she felt for women's literature of all types. She explained that it accounted for the majority of book sales in the country yet only a minority of the books published. Book clubs had mostly female members and the big ones preordered thousands of books, which helped to boost print runs, thus lowering the unit cost. George came back to the table with their drinks and listened quietly as Nancy spoke.

Sometimes Hilary interrupted with questions: Can you get an exact figure for that? Are there any other women-only publishers in the US? How many books could you publish in the first year with a team of, say, four? What percentage of the retail price of a book goes to the author? How much does it cost to produce the average hardback? How do book club deals work?

Nancy didn't know all the answers, but she felt gratified to be taken seriously. "Do you think there's any chance a bank might give me a loan to start up?" she asked.

"Only if you do this the right way," Hilary said. "I'm going to help you, but first I need you to fill all the gaps in your knowledge."

Nancy made notes as she counted off points on her fingers.

"Get me some market research on book sales to women. Analyze your competitors. Figure out how many books you can publish in years one through five. Find someone to handle sales and distribution, who can predict accurate costs. Think about where your office will be and what equipment you'll need. Then come back to me with your detailed estimate of how much you'll need to start the business and keep trading until you are profitable." Hilary grinned. "Simple, huh?"

Nancy felt daunted by the amount of work this would take. She couldn't even figure out where she'd get half the information. George caught her eye and grinned.

"Nothing worth having ever came easy," he said. "But if anyone can do this, you can."

* * *

RIGHT THROUGH FEBRUARY and March, Nancy spent all her leisure time on the case. Fanny Steloff yet again proved invaluable, introducing her to several of the publishers' sales reps who came to the store. They were happy to chat about their own experiences, but they were all men. Selling books didn't seem to be a job that women were hired for. Would she have to bend her self-imposed women-only rule?

One day she was browsing in a local clothes store when she overheard a young woman trying to persuade the store owner to stock a new range of pantyhose that came in multiple colors instead of the classic skin tones. There were even some with polka dots and psychedelic flowers.

"It's the latest thing in London," the young woman told the store owner. "In Barbara Hulanicki's and Mary Quant's boutiques, each outfit has its own coordinating pair of pantyhose. Did you see Twiggy on the Johnny Carson show with daisy-patterned pantyhose? Or that photograph of Marisa Berenson with rainbow legs sitting alongside Andy Warhol?" All the while she was spreading out the different colors on the counter, rearranging them so they complemented each other. "I can give you a five percent discount if you take twenty pairs," she coaxed. "I guarantee you'll be calling me to order more by the end of the week."

"I'd love a polka-dot pair," Nancy butted in, wanting to help her. "How much are they?"

"I can sell to you direct," the saleswoman said, then turned to the store owner and asked: "Or would you rather make your first sale?"

The store owner agreed to take twenty pairs, and immediately sold the polka-dot ones to Nancy.

Nancy waited outside until the saleswoman emerged with her suitcase of samples. "Can I have a word?" she asked.

Her name was Rachel Canvey. She said she was an avid reader and would love to try her hand at books. Selling was selling. And so she became the fourth member of the fantasy Harridan Press team.

* * *

WHEN NANCY HAD compiled all the information Hilary had asked for, she called to arrange another meeting. This time Hilary invited her to her office in a smart glass-and-chrome building downtown. She had a corner suite, with floor-to-ceiling windows on two walls. Hilary looked through the figures Nancy had produced and nodded slowly; they were enough for her to write a business plan and take the venture a step forward.

"I wish you could be part of the team if we get it up and running," Nancy said. "I don't have a clue how to handle money. . . ." She stopped, feeling embarrassed, because of course they could never afford to pay Hilary a fraction of the ginormous salary she must get in her banking job.

Hilary smiled. "I'll certainly be available to advise," she said, then glanced at her watch. "Do you have time for a quick lunch?"

Over salads in the staff canteen, Hilary asked Nancy if she had always been so ambitious.

"Not quite to this extent," she said, "but I've been working my socks off for almost eight years trying to get a promotion to editor, and it seems this is the only way."

Hilary scrutinized her. "What about your romantic life? Do you mind if I ask?"

"There isn't one." Nancy gave an involuntary shudder. "I've

been single for three years, after a bad experience with a man I thought was the be-all and end-all. I guess I've got my guard up now."

She'd dated a few men she'd met at literary evenings at the Gotham Book Mart, but none of them interested her enough to make it a regular arrangement.

"It's true men make you vulnerable," Hilary said, "but don't leave it too late if you want kids. I spent a year and a half with George, then another two years getting over him, so I was in my thirties before I met my husband. I'm lucky I was still able to have my children, Lucy and Adam, but I'm the oldest mom in the schoolyard."

Nancy didn't want to appear nosy but couldn't resist asking: "Why didn't it work out between you and George? You seem exactly the type of beautiful, successful woman I could imagine him with."

"Thank you." Hilary gave a wan smile. "It was bad timing, I guess. I started dating him just over a year after Amanda died and, frankly, he wasn't ready. He cried whenever her name was mentioned. He never let me stay over at his apartment, because I think he would have felt he was being unfaithful to her memory. I still haven't seen it to this day."

"I have," Nancy said. "I stayed there while he was filming overseas. I'm firmly in the friendship category rather than the romantic one, so maybe that's why he didn't feel I was transgressing any boundaries."

"What's it like?" Hilary asked, leaning forward.

"It's gorgeous," Nancy said. "An eclectic mix of travel-inspired décor. I was surprised to discover that George had such exotic taste but, come to think of it, perhaps Amanda designed it."

"She was a photographer, so it could have been her," Hilary

said. "In which case he hasn't changed the décor in the last ten years."

It was odd for Nancy to think she had been living in a dead woman's home, but she could see the comfort George must take from having Amanda's possessions around him, just as she felt when she looked through her mother's things at the Ossipee house.

"George tends to keep his life strictly compartmentalized, so I'm amazed he let you stay," Hilary said. "I never met any of his work colleagues. A couple of times I suggested flying out to join him after a shoot so we could vacation together, but he always blew me off. In retrospect, the only close friend of his I met was Jacqueline Susann. She insisted on checking me out and we became friends." She sipped some water. "Jacqueline helped me to understand when George broke up with me. She said he doesn't think he needs anyone else. He feels safer being self-sufficient, like an island."

Like Robin Stone in The Love Machine, Nancy thought in a flash of insight.

"It's soul-destroying when you love someone who likes you but doesn't need you. I hope it never happens to you," Hilary finished.

Nancy felt a pang of recognition. She loved George too, but had long ago accepted he didn't feel that way about her. Part of her was envious that Hilary had known that side of him, even though it had ended painfully.

After lunch, she had to rush back to Heywood & Bradshaw for the dreaded editorial meeting. She took a taxi to save time and noticed someone had left a gossip magazine on the back seat. She never normally read that kind of rag, but she picked it up and flicked through the pages to pass the time. Her eye was caught by a headline: "What on Earth Has Happened to Jacqueline Susann?"

Nancy looked at the photograph accompanying the article and flinched. Jacqueline's face was pale and bloated and her clothes were hanging off her. Had she overdone the pre-book-tour dieting? The magazine speculated that she'd had a facelift and the puffiness hadn't gone down yet, but to Nancy's eye she looked ill.

She tore the page from the magazine and shoved it in her handbag, feeling alarmed. How was Jacqueline going to get through the rigors of a book tour in that condition? What had she done to herself?

CHAPTER 47

Jacqueline
Manhattan, 1973

The *Once Is Not Enough* tour started in New York on March fifth. Jacqueline's schedule was crammed with chat shows, talk radio, and press interviews. She hadn't told anyone at the publishing company that she was ill, so as far as they were concerned it was business as usual. In fact, she had been forced to spend the second half of February in the hospital with severe fatigue, following the first round of chemo and cobalt treatments. All her life she'd had loads of pep, but suddenly it felt as if she'd been hit by a juggernaut. She couldn't sit up in bed without help, couldn't hold a glass of water for herself. At first she tried to fight it, but Irving persuaded her to look on the hospital stay as a rest cure to build her strength for the tour: "Think of it as a spa break," he suggested.

When the treatments began, back in January, Jacqueline had been hopeful she wouldn't lose her hair, but just three weeks in, it started coming out in macabre handfuls on the pillow. The dome of her skull was almost completely bald but, with grim irony, she had started growing a horrendous witch's beard and moustache. The nausea and retching she could cope with, the fever and chills were bearable, but the indignity of growing facial hair reduced her to tears. Irving hired a beautician to come and exfoliate her chin and upper lip while she was still in the hospital; she couldn't risk a bearded lady photograph getting into the press.

The enforced rest helped, and the irritating cough had eased, but she still wasn't happy with her looks. The steroid drugs had made her face puffy and no amount of facials seemed to help.

She experimented with contouring makeup to disguise the worst of it, and tried striking silver and turquoise eye shadow to divert attention: her eyes had always been her best feature. Irving went shopping and picked up some new outfits, including the latest Pucci silk pantsuits, which were loose, comfortable, and soft on the skin.

The tour kicked off with an interview with Barbara Walters for her show *The Bookshelf*. She asked Jacqueline how she felt about her bad critiques, including a *New York Times* one that said the novel was "nearly 500 steadily monotonous pages" and another that said her writing style was that of "a middling high-school student struggling to complete an assignment."

"These reviewers are patronizing the millions of readers who enjoy my books," Jacqueline replied. "You know, Barbara, if I wanted to be literary, I would load my novels down with meaningful metaphors. But there are already plenty of literary authors and most of them are starving in garrets. I write in simple, straightforward English because I don't want style to distract from my stories. Above all, I'm a storyteller."

"You've been criticized by some in the women's movement for your representations of women. How would you answer them?" Barbara asked.

"I've been into women's lib right from the start," Jacqueline said. "When I married Irving I told him from the outset: I'm not going to cook, I'm not going to clean house. I love you more than anything, but you need to know that my career is more important to me than my marriage."

Barbara laughed. "How did he take that?"

"I guess he already knew what he was letting himself in for!" She waved to him, standing off set. "If women want to be stay-at-home wives and mothers, I'm happy for them, but that was never me. The great thing about feminism is that it's given us all more choices—including the freedom to write novels with strong, independent women in them."

In the greenroom after the show, Barbara said, "You were brilliant! Are you OK, though? You look tired."

"My book tours are always a marathon," Jacqueline replied. "Four months of dawn-to-dusk interviews and events, but after that I'll be flying to a beach somewhere. Don't you worry about me!"

Next, in an interview with a reporter from the *New York Post*, Jacqueline was asked if she had tried everything she had her characters do—such as using a face mask made out of semen.

"Of course," she said, patting her cheeks. "It's rejuvenating, and you can have loads of fun obtaining your supply."

She made sure to give every journalist a headline quote. It made their lives easier, and increased her chance of getting on the front page. "Book Tour Jacqueline" was a persona she turned on, like flicking a switch. The wigs, the clothes, and the makeup helped. The studio lights and microphones were part of it. Her brain revved up into a faster gear. She made sure not a dull word crossed her lips. Sparkly, fun, entertaining, bright—those were her watchwords.

After each interview, she stopped to chat for five minutes or so, until Irving interrupted, saying, "Jacqueline, we're late . . ." Then she would stand to leave, waving gaily, never forgetting to thank everyone in the room—the camera and sound men, and the producer as well as the host. And once they were in the limo outside, she collapsed against Irving's shoulder and turned the switch off. This time around, it felt as if every single interview was draining her precious energy supply and leaving her pretty much running on empty.

* * *

WITHIN THREE WEEKS of publication, *Once Is Not Enough* was on the bestseller list, but it was May sixth before Jacqueline got a telegram from her publisher saying she had bumped *The Odessa File* off the number one spot. He said she had made publishing history by having three novels in a row reach the top, a feat that had never been achieved before. Jacqueline handed the telegram to Irving. She was too bone-tired to react.

They were in LA by then, staying in the Beverly Hills Hotel and doing interviews for *The Tonight Show, Merv Griffin*, the *LA Times*, and a host of other papers. Every morning she was undergoing radiotherapy treatments at Century City Hospital, dragging herself there to lie in a lead-lined room, like a coffin, while her chest was blasted with rays till it was red raw. Afterward, she pulled on her clothes, her wig, and her oversized sunglasses, went back to the hotel to fix her makeup, then proceeded to the next interview.

She was dreading one event in particular. She'd agreed to host a charity auction, to which she had donated four hundred signed copies of *Every Night, Josephine!* It had been arranged long before she knew about the cancer, and she didn't feel she could pull out because too many people were relying on her. For hours on end she would have to entertain the guests, including hundreds of booksellers, and persuade them to buy the auction lots. They'd be sitting in a marquee in the blazing LA heat and she'd have to stay "switched on." Would she be able to work miracles on the day? She wasn't sure.

One night, a week before the event, while Irving was asleep, she rang Jackie in London, and confessed her fear that she wouldn't be able to get through it.

"What if I pass out? That wouldn't look good. Or if I have to stagger out halfway through? The press would report I was drunk. Jeez, why did I ever agree to this?" She had hardly cried since getting the cancer diagnosis, but she started crying now. "I just don't think I can do it—but I can't let them down."

"Is there anyone who could cohost with you?" Jackie suggested.

"Not really, no. It's about books, so it has to be a bestselling author, and I don't want to bring in one of the old boys . . . Harold Robbins and co."

"I'm coming over," Jackie said, her voice clear and decisive. "I'll be your backup hostess. We'll do it together."

"Oh my god, would you?" Jacqueline sobbed harder. She never asked for help. It wasn't her style. But she knew she needed it now.

* * *

JACKIE ARRIVED IN LA three days later and came straight to Irving and Jacqueline's suite at the Beverly Hills Hotel. She looked young and chic, in a long, Indian-patterned skirt and multiple strings of beads. She rushed over to hug Jacqueline where she lay on a couch, and Jacqueline winced.

"My skin is raw," she explained, and waved away Jackie's apologies. "You weren't to know."

It was a relief to have another woman there she could be honest with. Jacqueline didn't like to upset Irving by telling him all the symptoms she was firefighting on a minute-by-minute basis—the peeling skin, the facial hair, the bone-deep pain, the excruciating headaches that came out of nowhere, the tight chest, the sore mouth, the never-ending nausea—but she could tell Jackie. Jackie listened, her eyes bright and skin glowing even after a twelve-hour flight. She was a messenger from another planet: the planet of good health.

The two of them talked through the plan for the auction. Jacqueline would start by greeting the guests, sitting on a tall stool inside the marquee. She would kick off proceedings, but Jackie would be seated on another stool nearby. As soon as Jacqueline began to fade, she would announce that the next lot would be introduced by her cohost and Jackie would take the microphone while Irving led Jacqueline outside. It would work.

Jacqueline woke early on the day of the event, and spent longer than usual on her toilette. She'd begun to notice a peculiar smell, like body odor, and hoped it was her nose playing tricks rather than her own sweat. Irving said she smelled fine, but she wasn't taking any risks. She bathed and perfumed herself liberally, then put on an ankle-length skirt and loose top, and a raven-black wig. The makeup she did herself, as always, sticking down her lashes and painting on eyeliner with difficulty as her hands were shaky.

Irving walked her to the marquee and she sipped a little water before taking up her position on a stool by the door. The bus bringing the booksellers arrived and they spilled through the entrance with a burst of noise. *Ping!* Jacqueline visualized switching on her magic switch.

"Ken," she called. "How are you enjoying fatherhood? You getting any sleep?" Next she waved to the man behind him who was hobbling on crutches: "Dan, you old daredevil, what were you doing on a motorbike? Tell Stella to confiscate those keys!"

She knew them all. Not a name escaped her. She clasped hands and smiled and bantered back and forth, and she was pretty sure not one of them guessed she was ill, although a few commented on her weight loss. Several congratulated her on making history with *Once Is Not Enough*, which was still holding on to its number one spot.

The first lot in the auction was a dress Joan Crawford had worn in *What Ever Happened to Baby Jane?* and Jacqueline announced it as the perfect outfit to wear when being served a dead rat on a platter by your sister. The bids flowed in, the drinks were served, the heat intensified. Jacqueline began to feel a little faint, but she was reassured whenever she turned around to see Jackie sitting there with a supportive smile pinned to her face, watching and waiting for her turn.

Almost an hour had passed before Jacqueline felt her head starting to spin. She turned to Jackie, planning to ask for help, but the words wouldn't come. She was going to faint.

Quick as a flash, Jackie snatched the microphone and announced, "I'm going to introduce the next few lots to give our marvelous hostess a break. Thank you so much—Jacqueline Susann, ladies and gentlemen!" The applause echoed around the room. Irving gripped her arm, helped her down from the stool, and half carried her out. As soon as she was in their suite, she collapsed.

But she wouldn't give up. After an hour on a portable oxygen machine, she insisted on going back to the auction. This time she and Jackie both held microphones and they bantered back and forth.

"Why are all your books about sex?" a man called from the audience.

"Because it seems to be all you lot think about," Jackie replied. "It's true, isn't it?" She turned to Jacqueline.

"It's a clear distinction between the sexes," Jacqueline replied. "If something terrible happens to a woman, like losing her job or her mom dying, sex is the last thing on her mind. But men can go through a devastating crisis and, if a hot girl happens to walk into the room and smile at them, they still think, 'Whoa! Maybe I can have sex with her!'"

A roar of laughter filled the room. Jacqueline felt it energizing her. She would get through this; she would. And afterward she would sleep for a week.

CHAPTER 48

Jackie

London, 1973

J ackie found it wrenching to say goodbye to Jacqueline the day after the charity event, but Irving reassured her they were coming to London in September. Jacqueline would have finished her treatments by then and he hoped she would be in much better shape. Jackie wondered if he was pretending to be optimistic for his wife's sake or if he really felt it.

On the plane home, Jackie worked on her fourth novel, *Love-head*, which was about a New York feminist campaigning to stop a Mafia boss from controlling the local prostitution trade. She was planning to let Nancy publish it as one of her first titles at Harridan Press, if she got her new company off the ground. It was such a brave and exciting venture, Jackie was keen to be part of it.

"Mort Janklow might not be happy about the level of advance I can offer," Nancy warned.

Jackie said she would deal with him. For her, the main thing was to find an American publisher who felt passionately about the book, and she trusted Nancy.

Jackie had loved both the book and the film of *The Godfather*, and could sense the dramatic possibilities of writing about crime families, but her only knowledge of their world came from Mario Puzo, and she had many questions he didn't answer. How could she research the Mafia?

Oscar met her at the airport. All had gone well, he said. There had been no disasters except when he served peas, not realizing that putting anything green on a plate rendered all other food inedible to children.

Jackie laughed. It was good for him to know these things, good that she could trust him with the girls. She described Jacqueline's fortitude and Irving's stoicism and related the highlights of the trip, while he negotiated the traffic outside Heathrow.

"Tell me, would you happen to know how much Mafia bosses pay to get someone whacked?" she asked.

"Depends who it is and how easy they are to reach," he said straight away. "Why? Who are you thinking of having whacked?"

"Not me!" She squeezed his knee. "My character. She's giving a speech in Central Park and I want a hitman in the crowd to take her out. How much would it cost?"

"About five hundred dollars at current prices," he said. "Unless she's very famous, then it would be more."

"Is that the cost of a life?" she mused. "What kind of people snuff out strangers by pulling a trigger? Do they have no consciences?"

"It's just a job to them," he said. "Like a worker in an abattoir killing cows."

Jackie glanced sideways. He answered with such confidence. How many hitmen did he know?

"After my character is killed," she continued, "three friends of hers decide to get revenge by targeting the sons of the Mafia boss. Where would they find them? Where might sons of Mafioso socialize in New York?"

He answered immediately, listing locations with such ease that she began scribbling notes on the back of her air ticket. She didn't want to ask why, or how well, her husband knew gangsters, but she might as well use his inside knowledge.

He put his arm around her and pulled her toward him. "You've never talked to me about your work before," he said. He had a smile playing on his lips. "But I like it."

"Do you think I could get myself into trouble writing about the Mafia?" she asked.

"Mario Puzo hasn't done too badly," he replied. "Just keep it fictional."

She smiled. "I missed you," she said, and it was true.

Being around Jacqueline had made her reflect how lucky she was to have a reliable husband, three adorable daughters, and a writing career that seemed to be going in the right direction. If she were ever to get cancer, heaven forbid, she knew Oscar would be by her side all the way, just as Irving was for Jacqueline. And if worse came to worst, she could trust him to bring up their daughters without her. Her eyes filled with tears and she leaned her head on his shoulder.

* * *

IN SEPTEMBER, W. H. Allen was throwing a dinner in Jacqueline's honor on the roof terrace at London's Dorchester hotel. Lots of showbiz folk would be there, and Jackie was delighted to be on the guest list.

Jacqueline and Irving were flying in earlier that day from a tour of France, where her books were doing spectacularly well. Jackie hoped that meant the treatment was working. She couldn't imagine the frail woman she had seen back in May having the energy for a back-to-back French, then UK book tour.

Jacqueline walked into the dinner, fashionably late, a broad smile on her face, wearing a hot pink, black-and-gold diamond-patterned shirt over hot pink bell-bottoms. She walked around the room greeting everyone before taking her seat on a dais, and Jackie saw she had gained a little weight. It seemed a good sign.

"Welcome, one and all," she said into a microphone. "I want to start by telling you that I have a major beef with Richard Nixon—and it's nothing to do with Watergate." Guests murmured to each other as she paused for effect. "I just heard that *Once Is Not Enough* has been knocked off the top of the *New York Times* bestseller list by a book about a goddamn seagull, and frankly I blame Tricky Dickie."

Jackie laughed with the rest of them. She had read *Jonathan Livingston Seagull*, by Richard Bach, a meditation on life and self-realization through the voice of a lone seagull.

"We all needed respite from corrupt politicians," Jacqueline continued, "a return to a more innocent time, and I guess that's why the seagull has beaten me this week." She stopped to clear her throat and have a sip of water.

"Since self-reflection is all the rage, I want to share with you my own philosophy on life." She paused theatrically, looking around at the assembled guests. "When you're climbing Mount Everest, nothing is easy. You just take one step at a time, never look back, ignore the rocks cascading about you—and keep your eyes glued to the pinnacle."

The audience burst into spontaneous applause. Jackie joined in, but she felt chilled. It was as though Jacqueline were talking about her current struggle, without admitting it in so many words. Was she still keeping her eyes on the pinnacle? She hoped so.

Jacqueline's editor presented her with a huge bouquet of pink roses, and she accepted them graciously, without getting up from her chair. Irving took them from her and laid them on an empty chair while the first course was served: *crevettes Marie Rose*.

Jackie watched throughout the meal and noticed that Jacqueline didn't swallow a morsel. She sipped at a glass of water, ignoring her wine, keeping up a stream of conversation with those on either side and engaging with everyone who came up for a private word or to ask for a book to be signed. She was bright, funny, and totally professional, but at ten o'clock on the dot, as soon as the dessert plates were cleared, Irving insisted that they had to leave and she didn't demur.

Jackie caught up with them by the exit to ask if she could meet them the following day, but it seemed W. H. Allen had booked Jacqueline on a frenzied round of media appearances.

"We should all have a vacation together," Jackie suggested, giving Jacqueline a cautious hug, in case her skin was still painful from the radiotherapy. "Sun, sand, and sea."

"You got it!" Jacqueline said. "Call me once I'm back in New York and we'll pick a date."

She left the roof terrace, Irving's arm around her, and headed toward the elevators. Only someone who knew the truth would have spotted that he was holding her up.

CHAPTER 49

Nancy

Manhattan, 1973

Over dinner with George, Nancy mentioned her worries about Jacqueline: not just the unflattering photo in the gossip magazine, but the fact that she hadn't called to interrogate her about her plans for Harridan Press. Irving must have told her. She hadn't even rung to ask how Louise was. It had been months since Nancy had spoken to her, and she missed her badly.

"Have I done something to upset her?" she asked him. "She confides in you."

He shook his head. "Jacqueline is a fifty-five-year-old woman doing a promotional tour that would fell a twenty-five-year-old," he said. "That's all she's focused on for now."

Nancy was relieved. "Talking of indomitable," she said, "Hilary has pushed through the loan application for my business. It's been a struggle, but she refused to take no for an answer. So it looks as though we're launching in spring of next year." She grinned so widely her cheeks ached. She still couldn't quite believe it.

"She told me." George grinned back. "How are you feeling?"

"Terrified." Nancy analyzed herself. "Excited. Daunted. Worried that it will go bust within six months and leave us with a mountain of debt to repay. All of the above."

"Yeah, it might," he said. "But I'd be surprised, because neither Hilary nor you are quitters."

Nancy watched his face. She was dying to quiz him about his relationship with Hilary. Did he regret breaking up with her? Her two kids could have been his. She had no idea how he felt about having children. They were close friends; she should be able to ask that, but when it came to marriage and kids, he put up a wall of privacy it would feel awkward to breach.

"Do you see her often?" she asked instead.

"No, we're both too busy, but she's a good friend. As is her husband."

"Any fresh notches on your bedpost lately?" she asked, with a cheeky smile, and was surprised to see that frown appear between his brows.

"I wouldn't dream of spoiling the Indonesian hardwood," he answered after a pause. "Why do you ask? Do you have any inappropriate new boyfriends I should be told about?"

"Dozens of them," Nancy teased. She had dated a couple of guys that year, but both had drifted away when she was too busy to see much of them.

Lots of the women she had met through the Gotham Book Mart were gay. It crossed Nancy's mind to wonder if she should try dating women, but she decided it was definitely men who turned her on. She remembered her obsessive lust for Steven in the early days when they couldn't keep their hands off each other.

Then she thought back to George talking about sex the first time they met at Toots Shor's. He'd told her to find a man who knew how to take care of a woman's needs, the implication being that he knew how. She felt her cheeks color. She looked at his hand resting on the table, with its long slender fingers, and her blush deepened.

* * *

IN NOVEMBER, JACQUELINE rang at last to say that she and Irving were back in New York and she wondered if Nancy was free for cocktails at the Navarro that Friday.

"I'd love to," Nancy shrieked. "I've missed you! I've got so much to tell you."

"George is coming too," Jacqueline said. "Seven o'clock." Her voice sounded husky as if she were all talked out from the year's book promotion, and she hung up immediately after the arrangement was made.

Irving opened the door on Friday and Nancy stepped into the familiar open-plan living room, delighted to be back after such a long absence. Jacqueline was lying on the couch in pale pink silk pajamas and within a few steps Nancy could see that she wasn't well. The bones of her skull were prominent beneath her skin and she looked deathly pale. Resting on her lap was a rubber mask attached by a tube to a metal tank on the floor alongside.

"Oh no!" Nancy gasped. "What happened?"

Jacqueline's eyes looked huge and dark, although she wasn't wearing makeup. "Let's wait till George gets here," she said, her voice a raw whisper. "I can't face saying this twice." She placed the mask over her mouth and nose and breathed slowly, in and out.

Nancy turned to Irving, her mind racing. She'd thought Jacqueline looked ill in that magazine photo and it seemed she'd been right.

"What can I get you to drink?" he asked.

"Whatever you're having," Nancy replied. She couldn't think about drinks.

As he crossed the room to the drinks trolley, she saw he was stooped and thinner than she'd ever seen him. Both of them looked like they'd been through the wars.

Jacqueline removed the mask and gave Nancy a warm smile. "Irving told me about Harridan Press, and I'm so proud of you. What's the latest? Tell me everything."

Nancy sat down and described the office they'd found in the Meatpacking District, the discounted deal she had negotiated with a New England printer, and the authors she had already signed up—including Jackie Collins, whose new novel *Lovehead* would be one of her launch titles.

Irving brought her drink, then the buzzer rang and he went to the door to welcome George.

As Nancy had done, George stopped short when he saw Jacqueline, then he hurried over to kiss her: right cheek, left cheek. "What is it?" he asked, urgently. "What's wrong?"

"It's cancer," she said, looking hard at him, then at Nancy.

George covered his face with his hands and took a few seconds before he spoke. "Is it linked to the breast cancer?" he asked, and Nancy blinked. She hadn't known about that.

"It is," Irving told him. "Ten years on—who would have thought it?"

"Have you been to Johns Hopkins?" George asked. "They're on the cutting edge of cancer treatment. I know a guy there . . ."

He stopped because Jacqueline was nodding. "I was there last week," she said. "I had some radiographs to see how the latest treatment is working, but I'm afraid it's not great news." She put the mask on to take a few breaths and Irving continued.

"The original tumors haven't grown, but there are signs that the cancer is in her lymph nodes." His voice cracked and he stood up abruptly. "Excuse me a moment," he mumbled, and hurried into the bedroom, closing the door behind him.

Nancy looked at George. So far she hadn't been able to react. "They'll cure it, won't they?" she asked him. "Cancer is not the killer it used to be."

She wanted George to reassure her, but his expression was grim. "What can I do, Jacqueline? Give me something to do."

Jacqueline took off the oxygen mask and spoke with determination. "George, I need you to look after Irving, OK? I'm relying on you for that. And Nancy, it's your job to look after George. That's why I'm telling you both together."

Nancy whispered, "I will."

"Is there nothing left to try?" George asked. He still hadn't sat down, but paced to the window and back, looking utterly devastated. "You've definitely called all the top people?"

"We have," Jacqueline said. "Next week I'm starting what they call palliative chemo. In return for feeling hideously sick and ill, I can buy myself a few more months of life. I don't love the terms of this particular deal, but it's better than the alternative." She looked from one to the other. "Come on, guys, get the funereal looks off your faces. I'm still here. Tell me what's going on in your lives. Have another drink. Irving?" she called sternly. "Get yourself right back in here!"

He sloped into the room, red-eyed.

"You three need to get drunk as skunks!" she ordered. "And I'll watch. I only wish I could join you."

Nancy looked at George. What she really wanted to do was put her arms around him and sob on his shoulder. He looked as if he felt the same way. She gulped her drink.

She couldn't bear to lose Jacqueline. Suddenly she felt twenty-one years old again, hearing her stepfather's voice on the telephone telling her that her mother had died. Eight years had passed since then, and she'd made a life for herself, but part of the bedrock of that life was knowing Jacqueline was there in the Navarro, dispensing cocktails and wisdom. Without her, the world wouldn't feel as safe—and she knew that, hard as the loss would be for her, it would be a whole lot tougher for George.

CHAPTER 50

Jacqueline
Manhattan, 1974

S ome days Jacqueline raged against the cancer, some days she cried, some days she felt strangely detached, as though the disease was ravaging someone else's body, not hers. Most of all she was weighed down by immense grief at the thought of leaving Irving and their darling son, and at everything she was going to miss. She, who liked to keep on top of all the minor ramifications of her friends' lives, was going to be forced to leave the party early.

Still she had only told a handful of her very closest friends. She couldn't face the news leaking out, because then she would have dozens of phone calls to deal with. She would end up having to comfort everyone and reassure them she was fine when she damn well wasn't fine. She dreaded the papers getting hold of the story and printing premature obituaries. There would doubtless be hundreds of sympathy letters from fans, but what use was sympathy to man or beast?

George had been calling cancer specialists all over the world, seeking someone, anyone, who could offer a new treatment with a positive prognosis. He bought her a huge bag of dried Chinese mushrooms, which were said to have cancer-fighting properties, and Irving brewed her a broth from them every day. George sent her medical notes to a French oncologist working on bone marrow transplants, an Italian doctor who was getting promising results from a new type of combination chemotherapy, and a German specialist who believed that cancer treatments should be tailored precisely to the individual patient. All of them expressed regret: Jacqueline was too weak to undergo intrusive procedures, too weak even to travel.

Nancy proofread her fourth novel, *Dolores*, for her, since the proofs arrived when she was bedridden from the grueling effects of the palliative chemo. And Jackie continued to be her truth-teller during their four a.m. calls, the one person she could say anything to.

"I'm afraid I won't be any good at dying," Jacqueline told her. "I'm not the type to slip away quietly, and that's going to make it harder for Irving."

"You'll probably be in hospital at the end," Jackie said, "and they'll give you pain relief that will make you drowsy."

"Your mother died at home, didn't she? I don't want Irving to wake up next to my corpse." Jacqueline shivered. "I've written about characters dying in my novels, but I can't actually imagine what it feels like."

"I'm not sure you should be trying to plan your death just yet," Jackie said softly. "Why not plan what you want to do while you're here?"

"I was thinking about taking out a contract on people who have pissed me off in the past, like Bernie Geis and Truman Capote. Do you think Oscar could arrange it?" Jackie had told her that she was both impressed and alarmed by the extent of her husband's knowledge of the criminal underworld.

"Then you would end up dying in some grotty prison hospital, where I'm sure they wouldn't have the standard of amenities you're used to," Jackie said. "Besides, I would rather you didn't take my husband down with you."

Jacqueline laughed, and it turned into a cough. "Once I get over this damn nausea, I'm doing a book tour for the paperback of *Once Is Not Enough*. We're kicking off March." That was something she could do, something she was good at.

"Blimey!" Jackie exclaimed. "Are you sure that's wise?"

"You know I love my book tours," Jacqueline said. "Irving's trying to talk me out of it. After thirty-six years of marriage, you'd think he'd know better."

* * *

JACQUELINE MADE HER last public appearance on April first, on a celebrity panel at a charity gala in LA. Helen Gurley Brown, another panelist, was horrified by her appearance.

"What did I tell you about not losing weight in midlife?" she scolded. "It always goes from the face." She put an arm around Jacqueline. "You're skin and bone. What do you weigh?"

Jacqueline smiled. Only Helen would ask such a personal question. "I'm under a hundred pounds. You're right, I need to eat more."

"Be careful because if you eat the wrong things, the weight will go on your ass, not your face." She regarded her carefully. "Did you shave your eyebrows? Big mistake! You should let them grow back. I'm going to give you the card of my New York beauty salon. Ask for Grace. You need a top-to-toe overhaul."

The panel was lively, and earned lots of money for the charity, but Jacqueline's strength had run out by the end. Helen looked alarmed when Irving had to come and escort her out, almost carrying her, because she was so frail her knees sometimes gave way beneath her.

Back at the Beverly Hills Hotel, Jacqueline loved to lie on a float in the pool, her aching bones buoyed by the sun-warmed, gently lapping water. You couldn't beat the West Coast light in springtime, creating glinting diamond patterns on the surface of the turquoise pool and turning the hills orange at dusk. It was so beautiful it brought tears to her eyes.

This would be her last spring. She could sense it in her body. Sure, she would talk to every last expert George found, and sip every cup of mushroom broth, but she could feel the life force ebbing away, like a tide that can't be turned.

* * *

IN JUNE, JACQUELINE and Irving flew to Texas to visit their son.

"Don't think the word 'last,'" Jackie advised her beforehand. "You don't know that for sure, and it will cast a pall over the visit."

It was all very well to say that, but the word echoed in Jacqueline's head. Was this the last walk through the airport terminal? The last drive in a hired car to the institution? Irving dropped her at the front door while he went to park, and she climbed, slowly, painfully, up the few steps. She wanted to see her son on her own, to explain to him in her own words, words she had planned carefully in the hope he would understand. It would be hard, she knew, but better that than disappearing from his life without saying goodbye.

An hour later, a nurse clutched Jacqueline's arm and led her out to meet Irving in reception. She felt as if her heart had been ripped clean out of her body. Tears were choking her, making it hard to get the words out.

Irving pulled her face against his shoulder. She could tell he was crying too but trying to hide it from her.

Jacqueline slid from Irving's arms and sank to the floor, then curled into a ball, her head in her hands. Usually she tried not to break down in front of him, because it was hard enough for him already, but this time she couldn't hold back. He crouched on the floor beside her, his arms enfolding her, and she could feel his body trembling as he tried to restrain his own grief.

"Let me die now," she sobbed. "Please. I can't live with this pain."

Irving didn't say anything. They stayed there, holding each other, knowing that their beloved son was nearby and yet so very far away.

CHAPTER 51

Jackie

London, 1974

That's it, I'm not saying any more goodbyes," Jacqueline told Jackie in one of their four a.m. calls. "The one with my son nearly finished me off. No matter what happens, I want you to say 'Cheerio' at the end of every call. Deal?"

"You got it!" Jackie said.

She could hear that Jacqueline's breathing was more labored. She often had to stop and gasp for breath mid-sentence, and sometimes she'd break off to inhale oxygen through her mask.

"You talk now," Jacqueline wheezed. "Tell me how *Lovehead* is doing."

"I'm in the UK bestseller list at number five," Jackie said, "and the reviews are better than I've had before. One of them called me a 'raunchy moralist,' which I kinda like. Nancy's done a great job with it in the States, but I still haven't broken into the hallowed *New York Times* list—that's your personal preserve. I'm coming over in fall to do more appearances out there, so I'll see you then."

Jacqueline didn't reply and the comment hung in the ether between them. Would she be alive in the fall?

"I saw a priest yesterday," Jacqueline said. "Not for the last rites—don't worry. I just wanted to ask him some questions about the afterlife. I wish I could know for sure that I'll be reunited with my loved ones in heaven: my long-lost pop, and Irving and my son when it's their time. Father Champlin couldn't offer any guarantees, of course, but it occurred to me that maybe that's why I converted to Catholicism all those years ago. The afterlife is like a free gift Catholics get in return for all those confessions and Hail Marys and communion wafers."

Jackie snorted. "Did you use the exact words 'free gift' to Father Champlin?"

"Yeah. Why not?" Jackie heard the hissing sound of oxygen and waited for Jacqueline to come back on the line. "On the other hand, they say 'Born a Jew, die a Jew' and part of me is drawn toward the rituals I grew up with." Jacqueline was silent for a moment. "I often dream about my father, and—don't laugh!— I wonder if that's him letting me know that he's waiting to greet me on the other side. Do you think that's wishful thinking?"

"No, not at all. I envy you your faith," Jackie said. "I would love to see my mum again and for her to know I've had two more daughters and four books published and that I'm happily married second time round. She never met Oscar."

"I'll tell her if I see her up there," Jacqueline said. "Elsa Collins, right? I'll look out for her."

* * *

THE CALL, WHEN it came, took Jackie by surprise. She was unpacking groceries in the kitchen and the radio was playing catchy but forgettable pop tunes.

"She's gone," Irving said, the words catching in his throat. "Yesterday evening. I'd been with her in the hospital all day, then I went for a quick dinner with friends. I headed back straight after, but she had passed away while I was out."

Jackie sat down on a kitchen chair. Her first thought was to wonder if Jacqueline had deliberately waited till Irving was out of the room, to spare him. Was that possible?

"I'm so sorry," she said. "It's a massive loss for all of us, but most of all you . . ." She trailed off. Words were inadequate. She couldn't take it in. The news felt monumental, as if a hole had been torn in the universe.

"The funeral is the day after tomorrow," Irving told her. "I know it's short notice but we'd love it if you can come."

"So soon?" Jackie squeaked. That didn't give her any time to make arrangements. She'd just have to book a flight and throw some clothes in a bag.

"I can't chat now," Irving said. "She left me a list of over a hundred people to call before the news is reported in the press and she'll kill me if I miss anyone."

Jackie wondered if he noticed his slip in tense: future instead of past. Was he talking of when they were reunited in heaven? Or just speaking from force of habit?

When they hung up, Jackie wandered over to look out the window at her back garden. The best of summer was gone: leaves were browning at the edges, the roses were shedding petals, and the temperature was dropping nightly. She supposed it would be headline news in the following day's papers. Perhaps she would be asked to comment. She should prepare something. What to say?

"Cheerio, Jacqueline," she whispered. "I miss you already."

* * *

JACKIE FLEW TO New York the following day, accompanied by Adam Cosgrove, Jacqueline's editor at W. H. Allen. Oscar had stayed behind to look after the girls because there was no time to find a babysitter. On the flight, she and Adam talked about the shock that had greeted the news: most of Jacqueline's friends hadn't even known she was ill and they were blindsided. The press obituaries talked of her trail-blazing approach to writing and promoting books and the world record she had set in topping the *New York Times* bestseller list three times in a row. Most of them called her "controversial," "sassy," or "pugnacious," and it seemed appropriate. She'd certainly been a fighter.

"She stuck her head above the parapet and took the worst of the incoming fire for daring to be a woman who wrote sexy books," Jackie told Adam. "It made it easier for me when I was published two years after *Valley of the Dolls*. She had responded to the critics with such articulate arguments that they had less ammunition to fire at me."

"You've still had a rough time," he said. "But fortunately you've got balls, like her."

The funeral was held at Campbell's funeral home on Madison Avenue, which was famous for hosting celebrity funerals, like Rudolph Valentino's and Judy Garland's. Irving had tried to limit the numbers, but so many folks turned up, it was standing room only by the time Jackie arrived.

She was surprised that the service was conducted by a rabbi. Jacqueline must have leaned toward her Jewish roots at the last minute. The casket was a simple wooden one, and Jackie focused on it, letting the unfamiliar words of the service flow over her as she imagined her friend's thin ravaged body inside. Was she already reunited with her father in the afterlife? Or had her consciousness simply ceased to exist when her heart stopped beating? Ashes to ashes, dust to dust. She had a lump in her throat that no amount of swallowing would clear.

Afterward, they congregated back at the Navarro apartment. Irving got room service to bring heaped platters of sandwiches and invited everyone to help themselves from the drinks trolley. It was unbearably sad to be there without Jacqueline bossing Irving around and forcing her guests to divulge details of their private lives, while she sat absorbing every word. Irving was smiling and talking and topping up glasses, but she couldn't bear to imagine how it was for him in private, when he was left alone.

Jackie didn't recognize anyone in the room apart from Nancy, so she went over to say hello. Nancy introduced her to her companion, a tall, slim man called George Carter, and she figured out he was the documentary maker who knew Johnny Gold.

"Jacqueline often talked about you," she told him. "You two must have been especially close. She was always saying 'George thinks this' and 'George is flying to that country' and 'George told me I mustn't ever do xyz.' You were a big influence on her."

"She was my best friend," he said, visibly upset. Nancy squeezed his arm protectively.

"I think most people in this room would say the same." Jackie looked around. "What a great legacy! Besides all she did for books, she touched so many of our lives."

"A good quarter of the items in my wardrobe were gifts from her," Nancy said, with forced jollity, as if trying to lift the mood. "She clearly thought I had no taste in fashion."

"You didn't," George said, and Nancy's eyes widened in surprise. "The first time you came to meet me at Toots Shor's, you were wearing a gingham dress and buckled sandals like Judy Garland in *The Wizard of Oz*."

"You remember that dress? It was very comfortable."

"Yeah, but you looked about twelve," he teased. "Everything you wore was baggy, as if you were trying to stop anyone from finding out what sex you were."

"That may be true," Nancy told Jackie. "I had to cover up at work to deter the perverts."

"I just thump them," Jackie said, and they laughed. "Or get them sacked," she added, and told them about finding out that John Perkins had been the one sending her condoms. He'd lost his job because of it, and she felt bad, but Nancy and George both agreed she'd done the right thing.

It was late when the crowd began to disperse, as if no one

wanted to leave because that would mean taking a step further away from Jacqueline. And poor Irving—how could they leave him?

When jetlag was making it hard to keep her eyes open any longer, Jackie went to say goodbye to him.

"She left a note for you," Irving said. He sorted through a pile of handwritten envelopes on the hall table and dug out one that said "Jackie C" on the front.

Jackie clasped it between her hands, touched beyond words. She'd only known Jacqueline for seven years, but it had been one of the most profound friendships of her life.

"Wasn't she great?" Irving said, giving her a goodbye hug. "Wasn't Jacqueline great?"

"She was the greatest," Jackie replied, and meant it.

She waited till she was back in Oscar's apartment before sitting down to read the note:

Dearest Jackie,

You've no idea how much our four a.m. conversations helped me through my illness. I could be honest, without trying to protect you from the blackest of thoughts, and I need you to know how much that meant.

Now that I'm gone, I want you to ambush that New York Times bestseller list and make it your own. Spend more time in America and find your people. Put readers first, booksellers second, and tell the critics to go to hell (as I'm sure they will). And when you get your first number one, know that I'll be raising a glass up here in whichever heaven will have me.

Grab it all, Jackie—you deserve it. With love always, J

Jackie clutched the note to her heart and whispered, "I will. I promise."

CHAPTER 52

Nancy

Manhattan, 1974

Nancy cherished her last note from Jacqueline, which felt like a warm embrace from beyond the grave.

I'm not worried about you, because I know you will be a huge success in whatever you do. That fresh, naïve girl who touched my heart when she appeared in my apartment, all alone and grieving for her mother, soon showed she had guts. Your hard work on Valley of the Dolls was an intrinsic part of its success. Do that for the books you publish yourself, and you'll rule the publishing world one day.

Don't forget about love. Have kids, don't have kids, but be sure to surround yourself with people you love, who love you in return. It makes all the difference.

Nancy framed it and hung it on the wall of her studio apartment. If she could have replied, she would have told Jacqueline that she couldn't have done it without her. Having someone so inspirational believing in her had given her strength when she needed it most.

In the weeks after Jacqueline's funeral, Nancy called Irving and George to check in every day. Irving was keeping himself busy dealing with Jacqueline's will, which placed most of her wealth in trust for their son, as well as containing a long list of charitable bequests. Until that moment, Nancy hadn't even known the couple had a son and was stunned they had kept such a huge secret from almost everyone. Irving spoke rapidly on the telephone, always sounding as if he were in a hurry, and she guessed his only tactic for coping with the loss was constant motion.

She was more worried about George. She knew he'd taken time off work, but he kept turning down her repeated suggestions that they meet for a drink.

"I'm not in the mood," he told her.

"Not even for a martini at Toots Shor's?" she pleaded. "You know Jacqueline would want you to."

"I'll call when I'm ready," he said.

"Did she leave you a note?" Nancy persisted, and he said yes but refused to tell her what it said, even after she read him hers.

"Mine's too personal," he said.

Nancy confided in Hilary that she was worried about him, and Hilary said she wasn't surprised he was mourning.

"George might be an island, but Jacqueline was always there, just across the bay. Now he's all alone and surrounded by ocean." She tilted her head sideways. "I've tried calling but he won't talk to me either. I guess we can't help him if he won't let us."

Nancy had promised to look after George, but how could she? Suddenly she remembered him telling her that after his wife died, Jacqueline had turned up at his apartment with pizza and vodka, and she decided to try the same tactic.

"I told you I don't want to see anyone," George said when she knocked on his door.

"You have to let me in," she insisted. "The pizza box is burning my hands."

He looked awful: unshaven, unwashed hair, baggy pajama bottoms, and a sweater that had seen better days. Nancy barged past, put the pizza on the bar, and poured them both a shot of vodka, then handed him a glass.

"To Jacqueline!" she toasted, and he swallowed his down like water.

The pizza never did get eaten as they sat side by side on the couch, drinking their way through a half bottle of vodka and sharing stories of their friend Jacqueline. Nancy wasn't a seasoned drinker and she got drunk very quickly, but it was the kind of inebriation in which she felt as if she were getting wittier and smarter by the moment. George was laughing at her jokes and she laughed too, glad to have cheered him up.

The vodka got finished but luckily George had more. Nancy felt her eyelids drooping but remembered George saying that Jacqueline had sat up with him all night so she struggled to do the same, until exhaustion finally took over.

The following morning she woke with the worst headache she'd ever had, as if someone was swinging a pickax at the inside of her skull. She lifted her head with effort and realized she had fallen asleep on George's shoulder, and his arm was squashed beneath her. How extremely mortifying! Their unfamiliar intimacy aroused all kinds of emotions she was feeling too sick to process. He was still sleeping soundly, skewed awkwardly across the couch with one leg on the coffee table, and a half-full bottle of spirits balanced on his lap.

Nancy extricated herself carefully and went to the washroom to scoop a handful of water into her parched mouth and search the cabinet for an aspirin. She splashed water on her face and checked her watch: eight thirty a.m. She had a meeting with an author at the office in half an hour.

Before she left, she removed the bottle from George's lap and covered him with a Mexican-style throw. With any luck he wouldn't remember she had fallen asleep on him—she sincerely hoped he wouldn't, and decided she wouldn't mention it unless he did.

* * *

ALL NANCY'S WAKING hours were spent at Harridan Press, with each day bringing fresh triumphs and new challenges. One moment there would be a brilliant review for one of her books in a national magazine, the next she'd receive a batch of returns from bookshops; an hour later she would be buoyed by signing a new author whose work she adored, then the mail would bring a bill from the printer that she knew she would struggle to pay. Everything was hand to mouth. There was never a dull moment.

In the evenings, the four women opened a bottle of wine and talked through the day's developments, trying to find ways to iron out problems. Hilary joined them roughly once a week. She'd become their unofficial financial advisor, and her wise head for money rescued them from many a scrape. She had an uncanny ability to persuade creditors to extend their payment terms, or to arrange a temporary overdraft when all else failed. Fanny Steloff was another reliable source of wise advice, and the Gotham Book Mart became the setting for all Harridan's launch parties.

Nancy had chosen people to work with who could perform more than one job, but she lost count of the number of roles she fulfilled herself. As editor-in-chief, she read submissions, chose the books they published, negotiated with agents to buy them, drafted contracts, then edited the text and wrote the copy for the covers. She helped with publicity when Lily had more than one author event on the same evening, or if she needed help stuffing hundreds of advance copies into envelopes and delivering them around town by hand to save on postage. Nancy was the bookkeeper, who kept records of income and expenditure; and she was very often the cleaner, who swept the floor and took out the trash before leaving at night.

She hadn't quite become an editor by the age of thirty, but she was CEO of her own company by thirty-one and that was beyond anything she could have dreamed of when she arrived in Manhattan clutching three letters inviting her to job interviews.

* * *

SHE KEPT RINGING George and Irving regularly, and was pleased to hear they had arranged to spend Christmas Day together: "We're going to get drunk first thing in the morning and stay drunk all day," Irving told her. Nancy was going to Ossipee to spend Christmas with her stepdad and stepbrothers, both of them teenagers who towered over her and spoke in deep voices she couldn't get used to.

Just before she left, George rang. "What are you doing New Year's Eve?" he asked.

"I've got a date," she said, but without enthusiasm. He was a poet, a perfectly nice guy she'd been seeing for a few weeks.

"Is he married?" George asked. "What's wrong with him? You never date men who're available."

She laughed. "If you're accusing me of avoiding commitment, you should look in the mirror first. Anyway, why did you ask about New Year's?"

"CBS is forcing me to attend a party they're throwing and I'm not sure I can get through it unless you come with me."

Nancy was pleased. "Does that mean you're finally ready to face the world?"

"I guess so," he said, and she could hear his tone was lighter than last time they'd spoken.

"OK, in that case I'll let my date down gently."

She dressed for the evening in clothes Jacqueline had given her: the black evening dress with rhinestone shoestring straps, and the brown suede coat with the white rabbit fur trim.

"I remember that dress." George smiled when she took her coat off. "You were wearing it the night we met at Jacqueline's party. I still can't believe you were planning to take the subway home in it. How green you were!"

"Yes, and how patronizing *you* were," she returned.

"I guess I was." He took a glass of champagne from the tray of a passing waiter and handed it to her. "Now I have to try and be sociable with my colleagues and I've forgotten how to make small talk. I'm hoping you can help."

The party was in a hotel banquet room, with a dance floor at one end where a few souls were bopping to disco hits. Nancy didn't keep up with pop music, but she recognized "Lady Marmalade," which seemed to have been playing in every bar she passed that fall. Other guests were sitting around tables or mingling by the laden buffet.

George introduced Nancy to his producer, his cameraman, his secretary, a news anchor, a set designer, and she chatted with each, asking about their roles and proudly telling them that she had started her own publishing company earlier in the year. She could sense they were trying to figure out her relationship to George, and guessed his love life was as much a mystery to his colleagues as it was to her.

They weren't far from Times Square, and at ten to midnight George suggested they go outside to join the crowds waiting for the famous ball to drop down the flagpole. Nancy had never seen it live before, only on TV. She retrieved her coat from the cloakroom and they ventured out along sidewalks thronged with shrieking revelers.

It was a mild evening for December and the square was exceptionally busy, but they found a corner with a good view of the ball, and the fireworks that George said would follow. They checked his watch, waiting for the seconds to tick down. Finally, the huge silver globe descended and the crowd cheered in a tsunami of noise that reverberated around the square. Ship horns hooted on the river and the opening bars of "Auld Lang Syne" were faintly audible above the din.

"Happy New Year, Nancy," George murmured and before she could reply, he grasped her coat collar, pulled her to him, and kissed her on the lips. Whenever he'd kissed her before it had always been on both cheeks, European style, but this was a different kind of kiss, a more intimate one. *Was he drunk?* His hands cupped the back of her head, while his kissing grew more insistent. She felt a wave of lust wash over her.

We're going to be embarrassed about this in the morning, she thought to herself. *It's even worse than me falling asleep on him.* At the same time, she didn't want to be the one to end it. In a flash, she realized she had wanted this all those years, since the first night they met.

George wrapped his body around hers, shutting out the world, so it was just them, kissing, holding each other, breathing each other, warming each other, and all she could think about was how absolutely right it felt, as if it had always been meant to be this way between them, and always would be for the rest of their lives.

S ix months later, Nancy was opening the drawers in George's bedroom looking for some nail scissors. She had spent every night with him since New Year's, and earlier that week a test had confirmed she was pregnant. They joked that it was as if the baby had been hanging around waiting for them to get their act together, and now it was impatient to be born.

There was no question of her giving up Harridan Press. She would take the baby into work and fit motherhood around her career. George had stopped accepting overseas assignments so he could help with childcare.

In his bedside drawer, she spotted a familiar-looking envelope and recognized the writing on the front as Jacqueline's. It must be her last note to him. Would it be terrible of her to read it? She knew she shouldn't, but, after a brief hesitation, she couldn't resist.

Dearest George,

For God's sake, will you just get a move on and <u>marry Nancy</u>! You told me you love her, and I know she loves you too. You have no idea how <u>unbearably frustrating</u> it is for me that I didn't get to attend your wedding.

Seriously, George. You need to take the plunge and let yourself love again. I can't promise that Nancy won't die young, like Amanda, but statistically it must be unlikely. What I can promise is that you'll be happy with her. So do it. Not for me, but for you.

You know I'm right. With love always, J.

"You got your way, Jacqueline," Nancy whispered. They had booked City Hall for September.

A voice spoke in her head, as clearly as if someone was in the room with her. "About time too," it said.

HISTORICAL AFTERWORD

Nancy, Steven, George, and Louise are fictional characters, with stories loosely designed to resemble the kinds of plots found in novels by Jackie Collins and Jacqueline Susann. Heywood & Bradshaw publisher and its staff are fictional, as are St. David's Press and Harridan Press, and I invented most of the staff members in Bernard Geis Associates and W. H. Allen. I read several memoirs by people who worked in the publishing industry in the 1960s, and gleaned insights from them about the way female staff members were treated. That fireman's pole at Bernard Geis Associates really existed!

In writing about Jackie Collins and Jacqueline Susann, I have tracked their real lives and tried to illuminate their true personalities but—spoiler alert coming up!—I found no evidence that they ever met. They certainly could have done. They had the same UK publisher, W. H. Allen, and both were published by Simon & Schuster in the US, although at different times. Jackie's sister, Joan, was at the wedding of Roman Polanski and Sharon Tate, as was Jacqueline Susann, and Joan was also at the casting party for *The Love Machine*, so their paths definitely crossed. But I invented the relationship between Jackie and Jacqueline that I describe in the novel—it was wishful thinking on my part.

There are two biographies of Jacqueline Susann, one of them written by her husband, Irving, and there are many articles by people who knew and worked with her. There's no full biography of Jackie Collins at the moment, although she richly deserves one, but there's an excellent documentary about her by Laura Fairrie, in which her three daughters, her sister, Joan, and several close friends reminisce about her. There are loads of online videos showing both Jackies being interviewed on TV chat shows, and these are illuminating as well as fun to watch. They were quick, smart, and always entertaining.

All dialogue, thoughts, feelings, and many of the events in the novel are fictionalized. Sometimes I moved an event to fit my narrative arc; for example, Jackie Collins was held up at gunpoint after she moved to LA in the eighties, and she put her foot on the accelerator and sped off, but I moved that incident back to London in the sixties and tied it to a fictional plot about protection money for Oscar's nightclub. I also moved the founding of Virago Press back from 1973 to 1971, to fit my timeline.

Where someone mentioned in the story is still alive—for example, Jacqueline Susann's son and Jackie Collins's daughters—I have avoided dramatizing scenes with them. They deserve their privacy.

I felt the treatment of Jackie Collins and Jacqueline Susann by the publishing industry, the media, and the public in the 1960s was an important story to tell. It's extraordinary how shocking it was considered for women to write about sex back then, even though the two Jackies' descriptions were never graphic or detailed. I wonder what they would have made of the 2011 bestseller *Fifty Shades of Grey* by E. L. James, and the huge genre of imitators that spawned? Their work was tame by comparison, but both were terrific storytellers, and that's the key to their phenomenal, continuing success. At the time of writing, *Valley of the Dolls* has sold over 31 million copies and Jackie Collins's thirty-two novels have sold more than 500 million copies. Not bad going for two women with challenges in their private lives, operating in what was still very clearly a man's world.

Thirty-five years after Jacqueline Susann died of metastatic breast cancer, Jackie Collins was diagnosed with stage four breast cancer. She lived a further six years, undergoing grueling treatments, but resolutely refused to tell any but her very closest family and friends. In September 2015 she came to London to promote her latest book and appeared on the TV chat show *Loose Women*. She looked very thin and gaunt, but managed to be sparkly and entertaining, as always. She flew back to LA and just nine days after that appearance she died, with her family around her. Jacqueline would have been proud of her.

Further Reading/Viewing

JACKIE COLLINS

Babitz, Eve, *I Used to Be Charming*, 1996

Collins, Joan, *Past Imperfect*, 1978

Fairrie, Laura, *Lady Boss*, documentary, with cooperation of family and friends, 2021

Obituaries in *The New York Times*, *The Times*, and *The Guardian*

Novels by JC: *The World Is Full of Married Men*, *The Stud*, *Sunday Simmons and Charlie Brick* (now retitled *Sinners*), *Lovehead*

JACQUELINE SUSANN

Arden, Sherry, *Jacqueline Susann & Valley of the Dolls*, documentary, 1967

Collins, Amy Fine, "Jacqueline Susann," in *Vanity Fair's Writers on Writers*, ed. Graydon Carter, 2014

Collins, Amy Fine, "Once Was Never Enough," *Vanity Fair*, July 2022

Davidson, Sara, "Jacqueline Susann: The Writing Machine," *Harper's*, October 1968

Goodman, Walter, "The Truth About the Bestseller List," *McCall's* magazine, 1967

Korda, Michael, "Wasn't She Great," *The New Yorker*, August 14, 1995

Mansfield, Irving with Jean Libman Block, *Life with Jackie*, 1983

Seaman, Barbara, *Lovely Me: The Life of Jacqueline Susann*, 1987

Books by JS: *Every Night, Josephine!*, *Valley of the Dolls*, *The Love Machine*, *Once Is Not Enough*, *Dolores*

BACKGROUND

Gold, Johnny, *Tramp's Gold*, 2001

Gurley Brown, Helen, *Sex and the Single Girl*, 1962

Korda, Michael, *Another Life*, 1999

Lazar, Irving, *Swifty: My Life and Good Times*, 1995

Pogrebin, Letty, *How to Make It in a Man's World*, 1971

The Autism History Project, University of Oregon

Whalley, Claire, *Virago: Changing the World One Page at a Time*, documentary, 2016

Woodhead, Lindy, *Black Tie & Tales*, blog on Sixties London: https://lindywoodhead.com/the-story/part-two/

Sources

Some quotations in the novel have been taken from printed sources, as follows:

Pages ix and 113: "Compared to Jacqueline Susann, Harold Robbins writes like Proust. . . . For the reader who has put away comic books but isn't yet ready for editorials in the *Daily News*, *Valley of the Dolls* may bridge an awkward gap." Gloria Steinem, *New York Herald Tribune*, April 1966

Page 119: "put their taste at Miss Susann's service" as they "guided her in cutting, inserting a new scene and bringing her characters into sharper focus." Walter Goodman, "The Truth About the Bestseller List," *McCall's* magazine, 1967

Pages 44, 50, and 105: "New York was an angry concrete animal that day" and "A man must feel he runs things, but as long as you control yourself, you control him." Jacqueline Susann's *Valley of the Dolls*, 1966

Page 89: "As if it was written by a slightly bashful fan of Harold Robbins'," *The New York Times*, February 4, 1966

You'll find questions for book groups at my website http://gillpaul.com.

ACKNOWLEDGMENTS

This novel was commissioned by my editors Lucia Macro in the US and Molly Walker-Sharp in the UK, with whom I had worked on several previous novels (six with Lucia, four with Molly). And then they decided to leave—*both of them!*—in the same month, June 2023. To lose one editor is a nail-biting experience for any author, and to lose two at once felt like being orphaned—but fortunately I've since been adopted and nurtured by Asanté Simons in the US and Amy Baxter in the UK. Grateful thanks to all four of them for being my editorial "A" team.

Thanks also to Mary Interdonati, one of the best publicists I've ever worked with, to Beth Silfin for sage advice, to Kim Lewis, my copy editor, for saving me from multiple blushes, to Lisa Flanagan for the award-winning audio narration, and to Yeon Kim for yet another stunning cover. Plus a special mention to Ella Young in the UK for always going above and beyond the call of duty.

Early readers were Karen Sullivan, Lor Bingham, Vivien Green, and my agent, Gaia Banks. Undying gratitude to each of them for the insightful feedback, and especially to Lor for explaining to me how metastatic cancer works. Thanks also to master storyteller Tracy Rees for talking through some tricky plot points and for her authorly emotional support services. And hugs to Karel Bata for taking photos, filming videos, and bringing me tea and snacks when they're most needed.

I'm always humbled by the bloggers, vloggers, and podcasters who invite me onto their sites to talk about my latest novels.

It's a huge amount of work to read the book, think up original questions, conduct the interview, then do the techy bits required to get it online, and I will never take it for granted. Heartfelt thanks to all of you!

Finally, my eternal gratitude to Jacqueline Susann and Jackie Collins for everything they did to advance the cause of women's writing. They were trailblazers for the kinds of novels that millions of readers enjoy worldwide, with glamorous settings, juicy plots, and generous servings of sex. The flak they took for daring to write sexy books was vitriolic and personal, but they carried on regardless. They were both colossal figures, and they paved the way for every single woman novelist who followed them.